Audley's End

Audley's End

Robert Hurst

To order additional copies of this book, contact:
Xlibris
1-888-795-4274
www.Xlibris.com
Orders@Xlibris.com
799153

Contents

For John,
the joy of my life and my epiphany.

Chapter I

Introit

His eyes grabbed me. They penetrated into my very being and broke through any composure I struggled to maintain. They burned into my soul. Dark eyebrows framed those icy blue eyes, which seemed to enhance their intensity. His piercing gaze followed me as I moved around the pub and would not release me from its grasp. I found myself mesmerized; my eyes attached to his, and I could not avert them. The overwhelming strength of their power repeatedly urged me to look away, yet each time, I was drawn back to them. I felt my heart pounding within my chest, and a sudden light-headedness overcame me. I had known for some time that this moment would finally come. I had planned and hoped for it. When the invitation was proffered, however, I shrank from accepting it. Yet I could not pull myself away either. Torn between desire and fear, I became transfixed. His reassuring "hi" did not break the spell.

I had discovered the Golden Lion in the classified ads in *Gay News*, but it had taken some time for me to gather the nerve actually to go there. At first, I had explored Soho on my own, expecting to find cinemas and bookstores catering to the gay community as I had seen in large American cities. I soon learned that London differed in this respect. Apparently, the licensing laws were much more restrictive in England, and such establishments were a rarity. They existed, if at all, only briefly until the Metropolitan Police caught up and closed them down. I did locate two gay theaters but never actually entered them. I looked in the door at the one on Berwick Street and

1

received a smile from the young man tending the counter inside. I found the admission set at five pounds and that I could, for that price, stay as long as I wanted. I felt, however, that the theater merely covered for prostitution, and I had absolutely no intention of involving myself in that quagmire. The other theater, the Lambda, was around the corner on D'Arblay Street. I could see in the door to the desk but not beyond the silvered streamers that separated the lobby from the center of "hot action." Once or twice, I stood outside the Lambda observing the clientele enter the building to attend the performance or, for those who did not require the formalities of a stage show, climb the stairs to the first floor. I wanted to mount that flight myself just to see what I would find at the top but judged it too risky. I noted that most of the customers were somewhat older than I was, dressed in formal business suits. Some went in confidently, while others, like myself, looked around furtively before entering. Likewise, I investigated some of the adult bookstores that abounded in Soho but also regarded them as unsatisfactory. Most had only a small stock of printed material aimed at the heterosexual male along with an amazing array of latex goods designed to stimulate even the most perverse. The magazines directed towards people like myself either did not exist at all or were tightly wrapped in cellophane to thwart those of us who had no intention of making a purchase. A few magazines on the shelves did contain pictures of naked young men, but they were so mild that even *Playgirl* began to appear hard core. On Wardour Street, I did locate a leather shop catering to the stud that sold magazines and provocative postcards to send to randy friends; but the leather and shiny zipper set made me rather anxious, and the postcards were, on the whole, very modest. In all London, there seemed to be not an erection in sight.

I took time one day to look through *Gay News* and read the classified ads in the back. London, I found, had a large number of groups that met weekly to discuss common concerns. Even a group of bisexuals gathered for lunch in a Ruislip pub on Wednesdays. Also listed according to location were the various pubs and discos aimed at gays. At once, I rejected the possibility of frequenting one of those haunts because it would force me to make too public a commitment to admit openly what I had known about myself for so long. Now that initial qualm seemed senseless because of my other, more flagrant indiscretions.

In the pages of one magazine, to my relief, I came across an advertisement about an exclusively gay bookstore that promised a complete collection of appropriate material, including a full line of California publications. The

Zipper was located near Camden Lock, and on one of my lunch breaks from the British Library several weeks after I had arrived in London, I made my way to its portals. The crisp November air braced me as I emerged from the Camden underground station. The weather had turned cold for the first time, and the Londoners now insulated themselves against the elements. Although the street seemed as bustling as any London commercial district a few weeks before, the shopkeepers and patrons standing outside the shops now directed their energies as much to staying warm in the unfamiliar cold as toward negotiating complicated business transactions such as haggling over the cost of a set of dishes or a piece of mutton. The greengrocer continued to chat up the overweight middle-aged women with insincere broad smiles and overzealous laughter, but he now handed them their little sacks of leeks or imported tomatoes with a hand covered with small gloves through which his dirty fingers protruded. As I passed by these people, I feared that they knew where I was headed, that they could look into the recesses and dark passages of my heart and understood its secrets. Still, I walked resolutely up the street.

The Zipper was situated a few yards away from the Lock. The plain-fronted shop had a large curtained window protected by security bars. The only means of identification was the red sign over the entry announcing that I had reached my destination. A small notice on the polished wooden door cautioned me that the store contained material adult in nature, which I might find offensive. I knew that I wouldn't. Once inside, I found myself in a small vestibule decorated with a large poster of Marilyn Monroe, which I considered strangely incongruous considering the nature of the provisions sold within. I passed through a set of louvered swinging doors into the shop itself. The doors reminded me of the saloon entrance that I had seen so often in Westerns at the Saturday matinee when I was growing up. But I knew that John Wayne would not be waiting, gun in hand, on the other side. Racks on two sides of the room displaying various leather garments richly decorated with silver studs and oversize zippers in mostly nonutilitarian locations first welcomed me. I did not muster the nerve to touch them. Behind the counter on the other wall stood two very attractive young men. They both sported light blue T-shirts bearing the name Zipper over the left breast. I thought my awkwardness had attracted their attention since they looked up briefly from their work, but they quickly resumed their quiet conversation over what appeared to be an inventory. Apparently, I was not as noticeable as I had apprehended. I concluded that they must have been cataloging the incredible array of rubber phalli displayed on one shelf in the corner. Although I walked over to look at them, I had even less desire to fondle them than I had to try on the leather briefs.

The merchandise I sought was in a second, slightly larger back room. A large display containing a vast gathering of uncellophaned magazines greeted me as I entered that part of the shop. In front of it stood six men, each leafing through one of the journals. Each peruser appeared to be somewhat self-conscious and held the magazines very close to his chest. Two of them seemed clearly gay. One was quite overweight and sweated profusely; the other very effeminate, the type that would have been called queer or faggot when I was in school. But the other four appeared to be as straight as anyone else, although obviously they enjoyed looking at the pictures of naked men in the magazines. One, dressed in a business suit, seemed particularly ill at ease. The others were attired in sloppy jeans and casual clothing. One had striking good looks. I could imagine him escorting an attractive young woman on a date and wondered if he had chanced into the wrong place.

I reached between two men to pick out one of the magazines that had the price tag in dollars. At once, I noticed that I wore my wedding ring and quickly pulled the magazine from the rack to hide that fact from those standing around me. I stuffed my left hand into the pocket of my jacket to conceal the ring. But I could not turn the pages of the magazine and hold it only with one hand. I was forced to expose myself to the world or at least the claustrophobic world of that tiny shop. As I turned the pages, carefully holding the magazine over the ring, I casually glanced at my fellow readers to see if any of them had telltale rings also. None did. Then I recalled that most Englishmen did not wear wedding rings; I might not be the only odd man out. Certainly, however, all of them saw my ring immediately and knew my terrible secret. Yet the readers in this peculiar library remained strangely unobservant of anything but the magazines they held. They stayed cloistered in silence among the minor tomes of literature they studied intently.

I also attempted to concentrate on the business at hand. I scanned the bookshelf and discovered intriguing titles such as *Honcho, California Boys*, and *Big Guys*. Many of the magazines were old editions, and I recognized one that I had seen on a trip to New York two years before. Nevertheless, they seemed to satisfy or at least partially fill that void within me. Most of the photos were in black and white; few had the color and sophistication of the major, heterosexual pornography. Young men, alone or in pairs, stood before me in often awkward or self-conscious poses and in various stages of excitement or climax. They were obviously aware of the presence of the camera even in their most intimate encounters. I knew that I could never assume some of their postures. While the photographs aroused, they also had an unnatural quality about them that, in the end, made them less than satisfying. After looking through about five magazines, I ceased to concentrate on the details. Erections became so familiar that they began to lose their uniqueness and attraction. Slowly, I became satiated.

I began to pay more attention again to those standing so close but remarkably confined to their private world of fantasies. The attractive young man in jeans, who was about twenty-five and had curly blond hair, captivated me. I wondered if he not only sought release through his readings but also searched for other outlets developed through chance meetings at the bookrack. In other words, did one cruise at the Zipper? I wanted to stare at him as I mused over this possibility but had difficulty keeping my eyes fixed on him. He did not seem to discern my furtive efforts. I really wished I had nerve enough to be aggressive, but my timidity always got in the way of my desires. When the fellow did look in my direction, I quickly averted my eyes and stared intently at my pictures. When I peered up again, I saw that he concentrated on his own magazine and not on me. Perhaps if I left the store, I reasoned, he might follow me; and we could arrange some suitable location to consummate our newfound kinship. Moreover, it was getting late, and my other books awaited me at the British Library. I therefore put down the magazine and ambled casually out of the Zipper. The two young clerks looked up briefly but resumed their work. Apparently, they were unconcerned if any of the readers made a purchase. In the half hour I stood at the rack, several persons had left without making a transaction, apparently just browsing (as I was) without any intent of buying. Others replaced them and entered the back room to study the literature. Only the fat fairy had actually purchased something, departing from the store with his masturbatory dreams concealed in plain brown wrapper.

Like most others, I left the store without a parcel. As I walked out the door, I looked back at the curly headed young man in hopes of catching his attention, but he continued his perusal. Thinking that perhaps he had noticed, I loitered outside the Zipper, looking in the window of the record shop next door. I contemplated what it might be like to explain to my wife how I had passed my lunch hour. I wasn't sure if she would be outraged, perplexed, or just hurt by that knowledge. The departure of the curly headed young man from the Zipper awakened me from the reverie. He glanced in my direction but seemed to look through me. Then he turned and walked in the opposite direction. Another fantasy had been sadly dashed. I would not, after all, snuggle in his arms this afternoon. Dejectedly, I walked back to the Camden tube station and resumed my other life in the British Library.

I returned twice to the Zipper within the next few weeks. The first time, I left my wedding ring in my briefcase at the library, but I worried so much that someone might steal it that I decided next time to wear it but on my little finger. That experiment failed since it bothered me a great deal; and in future, I wore the ring in its accustomed place, although keeping the left hand in my pocket as much as possible. These subsequent visits to the Zipper were not satisfying. The magazines did not change at all, and I tired of looking at the same bums each time. The stock became increasingly limited because the Thatcher government had curtailed the import of foreign goodies. Only the milder British publications, decidedly less titillating, were available in newer editions. I also found that no one really cruised at the Zipper, and my hopes faded of finding my secret lover there.

In the weeks that followed, I frequently took my lunch hour to wander through the backstreets of Soho, often passing two gay theaters. I would pause outside them and watch the patrons entering, hoping perhaps to see a familiar face from the British Library. At other times, I cased the sex shops but found nothing that interested me. Once when I was walking down an alley, a black prostitute accosted me, wondering if I sought her services. As I politely declined her solicitation, I took some pride in the fact that I appeared to be straight. Still, I was becoming bored and frustrated. I had resolved before coming to London that I would end my celibacy in this anonymous city. In the scheme of my life, it seemed to be now or never. "You only live to regret the things you haven't done," so I had heard, and this opportunity appeared to be my last. Yet Christmas was fast approaching, and I had done nothing to resolve my dilemma.

I sat daily in the British Library shifting through Dickensian materials and volumes on Victorian crimes and punishments. I took special interest in reports of buggery which seemed secretly to delight the Victorians. Occasionally, I would look around that enormous room filled with earnest scholars poring over their work. Ten percent of the males sitting in that great institution of higher learning were queer, I surmised. Perhaps the proportion was even higher because of an academic propensity in that direction. Certainly, many students of art and music as well as literature sat there, and everyone knew they all had tendencies. Yet how to discover the right one for me? I could not hold up a sign or wear a button advertising my desires. "Wanted: faggot for occasional afternoon of lust and adultery!" That would not do. Instead, I picked out a few likely suspects and cautiously watched them, but they did not respond to my look. I also realized that we academics were almost oblivious to our surroundings once engaged in arcane pursuits. Then I remembered that gay academics must eat lunch too. I often betook myself to the Museum Tavern for a ploughman's or a shepherd's pie before my excursions into darkest Soho. Perhaps some of my colleagues frequented one of the gay pubs in the area. It was possible that I could meet one there, and it was certainly preferable to the means I had attempted heretofore. I had set very rigid standards for myself. If I were going to sin, it must be safe sin. I did not intend to pick up just anyone; the threat of disease was too real to me. Of course, I would be much safer with the likes of a gay scholar than someone I might come upon at the Zipper. My scheme began to take shape. I picked out those whom I would be overjoyed to see in one of these gay oases. I was especially keen about one slightly younger and exceptionally good-looking man who I hoped was like myself. If only I could encounter him over a pint in the friendly local.

The next day, I went to a tobacconist that stocked *Gay News*. Surreptitiously, I picked up a copy and turned to the back. I was embarrassed when looking through magazines in the Zipper; I was even more self-conscious in such a public place. Finally, I found the list of gay watering holes under the heading of the West End. One called Stallions was located very close by but only opened in the evening. Then I came upon some regular pubs that catered to the gay trade. One near Euston station seemed too far for any of my compatriots from the library to walk for lunch. Another was on Poland Street, but I had no idea where that was. Then I made my grand discovery. The Marquess of Salisbury, catering to the theater crowd, was located on Saint Martin's Lane. That seemed ideal, close enough to walk from Great Russell Street and enticing to the sort of persons I sought. I also noted that another pub called the Golden Lion on Dean Street, while perhaps not as appropriate, would serve as an alternative.

I anticipated my new adventure with considerable excitement. When I would reflect on my enthusiasm now, I would be somewhat puzzled. I had broken another vow to myself never to go to one of these pubs. Like the gay theaters, they were often fronts for prostitution. The chances of contracting some venereal disease or hepatitis were much improved. Yet I must have rationalized that I was after not just any habitué of the pub, but some safe scholar whom I would recognize from the British Library and with whom I could strike up a conversation about the progress of research and my fascinating discoveries about the role of Charles Dickens in prison reform. It was going to be different.

At twelve thirty when I left the library the next day, I did not bother to stop for something to eat. The wintery day was dreary and overcast. Nevertheless, I walked briskly through the backstreets toward Covent Garden, along Long Acre to Saint Martin's. I soon found the Salisbury on the corner across from the Garrick Theatre. It reeked of Victoriana; it seemed more perfect for me than I could have imagined. The sizable building featured etched glass doors and windows. A pub sign depicting the portly Marquess himself hung prominently outside. In the alley between the pub and the theater stood a few metal tables and chairs, but on that chilly December noon, no one sat there. I walked in the front door and found that the interior was even more appropriate than the exterior. Semi-circular booths lined the wall across from the bar, and a huge, ornately decorated mirror framed by dark paneling highlighted each. Crystal chandeliers hung from the ceiling and followed the line of the immense curved bar. A red-carpeted staircase rose in the back corner of the pub, reaching up several stories to an elaborate skylight. In one corner of the bar, the publican had set out a large buffet of cold meats and pastries.

A mixed group eating lunch or drinking pints around the bar thronged the front part of the pub. Both men and women served at the bar, and in general, the patrons did not seem to be what I envisioned. These people looked like working folk on their lunch break, precisely what one would find in any normal pub. It did not match my expectations at all. I then noticed in one corner a pair of clones wearing matching plaid in intimate conversation. I knew at least that some of the clients were as described in *Gay News*, but perhaps the bulk of the gay element appeared in force only at night. My hopes seemed disappointed again. Then I found my way into a small back room furnished with hard benches around four walls and a few round tables scattered about. Here, I discovered what must be the gathering place. This area of the pub was deserted in comparison to the front. A few men sat around nursing their beers and watching carefully everyone who entered the room or even looked in. I decided to buy a half pint of lager and stay awhile. I stood sipping my beer in front of two gambling machines at the entrance to the back room.

I was quite aware that those around me were sizing me up. They probably were asking the same question about me that I had asked of them. Were they, or were they not? Finally, one aggressive gentleman made something of a direct approach to me. He was probably about fifty years old, which instantly offended me that someone so much older would assume my availability. After all, I was merely approaching my fortieth birthday, and my hair only hinted of gray. His hair was heavily streaked with gray, and one side was completely white. He was also not at all attractive to me, not like the curly headed young man in the Zipper. He looked at me and smiled. I looked the other way and concentrated on my beer. The more attention he paid to me, the faster I drank it. I tried to look at the others in the vicinity to locate any readers from the British Library, but I recognized no one. Still, the gray-haired man stared.

I finally decided that this place was not for me. I felt like a stranger in the world of glances and questioning looks. I was an intruder in an unfamiliar world. My dreams were not to be fulfilled here. The Salisbury contained nothing but businessmen and women who had none of my desires and a small collection of men who did not appeal to me in the slightest. Apparently, I had protected myself sufficiently that I would never lose my virtue. I finished my beer, replaced the glass on the bar, and exited into the alley.

I then remembered the other pub mentioned in *Gay News*, the Golden Lion. Dean Street was only a few blocks away, and I knew I could spare a few more minutes. After all, the Salisbury might not be typical. I walked down the alley to Charing Cross Road, passed the Hippodrome, and headed toward Leicester Square. Dean Street ran off Shaftesbury Avenue, and I had to wend my way through Chinatown to get there. I went by various stores displaying imported cloisonné and restaurants featuring Peking duck in the window. The streets were crowded with pedestrians trying to get by the various lorries parked halfway over the curb. At times, I had to walk in the street to pass. I was almost hit by a young Oriental driving his Datsun Sports coupe at a murderous speed. Yet this montage of images did not make the impression they might have on another day. I became increasingly depressed, thinking that I was to remain disappointed, that hopes of solving my problem were to be ever thwarted. I cursed what I was and my inability to sublimate it effectively. Why weren't pornographic magazines and movies enough? Why was I driven to roam the streets of London in search of something more? I knew that I was only leading myself to further frustrations.

Finally, I found the Golden Lion. It was located one block away from Shaftesbury Avenue on Dean Street. The pub was smaller and less attractive than the Salisbury. It had the obligatory leaded glass windows and wooden facade; otherwise, it lacked anything noteworthy. It had two entrances. The one on the south side opened to a flight of stairs that led to the lounge bar on the second floor. I could see the blue and red lights that shone through the second-storey windows. Just before the stairs, a small door led into the public bar beneath. The other outside door opened directly into the main congregating room. I walked into the pub and immediately discerned a different atmosphere from the Salisbury. The level of activity and noise excited me. Moreover, not a woman was to be seen. It struck me exactly as such a place should.

The decor of the interior seemed about as drab as the outside, yet the energy of the patrons overcame any sense of gloom. Underneath the windows was an upholstered bench, in front of which stood three small, circular tables. Scattered on the other side of the tables were a couple of stools covered in the same worn brown upholstery as the bench. Across the room, about six feet away, stood the small bar, complete with the usual set of glasses hanging from racks above. The wall behind was covered with a mirror almost hidden by bottles, various posters, and the cash register. I walked over to the bar and ordered half a lager from one of the young men. The price, forty-nine pence, I noted, was four pence higher than at the Salisbury. It puzzled me since the Salisbury was certainly a grander and more expensive-looking place than the Golden Lion. I should have been suspicious from the start.

Two young men tended the bar. One, a bleached-blond effeminate, flitted around the bar, doing his various chores. He was tall and rather good looking, but his mannerisms annoyed me. The other was short and had a noticeable harelip. His open-necked shirt revealed a heavy and dark chest hair that I found singularly unattractive. I always felt hairiness was the mark of one lower down the evolutionary scale. I prided myself in having adequate chest hair to demonstrate my masculinity but not so much to appear anthropoid. The harelipped and hirsute young man clearly slipped over the limits of manginess.

I stood facing the bar, with my left hand thrust deep into my jacket pocket. Looking down toward the end of the bar, I saw a clutch of men in animated conversation. As I watched, a man entered the bar, walked over to the group, and proceeded to kiss several of them on the lips. Although I had seen it before, I was somewhat taken aback by the openness of the gesture and its apparent acceptance. No one had done that in the Salisbury, although I had been there for about twenty minutes. Near this affectionate scene, a curved staircase ascended to the second floor; a board proclaimed the lounge bar open and the availability of hot food and snacks. I turned toward the other end of the bar, where similar male congregation drank and talked. On the wall behind them, I noted a jukebox with the name Panoram emblazoned on it and an Out of Order announcement covering the coin slot. The patrons, instead, enjoyed music from a stereo system behind the bar. A sign to the left of the Panoram stated that one could find the "gents" through the small door and down the stairs. I slowly turned around to explore the rest of the pub. Two slot machines, both engaged, stood by each entrance. I took special interest in the elaborate, cream-colored ceiling sporting Victorian designs and scrolls. A veritable jungle of fake ferns and flowers rimmed the decorative ceiling on all four sides. The flora appeared faded and quite dusty as if no gardener had bothered to tend it in some time. The Golden Lion certainly did not have the Old World quaintness the Salisbury enjoyed, but it had an almost sleazy character I found appealing.

As I continued to examine my surroundings, I became aware that someone watched me. None of the other patrons seemed to take the slightest fascination in me. The bartenders had not even demonstrated any interest that a new patron had entered their establishment. I had yet to observe anyone, like the gray-haired man in the Salisbury, was trying to attract my attention. Yet now I knew that someone had noticed me. He was seated facing me at the middle table with his back to the window overlooking Dean Street. I looked directly at him, and our eyes locked for the first time. Apparently, he had been staring at me for some time, for he had a well-it's-about-time look on his face. At once, his gaze hypnotized me and burrowed into me. It was more than a look of curiosity; it was an invitation. I tried with difficulty to look beyond the eyes. I knew that I remembered very little about him after that first encounter. Probably if I had seen him on the street, I would not have recognized him as the man in the Golden Lion.

I did note that he appeared to be rather young, probably in his early twenties, perhaps even younger. He seemed also to be thin and rather tall, although it was difficult to tell since he was seated. Yet he did not wear a coat the way the other patrons did, and I could get some measure of his stature. Most importantly, I saw that he was very good looking. At once, his physical appearance alone attracted me. I remembered very little else about him after we parted company.

I found that I had become paralyzed with fear, a reaction that I had not entirely anticipated. The young man matched my fantasies. I should have taken my beer and sat in the seat beside him. He had clearly suggested that was his desire. While that function of will would have been so easy, it was in reality entirely impossible. He looked at me invitingly, clearly implying that his interests coincided with mine. There was certainly nothing inscrutable about his look. His mouthing of "hi" only confirmed it. Still, I could not move. We continued to stare at each other for a few minutes; but to me, it seemed interminable, a confirmation of the theory of relativity. All the time, I had a running argument with myself, trying to persuade myself to act. Intellectually, I wanted to accept that summons; but physically, my body did not respond. Here, opportunity and desire met, but I could not persuade myself to move in his direction.

Instead, I downed my beer and almost fled from the pub. As I hurried through the door, I glanced over my shoulder and saw that he maintained his vigil. I lingered just outside the door, and we resumed our visual exploration. His eyes locked with mine, and urged by them, I started to reenter the pub. But my courage quickly failed me; and instead, I began walking up Dean Street. I crossed Romilly Street and stopped at the corner. Again, I inspected the Golden Lion. Through the open door, I could see him sitting at the table continuing to stare at me. Even at that distance, the eyes penetrated. I paused a moment more and then persevered toward my destination. At times, I felt as if I were running. My heart raced for some time afterward, and I had great difficulty completing any serious work that afternoon.

Chapter II

Kyrie

My father died of cancer when I was four years old. I do not actually remember what he looked like, only his image from a photograph of him in his army uniform. I do retain certain inchoate memories about him, mainly the scratchiness of his beard against my face when he carried me up to bed or the smell of a man whose work caused him to perspire a great deal. I also recall his solidness and the vigor of his hug. But the rest has faded from my memory. I believe that I had a much more vivid recollection of him when I was a boy, but I struggle now even to remember those images that survive. I occasionally study the photograph that still stands on the mantel in my mother's house, but increasingly, I see only a stranger.

My mother never forgave my father for dying. She deeply resented being left with two boys, especially me. She blamed my father for the way I turned out. Yet I suspect that I was quite the opposite from my father, a man who worked with his muscles rather than with his head. She also refused to absolve God for playing such a cruel trick on her. She remains a bitter person, someone I now avoid as much as possible.

My father, however, did not leave us destitute, the way Mother claims. He provided her with a small legacy and a life insurance policy that kept us out of poverty. But Mother really bridled at the fact that she had to work as a clerk at the five-and-dime to support us. She nurtured visions of gentility, which Dad's death shattered. She would often complain that her life would have been bountiful had Dad not left us. She constantly lamented her toil and was bitterly jealous of her sister, who did not have to work and had help once a week to do the cleaning. It appeared she half-expected that, when her sons were both grown, we would insist that she quit work and live off the ample income with which we would supply her.

Life, in reality, was not hard for us. Mother did not put in long hours at a sweatshop. A huge pile of leftover debts did not confront us. The small life insurance policy and some army benefits helped us over the worst times at the beginning. Dad had also worked hard to pay off the mortgage so that we continued to live in our small house. It was the typical white clapboard home with a porch equipped with wicker furniture in which most people in Selinsgrove resided. We lived up the hill away from the Susquehanna River; while considered to be an unfashionable neighborhood, it certainly proved satisfactory when the river overflowed its banks and the important people who had homes along the river were flooded out. In most ways, I remember my early life as relatively free from serious want. I only recollect my mother's bitterness about how fate had dealt with her. In that respect, she made both my brother Richard and me miserable.

Richard was ten years older than I so that he was fourteen when Dad died. My mother's constant moroseness finally drove him from the house. He finished high school and immediately took a job as a mechanic. He had a strong sense of responsibility, however—probably a lot stronger than I did—and always sent part of his paycheck to Mother each week. With him out of the house and the added income, things actually became much better, although one would not know it from my mother's complaints. Because of the great difference in our ages, I really did not get to know Dick very well. Now that we are both adults, we pretend to be close friends; but neither of us knows very much about the other, especially since our lifestyles now are so different. We have almost nothing in common; and when we meet for family gatherings, conversation is often strained and difficult. Even when Dick lived at home, he did not pay much attention to me. After he moved out, I only saw him when he brought the money by each week.

Mother made it particularly clear that my continued presence at home rankled her. I had been born at the end of 1946, a coming-home present for my father. Dad was in the army during the war and served in Europe, although I don't think he saw any real action. He spent most of his time in England, at least according to my uncle. My mother would brag to neighbors about his war record, but the next minute, she would berate him for leaving her destitute. I don't think Mother liked having kids, and the fact that Dad got her pregnant as soon as he returned home must not have pleased her. Mother was thirty-eight at the time and felt that she was much too old to have another child. She was probably correct, although I did not appreciate the constant reminders that I was a mistake. I do know that it made our life together an even greater burden for both of us after Dad died.

In many respects, though, I had a fairly normal childhood partially because of some of the other adults who had an influence on me. My mother's sister and her husband lived in town, and they often looked after us. I suspect that, occasionally, they even helped Mother out financially, although I never heard any word of gratitude from her. Uncle Frank owned a dry goods store and was regarded as one of the pillars of the community. I always enjoyed going to his house because he seemed to take a special interest in me. Uncle Frank always laughed, and Aunt Edna was the world's best cook, at least as far as my world extended then. A sense of happiness always pervaded their home, which was sorely lacking in my own. Moreover, their house sat by the river, and I would go fishing from their dock whenever we went to visit them on a Sunday afternoon. They even had a small rowboat; and whenever the river was more than two inches deep, Uncle Frank would take me out in it. I don't think I ever caught anything worth mentioning, but I always remember those experiences fondly. It was always a disappointment when Mother and I had to return home to our drabber existence. When I was about ten, Mother and Aunt Edna got into a fight about something. I still do not know what it was about, but the two were hardly civil to each other after that. Our Sunday afternoon visits to the house on the river then ceased, although Uncle Frank would, from time to time, take me fishing. I knew Mother did not like it, but she did not often refuse me permission to go.

The other important adult in my life was Pastor Robertson, our minister at the Saint Paul's Lutheran Church, where we went each Sunday. He spent a good deal of time with us after Dad died, trying to help Mother through it all. It seemed he even sought to be a substitute father to me. He had no children of his own, and when he had time, he would take me for hikes in the woods or just sit and talk to me. A few times, he took me to the movies, the first one being *The Wizard of Oz*. I can still remember that day vividly, even though I have seen the film many times since on television. Pastor Robertson was also the one who first got me interested in books. We never had any in our house except for a set of encyclopedias from my grandparents' house. Pastor Robertson revealed a whole new world to me when he bought me a book as a present. He then opened up the thrill of the library, getting me a borrower's card of my own. Mother did not appreciate his efforts, thinking books were for idle people. I had much more important things to do such as earning extra money by cutting lawns or later getting a paper route. Nevertheless, books assumed a central place in my life, and I have that kindly man to thank. I will always remember him fondly, even though he was probably the most boring preacher whom I had ever heard. He died not long after I went away to college, which perhaps is good in some ways since he never knew that I had lost the religious faith that he had struggled so hard to implant in me.

I was never a particularly coordinated child, and sports did not hold a keen interest for me. Therefore, my escape into books often protected me from the embarrassment of having to hit a baseball or some other means of making a fool of myself. I read the entire Hardy Boys series twice and even read a few of the *Nancy Drew Mysteries*, although I wisely never let any of my friends find out about it. Some of the rougher kids in the area, especially those who came from the surrounding farms, would make fun of my lack of physical prowess, but I tried never to let that bother me. Many kids my age lived in the neighborhood, so that I had a fair number of friends despite my sports handicap. My best friend David moved onto the block when we were both seven. His father had been transferred from Harrisburg, and it was exciting to get to know someone who had actually lived in a big city. Mother did not own an automobile, and we had to go everywhere on foot. Therefore, the confines of my world was extremely narrow. Only once did we take a train into Harrisburg so that Mother could see a lawyer. It was one of the most exciting days of my life. David now provided a new link to the world outside Selinsgrove.

David and I soon became inseparable despite the many fights and even major battles that raged between us. As we grew older, we began to venture off into the beautiful Pennsylvania hills that surrounded Selinsgrove. We would take our bikes and ride up Route 45 into the country and explore the woods and streams, which seemed to extend into eternity. David had about as much interest in athletics as I did, and we much preferred to walk in the woods, investigate the caves, and swim in the secluded lakes that dotted the forest. David, however, did not have the same devotion to books and school that I did. There always seemed to be a bit of jealousy on his part about the school grades that I earned.

From David, I first learned about sex and my sexuality. Mother never told me anything about the functions of human reproduction. It seemed if she had her way, I would still not know. Even when I was about to be married, she showed not the least concern that I might not have any idea what I was supposed to do when I got alone with my bride. Instead, I amassed my stock of knowledge about the facts of life mainly from playground discussions of the most uninformed sort. But my original initiation came in a form that produced a considerable shock to me. David and I were playing Clue in my room one rainy afternoon when we had nothing better to do. We must have been very bored since a two-person game of Clue was not particularly exciting. Mother did not arrive home from work until five o'clock, and it was about three thirty. David and I had both turned thirteen, and nature had worked her enigmatic ways on both of us. The hair had begun to turn dark on my legs, and pubic hair magically began to grow in secret places. I wanted desperately to ask my mother what was happening to me but did not have the nerve to approach her about such mysteries. I knew that she did not want to talk to me about dirty things like my body. That had been made abundantly clear to me in both verbal and nonverbal means. Therefore, I had not the slightest notion what the changes meant, although I did know from gym class that the same thing had occurred to other boys of my age.

Rather, it was David who initiated me into the secrets of the body. The funny thing about it was that David really did not understand that there was any link between what he was teaching me and human reproduction. He just described the fun part without the consequences of any of these actions. It was just another way of passing time. My mother coming home early interrupted our first lesson. As a diversion, David knocked over a glass of milk he had brought up with him.

"A fine mess you've made here." I doubted the wisdom of spilling the milk, but perhaps we could explain the mess that way rather than some other. "You'll have to pay to have that cleaned out of your paper money."

"But, ma'am," David said, trying to protect me, "I'm the one who spilled it."

"He should have known better than to let you bring a glass of milk up here. He'll just have to suffer the consequences for his stupidity." Mother always had a way of not mincing her words.

The whole experience so scared and flustered me that it still does not leave pleasant memories. I was certain that Mother had figured out what we were doing; and all during dinner, I feared that she would let go of one of her devastating strikes. She seemed concerned about my agitation and asked if I had been up to something. I prepared for her to fire the blast. When I explained that I was upset about the milk on the bedspread, surprisingly, she let it drop at that. That night, all I could think about was what David and I had done that afternoon.

For the next few weeks, my world revolved around this newfound knowledge. The changes that were rapidly happening to my body scared me. Not really knowing what any of it meant caused me to lie awake at night worrying about it. David seemed to be as clueless as I was, but it never bothered him. He just had a good time.

The wonders of sex had also become the main topic of conversation at school. It seemed that every other boy at school had the same preoccupation. We compared notes on the frequency of experiences, the duration of each occurrence, the size of the equipment, and other fascinating topics. Before long, I learned the whole burden of truth about what we had undertaken. In our science class, we touched (very lightly, of course) on the question of reproduction. When someone asked the ultimate question of human reproduction, Mr. Becker smiled knowingly and said that he could not pursue that topic and that we should ask our parents. I had not often pondered the secret source of babies; I knew they grew inside the mother somewhere but had not worried too much about how they got started. I had generated enough courage once to ask my mother when I was about six, but she calmly told me that I was too young to understand and waved aside further questions. Now my curiosity had really been sparked, and after class, I asked Tony Jenner if he knew.

"What? You mean you are that dumb that you don't know about fucking?"

I confessed my guilt and accepted the humiliation of having one of the slowest boys in the entire school lecture me. But through this misery, he instructed me about the usefulness of that mysterious white fluid that I so eagerly sought to discharge from my body. Now in possession of the cult secret, I could not wait to evangelize the rest of the world. I knew that David shared my ignorance, and I could not wait to proselytize him. We had agreed to meet at my house after school, and the idle chat and card games soon gave way to serious sexual activity. When we had both finished, I sprung my little surprise on him with all the tact of a great teacher.

"Do you know where babies come from?" I asked magisterially.

"Of course, they grow in the mother."

"But do you know why they start growing?"

"I don't know. I suppose when a women wants a baby, she goes to the doctor and gets a shot or somethin'."

"No, you ninny. A man sticks his cock in her." At this point, I was not exactly sure where. "And he jacks off inside her. That's how you got here," I said almost tauntingly. "Your father stuck his in your mother."

David's indignation could not have been more extreme. "My parents wouldn't do anything like that. That's sick." He gathered his things quickly and did not even help straighten up our little playroom. Instead, he marched out of the house and refused to have anything to do with me for several days.

Left to my own resources, I started hanging around another group of guys and eventually received an invitation to Bill Anderson's house. I met with him and some of his friends, but they did not interest me as much as David did. They tended to be shallow and primarily interested in girls. I never quite got into their enthusiasm, discussing this and that attribute of this or that girl. Bill had a stash of *Playboy* magazines that he had taken from his father. We sat around poring over the pictures, describing what we would do with each of those babes. I went along, trying to one-up the others with salacious suggestions. Yet I never got as excited about them as the other guys; they seemed contrived and frankly monotonous. Nevertheless, we often retired to the barn behind Bill's house and jointly relieved our pressures. Yet I never achieved the closeness with them that I did with David. There was an attraction, almost an emotional one, although I would not have identified it as such at the time.

Within two weeks, David and I became friends again. Apparently, he had checked out my information and confirmed its truth. He also must have forgiven the abruptness of my tutorial because he came up to me after school one day and asked what I was doing. What followed was a period of intimacy that lasted well over a year. We became inseparable friends and companions, enjoying each other's company and intimacies and learning about each other's responses, likes and dislikes, in an almost marital sense.

We spent many an afternoon that winter in my bedroom exploring the wonders of life. I had become rather uncomfortable about using my house, but David's mother did not work, making his home unsuitable. We sometimes joined the others at Bill Anderson's barn, but that was too public. There was also something unsavory about that group because of its lack of intimacy; it was too mechanical unlike what I experienced with David. My home remained the only convenient location for our secret rendezvous, but it had serious drawbacks. Once, my brother stopped by and almost caught us in the act. The closest call came when my mother arrived home early with a headache. David and I were in a compromised condition and no time to change, so David took his things and hid in my closet. I slipped my trousers on and shoved my hand in the pocket. It was just in time since Mother walked into the room. Fortunately, she was in so much pain from one of her migraines that she did not seem to notice anything awry. I falteringly explained that I had decided to change into old clothes to complete some work outside. (It was a very cold day, but I could think of nothing else quickly.) Mother paid little attention and took herself off to bed. After waiting to make certain she did not stir further, I smuggled David out of the house and practically froze to death, splitting some wood that Mother had been after me to do for weeks.

Winter passed into the spring of 1959. Dwight Eisenhower still guided our destinies from the White House, and "I'm Mr. Blue" was my favorite song. Spring afforded us an opportunity to move our activities to new climes. When the weather turned fine, we renewed our bicycle trips out Route 45; but now we added something extra to our agenda. We continued to explore the same trails and streams but would then find a secluded spot to conduct our intimacies. When summer came, we went almost daily to Crawford's Lake to swim. It was very isolated since most people would not endure the long uphill trek to get there. Many summers previously, we had gone there and swam naked in the cold waters. Now something else invigorated us. I know today that it was the happiest time of my life. I had all the enjoyment and natural fulfillment without the guilt and social stigma attached to it. We were free and alive, satisfying our basic animal drives with complete abandon. The experience could never be repeated when the adult world came crashing in on us.

The amount of time I spent with David disturbed Mother. I would generally finish my paper route early and then disappear with him until supper. Mother accused me of neglecting my chores at home, and to tell the truth, I was preoccupied with other things.

"I don't like you seeing so much of David Meadows," she said one night over the beef stew.

"Why? He's my best friend. What's wrong with him?"

"Nothing in particular. He's just different, that's all. You spend too much time with him."

She continued to eat without saying anything more about it. I worried that she had somehow found out about us. Only later did I come to understand that she really did not like me to have close friends, since she acted in much the same way about Ann.

In fact, I did not devote all my time with David. I continued to pal around with other guys in the school. I went to Bill Anderson's house on occasion to play rummy, and I developed a good friendship with Hank Bender, who had a fantastic train layout. I was certainly not unpopular with the other kids at school except for the athletes who despised anyone who did not concentrate all their energies on baseball. Most guys knew about one another's sexual activities since we all talked about them openly. At thirteen, none of us realized the horrible and unnatural character of our perversions. In many ways, David and I remained quieter about the character of our relationship than some of the others.

In the fall of '61, we entered high school, and life became quite different for all of us, more complex than it had been in elementary school. We struggled toward maturity, and adult mores forced their way into our world. For most of that year, David and I continued to meet in the afternoon in our usual fashion. But we heard the bigger kids talk about queers and faggots. Slowly, it dawned on us that our preoccupation was not considered cool. In fact, it was downright degenerate. None of us talked about our activities any longer; they became dark secrets. Some even denied ever having participated in them. The group at Bill Anderson's broke up. David and I continued but even more discreetly than before.

I began thinking seriously about what we were doing. Social pressure started to take its toll even on me. I became particularly alarmed about the fate of Onan, who, according to my Sunday school teacher, spilled his seed on the ground, and God slew him. He also talked in hushed tones about other sexual abominations, in which apparently David and I had engaged. I now know what that relationship meant to me, that it was an integral part of my being. Perhaps David felt the same way; I'm not sure. Neither of us was effeminate, although not of the football and baseball set. But I instinctively knew that somehow I differed from the others. I did not want to succumb to the admonitions, and the talk nagged at me until I withered. I should be interested in girls, commenting on their bodies. I participated in such dirty talk with my colleagues, but it somehow did not ring true with me.

Yet in the end, I decided I could not be different. I had even stooped to a flattop several years before, even though I looked ridiculous. Despite my inner compulsions, I found it necessary to conform. I would have to break off with David.

We met after school and began to walk toward our street. David was obviously quite happy. "I just got a B in Fisher's test." David was not a particularly good student, and the B represented quite an accomplishment. "Let's hurry to your place. I want to celebrate."

"David, we need to talk about something."

"You sound so serious. What's the matter?"

I stood outside of myself watching the scene transpire. "I think we should stop fooling around with each other." The voice was mine, but it sounded foreign and remote. It was forced and did not reflect my true sentiments. But I found that I had to say it. "I don't think it is a good idea."

David stopped walking and looked intently at me. "You're joking."

"No, David, I'm very serious. Listen, I've been thinking about this for a long time. I guess I'm just not in the mood anymore." The lies streamed from my mouth.

David's mood changed from surprise to anger. He tried to argue with me, but I insisted that we must stop. "It's just not right. None of the other kids are doing it any longer. Anyhow, I'm afraid we'll get caught."

We got to my house and stood outside for a moment in silence. Finally, David said with resignation, "Well, if you change your mind, give me a call." He turned and walked home.

David and I remained friends but not with the same closeness that we had before. I never did give David that call, although I had sat by the phone many anguished afternoons contemplating it. One year later, David's father received a transfer, and I never saw him again.

Chapter III

Lesson

Even before David and I ended our relationship, I recognized that girls existed. I had attended the school dances in eighth grade and had mustered the courage to ask girls to jitterbug. I did not find them repulsive or avoid them. To the contrary, I enjoyed their company very much. My evening fantasies included certain girls, although because of a total absence of practical experience, I lacked the precise details that I possessed about members of my own sex. When I entered high school, I discovered that dating had become accepted practice among my peers, but I found asking a girl out on a date terrifying. I was basically a very shy person and quite an introvert, yet social pressures forced me to make some effort for the homecoming dance.

One girl in my math class particularly attracted me. After waiting until the last possible moment, putting off the dreaded step, I asked her haltingly if she would accompany me to the dance. Her look of shock suggested that I was the last person in the world from whom she had expected an invitation and the last person in the world from whom she would accept one. But she kindly informed me that one of the football players had already asked her and thanked me anyhow. My ego was bruised but perhaps not crushed.

In desperation, I asked a rather plain girl in my Sunday school class who accepted with unseemly haste. David also had a female companion, considerably better looking than mine; and we decided to double-date. I emerged that evening from my room dressed in the only dark suit I possessed, one entirely too warm for that Indian summer evening. Starched and uncomfortable, I dreaded my mother's inspection. She did not approve of dating since it cost money; although I used my own earnings, which did not seem to matter to her.

"Did you have to buy such an expensive corsage?" She looked at me sternly, observing carefully the details of my attire.

"Mother, I didn't get her orchids. The school sold these for $1.50, which is pretty cheap."

She waved her hand dismissively. "I don't like Sarah much anyhow. You shouldn't have wasted the money on her." The idea of showing up at the dance with her did not thrill me either, but I deeply resented my mother's bluntness. The evening was not memorable. Sarah and I shared absolutely nothing in common. I was not an accomplished conversationalist to begin with, and trying to find something to talk about with her proved impossible. Instead, David and I spent most of the evening chatting with each other. I also hated to dance, mainly because of my own clumsiness. I really learned to dance only in college, and I recall those high school dances with horror.

On the other hand, I did enjoy my schoolwork. I had been an uncertain student during elementary school; but when I reached high school, I discovered the joy of learning. In particular, my English teacher built on the foundation already started by Pastor Robertson. She opened the world of books even further, and I now began reading extensively. I appreciated Mark Twain and Jonathan Swift, but I especially loved the *Iliad*, although I did not understand all its subtleties. Books slowly replaced, if only partially, the void left after David and I parted company. I immersed myself more and more in my studies, perhaps a means of sublimation. As a consequence, my grades improved significantly; and my teachers began to comment on my academic abilities.

Mother did not put much stock in my schooling. She just seemed relieved that I did not flunk out. She had much more concern about the profits from my paper route and looked forward to the day when I could take on a more lucrative part-time job.

I do not recall these years with fondness. Awkward and shy, I was also sexually frustrated. For almost two years, I had delighted in a steady relationship I found both gratifying and supportive. Now I was left to my own resources. I had abandoned my old world but had yet to find a suitable replacement for it. I masturbated a great deal. Halfway through tenth grade, I became aware of Ann. She had been in my classes before, but I had never taken notice of her. Slowly, I discovered her as a kindred spirit. Although certainly not the most beautiful girl in Regional High School, she did attract me. She was also even shier than I was. I often had the courage to ask someone to the school dances; or if I had no date, I would attend the dances with a group of the other guys. Ann never went to any of the dances even with other girls. We became acquainted when we sat together in Algebra II. My academic talents did not lie in mathematics, but she was hopeless. She began asking me questions about the homework, and I helped her. By the time the year ended, she had become heavily dependent on me for assistance. The more we worked together, the more I came to admire her qualities.

I actually did not ask her out on a date until eleventh grade to the homecoming dance that year. She seemed quite shocked that I thought of her in those terms and, at first, turned me down. But I persisted, and she finally agreed. When we had worked together on homework, we found a great deal to talk about; but on the dance floor, we moved around the floor in awkward embarrassment. I don't think ten words passed between us beyond "Do you want to dance again?" and "Yes, I guess so." Yet despite the discomfort, I had a pleasant evening and determined to see more of her socially.

One of the things that attracted me were her parents. Except for my aunt and uncle, I became fonder of them than anyone. I especially enjoyed Mr. Randolf's company, and he assumed the role of another father figure to me. He liked to read, and I now had someone with whom I could discuss books. He introduced me to Charles Dickens, who became a lifelong friend. Mr. Randolf taught English at Susquehanna University, and I admired him tremendously.

Mrs. Randolf also took keen interest in me. I think she understood that I did not get on well with my mother, although I never admitted that openly until after I married Ann. She wanted me to confide in her and allow her to serve as a surrogate mother. Much as I would like to have done so, my own inner reserve would not permit me to open up to her completely. She never became the mother figure whom both of us would have wanted. We did become good friends, which in many ways sufficed.

In some respects, I got to know Ann's parents faster than I did her. Her reticence persisted throughout our relationship. Conversation never came easily, even after we had married. We would often have long periods of awkward silence when neither of us knew what to say. Yet we continued to grow more comfortable in each other's company. We both enjoyed going to the movies, and whenever I was flush with extra money, we would go see the latest show at the Selinsgrove. Ann preferred comedies, especially Bob Hope, whom I had difficulty tolerating. I gravitated toward more serious dramas, but Ann usually won the choice. I did not have enough money for both.

We also shared an interest in attending the concerts at the university. Susquehanna had a reputation for its excellent music program, and they devoted much attention to Baroque music long before it had become generally popular. Ann often went to the concerts on Sunday afternoons with her parents, and I soon began to accompany them. If I owe nothing else to Ann, I will always be indebted to her for introducing me to music in general and Bach in particular. The choir regularly performed the Bach cantatas, and I became familiar with them. The university also possessed a fine organ, and noted virtuosos would travel great distances to play. Virgil Fox even performed a memorable concert. Ann never appreciated the music as much as I did, but she went to be with her family and perhaps to be with me. I knew that her father thought a good deal more of me because of this acquired taste for the Baroque. Like books, music became central to my life. Although Ann did not share the intensity of my feelings for either, she seemed to tolerate my enthusiasm.

Perhaps the strangest aspect of our relationship was its sexlessness. Although by twelfth grade I hardly went out with anyone other than Ann, we did not develop the affectionate responses and intimacies that most couples of our age did; we hardly ever did anything beyond holding hands, and I think that public display sometimes embarrassed Ann. I don't think I kissed her for several months after we started going together steadily. I did not try any serious advances until the senior prom, when we walked home along the river. I kissed her and placed my hand on her chest. She did not exactly get angry; but she moved away quickly, gently though firmly removing my hand. She seemed to anticipate that it would happen sometime and had practiced her response. I did not try anything again until after our engagement. I thought I had developed a normal, healthy lust toward girls; but for some reason, I could not treat Ann that way. I did not have any unusual respect for her virginity; and I don't think love prevented me, at least at first. Something about her stood as a barrier between us, not only a physical bar that would not allow me to violate her body, but a spiritual one as well. Although we grew to enjoy each other's company and came to love, this obstruction always stayed between us even after marriage. We remained close and distant at the same time. I could never completely bridge the gap that existed between us. At times, it even became a chasm into which I might fall if I had attempted to cross.

My sexual outlets had to come from other sources. I was not, by any means, sexually repressed or lacking drive; in fact, a towering sex drive that I found almost impossible to satisfy perhaps represented my biggest problem. Only when David and I engaged in our relationship, meeting three and even four times a week for sexual gratification, did I really feel fulfilled. I had great difficulty dealing with the celibacy imposed by Ann, yet I would not push our relationship further nor break it off out of frustration. I knew Ann would end our friendship had I persisted in my riverbank aggressions. The comfortableness of our association and my fear of being unable to develop another bond encouraged restraint on my part.

For quite some time, I dated girls other than Ann, although I always escorted Ann to the most important affairs. I shied away from making advances and did not rush into the good-night kiss. A few times, I got up enough nerve, but a rebuff or two kept me from trying too hard. Yet some girls seemed to expect and invited advances. I discovered the art of French-kissing from one particularly adventurous tenth grader who might have encouraged me to go even further had I not been so dumb not to recognize the hints. Before I completed high school, I did manage to lose my virginity. The first time that I went all the way was in twelfth grade with a highly experienced girl.

I had just celebrated my eighteenth birthday, and Bill Anderson approached me about joining him on a double date. He suggested it was in celebration of my becoming eligible for the draft. "How would you like to take a hot number to the drive-in with me tonight? Tony Bennings was supposed to go, but his father won't let him." He mentioned the girls' name; both were in the midtwenties and came from farms outside Selinsgrove. They sported reputations as easy conquests. I could well understand why Bennings' father would not allow it. "We're all eighteen now, so the police can't give us any guff." I had a sinking feeling that the plan was not just to watch the movie.

It sounded very interesting to me. I did not have access to a car, so that I had never taken Ann to the drive-in, a place moreover that I would not consider because of its infamy among my school chums. To go with someone else, however, intrigued me. "Sure, I'd love to go. What time?"

"I'll pick you up about eight. The movie doesn't start until eight thirty, when it begins to get dark."

I anticipated the evening with great excitement. I had promised Ann that I would watch television with her, but I now had to make an excuse to get out of it. I didn't feel guilty since I planned to take her to a dance the following night. I knew the history of the girls with whom we had dates and hoped for an educational experience. But I did not relish the thought that Ann might learn about it.

The movie was irrelevant to the evening's entertainment, although the story involved the California beach scene and starred Annette Funicello. The windows of Bill's Studebaker Hawk became fogged so quickly that it became impossible to see much of it anyhow. Bill got started at the beginning of the main feature after he had absorbed the cartoon. Obviously, my date expected to participate in the same activities; and while clearly not as professional about it as Bill, I knew most of the right moves. I attempted to pay attention to my companion while observing Bill's technique. Apparently, he had survived his homosexual stage without noticeable consequences. He certainly exhibited all the lusty qualities of an accomplished heterosexual, although without the slightest hint of finesse. I could tell that clothing was being shed in the front seat, and I attempted to do my part in the back. We had engaged in serious kissing, and I had moved on to the next plateau of upper torso petting. I reached underneath her sweater and attempted to feel under her bra. Finding that quite difficult because of the heavy underwiring that help produce the illusion of abundance, I tried to undo the fasteners that held the device in place. I fumbled for what seemed fifteen minutes, all the time trying to continue with the passionate kissing. It finally became clear to my well-experienced comrade that I would be unable to accomplish the feat, and she did it for me. It utterly embarrassed me.

Then she did something that, up to that time, no other woman had done; she went for my crotch and began to grope me. I became extremely self-conscious during the whole process and felt even more awkward as I began to respond to her touch. I understood that I should reciprocate but did not know if I wanted this thing to lead to its seemingly inevitable conclusion. I tried to see how far Bill had gone by, shifting around to get more comfortable. I could see Bill's bare buttock jutting up in the air and knew instantly that he headed in a direction hitherto unknown to me.

From the sounds coming from the front, I could tell that they, in fact, had reached that point.

I did not seem to have much choice since she took my hand and placed it on her secret parts and began to undo my trousers. Drawn inexorably on, we soon were both pantless. As I maneuvered into, I assumed, the proper position, I kept reassuring myself that I wanted to do this. The idea did not repulse me certainly, but it seemed somehow unnatural. Yet I knew that if I did not continue, my masculinity might be called into question; and I totally rejected that possibility. Before I could fully resolve my dilemma, the decision had been taken from me. The minute the end of my erection touched her, I ejaculated. I don't think I penetrated her at all. Looking up at me in disgust, she exclaimed, "You creep!" And she demanded to be taken home. Apparently, the mess on her insides did not bother her as much as the mess on the outside.

Bill was incensed at me. I don't know if he fully understood how I had spoiled her evening; all he knew was that it had ruined his. Then to make matters worse, a flashlight shone into the car. Officer Hendricks of the Selinsgrove Police ordered Bill to open the door. At once, he noted the state of our undress. "Let me see your identifications," he ordered. The two girls protested that they had nothing with them. "Oh, I'm not worried about you two slags. It's the boys here I'm concerned are underage." We both handed him our driver's licenses, showing that we were both eighteen. He looked disappointed. "One of you just made it," he smirked. "Well, don't worry, your parents will hear about this. Now get moving."

When I got home, it finally dawned on me that I could have made the young woman pregnant. I was even more worried about that than if my mother found out. I did not sleep the entire night, worrying about that possibility. The next morning, Mother asked me about my evening and seemed to notice my agitation discussing it.

For the next several weeks, I worried constantly that the farmer's daughter would walk up to inform me of the dreaded news about her condition. I envisioned having to quit school to marry her and taking a job in some garage to support the new family. She never did talk to me, however. Instead, she avoided me whenever I saw her in town. She would turn from me and commence deep conversation with her friends. Surely, she had reported to them my failure as a lover, how I had made an utter fool of myself that night. Bill never did ask me to go out with him again, and I resolved never to date another girl like that. Ann began to feel safer to me all the time, despite the lack of passion in our relationship. From then on, I dated Ann exclusively until graduation. Before I married, I had intercourse with only one other woman in college. Although I found it a satisfactory experience unlike the first, still that earlier memory cautioned me against repeated efforts; and I remained chaste until my wedding night. I never quite got why some many guys obsessed about that experience. To me, it was like my reaction to the photographs in *Playboy*. On a positive note, Officer Hendricks never did contact our parents. Obviously, his only concern was to catch the "slags" involved with underage boys.

One other problem continued to gnaw at me. I knew that I had never fully recovered from my experience with David. No matter how I tried to deny it, I recognized deep within me an attraction for males. I noted the physical appearance of the girls in my classes, but I also looked at the boys and found them appealing. I knew that was not "normal." When I changed in the dressing room for gym, I would carefully check out the genitals of other boys. I felt myself drawn to them despite my constant efforts to avoid it. I half-confessed to myself that I was a fairy but quickly reassured myself to the contrary. I could not admit that my experiences with David felt almost more natural to me than the events on the back seat of the old Studebaker at the drive-in.

Masturbation became my only sexual outlet. When I produced mental images for these times, girls only occasionally appeared. Once, I even snuck a *Playboy* into the house to generate proper fantasies. Too often, however, my thoughts turned toward David and our relationship. Even worse, they could become preoccupied with some good-looking guy in school. Although sickened by the perversity of my dreams, I could not avoid them. Yet I refused to admit that I somehow differed from the others. I could not accept that fact.

I also felt awkward about being with Ann. If she could only comprehend the focus of my secret life. If she understood how I spent so many afternoons before my mother came home from work, she would be sickened and angered. Ann and her entire family practiced a very devout Lutheranism. They took their religion much more seriously than I did, and Ann's strict moral attitudes stemmed from that belief. To think that she dated a pervert would have destroyed her. As a consequence, my life with Ann and my private life became completely separate. At times, I felt schizophrenic, like two different persons. With her, I played the upright Christian who enjoyed spending quiet hours with her. In private, I became the sex maniac, seeking gratification as often as possible in most unnatural ways. I was a *faggot*. The word screamed out at me from inside the calm facade as I sat quietly with Ann.

I tried to bury these thoughts under a pile of schoolwork. I enjoyed school very much but also found that I could divert much of my energies into it. My teachers considered me a good student in elementary school but somewhat of a star in high school. A number of my peers did not look on me fondly as a consequence because they regarded serious students as brownnosers or worse. I represented the most despicable combination of traits, studiousness and a lack of athletic ability. These folks assumed that something was basically wrong with me. It seemed that some of my forays with girls, overcoming my basic reticence about such approaches, resulted from my desire to maintain a heterosexual profile against these debunkers. My reputation, besmirched enough already, did not need the charge of queer added to it.

My grades in science and math generally remained good, but I excelled in English and history. I loved to write and even joined the school newspaper in tenth grade, but Mother made me give it up because it interfered with my work after school. I did contribute some articles to the newspaper and was delighted to see them in print. My proudest achievement in high school came with my selection for the National Honors Society in eleventh grade. The principal invited parents to the installation, and I pleaded with Mother to take an hour off to attend. She refused, however, claiming that the honor would not put any more food on the table nor help me find a job after high school. Ann's parents attended and invited me for dinner that evening to celebrate.

Just before the end of school that year, the guidance counselor called me into her office. "Have you thought about attending college?" she asked me.

"Not really, Mrs. Wharton. I know we cannot afford it. It just never entered my mind."

"You really should. Many colleges have scholarship programs for gifted students, and the state of Pennsylvania has just started a new loan program. There is certainly no reason with your records that you can't get assistance."

"Mother wouldn't let me go anyhow. She expects me to work as soon as I finish high school. She even talked about having me drop out at the end of this year."

"Perhaps if I talked with your mother, I could reassure her that it is quite possible that there would be no costs involved for her at all. Have you taken the SATs yet?"

I confessed that I had not since it did not seem worth my effort; and besides, Mother would not pay the fifteen dollars for them.

"Listen, they are going to be offered again in June. I'll send in the application for you, and you won't have to worry about the fee. That will be between you and me."

I knew that the effort would prove fruitless but agreed to go ahead with it. Mr. Randolf also talked to me about attending college, but not until Mrs. Wharton spoke to me did I begin to think seriously about it.

I loved to fantasize about being a student at Susquehanna University when I attended concerts there. I sometimes cut across the campus on my way to work in the afternoons, watching the students stroll their way to classes or, as was more likely, to the Rathskeller. I had used the university library on several occasions to work on term papers because Mr. Randolf had arranged a reader's ticket for me. College was something to be dreamed about but not taken very seriously.

Nevertheless, I agreed to take the examination and worked with Mrs. Wharton on my schedule for twelfth grade so that I would have all the academic credits I needed just in case college became a real possibility. Mother had insisted that I enroll in typing and other practical courses, but instead, I took another year of science and math, which I did not relish, as well as the honor's class in English. The manager of the grocery store let me off work on the Saturday of the SAT, and I made him promise solemnly that he would never reveal it to my mother. I rushed home from work each afternoon in the summer so that I could get the mail before Mother did. Of course, the scores came the day she beat me to the mailbox; and letting the opened letter dangle in front of me, she asked me what it concerned. I lied that the envelope just contained a survey sent to all new high school seniors, and I breathed easier when she did not press further. She probably had no idea what the Educational Testing Service did, and the test scores inside were as incomprehensible to her as they were to me. The next day, I rushed over to school, hoping to locate Mrs. Wharton there during the summer vacation. I found her in her office, just about to leave for lunch.

"You got 610 in math and 740 in verbal. They are fantastic scores. There is no doubt in my mind that you can get into a college with a good scholarship. If you are willing to borrow the rest, you should have no trouble. The loans don't have to be repaid until you have finished, and the interest rate is extremely low."

"But I'm sure Mother will not allow it." I did not tell Mrs. Wharton that Mother had been looking forward to added income for years.

We went ahead, despite my misgivings, drawing up a list of schools from which I would request admission materials. I had to write the letters secretly, late at night, so that Mother would not find out. I decided to apply to Susquehanna and the state university, but Mrs. Wharton also suggested that I try some of the smaller liberal arts institutions. We included Muhlenberg on the list. "Didn't Mr. Robertson go there? You should go see him about it. Perhaps he can help."

That Sunday afternoon, I went by his house to talk to him about his former college. He seemed delighted to see my interest in attending college. "I think it is all really a waste of time," I complained. "Mother is not going to allow it. She will insist that we cannot afford for me to go."

"But there are scholarships. Some are rather specialized, which few apply for. You should look into some of those. Perhaps there is one for a student who agrees to join the Peace Corps and go to Lower Zambia."

"That would be one way to get out of Selinsgrove," I quipped.

"Come to think of it, there is a scholarship that I read about in the *Muhlenberg Alumni News* that might interest you." He stirred through the pile of papers and magazines that cluttered his desk. "Here it is. Now let me see." He thumbed through the journal until he came on the article he sought. "This sounds too good to be true. The Fisher Foundation, it offers a scholarship for an orphaned Lutheran to attend Muhlenberg. You should definitely apply, even though you still have one parent."

My excitement about the prospect of college intensified. For the first time, I mentioned my thoughts to Ann. She suggested that I talk to her father about it. Mr. Randolf said that he always assumed I would go to college. "Certainly, a young man with your academic record would expect to go."

I explained my misgivings about the project, but he pushed them aside. "Your mother would never stand in your way if you were accepted to a good college and received financial aid." He was shocked to discover just how wrong he was.

That fall, I sent off my applications and also wrote to Muhlenberg about the Fisher scholarship. They wrote back politely that, although the scholarship generally went to a student missing both parents, they welcomed my application. Of course, all the letters came to the house, and Mother soon became aware that something was afoot. "Why are you getting all these letters from colleges?" she demanded. "You haven't gotten any foolish notions?"

"Mrs. Wharton convinced me that I should try. I'm a good student, and I want to continue with my education. She said that there are scholarships that will pay for the cost of college."

"And what do you think I'm going to do when you run off to college? I've counted on you to help out. I've had to slave to support you all these years, with no gratitude from you. Now you have to go out and earn something to help pay the bills. You shouldn't be going to school this year. You could have quit. Now you have these mighty, grand ideas about going to college. I bet it's your uncle Frank who put these ideas in your head."

"No, Mother. I told you, it was Mrs. Wharton who first brought it up. I also talked to Pastor Robertson and Ann's father about it."

"Why don't those busybodies mind their own business? You are not going to college, and that is final. Get those stupid ideas out of your head."

"But I thought you would be proud if I got accepted into. . . ."

"You thought! Well, you think again, young man. There's no way that you're going. Forget all that foolishness." She stormed out of the room, and that was the last we talked about it. I continued to submit the applications, more out of defiance than any serious thought that I would succeed.

The response to my efforts was gratifying. Some of the college representatives interviewed me at school and encouraged me to continue to seek admission. Finally, I received a letter from the Fisher Foundation about the scholarship. They notified me that they had selected me as a semifinalist and asked that I also meet their representative in Harrisburg for an interview. They wanted my mother to accompany me. I showed the letter to her, explaining that I now had a good chance of getting the scholarship that would assume the cost of college. She emphatically refused to have anything to do with it.

"If you don't go, Mother, then there is no way that I'll get the scholarship."

"That's just too bad because I'm not going to waste my time on a wild-goose chase. Nobody's going to give you money to go to school."

I knew that I could not persuade her to go with me. She objected that the cost of the train would be too high and that she would have to give up a day's work. In desperation, I went to my uncle Frank to discuss the problem.

"You see," I explained, "I really want to go to college. My teachers have been encouraging me. They think that I could do well there. I've thought about becoming a teacher, probably an English teacher. But Mother will not help in the least. She absolutely refuses to go to Harrisburg, and if she doesn't, there's no chance that I'll get the scholarship."

"I'll talk to her, son, but I have about as much influence on her as you do. Do you think Dick could help talk her into it?"

"No, I don't think so. Besides, he hasn't been very encouraging either."

That next Sunday after church, Uncle Frank stopped by our house to talk to Mother. I could tell at once that she resented his interference, and her anger toward me intensified because I had involved him.

"Frank, why don't you mind your own business? There's no call for you to come by here butting in where you don't belong."

"We're not talking about some minor problem, Martha. We're discussing the boy's future. He's a bright boy. He wants to go to college, and there is a good chance that he'll make it. I'll even drive you down to Harrisburg to the interview if that will help any."

"It's no use going. He's not going to college, and that's final. As soon as he's out of school in June, he's getting a regular job."

"Martha, you are totally unreasonable. You don't seem to understand what you're doing to him." I stood in one corner of the room as they continued to argue. The conversation soon reached the level of a shouting match. I knew that he wasn't getting anywhere and that there was no chance that she would change her mind. Uncle Frank stormed out of the house and roared off in his car.

"You'll regret ever getting him involved in the matter" were her last words to me as she left the room. The rest of the afternoon, I took a long walk in the woods, trying to resolve my life into some sort of order. I started to walk to Ann's house but decided against it.

The foundation had set the interview in Harrisburg for the following Friday. On Tuesday night, Uncle Frank stopped by the house again but asked to see me alone. "I telephoned the people at the Fisher Foundation and explained the problem with your mother. They were very sympathetic and agreed to my suggestion that I run you down for the interview myself. They said that they did not even have to talk with your mother." It seemed too good to be true. I rejoiced almost as much as if I had already received the scholarship.

At Uncle Frank's insistence, I did not mention the trip to Mother. That Friday, we risked the icy river road down to Harrisburg in his big white Pontiac. I sat nervously through the interview, but the three people I met reassured me and seemed very understanding. They expressed their admiration for my high school record and test scores but mentioned in particular the strong recommendations submitted by Mrs. Wharton and Pastor Robertson. Then they asked to speak with Uncle Frank privately, and I waited anxiously in the hall. He did not discuss what they had said, and we drove home without mentioning the interview further.

I heard nothing additional about the scholarship or any of my applications until March. The winter had been particularly cold and dreary; the extent of the delays lowered my spirits even more. Then in mid-March, I began to accumulate some replies. Susquehanna accepted me, which I had expected since Mr. Randolf said he had put in a good word. They could not offer much of a scholarship, and I would still have to pay $1,000, which I knew we could not manage. Then I got the letter from Muhlenberg, accepting me but not saying anything about financial aid. The next day, word came from the Fisher Foundation that I had received the scholarship to attend Muhlenberg. The amount offered covered tuition, room, and board; but I worried about the other expenses that I would have to meet. I knew that I could get a job and cover most of them, but I still had concerns.

I did not even bother to show the letters to Mother. We had hardly been civil to each other since Christmas, and I did not feel I was under any obligation to take her into my confidence. Instead, I rushed over to see Uncle Frank. He showed almost as much excitement as I had about the news. "Your aunt Edna and I have a surprise for you. Our boys have both finished school, and we know that college meant a great deal to them. We're fairly comfortable now and would like to help you out a little." He told me that they wanted to give me $200 each year so that I could spend more time with my studies. I would still have to work some, but I had become very accustomed to that from high school. My world seemed a much brighter place than it had for a long time. I had been delivered out of Egypt, and the Promised Land stood open, awaiting my entrance.

I also stopped by Pastor Robertson's house, even though it was suppertime. I showed him the letters but did not mention the generosity of my aunt and uncle since they wanted me to keep that to myself, even from my mother. "I knew you would do it, son. God meant you to go to college." He insisted that we kneel and say a prayer of thanksgiving. I felt very awkward and stumbled over a few words, leaving the bulk of the supplication to him. I kept wondering why God would want someone like me to go to college. I did not yet possess the maturity to deal with those existential questions.

I'm not sure why I did not tell Ann immediately. I had certainly confided in her about most things, although I knew that she remained quite reticent about revealing her inner feelings. A silent, semipermeable wall always stood between us. Few things of deep significance passed from her side to mine; a good deal more flowed from mine to hers. Yet even I did not discuss some things. Obviously, my confused sexual interests were one, but I did not tell her other things as well. The next Friday evening I spent at her house, and I told her and her parents at the same time. "Uncle Frank said that he would drive me over to Allentown in September and get me settled."

"How has your mother taken it?" Mr. Randolf asked.

"I haven't even told her yet. I suppose I should tell her soon, although I'd like to wait until I'm about to leave. Uncle Frank said that he doubts if she will stop me now that I have the scholarship. But she does have to sign an agreement."

Ann seemed very sad that night. Her parents went up to bed early, and we sat on the sofa watching television. I guessed the source of her mood had something to do with my leaving the next fall, but she never articulated it. I probably did not help much because I chattered excitedly about college and the courses that I wanted to take. Ann had declined to apply to colleges not only because she was a rather weak student but also because she did not have the drive that I had. That always puzzled me because her father was so bright and energetic about academics. Only later did I realize that he so overshadowed her that he stifled any intellectual sparks. Unfortunately, I had the same impact on her.

The scene with my mother the next morning turned out to be as ugly as I had expected. She received the news with great anger and positively refused to sign the required forms. I concluded that the possibility of college had now vanished and that I would continue to work at the Acme for the rest of my days. I talked to Mr. Randolf to see if any way existed for me to have the scholarship without her signature, but he knew of none. The situation appeared hopeless. It finally took another visit from Uncle Frank and a heated exchange between them to persuade her to relent. In the end, I think she regarded my departure from the house with some relief. I had informed her that if she did not sign, I planned to leave Selinsgrove and never see her again. Perhaps she hoped that if she consented, she might eventually realize some of the added income she craved.

Despite all the fighting, I remember the spring of my senior year as being particularly happy. I knew that I was college bound unlike the majority of my classmates. My relationship with Ann continued to grow, although I knew that my forthcoming departure upset her. One evening while sitting on her front porch, I finally got up the nerve to tell her that I loved her. She did not respond verbally but just squeezed my hand in recognition. I had not really expected anything beyond that since Ann was not a demonstrative person. The next week, I took her to the senior prom; and afterward on our walk along the river, I attempted to claim the prerogatives of a lover, only to be gently rebuffed. For a time, my inner torments quieted. That summer, the most serene period of my life, I worked hard at the Acme to earn spending money for the fall.

Chapter IV

Gradual

Uncle Frank drove me to Allentown on the day after Labor Day so that I could take up residence at Muhlenberg. Mother had kissed me farewell on the front steps but had declined Uncle Frank's invitation to accompany us. "I have to work to pay the bills. I'm all alone now," she said pointedly.

One might wonder why I became excited about the prospect of a drive to Allentown, Pennsylvania, but it represented the longest trip that I had ever undertaken. My world consisted almost entirely of the area around Selinsgrove. Except for two trips to Harrisburg, I had never been out of the area.

My new situation did not disappoint me. The college reminded me in many respects of Susquehanna, although it had one important advantage— its distance from Mother. When we arrived, an upperclassman showed me to my room and introduced me to my roommate, Carl Fleming. I understood that I would have a roommate since the college had written me about preferences. Because no one from my high school would attend, I had failed to return the form. Carl seemed nice enough; he came from Philadelphia and possessed an air of sophistication that I felt sorely lacking in myself.

Uncle Frank helped me unpack, gave me as close to a fatherly talk about hard work and perseverance as he could muster, and departed. For the first time in my life, I found myself left to my own resources. A grave uneasiness overcame me as I faced the prospect of the world alone. I had left behind all my traditional anchors. I had had a tearful goodbye with

Ann the previous night, and a deep emptiness overcame me immediately after we parted. But I also recognized that I would miss her parents, my aunt and uncle, and Pastor Robertson. I had grown very close to all of them. On the other hand, I felt a great burden lifted from my shoulders as I drove away from the sight of my mother. In the days before I left, she had tried to pile guilt on me for deserting her. She pleaded that she had become so dependent on me that she did not know if she could survive without me. I pointed out that I was only one hundred miles away and that Dick still lived close at hand. The more I remained guiltless, the more frustrated she became.

From the start, I corresponded with Ann every week, describing my new world to her. When she wrote back, a sense of sadness pervaded the tone of her letters. She had taken a clerical job at the university and was apparently satisfied with the position. Clearly, she envied my new experiences and felt increasingly confined by the atmosphere at home. She seemed to sense, as I had discovered, that another life existed outside Selinsgrove. For the first time, I noted a feeling of dissatisfaction in her. I also sent a letter to my mother every other week, detailing my room and classes, pretending that she might have a real interest in my new surroundings. I never learned if she did since she never wrote back. The only word I had from her came at the holidays when I returned home. Once, I complained about never hearing from her, but she brushed it off, saying she remained much too busy trying to survive. I continued to write despite the lack of response probably because I hoped it would make her feel guilty. It didn't.

Perhaps the most unique experience of college was having a roommate. I had never lived in such proximity with another male since my brother left home, and we had never shared a room. I was quite self-conscious about living so openly with one now. I had great difficulty getting undressed around him, although he did not seem to be bothered about it at all. He would stand naked talking to me, something that I remained too embarrassed to do. For a long time, I tried to schedule my showers at times when he was not around, although I did get over my uneasiness within a few weeks. The main problem was my morning erections. I would wait until it had subsided before getting out of bed. Sometimes a persistent one would keep me in bed so long that I arrived late once or twice for class. That plague did not seem to bother Carl since he jumped out of bed as soon as the alarm sounded. Never did I spy the telltale bulge in his pajamas.

Fortunately, I did not find Carl physically attractive. Pockmarks scarred his face, and I regarded him frankly as rather ugly. I did, from time to time, sneak a glance at his genitals, but the rest of him did not intrigue me. Thankfully, he did not possess Adonis qualities that I might have difficulty resisting. I did find several other boys in the dormitory very appealing, and I always enjoyed ending up in the shower room with one of them. I never made any overt approaches, maintaining a strictly heterosexual guise. I thought, at one time, that I noticed a guy named Jay sizing me up slyly in the shower. When I had finished, I turned around to discover him looking rather too intently at my privates. I looked at him, and he seemed definitely embarrassed. My only response was to nod, mumble a hello, and walk out of the shower room.

I thought about him afterward and even contemplated becoming friendly toward him in hopes that something might develop; but in the end, I considered better of it. Although he seemed interested in becoming better acquainted with me, I brushed off all advances. I tried to convince myself that these homosexual attractions were but an aberration. I was truly normal, and these strange, abnormal desires belonged to someone other than me. Yet each time I saw that boy in the hall, I knew that I was fooling myself.

Having a roommate posed other unforeseen problems. My usual means of sexual gratification now had to be curtailed. My frustrations grew apace since, apparently, no other possible release existed. I continued to fantasize, but that did not seem a satisfactory substitute. I made concerted efforts to make females the object of those fantasies, but male images continued to intrude. Girls did present a possible outlet, but none paid much attention to me. Men outnumbered women at Muhlenberg by a considerable proportion; therefore, the anxious and sophisticated sophomores quickly monopolized freshmen women. Any hope of getting a date with one was soon dashed since upperclassmen escorted them to all the dances and fraternity parties. I did not have a single date until the end of my freshman year. It turned out to be a long cold winter.

Throwing myself into my academic work with unusual vigor as a means of sublimating my frustrations, I found the work relatively easy and enjoyed most of my classes. I had decided to major in education and planned to become a high school English teacher. Of all my courses, however, I came to abhor the introductory education class. The teacher used perhaps the worst examples of pedagogical techniques, and the material bored me. At the beginning of my sophomore year, I switched to an English major. It seemed rather idiotic at the time since I could not teach without state certification, which required all those intolerable education courses. Moreover, I could do absolutely nothing with an English major. My uncle had suggested that I focus on business, but observing the intellectual capacity of the business majors in my dormitory convinced me that I did not want to be associated with those Neanderthals. It also seemed that one could not major in business unless one also majored in some sport. Clearly, I did not fit those qualifications. I therefore continued my foolishness of majoring in English, thinking that something might work out in the end.

Shortly after I arrived at Muhlenberg, I obtained a job in the campus bookstore, a position I kept during my four years there. At first, I did the stock work, loading boxes into the storeroom or unpacking books on the shelves. Eventually, I received a promotion to sales clerk, which did not require the same physical exertion. I enjoyed the work because it afforded me access to books; and when business dragged, I often sat by the cash register and read. The manager also permitted me to arrange my hours to suit myself, except at the beginning of the semester. The job provided me with the extra cash I needed to pay my expenses, and it also allowed me to exile myself when the world became oppressive. I found that, with growing maturity, I enjoyed solitude more than ever.

I did make one significant gesture toward socialization. I decided that I would join fraternity rush in the spring semester of my freshman year. It seemed that fraternity membership assured one of dates, and my extended chastity drove my decision. I joined Delta Chi; while not the premier fraternity on campus, it suited my personality and interests nicely. The guys seemed fairly serious academically, although I tended to study more than most of the others. But they enjoyed a good party on the weekends, which I appreciated also. The jocks all joined Sigma Nu, ate live chickens, and practiced other barbaric rites. The Delta Chis had their own crude initiation ceremonies, but they tended to be considerably more civilized. We drank large quantities of beer on the weekend and sang songs, and I greatly enjoyed the associations I made.

Of course, I strove desperately to appear as normal as my brothers did. I made crude jokes about queers and protested vocally against a prospective member who had slightly effeminate characteristics. That my actions involved any hypocrisy did not seem to bother me. Whatever understanding I might have had of my perfidy I quickly suppressed. I had become one of the guys and meant to keep it that way. Whether anyone in the house suspected anything differently about me, I did not discover at the time. I finished my four years at Muhlenberg without detection.

I knew the existence of a group of homosexuals at the college. They tended to gather regularly at one of the bars in Allentown with a reputation for attracting fairies. I discovered the bar and made a point, from time to time, to walk past it. I could not venture in since I did not possess the financial resources to have a forged Liqueur Control Board card like some did. Therefore, I could only observe. I never made a point of going there often for fear that one of my fraternity brothers might see me. Even in my senior year, when I reached the drinking age, I did not enter. The fear of chance discovery remained too great, and my proposed explanations for being there never fully satisfied me. So I only observed the place from the outside. Just before Thanksgiving of my senior year, I walked past the bar and ran into my former dorm mate Jay, coming out the door. We exchanged pleasantries and parted quickly. I realized that he had, in fact, watched me in the shower and that I had missed an opportunity from the first weeks of my college career. I speculated just how close I had come to a possibly complete transformation of my life.

Once I had joined the fraternity, I found that my social life improved considerably. Brothers began fixing me up with dates, often the lonely roommates of their steadies. Eventually, I came to know some girls on my own and dated several of them. Ann and I had an understanding that, although we proclaimed serious intentions toward each other, in my absence, we remained free to date others. I really don't think Ann ever took advantage of this agreement, but that did not stop me. I did not go out a great deal, yet the social pressures to have a date each weekend weighed heavily on me. I became quite attached to one girl in particular and dated her almost my entire junior year. She turned out to be my only actual sexual conquest since the girl at the drive-in. I would brag about my sexual experiences along with my other brothers late on Saturday night after we had taken our dates back to the dormitory. Surely, some of them told the truth. I never did.

During the summers, I would return home and resumed work at the Acme. I hated the prospect of summer since I detested the job, but more than that, I despised returning home to Mother. She did everything possible to make life uncomfortable for me. At one point, I tried to arrange to stay in Allentown for the summer; but the bookstore did not need me, and I felt some obligation to see Ann. We had to work hard each June to become reacquainted and renew our friendship. We passed days of awkward silences and forced conversation, but eventually, we became comfortable with each other again. I spent many hours with her; it avoided the prospect of having to go home.

The bad news that Pastor Robertson had died of a heart attack a few weeks before greeted me when I arrived home at the end of my junior year. The news grieved me since he had eagerly followed my college career and assured me that he planned to attend my graduation. He had also continued to take an interest in my religious well-being, which posed considerable difficulties for me. When I first arrived at Muhlenberg, I dutifully attended chapel every Sunday. I especially enjoyed the sermons, which sounded more profound than Pastor Robertson's. The music disappointed me, on the other hand, since it did not nearly achieve Susquehanna's level. But I attended throughout my freshman year, to the delight of Pastor Robertson. My backsliding began in my sophomore year. I found getting up on Sunday morning after a big party the previous night more and more difficult. Moreover, many forces around me challenged my basic religious understandings. For the first time, I came in contact with people who seriously questioned the tenets of Christianity. A number of my fraternity brothers avowed atheism and could argue rather persuasively against Christian doctrine. Things like the virgin birth and the resurrection did begin to appear silly to me. Perhaps the greatest blow came when I took a course on the history of Christianity. The professor in the Religion Department at this Lutheran college turned out to be an atheist, and he spent most of the semester debunking my religious beliefs. This onslaught soon began to take its toll, and I became a proselyte of this new religion of unbelief.

When I returned home, I continued to report my faithful church attendance to Pastor Robertson and, in fact, did go with Mother to Saint Paul's each Sunday, perhaps out of a sense of obligation because of the Fisher Scholarship or because I dreaded to reveal my hypocrisy. When with Ann, however, I would wax eloquent about my new religious convictions. At first, these revelations that I had fallen by the wayside, that I was the hard ground on which the seed of faith had at first sprouted but then withered from the lack of sustenance, deeply disturbed her. Eventually, I began to destroy her faith, and we grew equally cynical about religion.

Paradoxically, my missionary work succeeded much more effectively with her in the long term than my own conversion proved to be. After I learned of Pastor Robertson's death, although it deeply saddened me, I no longer made the pretense of attending church. Mother had to find her own way to Saint Paul's without me. I had long ceased attending chapel at Muhlenberg. If, as I had now become convinced, the entire Christian fable had absolutely no basis, then I would be hypocritical to attend even for the music. Life, it seemed, had no meaning unless the person made his own. Salvation seemed a hoax, and my own efforts at prayer and repentance appeared foolish now. Life emptied of its mystery and significance. I did not recognize at first just how much more alone I felt. Nevertheless, that would later change.

Attending the annual Bach festival in Bethlehem now became the closest I got to a church during my last year at Muhlenberg. I had gone every year to mingle with the crowds on the lawn outside the Moravian chapel and revel in the strains of the *Saint Matthew Passion* or the *Mass in B Minor*. Once, that music possessed profound religious significance to me; now I enjoyed it solely for its aesthetic qualities. Somewhere in the back of my mind resided the spiritual meaning the music once held for me. As its beauty invaded me, I felt nostalgic about its former import, now lost to me seemingly forever. The programmatic quality had disappeared, replaced by absolute music. When the strains of the *Matthew Passion* swept over me, the emotion engendered had nothing to do with the words sung by the choir. "O sacred head, sore wounded," they would sing, "defiled and put to scorn." The words ceased to have an impact; they became meaningless sounds disjointed from their original sense. "O kingly head surrounded with mocking crown of thorn! What sorrow mars Thy grandeur?" Those images no longer sparked the sense of piety they had when I was fifteen. "Can death they bloom deflower? O countenance whose splendor the hosts of heaven adore." The fable had lost its mystery.

I made two important decisions during the fall semester of my senior year. Several of my English professors urged me to consider graduate school, and I had determined to apply. During my freshman year, I had abandoned the idea of pursuing my original intention of becoming a high school English teacher. I now had a major that seemed to lead nowhere. I thought about law school but concluded that law held no interest for me. Likewise, journalism did not spark much enthusiasm. I knew that I wanted to teach but did not see how I could under the circumstances.

The Vietnam War had heated up, and the draft blew very close to me. So far, I had maintained a student deferment, but now talk circulated that a lottery would replace the draft. I had not participated in the antiwar efforts, which had been very limited on my campus. The national debate had begun heating up in 1967, but I knew already that I did not want to defend freedom in those Asian jungles. I had listened carefully but was unconvinced of President Johnson's rationale for the need to fight the Vietcong. The idea of graduate school, therefore, had a number of allurements. I could consider a career as a college teacher, and I might prolong the threat of conscription somewhat longer in hopes that the war would end. I began submitting applications to various schools, having much greater faith in myself than when I had originally applied to college. My grades remained very respectable throughout college, and I had done well on the standardized tests. I felt confident that I would gain admission to a graduate program probably with adequate financial help to support me.

The other decision that I made had to do with Ann. In many respects, the decision came after much more agonizing. I knew that I loved her, and we had had a silent understanding between us that we would eventually join our lives together. Ann had become comfortable to me, probably too much so. I took her for granted, and she did the same with me. I had problems about the prospect of marriage. The thought of remaining with Ann for the rest of my life did not concern me; I thought that I could do that easily. I had to confront the problem of my sexual desires seriously for the first time in a long while. I had pushed that problem out of my mind and buried it under academic work and an artificial social life; now when I thought about marriage, I knew that I had to be more honest with myself. Could I, in fact, carry on as a normal man? I did not really know. In the end, I pushed and shoved my doubts into the oblivion of my subconscious. I could not admit even to myself the dark truth. I had to present myself to the world as what I wanted to be rather than who I was in reality. Too cowardly to do otherwise, I pretended to be normal, at least as the world defined it; and marriage, children, and home had become part of that. My marriage resulted from the great urge toward conformity rather than out of conviction that I was a normal heterosexual male.

I decided to ask Ann to marry me when I went home at Thanksgiving. I would turn twenty-one that next month and felt that I now possessed the capacity to make adult decisions. I had managed to save some money from my work to buy Ann a ring. The cost seemed astronomical at the time, although the ring now seems embarrassingly small. Nevertheless, I determined at the time that if I married, I would do it properly. Of course, I did not show the ring to Mother beforehand, but I felt an obligation to tell my aunt and uncle about my plans.

"I pretty sure can get an assistantship that will not be enough to support us, but Ann can work as a secretary. We should be able to live on that." I sat in their living room, which now seemed smaller and dingier than I had remembered it as a child.

"I hope you aren't rushing into anything." Uncle Frank also seemed smaller and less awe inspiring than I remembered. He had aged noticeably and seemed tired. Mother, on the other hand, still maintained her vitality, which seemed to belie her cruel sufferings. "You might get called up by the draft," Uncle Frank continued, "and have to leave Ann behind to fend for herself."

"What if she got pregnant?" Aunt Edna interjected. "You couldn't just leave her with that to contend with." Edna seemed displeased that I considered going to graduate school as well. Both could understand college, but the thoughts of further education and an academic career was foreign to them. I knew that my decision not to major in business, after giving up the idea of being a school teacher, had disappointed them. "I'm sorry that you seem to have all these dreams that are so unrealistic."

"I've really thought about all this." I found that I had become much less dutiful to both of them, which also irritated them. "I know what I want to do and haven't found anything that should stand in my way." I thought of my private concerns about marriage when I finished. I saw them shift uncomfortably in their chairs. Why, they must be thinking, hadn't I consulted them beforehand about buying the ring as I had with everything else in the last few years?

"How did you afford to buy that ring?"

"I worked extra hours and saved the money. My schedule is demanding, but I'm taking mostly reading courses. I can do much of it at work. Besides, the diamond is probably the smallest known to man. The ring only cost $200." The figure came leaping out at me, the same amount they had given me each year. I felt suddenly less sure of myself. "Honestly, Uncle Frank, I really think we'll be all right."

"Well, I hope you know what you're doing," Uncle Frank retorted, a touch of bitterness in his voice, although I doubt it was because he had made a connection between the cost of the ring and the size of his largesse.

"You should have a job and some savings before you rush into marriage. You know we won't be able to bail you out this time if you run into trouble."

"I don't expect you to. I am almost twenty-one. If we had problems, I could always quit school and get a job. Even if I'm drafted, Ann could work while I'm in the service." My assurances did not seem to satisfy them, but they ceased pressing their concerns. I hated to alienate them since they had supported me so much in the past. I knew they did not understand why I seemed to be rushing into marriage, and frankly, I was puzzled myself. No real reason existed not to delay until I had finished school. *Ann will still wait for me*, I thought smugly. Yet the more I contemplated marriage, the more I became convinced that it represented a way out of my dilemma. Running into Jay a few weeks before had scared me. I had already thought about asking Ann even before that incident, but it had forced me to flee from myself and my inner thoughts even more. Marriage became a way of proving my masculinity to myself, a further means of stuffing those doubts about myself even deeper into my psyche. I knew that once I married, the hidden desires and perverse fantasies would disappear. I would become like every other male.

I planned to remain home for the weekend, returning to college on Sunday afternoon. I thought Saturday the best opportunity to ask Ann the big question. I took some delight in speculating that she had no inkling of my intentions. I just told her that I needed to discuss something with her and left it at that. Friday night, I had great difficulty sleeping, repeatedly turning my various doubts over in my mind. It represented perhaps the most tormenting experience I had yet faced. I knew the step was irrevocable. Once I made the commitment, I could no longer turn in other directions. For perhaps the only time in my life, I confronted myself honestly. In the end, I concluded that I had no alternative. I could not exist in any other guise except that of a normal person. I succumbed rather easily to social pressures; and just as I walked out on David many years before, I now committed myself again down an irreversible path.

"You sounded so serious last night." Ann had greeted me the next day with a look that suggested that she also had worried. "Is there anything wrong?" I must have appeared dourer than I supposed. Obviously, Ann felt that something was quite amiss.

"No, actually, I hope you will think it is very good news."

"Don't keep me in suspense," Ann almost snapped. She did not appear relieved.

"I don't want to talk here. Let's take a walk down by the river."

The significance of the choice of location did not strike me at the time. The frosty air along the river invigorated me, and I thought it might cover any tone of uneasiness in my voice. I knew that I must be quite convincing. As we walked along, I put my arm around her. "Ann, next year, I hope to go on to graduate school. I've already submitted my applications and my adviser thinks I have an excellent chance of getting in." I had discussed my thought about graduate study with Ann but had never confirmed to her that I had determined to go ahead.

"I'm very happy for you. I know how much it means to you." I sensed that Ann perhaps expected me to use this opportunity to break off our relationship.

The thought of my real intention spurred me on with greater courage. "I may go out to the West Coast. Berkeley has a great department, and one of the most important Dickensian scholars is there."

"It's so far away," she interjected wistfully.

"That's the whole point. I don't want to be separated from you any longer." Her eyes widened as it dawned on her where this conversation headed. "I'd like you to marry me this summer so that we could go out together." She made no response but just studied me. "You could get a job, and with a decent assistantship, we could make it. We might have to alter our plans if something doesn't work out, but I'm pretty confident."

I said nothing more, waiting for some response. We walked along silently for several minutes. I did not have the nerve to look directly at her. I just stared intently along the sweep of the Susquehanna, fringed with bare trees and shimmering in the cold. Finally, I looked down at her. She was crying, and I pulled her closer to me. "Well, what do you say?"

"I just never expected . . ."

"I have a ring in my pocket, if you are willing." I pulled it out and opened the box. The clear sunshine made the small stone glisten and appear larger than it was. Ann looked at it in disbelief and wept ever more. "Come on, Ann, say something."

She finally swallowed and stammered, "Of course, I will. You know I love you." It may have been only the second time that she had ever admitted it.

I turned and kissed her. Then I slipped the ring on her finger, praying that it had some semblance of a fit. Afterward, we walked slowly back to her place. We did not say a word to each other.

We walked into her house, and Ann ran upstairs. She obviously had been crying, and she did not want to meet her parents. I walked into the living room and greeted the Randolfs. "What's wrong with Ann? She looked upset," Mrs. Randolf asked with concern.

"Would you be upset if I just asked you to marry me?" I quipped.

The Randolfs looked at each other in disbelief. Then Mr. Randolf jumped up with a broad smile on his face. "You aren't kidding, are you?"

"No, sir, I'm quite serious. And I think she accepted me."

"That's great news!" he boomed. Mr. Randolf had remained very fond of me, especially after I suggested that I would go into the same scholarly discipline. Ann was an only child and not academically motivated. I had become a scholar surrogate son for him. "When do you plan to marry?"

"We haven't gotten that far yet. I suppose this summer before I go to graduate school." Ann had just walked into the room, evidence of a quick repair job on her face. Her mother went over to hug her; Ann seemed comforted that I had already broken the news.

We discussed the possibility of taking Ann with me when I went home to tell my mother. Since I anticipated our usual scene, I thought the strain might be too much for Ann, and I did not believe Ann's presence would temper her conduct. Mother's first reaction was to laugh. "And what do you think you'll live on? Certainly not your good looks." She had a way with clichés.

"Mother, I knew that I would get some intelligent comment like that from you. I should get an assistantship sufficient to meet most of our expenses, and Ann will get a job. We shouldn't have any problems."

"What if she should get pregnant?" Mother was the second person to raise that issue, but both times, I dismissed the suggestion as ridiculous; it was a foreign consideration. "Her parents will never allow it."

"They've already agreed to the idea," I said with a note of triumph.

"I bet they have," she muttered. "Probably think they'll never get rid of her."

I made no reply to that last comment, although I thought, *Bitch*. But I did not vocalize it.

Preparations for the wedding consumed the next few months. I returned to school and continued to make plans for graduate school, sending off applications and requests for financial assistance. Ann remained home, getting ready for the wedding, which was to be a large one. Ann and I had originally hoped for something rather simple, but Mrs. Randolf insisted that it must be done right. Ann was her only child, and she wanted a dream wedding for her. Unfortunately, Ann did not share the dream; and I knew the preparations proved burdensome to her. The thought of being the center of attention in this way did not at all please Ann.

At Christmas, we had a long discussion about where to have the service. Ann and I were somewhat uncomfortable about a church wedding because of my lack of religious convictions and Ann's growing doubts. But her parents, who were not totally aware of our skepticism, remained pious and wanted the marriage suitably blessed. We considered the chapel at Susquehanna but, in the end, agreed to have the wedding at Saint Paul's. We talked to the new pastor, who had replaced Mr. Robertson, about the arrangements. I took instant dislike to the man because of his superficial joviality and exaggerated friendliness. I became disenchanted by the entire process and divorced myself from the preparations. It now became the Randolfs' wedding and I a casual participant. I returned to school after the holidays and buried myself in academic work.

Easter brought a new crisis. The responsibilities of marriage slowly began to sink in. I continued to ask myself why I had rushed into this decision so precipitously. Comments about children continued to bother me. What, in fact, would we do if Ann got pregnant? I approached Ann with the problem when we saw each other again at Easter.

"We need to take some precautions. A family will have to wait until I get established in a teaching position."

Ann probably had not considered that side of marriage either. That sex would become a part of her life seemed to be the farthest thing from her mind. She must have taken my comments to heart since, a few days later, she told me that her mother had made an appointment for her with a gynecologist. When I returned home in June, a few weeks before the wedding, Ann told me she had started taking the pill.

Preparations for the wedding had now reached their final stages. Mother had been totally uncooperative in the entire process, and I had to supply the list of names from our side of the family because she insisted she did not have the time. She also refused to buy a new dress for the ceremony, being emphatic that the one she normally wore on Sundays would suffice. She appeared drab and worn at the wedding in comparison to Ann's parents, who glowed with pride. Only the fact that it would probably be the last time I would have to sleep in her house heartened me.

Between graduation from Muhlenberg and the wedding at the end of June, I resumed my job as stock boy in the Acme. The thought that a holder of a bachelor's degree in English would work in such a position astounded a number of people who saw me. I also did not relish the idea of continuing this drudgery until we left for graduate school. I often talked with a girl named Julie who had worked with me for many years. She also planned to get married that summer to a fellow who worked in my brother's garage. One day when business was particularly slow, she walked over to me and began discussing her wedding. Then out of the clear blue sky, she added, "You know, if I didn't know you were getting married also, I would swear you were a homosexual."

My heart sank to the pit of my stomach. I tried not to appear flustered. "How's that?"

"Well, I often notice that when guys come into the store, you looked them over very carefully—you know, study them from top to bottom."

I was not aware that I had that habit and certainly did not imagine that other people could detect it. "Oh, I do that to everybody, I suppose." I did not want to protest too much about the question of homosexuality and allowed her comment to pass off casually.

"Well, I just notice it, especially with the guys. But I guess it's nothing."

She shrugged it off and continued discussing her wedding. For the next few days, I made a conscious effort to look girls up and down with special intensity. I was not sure if Julie paid any attention, but I would not take any chances. I also became aware that I did, in fact, have a desire to do the same with men, although I avoided it scrupulously whenever I was in Julie's presence.

In the final days before the wedding, I became overcome with ennui. Internal depression almost paralyzed me, and I continued to be plagued by doubts. Was I making a fatal mistake? Was I ready for marriage? Would I ever be ready for marriage?

The scene at the Acme haunted me continuously. One afternoon I lay on my bed listening to records. I had put on Rachmaninoff's *Symphony No. 2*, and the emotion of the music engulfed me. The mournfulness of the third movement matched my own mood, and its sorrow plunged me to even greater depths of despair. Yet I could not extricate myself. I had gone too far to turn back. I loved Ann and knew that, in many ways, we were well suited to each other. But there was an inner self bursting to be released that I knew I must keep caged for the rest of my life. I feared that I did not have the strength. Only the momentum of events kept me going. I tried to put on a good front, but Ann knew something bothered me and tried to encourage me. At one point, she even assured me that if I wanted to back out, she would not object. Yet despite her valiant efforts, I remained morose and disheartened.

The wedding itself went without a hitch. The service was beautiful in spite of the repulsively effusive pastor. His saccharine sweetness almost seemed appropriate to the occasion. The only moment that gave me pause came when the minister demanded that if either of us knew any reason why we should not be united in marriage lawfully and in accordance with God's Word, we must confess it. Well, of course, I knew very plainly of such an impediment: I was a flaming faggot who had no business marrying anyone. I let this last chance slip by without doing my moral duty, however. The minister had not really provided me with an adequate opportunity to mull these thoughts over; he continued on with the service without a pause. Only later did the import faze me.

The Randolfs held reception in the student center of the university and had gone to great expense to make it a festive afternoon. They even hired a band, which played dance music badly. At one point, I danced with my new mother-in-law and, at her insistence, even called her Mom. As we circled the floor, she began talking with me seriously. "You know, Ann is very apprehensive about tonight. Please be gentle with her. We had some talks, and I tried to calm her fears, but there is only so much I can do. You will have to comfort her and keep it from being a bad experience. Can I trust you to do that?"

"Of course, you can" was all that I could say. I was not exactly an experienced lover who could skillfully guide my bride to new heights of ecstasy while soothing her fears. My own awkwardness and discomfort did not make the situation any easier.

In fact, the wedding night turned out disastrously. Uncle Frank had given us his hunting cabin to use for a week since we could not afford to go anywhere for a honeymoon. First, I had trouble finding it since I had never driven there before. At one point, I drove the Randolfs' car into a stump and damaged a fender. When we finally arrived, we discovered a dirty and unkempt cabin, which had no semblance of a honeymoon cottage. It smelled of stale beer and must; no one had used the place in months. We sat in the main room amid the clutter, trying to be appropriately romantic, but the atmosphere proved inconducive. We delayed retiring to the bedroom as long as possible. I tried to be as reassuring and light about everything, but my own awkwardness only made matters worse. I discovered very quickly the extent of Ann's modesty, a characteristic that did not alter with time. I did not think she ever took off her clothes in front of me; and to this day, I wouldn't recognize her headless, naked body. What I remember most about that night was the amount of weeping Ann did. It was not an auspicious beginning.

After our first week, we returned to Selinsgrove and moved in with her parents. That proved an uncomfortable arrangement, although thankfully only temporary. I worked for the last time at the Acme, saving up money for our trip to California. Berkeley had accepted me, and I had won a scholarship sponsored through the National Defense Education Act, which handsomely paid my graduate expenses. We planned to take a train to San Francisco in the middle of August to set up housekeeping and buy a car before classes began. The Randolfs had generously given us cash for a wedding gift, and Ann had saved a good deal of money from her job. We seemed to have some financial security and had survived the initial traumas of marriage. With much relief, we boarded the train in Harrisburg, on our own for the first time.

Chapter V

Epistle

Life at Berkeley was like nothing we had ever experienced before. The first exposure to Telegraph Avenue swept Ann into a state of shock and disbelief. Nothing in Selinsgrove had prepared her for this scene. We took an efficiency apartment on Warring Avenue, which allowed me to walk to my classes in Wheeler Hall. We rented a few pieces of bedroom furniture from the Graduate Housing Office and made do with makeshift for the rest. I carefully placed my books in a bookcase made of bricks and boards, and we ate supper sitting on folding chairs at a card table. We also bought two beanbag chairs, our only other means of sitting. I did not want to purchase a television, but Ann insisted because she became so bored at night while I worked on my papers.

Ann's father had arranged through a colleague in the English Department to get Ann a position as a secretary, and we found that we could live a comfortable although Spartan existence on her salary and the proceeds from my fellowship. We rarely went out for dinner, although we loved the ethnic food available there, and our main form of recreation remained movies. I succeeded in elevated Ann's tastes somewhat, and we took in a few foreign films. Peter O'Toole's *The Ruling Class* had a particular impact on her. Otherwise, we spent most of our time at home. Ann seemed satisfied with this arrangement since we shared a great deal of time together.

Both of us, however, experienced a deep cultural shock by the lifestyle we found surrounding us. We had lived sheltered lives up to that point, especially Ann, who had never ventured out of Selinsgrove. Even Allentown seemed painfully provincial beside Berkeley and the Bay Area. We knew that hippies existed but only through the filtered experiences of television. Neither one of us had come into contact with drugs, and now we found them almost universally accepted and openly used. People in offbeat attire wandered the streets and campus of Berkeley, and evidently, the campus community swelled by twice its size because of the influx of outsiders attracted by the excitement or the prospect of being able to proselytize in this fertile soil. Ann seemed disconcerted and repulsed by much of what she encountered, and I became aware of her unease. I hoped, eventually, she would become accustomed to much of the carnival atmosphere and, in a sense, appreciate it. But she was never happy there.

Living in Berkeley in those years seemed tremendously exciting to me. The war in Vietnam had heated up; and the protests against the war, some violent, became a common feature of campus life. I sometimes became annoyed when the demonstrations interfered with classes or getting to the library. The acrid smell of tear gas often filtered into the classrooms of Wheeler and made concentration difficult. I watched brutal clashes between police and students as campus authorities attempted to clear Sproul Plaza of demonstrators. They clogged Sather Gate and moved like waves across the campus, outwitting the feeble attempts of the security forces to control them. I strongly supported the protests against the war, but I never became actively engaged in the movement. I felt a sense of responsibility about my academic work and family concerns, which would not permit me to slacken. I cannot say the same for many of my colleagues in the graduate program.

The draft loomed as a particular threat to me. Like all eighteen-year-olds, I had registered for the draft; but at that time, no one had even heard of Vietnam. In those days, we all expected to have to go off to Cuba to fight. Now the widened war in Southeast Asia became the focal point of our attention. My draft board had renewed my student deferment once I went to Berkeley, but I feared the calls for removal of the "privileges of the rich." I didn't know what I would have done had I received that unwelcomed greetings. I opposed the Vietnam War and, in an inchoate fashion, struggled to define general attitudes about war. The vast movement of young men to Canada and Sweden had not yet begun, although one associate in the graduate program had disappeared when his draft board refused to grant him a fifth extension on his student deferment. Ann and I rarely discussed the problem until later when President Nixon introduced the lottery.

The years at Berkeley opened both of our eyes to the wider world around us. Ann had never come in contact with such a variety of types, and this new awareness did not always comfort her. She expressed a sense of homesickness once or twice when we first arrived; but I dismissed it, and she stopped voicing these concerns. Since we did not have the resources to travel home, we did not see our families for long stretches. At the same time, no one in Selinsgrove would have considered coming to California to visit us. I read about the fact that San Francisco had become a growing center of the gay community, and I even became familiar with the names of the sections of the city where they tended to congregate. Yet this knowledge never really tempted me to explore the Castro and satisfy my curiosity. I sometimes went into the city but did not feel compelled to venture into that part. My cravings remained surprisingly quiet during these early years of our marriage.

By December, I recognized Ann's discomfort at Berkeley and worried that it proved too much for her. One evening not long after a particularly violent protest march at the university, I spoke to Ann about my ruminations. "I thought that perhaps I would apply to some schools back east to complete my Ph.D. Wouldn't you be happier in Michigan or Wisconsin?"

"You really need to do what is best for you. Don't worry about me. I'll get along fine."

"Now, Ann, be honest. You aren't really happy here. I've seen you try, but I know it is too foreign."

Ann persisted in her claim that she could adjust if she had enough time. At the same time, I discussed the possibility of a move with my advisor. Without saying it openly, he certainly hinted that I would be very foolish to leave. He also pointed out that the two institutions I had considered also had experienced violent protests against the war. Persuaded by his counsel, I determined to complete my degree at Berkeley. Shortly after I had made our decision, the Tet Offensive again sparked a renewed round of demonstrations more violent than preceding ones. The focus on academics became less and less important to most of the students. Many became involved in the presidential campaign, stumping for either the McCarthy or Kennedy campaigns in an effort to stop the election of Humphrey, whom we all regarded as a stooge for President Johnson. Although I got caught up emotionally in these various political disputes, I felt restrained from taking on an active role. While Ann voiced her support for my decision to stay, I could tell that she would have preferred to be elsewhere. Yet either institution I consisted also saw violent protests culminating in the bombing of Sterling Hall.

Ann never fully acclimated to the offbeat lifestyle of the Bay Area; the drug culture that surrounded us particularly disturbed her, and she took offense when offered pot at a party we attended. Incense and temple bells did not suit her personality. I must confess that I tended to be more conservative in my lifestyle than many of my colleagues, but I found that I could tolerate differences much more than she could.

Demonstrations continued to disrupt classes, and the debate over the war seemed to take a higher priority than academics. These years seemed very exciting to me. I remember fondly the protests, especially following the Kent State massacre, in which I actually took an active role for once, abandoning classes and turning in an assignment late because of it. I suspected that, in that case, the professor who was rabidly antiwar thought more highly of me because he had previously regarded me as somewhat suspect in my political thinking. The demonstrations continued, it seemed, almost daily. I took special interest in the trial of the Chicago Eight; here were men willing to stand up for their convictions, in the face of oppression. It was an invigorating period to be alive.

Yet despite the turmoil of these surroundings, it seemed another peaceful period in my life. I enjoyed the work and had a good rapport with my professors. Ann and I adjusted to marriage with a good deal of success. Living together proved an interesting experience for both of us. Ann's modesty did not abate over time, and I thought that she was often upset that I was not more modest myself. She objected especially to the fact that I did not wear pajamas. Her father had always worn them, and I suspect she thought that something was wrong with me because I preferred my shorts or even nothing at all. She never told me this directly since we rarely communicated these things verbally. I could just tell by her expression or the haste with which she shut off the light if I returned from the bathroom with nothing on. I probably should have been more sensitive, but I wasn't.

My own internal torment seemed to have vanished during this period as well. I thought that perhaps it had disappeared with maturity, never to bother me again. I still looked at men admiringly, but I found that the strong desires about physical contact seemed to have waned. My sexual relationships with Ann did not prove a substitute since they did not increase in number or variety over time. Sex was something that must be done out of obligation and marital duty; Ann never really seemed to enjoy it. I attempted to introduce some innovations into our physical relationship but with no success. Once, I even mentioned oral sex, and Ann became physically ill when I explained what I meant. I even thought that her regard for me suffered for suggesting such a thing. Yet somehow I was able to sublimate my natural desires in my work. I did not seek release through any external means and contented myself with self-imposed gratification when the opportunity arose. My fantasies, however, still had a healthy dose of all-male content.

The other matter I thought less about was religion. I became a convinced atheist, and my thought processes had grown thoroughly secularized. We did not bother to attend church at all since we left home. Once when we had returned to Selinsgrove for Christmas, we refused to attend services at Saint Paul's, much to the discontent of Ann's parents. We remained unabashed in our convictions and explained forthrightly that religion and Christianity no longer held any meaning in our lives. I remember delivering a grand sermon about the fact that we must mature as human beings, take our fate into our own hands, and face the world with our own resources rather than depending on myths and legends that had no bearing on our own times. Yet I did not recognize the similarity between the message of humanity I proclaimed in line with the liberal humanists who influenced my thinking and what I had been taught as a youth.

Toward the end of my graduate program, I began work on my dissertation, focusing on the relation between Charles Dickens' writings and liberal reform efforts in England. I had long held a fascination for Dickens, and my major professor suggested that this was a suitable topic, especially considering contemporary events. Dickens' later novels such as *Bleak House*, *Little Dorrit*, and *Our Mutual Friend* especially interested me. I planned to examine the reforming themes in these novels and explore the extent to which Dickens' contemporaries depended on his inspiration to bring about social reform. The research took me on my first trip to London to do research at the British Library. During the spring semester of 1972, I spent a few months in London, living at London House, located near the museum off Russell Square. The expense prevented me from taking

Ann along. At that time, the pound was quite high and the cost of living in London astronomical. Ann did not seem to mind staying home to work.

After I returned home, I began the serious work of writing the dissertation and looking for a job. I had thought of remaining in school for as long as possible because of my draft deferment, but then Nixon altered the system and introduced the lottery. Perhaps for the only time in my life, I was lucky since February 9, my birthday, was number 317 in the lottery. Although I lost the deferment, the new system made the possibility of getting drafted highly remote; I could therefore go about planning my life like a normal person. I never did feel a sense of guilt about avoiding the military. The war had never really touched me; a few young men from Selinsgrove died in Vietnam but no one to whom I was close. I had not done manly deeds on the battlefield as they had to defend freedom. Like the wimp that I was, I had remained close to my books, avoiding the challenges of life. I had also not become deeply immersed in the antiwar movement. Although I did attend some of the rallies, I did not involve myself in the various organizations that fought against the war. My life was never as torn up as many of those who fought in the war, only to return home to an ungrateful and guilt-ridden nation.

Getting a job proved harder than I had anticipated. The universities turned out English Ph.D.s at a fantastic rate, drying up the job market rapidly. Fortunately, my major professor had a friend at Dickinson College in Carlisle, Pennsylvania, where an opening existed. Ann was very excited when I told her about the prospect since it was less than one hundred miles from Selinsgrove. I interviewed there in April 1973 and received an offer of a position. Since a place in a community college seemed to be the only other possibility, I accepted the job with glee. I now would have a real job that paid reasonably money. No more Acmes to sweep or shopping bags to fill. No more constant worry about whether we would be able to make it on our small incomes, although since we had no children, we had a much easier time of it than some in the graduate program.

The security of a job encouraged Ann to consider changes in our situation. She often talked about having children, but she seemed to understand that, as long as I was in graduate school, we would have to wait. Now that a secure position seemed assured, she began talking about the need to start our family. Ann always had a deep love of children, and she seemed to have a natural way with them. I was not at all surprised when she began pressing me about having one of our own.

"I'm almost thirty. I'm worried that if we have any trouble with having a baby, I'll get too old if we wait much longer."

"But don't you think we should get settled at Dickinson first? After all, the job might not work out, and we'd have to move again." Not convinced about the entire idea of children, I had trouble envisioning myself as a father. I wondered if a man with my problems could really be suitably paternal. Moreover, I worried that my condition might be hereditary, although I didn't really understand much about its nature. I did not begin reading seriously the psychological studies of homosexuality until much later. All I knew was that I might not make a satisfactory father. "Can't we wait another year?"

Ann began to cry when I became negative. "I've waited so long. I want a child very badly. Please wouldn't you see my side? You worry entirely too much about the costs." I had also expressed concern about the financial impact of children to try to discourage her. "I'm sure we can make it." In the end, Ann prevailed. I knew that she was so unhappy about further delay that I decided to relent. I also supposed that it would take some time before she could get pregnant. In May, Ann stopped taking the pill; and in June, she became pregnant. I never knew that I possessed such virility.

That August, I defended my dissertation successfully, and we packed up to move back to Pennsylvania. Carlisle, in many ways, reminded me of Selinsgrove, not always a fortunate comparison. I knew Ann delighted in getting back to familiar settings, but the experience in Berkeley had opened up entirely new vistas for me. Returning home did not hold out the same promise as it did for her. Yes, the mountains seemed as beautiful as ever, but the same small-town atmosphere of my youth quickly became oppressive. The English Department at Dickenson was a solid one, although most of its members were considerably older than I was and did not share much in common with me. Politically, they were all quite conservative; and while Ann and I celebrated the night Nixon resigned, the others appeared in deep mourning. I wanted to try some new courses, which I thought might appeal more to the students, but the other members of the department eschewed change with vigor, the only thing about which they ever became animated. Surprisingly, I eventually did receive tenure, even though they regarded me as something of a Young Turk and a troublemaker. I tended to remain to myself, engaging in my research or spending time with the students, again something my colleagues avoided. I released my frustrations by taking up jogging and soon ran about five miles a day through the serene countryside that surrounded our house.

That March, Ann gave birth to a boy whom we named after my father. Thomas' arrival produced remarkable changes in Ann and in our relationship. Ann had a natural maternal instinct, which caused her to blossom in ways that I had never seen previously. She seemed radiant, aglow with a warmth and affection I had never experienced. She extended this new feeling primarily to the child, but I also became a recipient. Even our sexual interludes warmed from this new power within her. Had I known the impact of having a child, I would have had one long before.

I had not particularly wanted a son. I had great discomfiture about having another male in the house and had hoped all along that we would have a daughter. In the end, though, I was very pleased about Thomas, but I wanted to make certain that he did not turn out to be like me. He was going to be a true man and not share my ambiguities. Soon after he was born, I rushed out to buy a variety of sports equipment and a lifetime supply of GI Joe toys. If I could not be macho, Thomas would. Ann was quite surprised at my seeming turnabout in attitude. I practiced tossing a ball to him shortly after he began to walk, and when he turned two, I began taking him out every Saturday afternoon to play ball or hit with a bat. One such occasion would remain forever etched in my memory. I had been pitching a ball to Tom so that he could hit it with a bat. For a long time, he had failed miserably. I instructed him in the fine art of batting, of which I knew nothing myself, but spoke with great authority. "Now watch the ball carefully and swing just before it gets to you."

The ball went whizzing past him as he swung furiously at it as if it were some phantom in the night. "Tom, I don't think you were watching." I got a great deal of exercise chasing after the ball since depending on him to retrieve delayed our game immeasurably. "Swing at the ball in a straight line. And you don't have to try to hit it so hard." He just smiled at me as I ran back to my original position.

"Do you want to fly the kite now, Daddy?" he asked, obviously bored with my efforts to turn him into a Stan Musial.

"Not yet, honey. Just a few more pitches. I think you're really getting it." Another ball sped past him, unmolested by the bat except perhaps for disturbances in the air currents. "We'll give it another try. I'm sure you'll hit it now. Just watch the ball."

I pitched the ball one more time. I had resolved that it would be the last effort of the day before we retired to the more leisurely pursuit of kite flying. Tom watched the ball intently and swung with all his might. Of course, it was just plain luck that he connected, but that did not alter the result. The ball hurled toward me with tremendous speed and strength. Catching me in the middle of my stomach and knocking me to the ground, it dazed and completely winded me. I lay semiconscious on the ground until Tom came over to me. He picked up the ball and stood looking down at me. "Are you all right?" His lyric five-year-old voice created a melody out of the question. I will never forget the poignancy of his look and tone. His words of innocent concern instantly overcame the anger that I initially felt when the ball plowed into me.

"Yeah, I think I'll be okay." I picked myself up and looked again at his small face looking intently at me. "Don't worry, I'm fine." I pulled him close to me and hugged him. He still mixed surprise at the impact of his hit with fear that I was either seriously hurt or angry with him. I tried not to show that the impact of the ball still hurt and walked as upright as I could manage to the car to stow the bat and ball. "I think we better go home. It is starting to get dark." I smiled to myself, thinking that perhaps Tom did have the makings of a star Little Leaguer.

It became almost an obsession with me that my son was going to be a jock. Funnily, Tom seemed much happier about doing puzzles or looking at a picture book. It seemed that he tolerated our Saturday sports extravaganzas to humor me. It soon became apparent that Tom shared my lack of coordination and had the same difficulties in catching a ball as I did as a boy. Ann sometimes became annoyed with me because she felt that I was pushing sports on him, claiming that it seemed rather peculiar for me and quite out of character since I would never ordinarily spend a Sunday afternoon in front of the television watching a Steelers game. Even though I realized that I could not alter Tom's inborn character, I enjoyed tremendously the time that I spent with him and now am exceedingly thankful that I did.

My own work seemed to benefit from this new source of strength. I found that I enjoyed teaching tremendously and developed good relations with students, although perhaps it stemmed primarily from the fact that I was so much closer in age to them than most of the other members of the department. The responsibility for producing a series of new courses weighed heavily on me, and I found that I had to spend long hours in my office or the library preparing for classes. I got to pass less time at home because of these demands, and Ann understandably resented the fact that I was not around even as much as I had been in graduate school. I tried to devote as much time with my new family as possible, but it was really not enough. Moreover, since Ann did not work once the baby arrived, she found that she had much more time at home; and my absences became more obvious.

Thomas had reached the age of six before we had another child. Sarah was born in June 1979. I had already received tenure and promotion to Associate Professor, not without some misgivings from my older colleagues who showed signs of resentment. Because of the uncertainty of the job, we waited to enlarge our family until I had a sense of job security. With fewer burdens placed on me than as a new teacher, I now found time to do a great deal more with the family. Yet I never became as close to Sarah as I had with Tom. I did not really know what to do with a daughter. Tom was very active and outgoing, while Sarah was extremely shy like her mother. I did not enjoy playing dolls with her, nor could I force the same enthusiasm to play ball with her as I had with Tom. Our relationship was, for many years, restrained and even awkward; not until recently did we begin to develop some sort of closeness. Ann always resented that I showed too much partiality to the boy.

A few weeks after Sarah's first Christmas, Tom developed a bad chest cold, which he could not seem to shake. Because of the extremely cold weather, we did not think that it was unusual and gave him the normal treatment, allowing him to stay home from school once or twice. Ann's mother came to visit us a few weeks after the cold set in, and she became instantly alarmed. She urged Ann to take him to a doctor, which we had been reluctant to do since we had not found a satisfactory one in Carlisle. Ann did take Tom to a doctor we used occasionally, and he seemed worried about the condition and urged Ann to take Tom to a specialist at the Hershey Medical Center outside Harrisburg. Since Ann's mother remained with us, she agreed to take them so that I would not have to miss any classes. We had no idea what the problem might be and dismissed both Mrs. Randolf's and the doctor's concern. When I returned home from work, Ann and her mother had just arrived back from Hershey. Ann was crying, and her mother greeted me with a somber and drawn look. "What's the matter? Where's Tom?" A sense of panic overtook me.

"We had to leave him at the hospital," Mrs. Randolf replied. Clearly, Ann could not speak. "We needed to collect a few things and planned to drive back tonight with you."

"But what's wrong with Tom?" I asked urgently.

Ann mustered the strength to mutter, "It's leukemia."

I felt myself turning light headed, and my head began to swim. "But. . . ."

"You'd better sit down." Ann's mother put her arm on my shoulder and guided me over to the sofa. Ann sat down across from me; she did not bother to remove her jacket. "The doctor took some blood tests and said that there might be a problem. Tommy's white cell count is way up. He didn't tell us exactly what it was but thought it might be serious. He wanted Tommy admitted to the hospital at once to do further tests."

"I know it's cancer." I could hardly understand Ann. Her voice trembled, and the soft sobbing muffled her words. "I should have taken him to the doctor sooner. We might have. . . ."

"Don't blame yourself, Ann. It just seemed like a bad cold. You couldn't have known."

"No, I should have taken him immediately. The doctor wanted to know how long ago the symptoms had appeared, and he seemed concerned that it was over two weeks. Probably they could have done something."

As we talked, I tried to recover my equilibrium. I saw that Ann had lost almost complete control of herself and that her mother, while struggling to avoid breaking down to help her daughter, had increasing difficulty doing so. I knew that I had to maintain my composure as much as possible so that all of us were not incapacitated. "Ann, did the doctor tell you it was leukemia?"

"No, but. . . ."

"Well, don't jump to conclusions yet. Wait until the tests are finished. Let the doctor do the diagnosis. Don't get yourself worked up needlessly." I tried to sound much cooler than I felt inside. "What are we supposed to do?"

Mrs. Randolf, sensing that I was trying to quiet the situation and soothe Ann somewhat, seemed to regain some of her own composure. "We drove home really just to get you. The hospital will allow a parent to stay in Tommy's room at night. We haven't told him that something's wrong, but I'm sure he senses it. The doctor thought that one of you should stay with him so that he does not become unduly fearful of the hospital. We were going to grab supper somewhere and drive right back this evening. I wanted to leave Ann there, but she needed to be here when we told you. She knew how much you would worry." Of course, ironically, I seemed outwardly to be a tower of strength in comparison to Ann, who verged on hysterics.

"Well, let's go then." Ann stuffed some clothing in a case while I telephoned the head of the English Department at his home to explain our problems and asked him to cancel my Friday classes. I told him that I would call again from Hershey if we would be delayed beyond Sunday. Ann had gone next door where Sarah was staying to ask our neighbors if they would keep her for a day or so until I returned. The Hingstones, a retired couple, treated Sarah like a granddaughter and were pleased to be able to help out. Then we jumped in the car and began the drive to Hershey. We found the hospital shortly after nine o'clock after a rather too fast drive down the Pennsylvania Turnpike. We decided that Ann should remain with Tom, while Mrs. Randolf and I stayed at a nearby motel. I went up to Tom's room first, after some argument with the rather officious hospital staff, to say good night. I found him still awake, watching *The A-Team*, something we did not normally allow.

"How do you feel, sport?"

"Daddy, I don't like this place. Can we go home now?" He did not appear to sense the potential seriousness of his problem. At this point, he seemed more bored than concerned.

I fixed his pillows and straightened out his covers. "No, honey. You'll have to stay here tonight, but Mom's going to sleep in the other bed. She'll be here all night." He looked so small and frail in his hospital gown amid the covers. Suddenly, he appeared to be weak and vulnerable.

"But I want to go home."

"I bet the doctor will let you go home tomorrow, and when we get there, I'll take you ice-skating on the lake like I promised." I took his hand and gave it a squeeze.

"Can't we go now?" he asked plaintively.

"Mom's going to spend the night here with you, and Gram and I will be close by. Tomorrow then we'll go home." The last seemed almost like a prayer. I felt the urge to pray, but I was not sure to whom, perhaps to the doctor.

I kissed Tom good night and walked down to the nurse's station. Ann and her mother stood talking with one of the night staff. "I'm sorry, ma'am, but there's nothing more I can tell you. Dr. Higgins ordered a series of tests for the morning. We can't tell you anything until the tests are completed."

I could tell Ann had been crying again. "Please try to pull yourself together. The nurse is right. Don't jump to any conclusions. Tommy is liable to be scared enough. You need to be in a condition to support him." Ann did seem to rally, and by the time she entered Tommy's room, she had managed to gain control of herself again. Mrs. Randolf and I left the hospital and checked into the Holiday Inn nearby. I spent a sleepless night worrying where I would get the strength to support both Tommy and Ann. I didn't think that I could pull it off.

The next day, we sat in the sterile waiting room of the hospital during the completion of Tommy's tests. The atmosphere of the room only intensified our anxiety. Tommy returned to his room about eleven thirty, and we spent several hours in there trying to cheer him up. Some of the tests had included taking samples of his bone marrow, which had been extremely painful. We had to wait for two days for some of the results. We all took turns over that endless weekend trying to cheer Tommy. Finally, on Monday morning, Dr. Higgins asked to see us in his office. "I'm afraid I have some pretty bad news. We did extensive blood work and also examined his marrow. I'm afraid he has an abnormality called pancytopenia, which is seriously advanced. I've ordered preparations for chemotherapy to begin as soon as possible. He'll have to stay here several days and perhaps for a week, but we should be able to transfer him to a hospital closer to home to complete the treatment."

I felt my entire body chill with fear. I looked at Ann and saw that the impact of the news had not fully struck her. I started to take her hand, but it trembled so much that I thought I would only make the situation worse. "What is pancytopenia?" she asked. Now I knew why she had not broken down completely.

"It has produced a cancer of the white blood cells, leukemia." The doctor spoke the words that Ann had dreaded. She began to collapse, but I managed to grab her. The doctor continued talking hurriedly, trying to reassure Ann. "I am fairly certain that he suffers from acute myeloblastic leukemia. Several years ago, such a condition was always fatal. But with modern treatment, the chances of survival are improved. Your son's condition is more advanced than we would like to see, but don't give up hope. He's a good, strong lad and may be able to pull through." The doctor's comforting words, however, fell on deaf ears. Ann had already given up our son for lost.

We decided that, before we saw Tommy again that day, we should regain some composure. We went out to a diner to have an early supper and talked about what we must do. "We have got to maintain calm in front of Tommy. We don't want him to become alarmed about his condition. I know that he is already worried about being in the hospital. We don't want to make it worse."

Ann agreed mentally, but control of her emotions seemed another matter. She broke down several times during the meal and sat most of the time wringing her napkins in her hands without touching her food. "It's a lot easier to say than do. What are we going to do?" she added in total desperation. "Should we see another doctor to confirm the diagnosis?"

"Ann, we can't deny what he has. We have to do what the doctor says and hope for the best."

"You could also pray," Mrs. Randolf interjected. I didn't think she meant to be sarcastic, but the remark stung me.

"How could a God allow this to happen to a helpless boy?" Ann shot back. For the first time, she made a public declaration to one of her parents about our religious views. Ann's mother, also feeling the tension, mumbled something about Tommy's lack of religious training. I had never seen sparks fly between them in that manner before.

"We can't get into this now," I interrupted. "We are all under a strain. We've just got to pull ourselves together."

We sat in silence through the rest of the meal and then walked back to the hospital. Ann wanted to remain in the hospital with Tom again that night. I went into his room to say good night. I struggled to maintain my composure. "Well, sport, you've had a big day. Get some sleep, and tomorrow I'll come back and read to you."

"Daddy, am I going to die?"

I had not expected the question, and its impact almost floored me. "Of course not, son. You're going to be fine. You have to take some medicine and stay here for a while. But everything's going to be fine."

"Dad, I'm scared." Perhaps we had not maintained our confident expressions, or perhaps he just had some instinctive understanding of the nature of his illness. Somehow he sensed that I did not speak with full assurance about his condition. We talked for a few minutes more, and then I left to return to the motel. That night, I cried for the first time since I was a teenager.

Monday evening, I left Ann with Tom and returned home with Mrs. Randolf. There did not seem much that I could do, and the doctor felt that Tom could be moved to Carlisle within a few days after his initial treatment. Therefore, I decided to return to my classes to fulfill my teaching obligations. Ann's mother had agreed to keep house for me. Shortly after we arrived home, the phone rang. Humphrey Johnson, dean of the chapel at Dickinson, had called to see if he could help. Apparently, my chair had spread the word about Tom's illness. I explained to Humphrey that the doctor had diagnosed the condition as cancer. "Can I stop over at your office tomorrow?" Humphrey responded. "Perhaps we could talk about it." We agreed to meet for lunch.

I did not relish the thought of discussing my personal problems with him not only because I did not know him that well but also because I did not look forward to the religious soft sell that I anticipated. I made a pretense of teaching my morning classes and then went to the faculty dining hall to have lunch with him. "How is Ann handling it?"

"Not very well. She broke down several times, but she has managed to keep her wits when she's with Tommy."

He asked about the prognosis, and I explained that the doctor had been rather noncommittal about it. "Have you prayed about it?" I knew the question was inevitable and resented the fact that Dickinson had to have a chaplain who actually took religion seriously. I had enough troubles dealing with Tom's illness without having to feel guilty about my lack of religious beliefs. I did not, however, have to answer the question. Apparently, my expression suggested my annoyance. "I don't mean to pry into your personal beliefs. Perhaps I shouldn't have said "prayer." I only mean that it helps to talk about these things to someone else, either to God or another person. Just don't hold it inside you. It only makes it worse."

Thereafter, he dropped the God talk and discussed his own experience with a seriously ill child. In his case, his daughter recovered, but the situation appeared very grim for a long time. I found that talking with him did allow me to open up somewhat, something that I had not been able to do with Ann. I did want to talk to someone, but opening up with Ann only made the situation worse for her. I discovered that Humphrey was not a stuffy and pious clergyman at all but a man sincerely concerned about the hurt that I was feeling and desiring to help if he could. Over the next several months, we developed a deep relationship, meeting frequently to talk about Tom's condition. Humphrey filled a void for me at a critical juncture since Ann and I began to grow apart as Tom's condition worsened. Although I tried to support her, I found that she increasingly withdrew within herself, putting up barricades so that my efforts to reach out proved fruitless. I tried to arrange for Humphrey to talk with her, but she refused.

Tom returned to the hospital in Carlisle after a week's stay in Hershey. Although the doctor felt that Tom had a chance to overcome the cancer, he warned us of its rapid progress and Tom's weakened condition as a result. The chemotherapy seemed to have slowed the advance of the cancer, but remission had not taken place. Tom remained in the hospital for over a month, receiving further treatment. He looked like a bald dwarf, and his appearance and the constant testing seemed to discourage him. Although we assured him that he was getting better, he became more and more depressed. He finally came home after staying in hospitals for almost two months. The course of the disease stabilized for several months, but then he began to deteriorate. We had to place him back in the hospital at Carlisle, but soon we transferred him to Hershey again because the facilities in Carlisle could not cope with his worsening condition. There, the doctor told us that the cancer seemed to be defeating their efforts to combat it. They felt that Tom had only a few weeks to survive.

During this period, I attempted to keep up my classes as much as possible while spending hours driving between Carlisle and Hershey. Ann's mother became a tower of strength for both of us since she realized that I felt the strain nearly as much as Ann did, although I forced myself to carry on. Ann, by this point, had given up in despair. The doctor finally came to me and suggested that we should begin to prepare Tom for death. "I think the boy understands already that he is not going to recover. In these cases, it seems to make things easier for the child and the parents if we are honest about his condition."

Ann became quite incapable of handling the situation any longer. I found it increasingly impossible to try to help Tom and deal with Ann at the same time. Finally, I determined to seek help from Humphrey Johnson since I did not seem capable myself of dealing with the situation. "The doctor has been quite unhelpful about how to deal Tom. Clearly, he is going to die soon, but the doctor has not said anything about how to tell him, just that we should."

"That's part of his own defense mechanism. Doctors hate to admit failure, and death is the ultimate form of failure. Telling Tom directly that he is about to die, it seems to me, is not going to help much. What you need to do is to help him avoid fear. That's what makes it more difficult."

"Again, that's fine for you to say, but it still doesn't help me much."

"You need to avoid bitterness yourself. That won't help Tom either. You need to accept his death as much as he does."

Now the flood of emotion began to burst forth. I had tried to be a source of strength to both Tom and Ann. "Why does it have to happen to him? What has he done to deserve this?"

"He's done nothing. That is one of the great tragedies of life, which we can't explain. It's good for you to cry to release some of the pent-up anger. Don't try to find someone or something to blame. It's no one's fault. Just go to Tom and tell him softly that you love him, that you want to be with him as much as you can, and leave it at that."

The next day, I returned to Hershey to find that Tom's condition has worsened considerably. I went into his room and sat by his bed. I took his hand, and he awoke and smiled at me. We just sat there for a long time, his hand in mine. Finally, he said, "Tell Mom not to be so sad. I'll be all right. She needs to stop crying so much. It makes me very sad." I sat with him for another hour, a feeling of total helplessness overcoming me. What could I do? Where could I turn for help? I had never felt so depressed. Ann finally came into the room again, her face strained with grief. Life seemed to be ending for her as much as for Tom. I felt empty and alone.

I found that talking with Humphrey helped a great deal. I had even tried again to persuade Ann to meet with him, but she refused. Trying to maintain my classes and driving over to the hospital every few days drained me, but I would set aside an hour every few days to talk with Humphrey. He kept repeating to me that it was natural for parents to blame themselves and that I must understand that we were not responsible. He also lamented the fact that we did not share a religious faith, which would help us through this time. He gradually began talking more about God, something that he had avoided after my initial negative response.

"How can you talk about a loving God," I asked, "while I watch my son dying from cancer?"

"Evil exists in the world. Tom's illness is a manifestation of that evil. Why it exists, I don't know. Lots of men have tried to explain it, but I find their explanations as unreasonable as you do but in terms of human reason.

I know that, in times of trouble, I have a source of strength that I can turn to for help. My first wife died in a car wreck. I watched her life slip away. I don't think God caused her to die any more than I think he is killing Tom for some desire to have him. Perhaps God is powerless to prevent the evil that exists. I don't know. What I know is that God helped me when I lost Alice. God does not want us to suffer, and when we depend on him at these times, he will support us. He understands our pain. He experienced human pain himself and overcame it."

"It sounds very nice. I only wish I could share your confidence." I marveled at this man who had suffered so much personal tragedy and still could maintain such a strong faith.

"Just be open to Him. If he comes to support you, don't turn Him away." Humphrey suggested that we have Tom baptized in the hospital and volunteered to drive over to Harrisburg to do it. "I'm certainly not suggesting that God won't take the boy if he is not baptized. I know he will. It's for your sake more than anything. It just puts one thing out of the way that you might later regret not doing. It's not a feat of magic." At first, I rejected the suggestion out of hand but later did speak to Ann about it; we agreed that it would be hypocritical of us to do it. Then I thought better of it and decided to have Humphrey go ahead. I also determined not to tell Ann since she had reacted strongly against doing it. Ann's loss of her religious beliefs seemed to make the entire problem with Tom worse than had she perhaps retained her faith. Ann's mother heartily approved of my idea of having Tommy baptized; it had been a concern for her all along. She agreed to take Ann out of the hospital while Humphrey was there.

"How are you doing today, Tom?" Humphrey asked. Tom had had a particularly bad night and could only smile weakly. "Tommy, do you know about Jesus?"

Tom nodded in the affirmative. Apparently, his grandmother had been talking with Tom privately also.

"He is a special friend of little boys your age. He was always sorry to see anyone sick and tried to make them feel better if He could. I know that He is concerned that you are so sick."

"Jesus lives in heaven. That's what Nana says."

"But Jesus is also right here with us now. You can't see him, but I know He's here. And He's very sorry that you don't feel well."

"Why doesn't He make me better?" That was the very question that was going through my own head.

"I guess that He would like to. I know that when all of us get to heaven after we die, He makes us better. Then we can run and play ball just like we did when we were better. In heaven, there is never any sickness, not even a runny nose."

Tommy managed a giggle at that comment. I wished that I had his innocent faith. Perhaps at one time I did.

"Jesus wants you to love him just as much as He loves you. He wants to be with you all the time. Would you like that?"

Tommy's simple affirmation touched me. *Suffer the little children to come unto Me*, I thought. *Too bad that grown-ups lose that innocence.*

Humphrey walked over to the sink and got a glass of water. "Jesus wanted all His friends to be baptized. That was to show that you love Him the way He loves you. We are going to say a prayer to Jesus, and then I will pour a few drops of water on your head. When Jesus was a young man, he was baptized in the same way. Would you like that?"

Again, Tommy nodded his assent.

As Humphrey continued, I too became caught up in what he was doing. Wouldn't it be lovely if there were a heaven where Tommy could go, if life was not just snuffed out, if we were not just discarded like so much waste?

"Dear Lord, we cannot always understand your purposes for us. Sometimes your face is withdrawn from us when we cry out to Thee. But in the hour of trial, you are always near. We need only look. Be with us now, especially with this child, who so desperately needs you. If it be possible, bring us a miracle. But if not, be with Tommy and his parents. Help them endure. Accept this boy as your own. Take him to you and comfort him. Make this water a symbol of your love. Wash Tommy with your love and make him whole."

Humphrey then dipped his fingers into the glass and allowed a few drops of water to trickle onto Tommy's brow. "Tommy, I baptize you in the name of the Father, and of the Son, and of the Holy Spirit. Amen." As the water ran down Tommy's checks, I began to cry. Oh, if it were only true.

"Mr. Johnson, when I die, will I see Jesus?" Tommy clearly had accepted his fate better than we had.

"Of course, son. That's why I baptized you, to show Jesus that you love Him and want to be with Him. If you die before your parents, you can go to heaven and wait for them. You can find a neat place to play football with your dad and another where you can sit and talk with your mom. It won't be a long wait." I increasingly felt the burden of my own mortality. "And

Jesus will be there to keep you company. I hope to be there soon myself, and perhaps we can play checkers. I'm not much of a footballer." Actually, the checkers sounded better to me than the football, but I did not bother to bring that up.

A few minutes later, I walked Humphrey out to his car. "Thanks for coming over. I'm glad now that I decided to go ahead with it. I just hope Ann isn't too upset."

"Why is she so hostile to religion? It seems so out of character for her."

"She came from a very religious background. I think it's her one form of rebellion against her parents and her life in Selinsgrove. She has retained everything else. Religion, perhaps, was the safest to drop. I guess it is also something that we could share since, in many ways, we share so little else." I surprised myself about my openness with Humphrey, a man whom I knew as a colleague but certainly not as a confidant.

"I can only pray that this problem with Tommy will bring you closer together. So often, the illness of a child results in recriminations with the parents. I have known a number of couples who have lost children only to see their marriages decay as a result. I hope you won't let it happen to yours."

I said good night to Humphrey, and he drove off toward Carlisle. Although the days were getting longer since it was approaching May, we had been in the hospital for quite some time, and it had gotten dark. I admired the self-sacrifice of the man, a casual friend who would take the time to drive all that way and then have to face a class at eight o'clock the next morning. I wished I had his strength.

Tommy hung on for a few more weeks. The doctors had first diagnosed the leukemia in February, and he succumbed to the onslaught in May. I sat by him at the end, watching his short life slip away. The doctors had heavily sedated him to relieve the pain he suffered. They told us that the pace of his decline had been remarkable since, in many cases, children with this form of leukemia can linger for several months. In some ways, perhaps it was a blessing that he did not. I don't think I could have taken much more. In his final hours, he struggled for breath and seemed to be disturbed by hallucinations. Ann and I took turns sitting with him. I remained in Hershey for the final week, and colleagues in my department picked up my classes for me. I was overwhelmed by the support that we received from our friends. When the end did come, I sat with Tommy while Ann left to get some supper. She had lost a good deal of weight, which she could hardly afford, coming to resemble a zombie. During my stays in Hershey, we hardly communicated at all. I would try to support her as best I could, but she seemed to want to be alone.

I sat on the edge of the bed and watched Tommy struggle for breath. He had been comatose for about a week, and we had not had any sign of recognition from him. I continued to talk with him, however; and the sound of my voice seemed to have a calming effect on him. As I sat there watching him, I heard him give a sigh and fall completely calm. I saw no further efforts to breathe. My first thought was to get some help, but I saw it was too late.

We had been told enough times the end would be a blessing for Tom. Instead of rushing out, I took him in my arms and hugged him. I kissed him several times and then laid him out again. I knew that I could not bear to touch him once he was cold; I wanted to hold him one last time while he still felt real before I let him slip away from me forever. I looked at him lying there peacefully as if he was only sleeping. I thought back to the time in the playground when he had knocked me over with his pitch, how vital and alive he had been. I remember his words of concern in that sweet boyish voice of his as he peered down at me lying on the ground. Now the roles were reversed. I wished that I could help him now, but he had slipped beyond that point forever.

I walked out into the hall and met Ann and her mother walking toward me. I did not have to say a word to her; I supposed she could tell from the look on my face or the fact that I did not remain in the room while she went out for dinner. She pushed past me and into the room. I heard a cry and then silence. I ran into the room and found Ann slumped over the bed. I summoned a nurse who was passing in the hall, who tried to revive her. Finally, we managed to contact the doctor, who administered a tranquilizer to her. She remained under sedation until after the funeral. We did not communicate at all until that time. She did not utter a word from that time until funeral.

The burden of dealing with arrangements fell to me. Although I asked Ann's opinion about things, she just waved me aside. I knew that I did not want a service in a funeral parlor, standard practice in that part of Pennsylvania. At one point, I thought that we might save ourselves the burden of a funeral altogether but decided to consult Humphrey about it first. I spent almost an hour on the phone with him talking more about how I was doing than about the preparations. Humphrey insisted that I leave everything to him and try to deal with Ann the best I could rather than worrying about the funeral.

Within an hour after we hung up, Humphrey called me back to tell me that a funeral director had already collected the body, which was to be sent back to Carlisle. He had arranged to have the funeral in the Dickinson chapel two days later. "The choir has agreed to sing. Do you have anything special you would like them to do?"

"But haven't final exams started?" It dawned on me suddenly that I was scheduled to give an exam the next morning and had not even prepared it yet.

"Don't worry about trivialities. Now what do you want the choir to sing?"

"Well, Ann and I both love Bach. Could they sing 'Sheep May Safely Graze'?"

"I don't see why not. Now don't worry about a thing. I have already taken care of your exam tomorrow, and you can decide what to do about the others later. Just take care of Ann and come home."

I tried to do what Humphrey wanted, but Ann was too disconsolate to allow me to be of any assistance. Both her mother and I tried to deal with her but without success. Even her father, when he arrived, failed to comfort her at all; and he, in many ways, remained her closest friend even after our marriage. The doctor felt that we could only hope that she could pull herself together and recommended that, at least for the time being, she remain on the pills.

The next two days were a total blur. The telephone never stopped ringing, and people dropped by constantly to express their sympathy. In some ways, that level of activity was better than when we were alone at night; the desolation made it much more difficult to bear. The hardest part was trying to explain to Sarah that she would not see her brother again. The poor girl had been almost totally neglected during this long ordeal. We had placed her in a day care center, but I took care of her at night when I was home. During the last three weeks of Tommy's life, when I spent most of my time driving back and forth to Hershey, Sarah had remained with the Hingstones. Now we brought her back into the house, an only child.

Tommy's funeral was held on a beautiful May morning. When we entered the chapel, we found that it was filled to capacity, including most of the faculty and a good many of my students. Even members of Tommy's third-grade class attended. I had to keep back the emotion that almost filled my eyes. Tommy's small coffin sat in the center aisle between the front pews, three large candles on either side of the bier. Flowers stood on the altar, but we had requested donations to the Cancer Society rather than flowers to be piled on top of the grave and left to become a decaying mass after the funeral. One of the most depressing sights in the world to me was the appearance of a new grave, the freshly dug earth peeking out from under the heaps of withered flowers. Death became even more depressing when viewed from that vantage. These thoughts wandered through my mind as I sat almost mesmerized listening to the service. I also thought about the little boy in the coffin, my son, and how I had hardly gotten to know him.

I don't recall much about Humphrey's sermon. I know that he repeated some of the things that he had said to me about the existence of evil in the world, about the seeming cruelty of the death of a child. He based his text on the verse of 1 Corinthians, in which Paul wrote that "for now we see through a glass darkly; but then face to face: now I know in part, but then I shall know even as also I am known." "We do not know God's purposes. We do not understand why someone like Tommy dies, although we can be sure that it is not God's will that a child suffers. We can only hope that, some time, these great mysteries of life will come clear to us. In the meantime, we can only celebrate Tommy's short life, what he meant to his family and his friends. We should be glad that we had Tommy as long as we did and rest assured that he is now in a place where there is no pain or grief but light eternal." I listened, numbed by the entire experience, hoping that it might be so but fearing that it was not. I wanted very much to know that there was the sort of loving God of whom Humphrey spoke, but I thought that perhaps more likely was the cruel and mocking god that I found in the novels of Thomas Hardy, the god who destroyed innocent, well-meaning people like Tess or Jude. Besides, did I want a heaven in which I shall know even as I am known?

After his address, the choir sang the chorus that I had requested. I felt the presence of the coffin looming up next to me as they sang, "Flocks in pastures green abiding, safely with their Shepherd rest." The tears welled in my eyes, and I finally had to succumb to them. "With the food of life, He feeds them. To the fold, He gently leads them, there to dwell forever blest." I looked over at Ann, but she only gazed steadily ahead. I doubted if she had heard any of it or felt any of the comfort that broke over me as they sang.

Oh God, if it could only be true, I thought.

That melody always came to remind me of Tommy, not his funeral but when he was alive and vibrant. Afterward, I often hummed it to myself. Eventually, the tune also became associated with Audley in my mind, although I did not for a long time understand why.

At the end, the pallbearers—members of my department—wheeled the coffin to the back of the chapel and out the door, where it was placed on the hearse. Ann and I walked behind it to the rear of the church, where we stayed to greet the congregation. As the various people streamed by us to give us their condolences, the organist played Bach's *Great Fantasia and Fugue in G Minor*. After the church had cleared, Ann, her parents, and I drove into the bright and verdant Pennsylvania countryside to the cemetery for the private burial. That final farewell proved the hardest of all.

Chapter VI

Sequence

The months after Tom's death proved a difficult period of readjustment for both Ann and me. The chasm in our lives did not become apparent until almost a month after the funeral. Friends continued to support us regularly, and for many days afterward, we did not have an opportunity to assess our loss. Eventually, our friends resumed their normal routines and left us increasingly to our own resources. Ann had mourned Tom's passing much longer than I had since she had begun the grieving process even before his death. The realization that Tom was in fact gone struck me suddenly. I had to come to terms with it much later than Ann, discovering just how large a part he played in my life, how he filled voids and vacuums that had existed until he came along. The old emptiness reappeared but now seemed much deeper since I had known what it had been like to have it filled.

The loss put a strain on our marriage. I felt, at times, it would destroy it. We hardly spoke to each other after the funeral, not out of anger but out of emptiness. We had built the strength of our relationship in the last several years on children. In much the same way that he had bolstered me, Tom's birth had served to fulfill Ann in a way that I could not. Although we still had Sarah, she did not serve the same function for us. I never became as close to Sarah as I had to Tom. I tended to treat her like a china doll, too delicate to handle lest she break. Tom's death did not lessen that distance. Ann, on the other hand, seemed to compensate for me. She smothered Sarah with affection, perhaps in desperation that she might be taken from us also. In some ways, Sarah became a bone of contention between us since Ann now noticed how differently I reacted to Sarah.

"You don't have to take Tom's death out on Sarah," Ann would say in an accusing tone.

"I'm not doing anything of the kind. But I can't take her to play baseball. She doesn't like that anyhow." I had no independent verification of that last remark.

"You don't spend time with her doing anything." That also was a falsehood since I did try to devote as much time as I could to her, mostly reading or telling her stories. But Ann was right; there was a qualitative difference in our relationship, if not a quantitative one. I did not feel that warmth toward her that Tom had generated in me. Perhaps I just had not tried to get to know her as well. Whatever the cause, I did not develop, at that time, a strong relationship with her, although I don't think I neglected Sarah as much as Ann charged.

At one point, I seriously suggested to Ann that we have another child. "Not to make up for Tom. I know we can't do that. But it may help fill a gap."

Ann would become testy with me at these suggestions. "Don't talk nonsense. I'm getting too old, and besides, you've had a vasectomy. You can't have another."

"That can be reversed. It's expensive, but if you wanted another child, it would be worth it."

"I can't put myself through that again with the possibility that I would lose another. I just can't."

Her conversation was intermingled with this mixture of hostility and sorrow. I did not fully understand why Ann, normally such a mild person, had become so aggravated with me. Perhaps she blamed me for her sorrow since I had impregnated her in the first place. Had she never had Tommy, she would not have to face this grief. Maybe she felt I should have insisted sooner that Tommy see a doctor about his illness. I knew that she could never forgive herself for that, although Dr. Higgins had assured us that the disease had been long in progress before we noticed any symptoms. A week or two difference in seeing a doctor would not have altered the course of the disease. Nevertheless, Ann could never shed the guilt. Her bitterness was also directed at others, including her parents; and I had long talks with the Randolfs about her attitude. We all tried to persuade her to see a psychologist, but she stoutly refused. The resentment subsided after a few months, but the gulf between us did not. We never regained the closeness that we had shared during the life of our son. That feeling had vanished.

A decline in our physical relationship matched our spiritual. Our marital intimacies came almost to a complete end as soon as we learned about Tom's problem. The long absences we experienced when he was in hospital made physical relations impossible; but even at home, Ann's moods would not allow her to consent to my desires, which did not abate despite the sorrow I felt for Tom. Only occasionally did I enjoy my marital privileges. After Tom's death, all such closeness came to a complete halt for several months. Whenever I suggested that we try to get our marriage back into order, she would exclaim, "How can you think of something like that now?" For a while, she even slept in Tom's bedroom to get away from me. I tried to be as understanding as possible and did not push my suit. But I did fear that our sexual relations might end permanently. I became preoccupied with my desires, and I came to envision myself like some Beardsley drawing with a gargantuan erection overwhelming my entire body.

After several months of abstinence, I became more direct in my approach to her about the subject. "I just can't bring myself to do it" was all the explanation that I got. I urged her to seek professional help not only because of what her moroseness did to her but also what it was doing to me. It availed nothing since she refused to seek assistance. Again, I pressed her parents into the problem, although not revealing the full extent of the change in our relationship. Nothing seemed to help persuade her to change her mind. "I'll have to handle it myself," she would argue. "I am not going to get anyone else involved with my affairs." She failed to recognize it as our problem. In the meantime, I had to resort to my old methods of relief.

Finally, Ann seemed to come to grips with the fact that life had to continue and that her attitudes would not bring Tom back. She did allow normal marital relationship to resume, although always on a limited basis. Whenever we became intimate, she kept the barrier ever in place. She was cold and mechanical, almost distant in her attitude. I never sensed any degree of pleasure on her part; it represented a duty most regrettably she had to fulfill. Our relationship chilled until we became two people living in the same house without any sense of intimacy whatsoever. My sense of loneliness continued to increase after Tom's death because of my isolation from Ann. Yet the change in our relationship did not bring about the rise of the other side of me. I cannot, in all honesty, blame that on Ann even if I wanted to. In fact, the reawakening of my homosexuality came even before Tom's illness. It had always been there, under the surface; but marriage, a family, and the demands of my profession seemed to sublimate those pressures. Certainly, I continued to admire men and felt a muffled longing, but it was something I thought I could control. I had convinced myself that immaturity had given rise to it and that, as I grew older, it would disappear entirely. Yet it seemed the lack of opportunity, more than any changes in me, kept the feelings at bay. There was no evidence whatsoever of a gay community in Carlisle. Of course, Dickinson had the usual number of gay students, but professional fear kept me from ever exploring that reality. Once I discovered that hidden world outside Carlisle, the homosexuality within me blossomed as if it had been held dormant in the cold winter and burst forth again with the coming of spring.

My first introduction to this strange world, one that would emerge increasingly as my own, came when I attended a conference of the Pennsylvania Council of Teachers of English in Philadelphia. It was about a year before Tommy became sick, around March 1980. The conference met at the Benjamin Franklin Hotel on Chestnut Street, and during breaks, I would roam around the city. I had not been out of Carlisle much in my first years there, and the big city atmosphere I had missed since living in California fascinated me. I always liked the vitality of a city and enjoyed watching the many strange and interesting people who wandered the streets. I had started down Thirteenth Street when I came on a sign proclaiming the Top Cat Shop. A set of stairs led down into a basement door. The mysteriousness of the place sparked my curiosity, and I decided to venture down. The discovery I made was completely serendipitous; I had absolutely no intention of getting involved in that world. I might not have gone down those steps had I known what was at the bottom, although in retrospect I probably would have.

I discovered I was in a bookstore, a rather unique one for me since I did not know that such things existed. This bookstore catered to men who had unusual interests. I had seen many heterosexual bookstores in Soho on my brief visit to London. I was only dimly aware that any existed for the homosexual as well. Although I had lived just outside San Francisco for several years, I had never really explored that aspect of the city, something amazing to me today. The Top Cat consisted of a rectangular bare room with a cement floor around the walls on which were magazine shelves and bookracks displaying the wares. Many were wrapped in cellophane, but fortunately, a few were available for perusal. Two men stood by the racks, leafing through magazines. I first surveyed the scene and quickly caught on to what was available there. I speedily became embarrassed and started up the stairs. *What if someone from the conference sees me here?* I thought. Before I reached the top of the stairs, my curiosity got the best of me again. Here was an opportunity I might never have again. I was in a strange city where no one really knew me; it was a perfect opportunity. I descended the stairs again. The sales clerk, who sat behind a raised desk, took notice of me this time. He had been seriously reading when I had first entered the store. Now he looked me over curiously. I realized that now someone knew me for what I was, a queer. For the first time ever, I had actually proclaimed myself, and I didn't like it. I uncomfortably walked over to the bookrack, constantly aware of his eyes on me. One of the customers also looked up, to my mortification. I tried to ignore them, although I was sure that everyone in the store was looking at me, and picked up one of the magazines. To my wonderment, I gazed for the first time on a picture of a smiling young man with an erection. My eyes were riveted on his penis, and my hands began to tremble. I flipped through several pages and found similar young men in various states of excitement. By this point, my nerves got the best of me. The presence of others disturbed me, and I suddenly feared that a Dickinson student might happen to walk in and see me. Then my entire world would know the horrible secret. I could not take the pressure any further and decided to leave. But to make certain it appeared that I had ventured into the wrong place, I pretended to laugh to myself, put the magazine down, and began to walk out. As I passed the attendant, I shook my head as if in disbelief and disgust. I tried to declare myself as the healthy heterosexual who had inadvertently entered the wrong place.

The facade did not last long. That evening, I thought about the smiling man in the photograph. I knew that I wanted to see more. I had tasted the forbidden fruit, and the flavor intrigued me. I determined that my fears were groundless. The chances of anyone recognizing me there were extremely slim while the other patrons in the shop were as queer as I was. I decided, therefore, to return the next day.

I walked with greater confidence down the stairs this time. I had gone there on my lunch break and discovered that the shop was much more crowded than it had been in midafternoon the previous day. For some reason, the larger crowd made me feel less conspicuous, and I had less trouble picking up a magazine and looking through it. The one I found this time showed groups of men engaged in sexual activity—activities similar to those in which I myself had participated with David. I found looking at these men committing unpardonable abominations on each other very appealing. I discovered that I not only responded mentally but, much to my consternation, physically as well. I became quite embarrassed thinking that someone might detect it but found that I was so arranged that it only hurt because it was not free to expand naturally.

I spent time much longer in the shop than I had expected. I looked at most of the magazines and even read passages from some of the novels. They certainly did not have any literary quality, but their authors' ability to describe sexual contacts in graphic details would have embarrassed D. H. Lawrence. I glanced around the room to look at my fellow readers. They pored intently over their magazines, and I recognized them as kindred spirits. I also discovered that the back room had film cabinets where, for twenty-five cents, I could view delectably explicit sex scenes. I was wise enough to realize that the cost mounted quickly since I heard the machines turn off repeatedly, followed by the sound of a coin dropping into a slot. I noted that the sign on the booths promised complete privacy, and I could easily imagine what was going on behind those locked doors. I saw one older man emerge from a booth, his hands covering his crotch. I tried unobtrusively to get a look at what he was hiding; the bulge in his trousers made it quite apparent.

The whole scene had a negative effect on me. Here was a secret underground society hiding from the glare of the sun. It was perverse and dirty. It disgusted me, and I became ashamed for being part of it. I felt low and unclean, as dirty as the floor in that bookstore. Why did I enjoy looking at those pictures? Why did I too want to watch those films in the stifling booths? These thoughts plagued me for quite some time.

I left the Top Cat and avoided the area for the rest of my stay in Philadelphia. I was torn between my shame and the knowledge that I had delighted in the pictures, that given the opportunity I would do it again. It began taking possession of me. Of course, I mentioned none of this to Ann, though I often wondered what she would do if she knew. She had never said anything about homosexuality, and she generally was a tolerant person; but I could not imagine that she would take the knowledge of what I had been up to easily.

After I returned home from the conference, I pondered what I had done for some time. The embarrassment and guilt that I had felt initially began to wane while the memory of the pictures remained fresh. I hated to admit it to myself, but I enjoyed looking at them. I lay next to Ann in bed thinking about those magazines, remembering the expressions on the faces and the shape of the vital parts, thinking to myself about the peculiar irony under which I lived. Here I was, the happily married man next to my sleeping wife, fantasizing about naked men. I kept wondering what was wrong with me, what had caused this unnatural interest. I had heard from the television preachers that homosexuality was the sinful choice of those involved. I knew that I had not voluntarily chosen to be this way, that no matter how hard I wished that I weren't, it would not go away. I had also read that homosexuality developed from psychological factors of early childhood, such as a domineering mother. Perhaps that was the case since I certainly had a mother who attempted to dominate, although with little success. Yet the fact remained I desired to look at those pictures again; I could not get that out of my mind. I decided that I needed to know more about me and went to the library to read books on homosexuality. I knew that I could not check them out since the student on the desk would certainly wonder why an English professor was checking out such literature. I could envision the rumors already. No, I had to go into the stacks and pull the books off the shelf quietly so that no one would see. I usually went to the library on Friday afternoon when no self-respecting student would be found in the place. Still, I had to be very cautious that no one saw me reading these books. I learned a great deal about homosexuality and the lifestyle associated with it. I found that I was an inserter rather than an insertee, meaning that I was aggressive rather than passive, a fact certainly surprising to someone as shy as I was. Most of all, I discovered that the so-called experts were in complete disagreement about the causes of the affliction. They did agree, however, that it was not the result of a conscious choice, to the contradiction of the television preachers. None of the information seemed to do me much good and left me discouraged about shaking it. Although some psychologists claimed that they had been able to "cure" homosexuals, the studies I read generally gave little hope even for the most motivated. I felt that I fell into that latter category and despaired.

These thoughts left me during the time of Tom's illness. When our troubles began to develop after the funeral, my mind turned increasingly to those considerations I had pondered several months before. But opportunities were rare in coming. The summer after Tom's death, we spent much of the time in Selinsgrove with Ann's parents. Ann seemed to want to get away from our home because of the memories associated with it. Perhaps she wanted to return to the simpler, pristine days of life in Selinsgrove. I had suggested that we travel, perhaps take a trip to Europe since Ann had never been there, but she insisted on Selinsgrove, and I thought it best to go along sheepishly. I was uncomfortable and bored. I did not enjoy seeing my old friends again since their lives were now so different from mine. They wanted to talk of sports and the Phillies, and I longed for more elevated conversation. I saw Bill Anderson now married with three daughters and managing a Woolworths, and thought of our evenings in the barn. How simple and carefree it all seemed, with none of the guilt that now haunted me. I also had to spend time with my mother, which was totally disconcerting. Even Ann admitted that perhaps coming to Selinsgrove had been a mistake on that ground. Mother said tasteless things about Tom's death and hurt Ann's sensitiveness about her part in it by suggesting that we should have been more alert to the symptoms. I hated her more than ever because I recognized that my sexual dysfunction probably stemmed from some deep psychological problems engendered by her. At least I had a convenient person to blame.

My next real encounter with my other nature came in the December following. I attended an MLA conference in New York, leaving Ann behind with Sarah. Even before I left, I had decided to see what outlets for my fantasies were available. I knew that if such things as the Top Cat existed in Philadelphia, an exciting new world must be present in New York. When I got there, I began exploring the city, especially the area around Eighth Avenue. It was not long before I confirmed my worst suspicions; New York was a mecca for queers like me. I discovered not only bookstores with treasures unknown in the Top Cat but also movie theaters promising hot action on the screen. I also found one theater that also had live sex acts on stage, but I decided that I was not quite prepared for that yet. I determined that I would go to the Adonis Theatre at Fiftieth Street to see something starring Jack Wrangler. I decided to cut one of the sessions that did not hold any interest for me and go to the film instead. After lunch, I took a walk up to Central Park because the day was unusually warm, and I wanted to get some air after spending the entire morning with my fellow academics. The park, even in winter, was beautiful. The joggers were out that lunchtime in their shorts, which I thought was somewhat obsessive since it wasn't that warm. After walking a few minutes, I looked at my watch and decided that if I wanted to get to the Adonis at the beginning of the feature, I needed to leave. I thought of how pathetic I was standing in this beautiful spot, looking at the soaring buildings that framed the park, about to leave this quiet glade to go into that movie theater, which, if it were as grungy on the inside as the outside, opposed everything natural. Yet I felt compelled.

As I walked down Eighth Avenue toward the theater, I pondered how I had gotten into this condition. Why was I so unlike the other people who passed me on the street? How had I come to be cursed? For a moment, I had a tinge of anger at my father for leaving me at the mercy of my mother and momentarily blamed him for my condition. Then I realized that I was thinking like my mother and became quite annoyed with myself. I began to worry that, in fact, my father could see me walking with deliberation toward that theater, that he would know the hidden secrets of my heart; and I again felt shame. It became all the more reason not to hope for a heaven because it would then be possible for my father to know the true disposition of his son. In some perverse manner, I really didn't care that much if my mother knew. Perhaps it would cause her some suffering in the way it had caused me, but I doubted that she had the capacity for remorse.

I finally reached the theater and paused before I gathered the nerve to enter the large lobby. I felt as if I were invading a surrealistic world. The lobby, which sloped uphill at an almost exaggerated pitch, was decorated with photographs from the coming attractions all illustrated with muscular young men in various stages of undress. I approached the upper corner of the lobby, where the box office stood; the black woman behind the counter did not even look up as I muttered, "How much?" She merely pointed to a large sign that I could not possibly have missed that stated that the cost of admission was five dollars. I almost balked at the price but felt that I had gone this far and could not retreat. I began to pull my wallet out, simultaneously becoming painfully aware of my wedding ring and also that my hands were sweating and trembling slightly. I pulled the bill out of the wallet and shoved it through the window. She then motioned me through the turnstile, and I passed a curtain to get to the auditorium. At first, my eyes had trouble adjusting to the dark, but I became quickly aware of the action on the screen. A sense of panic overcame me as I saw a close-up of a man performing fellatio on another. The film was grainy and slightly out of focus, but I could not mistake what was happening. The soundtrack combined heavy breathing and moans, accompanied by overloud rock music with a heavy drumbeat. Every once in a while, a male voice would utter, "Oh, that's great" or "Suck harder" or even "Suck that cock." I stood at the back of the auditorium for a few moments, observing the film, until I became more aware of my surroundings. The theater was cavernous and had obviously been used as a legitimate film theater until it had fallen on hard times, although the thought crossed my mind that the owners might have made a wise business decision. It was not crowded, and men generally sat individually scattered around the auditorium. In a few cases, I saw couples in deep embraces, more concerned about each other than the film.

I finally resolved to sit down and watch the film, and I groped my way about halfway down the aisle into a seat. I sat across the aisle from one of the couples, and I noticed at once that the one man was performing the same act on the other that I had just witnessed on the screen. The man's head bobbed up and down while the other gently stroked his hair. My eyes became riveted on this scene, and I felt my stomach begin to tie itself into knots. I tried to divert my attention back to the film, seemingly little more than one sex scene after another. The producer had not bothered about intricacies of plot, although I gathered that it concerned an innocent young man who had gone to work on a ranch in the old West. Although the cowhands portrayed themselves as machos, they all constantly engaged in homosexual acts. Eventually, the young innocent was swept into this circle of activity and was had by all the other men on the ranch, much to his delight and theirs. One could not accuse any of the men on the screen of being actors; and they often painfully acknowledged the presence of the camera, getting stage directions as they attempted to maneuver themselves into various unlikely positions. Since the soundtrack had been dubbed over, the audience was not supposed to be aware of all this.

As I watched the film, I sensed a great deal of activity around me. In addition to the lovemaking across the aisle, I observed a number of men wandering up and down, looking intently at the various members of the audience. At one point, a heavyset man of about fifty slipped into the row behind me. As he passed, he ran his hand over my shoulders. I reacted with revulsion, quickly sitting forward, pulling away from his touch. He sat down a few seats from me, and I became quite aware that he continued to watch me. I became so uncomfortable that I almost left. I also noticed that quite a few would walk down the side aisle and into a curtained area beneath an Exit sign. It became increasingly obvious that a good deal of traffic headed in that direction. Finally, my curiosity got the best of me. I too wandered down the aisle toward the exit. I walked up into the area but recoiled when I saw the glow of cigarettes in the darkness. I could not see what was going on; but it did not take much imagination, and I wanted no part of it. I walked back to resume my seat but decided instead to explore further. I had observed a balcony and seen a number of men climb the stairs. I decided to follow and found the balcony more crowded than the section downstairs. Apparently, the downstairs was designed for the more serious moviegoer while the balcony was reserved for love trysts. I saw various couples participating openly in heavy sexual activities. One couple even engaged in anal intercourse, something from which teenage memories repelled me. A number of men looked at me inquisitively; but I averted my eyes and, aware of the danger, moved away. I walked downstairs again to use the men's room, again not realizing the obvious. I entered the men's room and found a great deal of activity there also. The stalls all seemed to be occupied with men sitting on the toilet, holding their erections. The doors stood slightly ajar to make observation easy. I assumed that they would have welcomed company since other stalls with closed doors were clearly occupied by more than one person. Around the rest of the room stood a number of men watching or smoking and obviously waiting. With some difficulty, I got up enough nerve to do what I had come to do. As I stood at the urinal and unzipped my trousers, I felt tremendously conspicuous since, apparently, no one else intended to use the facilities that way. I finished as quickly as possible since a man came up to the urinal next to mine and made no pretense whatsoever of looking at my exposed penis. I stuffed it back into my pants so quickly that some urine ran down my leg.

I hastily returned to my seat and tried to watch the picture. But so overwhelmed by what I had discovered, I had difficulty concentrating. I didn't think in my wildest imaginings that I could have envisioned the scenes I had witnessed. I felt as if I were in some dream world. The semidarkness of the theater gave the whole episode a sense of unreality. The faces that I saw I could only make out dimly; I was never sure if the man approaching me was young or old, good looking or hideous. I could only imagine in my mind's eye what they looked like. I found it all repulsive and degenerate. I tired of the film and walked out into the now cold gray of Eighth Avenue. When I had gone in, the sun had shone brightly; now the winter gloom descended on New York. That same gloom had fallen onto my soul. What I had witnessed had been too much for me to digest at such a pace. It was a sick world of degenerates in which I had found myself. But I could not merely disassociate myself from it. I could not dismiss these men as sick perverts because I was one of them. I watched as a stranger yet participated vicariously in it. I had looked at those men, and I shared their desires and passions. I tried repeatedly to deny it but could not. I too wanted to take another man in my arms, to fondle him and have him caress me. I watched the men on the screen and wished that I had been in their place. If these men were all sick, so was I. And I could not understand the reason why I had been singled out to be thrust among these people. I walked down Fiftieth Street in a mood of despair. I had arranged to meet colleagues at seven o'clock for dinner. Since it was just five o'clock, I walked up Fifth Avenue to help release some of the tensions building up within me. I passed Saint Thomas' Church and heard the sound of voices coming from inside. Out of curiosity, I climbed the steps and entered the narthex. A choir of men and boys confronted me as they began to process down the aisle toward the elaborately carved altar screen. An usher rushed over to me and, with smiling enthusiasm, handed me a program.

"Just made it in time," he said approvingly. I had not expected to stay but felt compelled by the situation to walk down the side aisle as he directed and find a seat toward the back of the long church. I was struck immediately by the sound of the choir reverberating off the lofty stone vaulting. The voices of the boy sopranos gave the sound a particular quality I had not really heard before. I found it sublimely beautiful, and it helped me forget my torment. The beauty of the strikingly blue stained glass windows gave a particular hue to the entire scene.

I decided to remain for the duration of the service and hoped that it would not last too long. I really did not fully appreciate what was going on since I had never been in an Episcopal Church before and did not understand the liturgy, although in some respects it resembled the Lutheran Church in which I had been raised. All I knew was that it involved a lot of movement. We stood and then sat and stood again while the choir sang. I tried to follow the service in the bulletin, but since I had only begun to pay attention to what was being done after it had started, I found it difficult to determine where we were. Only at the end did I catch up with everyone else and knew to respond, "Thanks be to God," after the minister had said, "Let us bless the Lord." But despite the fact that I could not fully comprehend what was going on, I found myself filled with what can only be described as a religious sensibility by the beauty of the service. Not only did the music inspire me but also did the quiet dignity of the service. At one point, the minister prayed for All Sorts and Conditions of Men, and I thought that he must have me in mind when he prayed for those who were distressed in mind, body, or estate. I recognized my distressed mind. The small congregation stood as the choir, preceded by a young man carrying a large cross, recessed. As the cross went by, the people bowed deeply, and I found that I did the same when it passed me. When the procession had finished, the people knelt down again before going out of the church. I also knelt and began thinking about myself and what I had seen that day. *Oh, God, if you could only cure me,* I thought. *If you could only make me like other men and drive these desires from me.* Why had I been made this way? I knew that it did not come from any perversity or will on my part. It was something I could not seem to escape. If it were a disease and if there was a God, could he make me free of it? I mulled these thoughts over for several minutes, half-praying to the unknown God, half-contemplating to myself, until I noticed that the usher who had handed me the program stood discreetly near me.

"Whenever you are done, sir, we will close the church." I realize that I must have been there longer than I had thought because the church was entirely deserted except for the two of us.

"Oh, I'm sorry. I didn't mean to keep you."

"It's no bother. We never want to interrupt a person's devotions." Then he added as if as an afterthought, "If there is something bothering you, I could get one of the priests to talk with you. I think Father Saunders is still in the sacristy."

I thought for a moment that it might be useful to talk with someone but then realized that I could not divulge my thoughts to anyone, particularly a minister. "No, I'm fine. Thank you for your help." I got up from the kneeling position, grabbed my coat, and started to walk out. I noticed that the usher genuflected and then followed me out. I was not used to the amount of ritual used in this church. Saint Paul's had been vigorously Protestant, and on the last Sunday of October, the pastor always delivered a vigorously anti-Catholic sermon. I was surprised to find in this supposedly Protestant church so much Catholic ritual and gesture used. I think I was originally attracted by the music, which was perhaps the most beautiful I had ever heard; the mystical nature of the service; and the elaborateness of the ritual. It was not by any conviction that the God I had prayed to had any power to help me.

I pondered the two images of that day, which seemed, at the time, totally at odds. I envisioned the darkened theater with the open sex acts and the stealthful men seeking their own gratification, the symbols of erections and anuses. Then I thought of Saint Thomas', brightly bathed in light and accentuated by the blue of the glass glowing softly in the twilight. Here, the small congregation—mostly of older women—listened to the heavenly music filling the vaulting. Here, the symbols were crosses and candles. How different they seemed. By the time I reached the Roosevelt Hotel, it was the first image that had triumphed over the second. I knew that no matter how disgusted I was with the initial images and with myself, I wanted to go back. I went to my room to get ready for dinner. I stood looking at myself in the mirror and hated what I saw and felt. Finally, I released the unbearable tensions rising within me. I felt a sense of relief and shame at the same time.

For the next week, I was obsessed with those scenes I had witnessed in New York. I would lie awake at night listening to Ann's quiet breathing and think about what I was and the contradictions in my life. I had a wife and child and lived an apparently heterosexual existence. Yet deep within me were these secret drives over which I seemed to have no control and that apparently took charge of my life. Each time I sought to satisfy them, they became bigger and more uncontrollable. Like Malthus' theory of population, they seemed to grow exponentially while my ability to satisfy them expanded only arithmetically. It was like some cancer spreading within me mortified my spirit in the same way that it had killed Tom. I had a great desire to talk with someone about it all, but obviously, that was impossible. I had even thought of confessing all to Ann but knew that she could not help me and that I would only destroy her further. I was thrown back on my own resources again, inadequate as they were. I fell into a deep depression, which Ann, because of her own state of mind, apparently did not even notice, or at least she said nothing about it. But some of my colleagues noticed it, and the department chairman made a special point to call me into his office. He had just come the previous year, replacing the former chairman of twenty-three years, who had finally given up the ghost. A younger man, his attitudes corresponded much more closely to mine.

"I've noticed that you have been rather down lately. We all thought that you had adjusted to your son's death, but I guess you are still having problems." The last was more in the form of a question than an assertion.

"I guess it was the first Christmas without him that made it all come back again." Actually, Christmas had been very rough for both Ann and me, but that was not the only thing bothering me. "Don't worry, I'll pull out of it. I didn't know that it was obvious."

"It is to all of us. We are all very concerned that you don't try to depend so much on yourself and seek help if you need it." I thought of the usher in Saint Thomas'. "You know that you have long been overdue for a sabbatical. You have left that project drift on Dickens' influence on prison reform for a long time now. Isn't it about time that you got something published on it? Why don't you plan to take a sabbatical and finish the research? You deserve it."

"You've been pushing that sabbatical for a long time now. It sounds as if you would like to be rid of me for a while."

"You know I have a lot of respect for your scholarship and want to see you finish the book. But you also need the rest. You've become a workaholic. You won't be of any use to us if you drive yourself to a nervous breakdown. And you won't be of any use to Ann either. Please think about it. It's too late to take off '82–'83, but certainly, you could arrange for the following year."

"I had thought about applying for an NEH but just haven't been able to get myself motivated to fill out all those forms for what is probably a waste of time."

"Don't be so sure of that. Prison reform is big these days. There's talk of going back to torture and inhumane treatment again to cure our social ills. There would be nothing better than a project that would show that the problems today arose not only from ending prayer in the schools but also from a fuzzy-headed liberal like Dickens. It would sell well down in Washington."

Prompted by the chair's urgings, I did, in fact, begin to apply for the sabbatical. I was unable to land anything for the next year but was wildly surprised when the National Endowment did agree to support a year's research in London for the 1983–84 academic year. Shortly before I made a second round of applications for a research grant, I had gone to Washington for a week to complete some research at the Library of Congress. I had urged Ann to bring Sarah along because I thought it would be good for her to get away from Carlisle. After Tom's death, we had not gone anywhere as a family except for the few weeks in Selinsgrove, which had not been my idea of excitement. I had attended a number of conferences but failed to persuade Ann to accompany me to any of them. She seemed content staying at home, dwelling on the death of our son.

It seemed almost pathological, but every effort that I made to get her out of her depression or to seek any sort of help failed. Therefore, I went unaccompanied to Washington as usual.

I worked diligently for three days, avoiding the haunts where I often found myself on such out-of-town trips. At breakfast on the fourth morning, I leafed through the *Washington Post*, where I discovered an advertisement for the Follies Theatre on O Street, just a few blocks from the library. My original determination to avoid these places melted quickly as it always did, and at one o'clock, I left the library for my lunch break and headed for the theater. I now walked up to the box office with more confidence than I had the first time I attended the Adonis since I was considerably more experienced now. I made a point to have the money in hand before I arrived at the theater so that I could keep my left hand thrust in my pocket. I had never been to the Follies before, but it resembled all the other gay movie houses that I had entered. I took my seat and began to watch the all-too-familiar activity on the screen, which I found just as appealing as ever. That also had not changed. Once my eyes became accustomed to the gloom, I began to look around and saw that the same cruising was going on at the Follies as elsewhere.

I had resisted any temptation so far to become actually involved in these activities, contented to be an observer. I had a strong sense of guilt associated with my activities, and I also felt sincerely that I had made commitments to Ann that I did not wish to break. I did not want to become an adulterer. A strong additional motivation prompted my celibacy. In recent months, news reports of diseases associated with the gay activity had been increasingly widespread. Of course, I knew about syphilis and gonorrhea, but now there was ugly talk about hepatitis and herpes. Moreover, a strange form of cancer called something-or-other sarcoma seemed to develop in the gay community. I was not yet aware of the major scare that would come as medical evidence about AIDS began to spread. All I knew was that I did not want to acquire any of these ailments and especially did not want to take them home to my wife.

I noted, as I looked around the theater, a wide aisle on the right side filled with a line of young men who stood watching the movie but also observing one another and those in the seats. One young man in particular attracted me because he smoked one cigarette after another. His nervous mannerisms and apparent intensity caused me to continue watching him. I also quickly recognized that he was extremely good looking, perhaps better looking than any of the others whom I had seen. I kept thinking he could not possibly be gay. He possessed none of the typical characteristics, no hint of effeminacy, just incredible good looks. The more I looked at him, the more he returned my glance. Finally, I became uncomfortable and attempted to concentrate on the movie with considerable difficulty since it was one of the most poorly made I had ever seen.

Finally, I looked again to my right and discovered that he was no longer standing there. I was somewhat relieved until I noticed that he had slipped in two seats away from me on the left. He looked at me steadily and conspicuously rubbed his crotch with his hand. I looked at his hand and then back up to his face. He looked at me with a longing stare, an unmistakable invitation. I then watched in some disbelief as he pulled down his zipper and slipped his pants down to his knees. He had no underpants on, and his rather large erection immediately became apparent. He began stroking it up and down, continuing to look at me intently. His look became almost pleading, and I could plainly hear him breathing more heavily. He patted the seat between us in an obvious gesture that I join him.

I knew that I stood at a crossroads. The desire to sit next to him, to touch him, and to have him touch me was overwhelming. He attracted me with an intensity that I didn't think I had ever felt before. I actually started to get up, but then thoughts of infidelity and disease rushed into my mind. I sat frozen in my seat, watching him continue to pull on his erection and look at me in that sorrowful, longing way. I neither accepted nor refused his invitation. I did nothing. Finally, he looked sadly at me and began to pull his jeans up again. He then moved away from me and back to his original standing position. Later, I saw him having oral sex with another man in the back of the theater as I was leaving.

The surprising thing about this incident was not my desire to have sex with that handsome stranger but the anger I felt afterward because I had been too cowardly to respond. I realized that I had missed an opportunity I had fantasized so long about, and now it was gone. It would have been so simple to move over that one seat. The thought of my cowardice saddened me. At the same time, my rational side told me that I probably avoided some serious venereal disease or worse since he was clearly not particularly selective about his sexual partners. I also could return home to Ann knowing that I had not broken my marriage vows. But I had come very close, and I knew that I would have great difficulty holding out again.

The whole scene rushed back into my mind a few weeks later when talking with an elderly trustee of the college at a cocktail party. "Take it from me, young man," he had quipped. "You only live to regret the things you haven't done." I really think he had business investments in mind, but I took his prophetic words in an entirely different sense. I did not know if my courage would fail me again when I did meet that or another attractive young man.

Chapter VII

Gospel

This road led me to the Golden Lion that December afternoon. Yet my nerve had failed me; and, despite my resolve to gratify my other nature, I found I could not. It seemed I would forever look at that world as an outsider, never fulfilling my fantasies. I could not gather the fortitude to return to the Golden Lion for several weeks after my initial visit.

The coming of the Christmas season, for one thing, distracted me. I now spent many of my lunch hours running to shops to get presents for Ann and Sarah. Christmas in London, with its shops glistening with bright decorations and thronged with excited shoppers, lifted my spirits. A walk down Oxford or Regent Streets at the end of the day to take in the colorful lights or browse along the row of tastefully adorned shop windows especially delighted me. The gaiety and brilliance of the season seemed to overpower the confusion in my own soul.

I also busied myself getting ready for our first expedition. We had carefully avoided the possibility of a visit from my mother, who had threatened to join us now that she had retired. For a woman who complained all her life about lack of money, she located with relative ease the sum necessary to cross the Atlantic. We had therefore taken precautions to make it difficult for her to surprise us. For that reason, we planned a Christmas trip to take us far from home.

Moreover, we had purposely let a very small flat barely suiting us, let alone company. In Amersham, we had discovered precious accommodations in a former almshouse converted into apartments. We rented a two-bedroom garden flat in the U-shaped brick building, which opened onto the main road running from Gerrards Cross to Wendover. The street, lined with Georgian houses and a few of an earlier vintage, boasted one pub for every five houses. We often frequented the one directly across from us, the Eagle, for a pint on a Friday night after Sarah fell asleep. At the center of the town stood an eighteenth-century covered market close to the village church, Saint Mary's, where the change ringers would practice every Sunday afternoon, providing the backdrop for tea at the Willow Tree Restaurant on the high street. Our location could not have been more idyllic.

We did not wish Mother to intrude herself into this quiet paradise we had discovered. Yet she kept writing, almost weekly it seemed, that she had gotten her passport and wanted to work out a time when she could tear herself away from her sowing group. When she first suggested Christmastide, I quickly made reservations for the three of us at Castle Combe for the holidays and informed Mother that, although we loved the idea of a visit, we could not alter our reservations.

In our tiny flat, we celebrated a traditional Christmas complete with a tree decorated with homemade ornaments. I had done most of the shopping because Ann did not like to venture out and would not travel into London alone. Although I had anticipated that the new atmosphere would help bring Ann out of her shell, very little change occurred. She still suffered fits of depression and would not communicate with me for several days. Although she seemed happier than she had been at home with all its memories, the improvement proved ephemeral. I hoped that, once we began to travel, she would relax even more. On Boxing Day, we picked up the rented car and started toward Bath and Castle Combe. I wanted Ann and me to use this time together to strengthen our relationship, but when I suggested that we place Sarah in an adjoining room, she refused. She reminded me that Sarah was only five.

"She would be in the next room. It would give us some privacy."

"Is that all you ever think about? I want Sarah in the room with us."

That was her final word on the subject, even though we often left Sarah alone on Friday evenings to step across to the Eagle. I dutifully booked a triple room located in the renovated stables of the manor house. We actually did have a nice time, taking long walks in the country and exploring the tiny village. I even got a chance to see one of the three ghosts that the manor house boasted. The desk clerk explained that I had encountered the

Roman centurion when I described the strange glow in the cold night air. Initially, Ann seemed cheered by our little holiday, and I hoped that she had finally come to grips with herself. Then she became very moody again and began thinking about Tom, wishing that he still lived to share this. I tried to distract her, but she continued to return to more maudlin thoughts. Finally, I pleaded, "Ann, you've got to begin living for yourself. You can't forever live vicariously for Tom. He's dead. We can't have him back." The words barely slipped from my mouth when I recognized my error.

"You're heartless," she snapped back.

"Ann, it's been over two years. You can't constantly return to these preoccupations. It's not healthy."

"You don't give it any thought at all."

"Ann, don't you think I grieve for him? I loved him as much as you did. But you act as if you are the only one who cares. Piling recriminations on both of us won't do a bit of good. You'll destroy us all."

Without saying another word, Ann returned to the room. I tried to apologize but to no avail. She remained cloistered in the room while Sarah and I went for a long walk. The unusually mild December afternoon made the walk quite pleasant. We explored some woods near the manor house, and I pointed out the bracken and other plants I recognized. The amble in the dark woods swept me into my own thoughts. I grew angry with Ann and then at myself for lacking compassion. Alternatively, I felt sorry for myself and then guilty.

Increasingly, my thoughts turned to ways of alleviating my frustration and particularly to the young man in the pub. Like the time in the Washington cinema, I regretted that I had not sat down with him. I resolved that, after our return to London, I would go to the Golden Lion. I knew that I had to seek him out again. This determination included all the subsequent consequences that might arise from it. As I walked through the woods with Sarah, I knew I must fulfill what had clearly become my destiny.

My spat with Ann put a damper on our last day at Castle Combe. We went home in silence; only Sarah's chatter in the back seat broke the silence. The sound of a five-year-old's soliloquy would have otherwise annoyed me; now it blessedly filled the emptiness. I had once suggested to Ann that we hire a babysitter for New Year's Eve and join the revelers at Trafalgar Square. Ann vetoed the idea after we arrived home, and we spent a quiet evening watching the festivities on television. She even refused to walk across to the Eagle for a toast. The trip, instead of holding out its promise of hope, swept Ann back into a period of depression lasting about a month. What began so auspiciously became another failure in my efforts to restore Ann to healthier attitudes. I hated to admit it, but I approached the point where I really didn't care to try further.

Two days after New Year's, I resumed my research at the British Library. The first noontime, I had to run some errands, returning a few presents that did not fit. The next day, however, the Golden Lion and the intriguing young man became my destination. I went boldly to the pub but then entered with a sense of trepidation. I looked around and recognized a number of the men who had been there on my first visit, but I was almost relieved when I failed to spot the man who had drawn me there. At the bar, I ordered a pint of lager from the effeminate blond, who took as little interest in me this time as he had the first. I took my beer to one of the empty tables, the same table where the young man had sat previously. As I sipped my beer, I watched the two entrances and anyone entering, afraid and eager to see the entrancing eyes. They did not appear that day. As I waited, I pondered the reality of the situation. How would I strike up a conversation? Would I just walk over to him and introduce myself? Would I use my real name? I hoped he would be the aggressive type since I knew that I could certainly not muster the courage to proposition him. But what if he played coy? How would I suggest that I had an interest in more than just a casual chat?

Then an even greater difficulty posed itself. Where would we go? I had never really even considered that problem. In my experience, I had observed most intimacies carried out in public view in the rows of seats or the men's rooms of movie theaters. Nothing of that description existed in London. If he was obliging, I could only pray that he had a flat where we could retire. I thought about taking the underground to our secret location, where we would consummate my fantasies. *How long would it take?* I wondered. I had no real idea of how to proceed. I had seen a good deal of activity on movie screens and had worked out scenarios in my imagination, but now I was involved in serious business. Then I realized that, on Fridays, the British Library closed early. Should I collect my books before retiring to our hideaway? These random speculations passed through my mind as I sat nursing my beer and watching the doors of the pub expectantly.

Finally, I exited from the Golden Lion in a depressed mood. Would I ever see him again? He might have been there that one day, never to return. I found it somewhat encouraging that I recognized many of the patrons of the pub from my first visit. I hoped my young man was one of these regulars; and if I didn't encounter him today or the next, he would reappear into my life. I seemed prepossessed with these thoughts during the weekend. We took Sarah to see the "stuffed animals" at the Natural History Museum, and Ann commented on how distracted I seemed. Slowly, the enormity of my intentions had sunk into my brain. What if I did engage in sexual activity with him? What if I picked up some serious disease such as herpes? My better judgment, at least for a time, took hold of my passions. I tried rationality about the entire situation. Why couldn't I be satisfied? I had a good wife and lovely daughter. Yet I had become obsessed with sexual desires that did not bother normal human beings. I was a sick, driven man. While I thought of these things rationally, I knew that I could, in fact, not control myself. My drives had taken charge of me. Ann might note my unease, but I was beyond her or anyone else's help.

On the Monday after, I returned to the Golden Lion, again in search of the man with the eyes. Again, my hopes of meeting him were to be disappointed. I stood in the corner with my beer, waiting in vain hopes of seeing him walk through the door. Failing to see him on Tuesday and Wednesday as well, I concluded that he must come at different times. I had always gone at one o'clock and remained each time until about two fifteen. The pub closed at three; was it possible that I had been just missing him each time? I resolved to come later on Thursday in hopes of meeting him. I also determined that I must give up this endeavor as a lost cause if I did not see him on the next visit or so. I pondered these logistics when another young man whom I had noted on my two previous visits walked into the pub carrying a very long, thin case. We looked at each other, and I inadvertently smiled at him. Quite muscular and having a day's growth on his chin, he did not exhibit any of the effeminate qualities of some patrons. He appeared to be quite tough and streetwise. He possessed a certain amount of swagger in his stride. I drank my beer, determined to give up again, when he approached me.

"Come over here to this table and sit down. I want to talk to you." His accent was clearly lower-class London. "Hi, my name's Ed. I've seen you in here a lot lately." He spoke in a rapid, clipped manner as if afraid someone might overhear him.

"Yes, I've been here a couple of times," I replied. I felt quite uncomfortable and threatened by him.

"Are you married?"

The question caught me off guard. I guessed I was more obvious than I had hoped. "Yes."

"Any kids?"

"I have a little girl."

He sat there for a moment sipping his beer. He looked up and smiled. "How would you like to do some business?"

I understood his drift instantly. No question existed in my mind about his meaning. I decided at once that I must squelch it. "I'm afraid I don't do business."

"You mean you want it for free? You've come to the wrong place for that, mate. Don't you know what kind of place this is?"

"I had my suspicions, but I wasn't sure."

"All these young guys here, they're rent boys. If that isn't what you wanted, you shouldn't have come here."

"Sorry. It just seemed like a nice place, that's all." I became angry with myself for my defensiveness.

"You should try the Salisbury or the Kings Arms. That's where guys pick each other up." I stood up, thinking that our business conference had concluded, but he motioned for me to resume my seat. "Don't go away," he blurted as he tried to gulp a mouthful of beer. His entire manner now changed. Aware that I was not a potential customer, he reverted to a more conversational tone, abandoning the hushed tones of our previous discussion. "You're American, ain't ya? How long have you been here?"

"Yes, we've been here for about five months," I said, trying to answer both questions at the same time.

"You just started to come in here recently?"

"This is my third or fourth time."

"I could tell you wasn't a regular." My nervous mannerism must have stood out very clearly. I felt my face turn hot as I thought of it. "Listen," he continued, "I'm a little short of cash. Do ya think you could buy me a pint?"

One gets hustled one way, I thought, *or another*. The request angered me, but I decided to avoid a scene that might be explosively embarrassing and buy him the beer. Handing him two pounds, I asked him to get me a refill. He brought the beers back and laid the change on the table. Since we seemed destined to share the table for a few minutes, I felt obliged to make light banter. "What's in the long case I see you carrying all the time?"

"It's my pool cue."

"Oh, are you a professional?" My naiveté only became apparent to me when he chuckled.

"Nah, I just fool around. I pick up some cash once in a while playing against suckers."

Another way to hustle, I thought.

"How long do you plan to stay in London?" He seemed to want to keep the conversation going as well.

"Until next September. Then I have to go back to teach."

"What are you doing here?"

"Doing research at the British Library." I only volunteered that much since he had no obvious interest in the details.

"Are you living around here?"

"We have a flat in Amersham."

"Where's that?"

I knew he had never ventured into the suburban region; he had probably never set foot outside London except for the odd weekend to Brighton or Southend. "It's pretty far out in the country, to the northwest of London."

"Oh." He didn't have any real interest in where I lived or in me. I was just a potential source of money in one form or another.

"Well, it's been nice chatting with you, but I better get back to work."

He eyed a man in a business suit who had recently entered the pub. Clearly, Ed wanted to size up this potential client. "Guess I'll see you in here again." Then as an afterthought, he added, "Remember, if you ever have an interest, I'll be here." I thanked him, finished my beer, and walked out. I had almost resolved that I would never return to the Golden Lion again. Ed was probably right. I should try some of the other pubs suited to my purposes.

Two days later, I returned to the Salisbury in hopes of encountering someone not in the business of selling sex. I spent more time there than on my first visit, but the people still did not impress me. The same gray-haired man perused me as I drank my beer, which did not bother me as much this time; I found, in general, I became much cooler about these situations. I even struck up a conversation with a man about my age, although he clearly bided his time in idle conversation, waiting for someone more youthful than I was. He inquired where I came from in the States and the other usual things Englishmen ask foreigners. We spoke not one word about the nature of the pub or why we were there, which quite relieved me. For the most part, I found the Salisbury somewhat too reserved. The Golden Lion had more vitality, even though I presumed that most of the men there either sought services or offered them for sale. It nevertheless seemed more open. The people did not perform the same ballet as the clientele of the Salisbury, trying hard to attract attention but being somewhat suspicious of the others in the pub. No one really seemed relaxed about it.

On Monday, I decided to try another pub mentioned in *Gay News*, the Kings Arms on Poland Street. The previous night, I had examined our *A to Z* and found that Poland Street ran off Oxford Street not too far from Tottenham Court Road. I had no difficulty finding the very crowded and lively pub. As I pushed my way to the bar to order a drink, I encountered quite a mixed group. A number of men in business suits stood alongside a large number in casual dress. Most engaged in animated discussions, and I did not sense merely a collection of men studying one another as I had found at the Salisbury. The men seemed to know each other, and I observed less obvious cruising. This feeling made me feel somewhat like an outsider. Few men stood alone, whom I felt I could approach. Striking up a conversation with a stranger was hard enough for me, let alone under these circumstances. But I decided to give the place a chance since it seemed a good compromise between the unduly staid Salisbury and the place of ill repute, the Golden Lion.

As I went to get another pint, two patently drunk young men attired completely in leather came tumbling down the stairs from the lounge bar and practically knocked me over. They held each other in a tight embrace and came to a stop next to me to engage in a probing kiss. One looked quite silly, dressed in very short leather pants and opened leather jacket revealing a bare chest. After the two paused for an affectionate moment, they stumbled through the pub and out the door. The young man's attire was certainly inappropriate for the February cold. What surprised me, though, was that no one around me seemed to take the slightest notice of the couple as if it were the most natural thing in the world.

With the thought of becoming a regular at the Kings Arms and getting to know some of these people, I returned the following Monday. I recognized some of the same faces but still had the strong sense that I continued to be an outsider. I was clearly an American; I did not try to dress like the English. At both the Salisbury and the Golden Lion, I had detected at least one American. In this particular pub, I did not see any at all. Perhaps that was the problem here; perhaps they did not welcome strangers. The fact that I found few of the men at the Kings Arms attractive as much as the young man at the Golden Lion also discouraged me. *Perhaps*, I thought, *I should give the Golden Lion one more chance.*

I planned my next adventure while in bed at night, trying to fall off to sleep. The perversity of it often struck me. Here I lay next to my sleeping wife, plotting which homosexual pub I would frequent next to pick up some guy with whom to make love. At times, guilt would well up within me; but at others, I could be coolly dispassionate about the whole thing. I often reassured myself that, despite all my planning, nothing would transpire; I would chicken out. For all I might resolve that given the right circumstances I would plunge ahead, I felt those conditions would never be met or that none of the pub dwellers had an interest in a married thirty-eight-year-old American queer. I never considered myself particularly attractive, and I was positive that the young man in the pub had no real interest in my body. I had not thought much about the possibility that he was a hustler and might be interested in my money. The hustlers were the regulars, the ones I had seen each time I had gone in there.

The next day, I dragged myself back to the Golden Lion without any enthusiasm. I figured I would give it one more try; perhaps he would be there this time. As I walked in the door, I was thunderstruck when I saw him standing in the corner of the room surrounded by a group of young men I did not recognize. As I drank my beer, I felt nervous standing within a few yards of the object of so many of my thoughts. I had calmed down considerably by the repeated visits to these various pubs. It no longer seemed strange to enter a place frequented by homosexuals. But now the panic returned. I studied my glass; I dared not look in his direction since it would only make matters worse. I did not think he had noticed me when I walked in, but I stood within clear sight of him now. Finally, I glanced up, and our eyes met. He apparently had seen me standing and had continued to look in my direction. Our eyes locked the same way they had the first time. He continued to carry on his conversation but frequently stared at me. I could not keep my eyes off him. Studying him carefully, I found myself strongly drawn to him. The more I watched him, the more physically excited I became, even to the point where I felt a rumbling in my trousers.

He finished the contents of his glass and walked over to the bar close to me. He ordered another pint and, once he had received it, turned around with his back to the bar. We stood next to each other. "Hi, how're you doing?" He allowed his eyes to look away from my face and follow the contours of my body.

"Fine" was all I could muster as a response. My heart beat wildly.

"What's your name?"

"Sim," I replied.

Shit! I thought to myself. *Shit! Shit! Shit!* I almost collapsed in a panic. For days, I had practiced "Frank" as the response to that question. I had rehearsed the name over and over again. It was an easy name to remember, even if not my own. Any fool could have pulled it off. But I couldn't. In my fluster, I had given my real name. Visions of blackmail and other horrors raced through my mind. Now this guy actually knew my name, something I had wanted to avoid at all costs.

"Sim?"

"That's right. Sim." I saw no way out of it now. "It's short for Simeon. I was named after my grandfather."

"I like it."

"What's your name?" I countered.

"Audley."

"Audley? That's really usual too. I don't think I even heard a name like that before." It was all hopeless small talk, but the more we chatted, the more relaxed I became. "Is it a family name?"

"No, I was named after a house."

"A what?"

"A house. Audley End. It's in Essex, just outside London." I began to comment, but he did not seem to want to pursue that topic further. "You're an American, aren't you?"

"How could you tell? The color of my socks?" I asked flippantly.

He smiled for the first time. Up to that point, his look had been quite serious, his eyes ever probing mine or examining me. "Do you come in here often?"

"Yes, I've been here a few times."

"I remember seeing you here a couple of weeks ago." Actually, almost two months had elapsed. "I don't get here too often, every once in a while." He did not have a London accent, and I guessed he came somewhere from the north of England, although I was not expert enough on accents to be able to place it. I wanted to think of something intelligent to say but could only fumble nervously with my beer.

"Have you ever been to the Heaven?"

I'm there right now, I thought. The more I talked with him, the more attractive I found him. He had a cute youthful face, slightly curly black hair, and an angular build.

"Heaven?" I inquired.

"It's a night spot under the arches at Charing Cross."

"No, I've never been there. Never heard of it before. Why did you ask?"

"No reason. I just thought I recognized you. Thought I might have seen you there. I go there a lot."

"What's it like?" I desperately tried to keep the conversation going, hoping that it would lead somewhere.

"It's a place where men like me hang out."

That sort of place, eh? I thought. *Now we are getting somewhere.* "Do you think I would like it?"

"That depends."

"On what?" The sparing continued.

"I guess on what sort of men you like."

Just then, one of his friends called over to him. "Hey, Aud, let's go now."

He turned to me and looked at me with his intense eyes. "Listen, I've got to leave. I hope to see you in here again." With that, he put his glass on the bar and walked out with several others. I watched him carefully as he departed and then stood nursing my beer, trying to calm myself down. I reached several important conclusions. First, I concluded that Audley was not a hustler. Second, he had some interest in me. He could have gone to a closer spot at the bar to get his refill. Instead, he deliberately had stood next to me. I felt as if an entirely new world had opened up to me. Perhaps, indeed, my fantasies were to be fulfilled.

Nevertheless, that night, I had some qualms about it. I felt myself being too animated in talking with Ann, and I suspected that she noted my agitation. To avoid talking with her too much, I went into the lounge and read Sarah a book while Ann completed dinner. That alone should have raised Ann's suspicions since I normally did not read to Sarah before dinner. Finally, at dinner, she commented, "You seem to be preoccupied with something. Anything happened today?"

"Nothing unusual." I then proceeded to recount the material I had examined that day, which quickly lost Ann's interest. Almost in midsentence, she interrupted to tell me Sarah had contracted a cold. For the rest of the evening, I engrossed myself in some reading to avoid further conservation.

I had the weekend to contemplate what I would do next since I had to wait until Monday to return to the Golden Lion. On Saturday, we boarded the train into London to take Sarah to the Science Museum. Later, we poked around Harrods because Ann wanted to get an anniversary gift for her parents. On Sunday, I suggested we should go to church at Westminster Abbey or Saint Paul's Cathedral. "Are you kidding?" Ann said dismissively." You can go if you like, but I'm not sitting through a church service with Sarah."

"But she might really like the music." I dropped the suggestion when I noted her resistance and instead remained home to read the *Sunday Times*. During the afternoon, we walked up the high street to have tea at the Willow Tree Restaurant, where the smiling young proprietor always slipped Sarah a cookie when we paid our bill. We strolled home in the darkness as the change ringers practiced their art in Saint Mary's Church.

Throughout the weekend, I thought a great deal about Audley. It seemed strange to connect a name with those eyes, which had haunted me for so long. I wondered if my marital status would make a difference to him. Did he work days and could only meet me at night? Of course, an evening rendezvous was out of the question since I could not produce a legitimate excuse to go into London by myself at night. The more I thought about it, the more hopeless it seemed. Yet I resolved to revisit the Golden Lion on Monday.

Monday came but without Audley. I went to the pub as usual and wasted almost two hours hoping he would come in. I returned almost every day for a week, if only to stick my head in, but no Audley. Finally on the following Friday, I stopped by the Golden Lion on my way to the Leicester Square ticket office. Ann had planned to meet me for dinner and a play if I could acquire cheap tickets. I had, therefore, dressed in a coat and tie, not my normal sabbatical attire. I ordered a beer and started to drink when Audley walked down the steps from the second-floor lounge bar. He walked over to me and smiled broadly.

"Haven't seen you in a long time. Where have you been keeping yourself?"

"Oh, I keep busy," I said coyly. I didn't want to appear inexperienced.

"Have to go back to work today?"

"Well, I probably should."

"You had your day off when I saw you last week? Sorry I couldn't stay around."

"No, I worked last Friday when I saw you." I knew exactly which day of the week and even the approximate time when I had last seen him. "I work pretty much according to my own schedule."

"What are you, a banker?"

"Nothing that exotic. I'm a college professor.

"You're all dressed up. I thought you were a business type."

"I'm afraid I'm not very important. I'm just over here doing research at the British Library."

Audley laughed. "Guys can do just about anything they want to on me. But I don't want to be researched."

"Actually, I teach English, and my research concerns Charles Dickens."

"I think I read a book by him. Bloody boring."

I could tell that Audley was no intellectual. But that didn't matter at this point. I wanted to say something to make clear my interest in him. I stared at my beer trying to muster the courage, but each time I opened my mouth, nothing emerged. If only Audley would take the initiative, but he didn't. Finally, I thought I might prod him by suggesting that I was about to leave and he better take advantage of me now. "Well, I guess I should get back to work now, although I'd much rather stay here." *That should get him*, I thought.

Instead of a proposition, I got "Sorry you've got to go. Probably see you next week."

I didn't know how to get out of leaving. I finished my beer and retired to the British Library, condemning myself for not having more nerve. Again, the following Monday, I returned without much hope of seeing Audley. He must work, and Friday was his day off, I concluded. Therefore, to my surprise, I spotted him there with another chap. They approached the bar, and Audley smiled at me. He introduced me to the other young man, also an American. "Hank, this is my friend . . . ." He paused, obviously having forgotten my name.

"Hi, my name's Sim."

"Hank comes from San Francisco. He's been to Mecca." As Audley spoke, his youth and immaturity struck me.

"Actually, I just graduated from Berkeley," said his embarrassed companion.

"I went there too," I replied, "although it was a long time again. I did graduate work in the late sixties." I knew I had revealed my age to Audley, but he had certainly figured out I was no longer twenty. The three of us chatted for a few extremely frustrating minutes; I wanted to talk to Audley alone without this intruder. Again, I met defeat since Audley and Hank had already made plans to go elsewhere. They departed, leaving me in a dark funk.

That night, Ann consented to allow me my marital privileges. It had been two weeks since our last encounter, and desire filled me. My encounter with Audley may have heightened my urges, although I tried to eliminate those thoughts from my mind. Yet his face continued to press its way into my imagination the entire time of our intimacies. Ann did not help much since, as usual, she clearly consented out of a sense of obligation rather than from any real passion. It was as if she felt that our marriage contract obliged her to perform twice a month, enough to satisfy any normal human. I resented the attitude but at the same time felt compassion because I knew the deep hurt continued to fester within her. Even before I married Ann, I should have realized what it would be like.

The following morning, I arose early to take a bath to wash away the sweat of passion. Afterward, I stood at the mirror in the tiny bathroom, shaving. My thoughts once again turned to Audley. *Should I go to the Golden Lion today?* I thought. The answer, despite the release I felt from the previous night, was yes. I imagined my encounter with Audley there, how we would again strike up a conversation, this time without Hank. He would eventually suggest that I stay around this afternoon rather than rushing back to the British Library. I would consent, and after some more chat, he would invite me over to his flat somewhere in Wimbledon. The scene then shifted to his humble digs. Here, he would put his arm around me, and we would embrace. Then his hand would slip down to my crotch and mine to his. Another scene change, and we were in bed engaged in the most exquisite sex, the type I had seen portrayed so vividly on the screen at the Adonis and the Gaiety. Ann opened the bathroom door, rudely awakening me from my reverie, and reacted with some annoyance. "What's wrong with you?"

"What do you mean?" I had some difficulty reorienting myself to the reality of my situation.

"What if Sarah should walk in?"

I then realized that I stood stark naked with an almost complete erection. "Oh, I see what you mean," I faltered. "Just thinking about last night." I needed to add some explanation for my physical condition.

"Please have some common sense," Ann retorted as she left the room, closing the door behind her.

I felt sick about the excuse I had used afterward. The most perverse person in the entire world, I could fantasize about Audley just a few hours after making love to my wife and then lie to her about the cause of my excitement. This whole thing had to stop; I could not persevere. That day, I did not return to the Golden Lion but sat in the British Library, sulking. My resolution to mend my ways lasted, however, only one day.

On Wednesday, I entered the Golden Lion with a great deal of anticipation. This time, I would approach Audley directly and try to work out some arrangement. He seemed to be free enough so that we probably could find an afternoon together. The only difficulty I foresaw was a suitable location; but I willingly would pay for a hotel room, so anxious was I, to consummate. My heart leaped when I observed Audley standing on the other side, talking with a group of young men. At once, my nerve began to slip away. How could I approach him? I had never propositioned anyone, male or female, before. I went to the bar, ordered my drink, and stood there watching him, hoping for an opportunity to speak with him. He soon noticed me; our eyes again locked on each other. My heart raced inside my chest, even though he had, by now, become a familiar sight. He stayed with his friends but frequently gazed in my direction. The passion rose steadily within me, and I became oblivious to anything or anyone around me. Only vaguely did I hear Ed say, "You in some sort of trance?"

"Huh? Oh, I'm sorry. Were you talking to me?"

"Have been trying for the past few minutes, but you seem so engrossed in thought that I couldn't get your attention."

Ed's interruption of my reverie somewhat annoyed me. I couldn't very well talk to him and hold my sights on Audley. I also did not want Audley to think I spent time with hustlers like Ed. Moreover, Ed only wanted to borrow money from me or solicit me for a beer. "I'm sorry, Ed, I was just deep in thought." Beyond that, I did not attempt to carry the exchange. Ed soon got the idea and slipped off to talk with someone else. I continued to watch Audley as he carried on his conversation with the two young men. Every once in a while, he would look over in my direction, and our eyes would meet. At times, he seemed to be paying more attention to me than to his friends. I wanted desperately to go over to him and join the group, but my nerve would not allow it.

Finally, Audley and one of the young men left the group and descended the stairs to the men's room. On an inspiration, I decided to follow. When I got there, I found the two standing in the corner by the washbasin. Turning to the urinal, I felt embarrassed since I was already somewhat aroused, and I feared someone else might detect it. No partitions separated the urinals. I looked cautiously over my shoulder and could hear the two discussing what they had done the previous evening. The dim blue light of that room prevented me from seeing them distinctly. Audley washed his hands—I gladly noted his cleanliness—and grabbed a paper towel. After discarding it, he turned to his friend and held him in his arms, running his hands down the other's back and squeezing his buttocks. They pulled each other together in a muscular embrace. I heard Audley say, "What if someone could see us? What would they think of two men hugging each other?"

Then Audley added, "I really don't care what the fuck they might think. I know I like it." He spoke in a loud voice, I concluded, solely for my benefit.

Having finished my business, I walked next to them at the basin and washed my hands. They proceeded out the door, and I followed closely behind. Audley held the door for me, and I put my hand out to catch it. He put his hand on top of mine. For a brief moment, we stood there holding the door, his hand covering mine. He looked at me deeply, and I felt a thrill, the likes of which I had never experienced before. He then released my hand and went up the stairs quickly. I paused for a moment and followed. By the time I reached the top of the stairs, I saw Audley and his friends slip out the front door onto Dean Street. For a moment, I thought of pursuing him. Instead, I walked over to the bar and retrieved my glass, which to my surprise still stood there. In America, the bartender would have removed an abandoned glass even if completely full. After I gulped it down, I returned to my work. But I could not concentrate for the rest of the day. I had become so emotionally high from the mere physical contact with another man, with Audley, that I could think of little else.

I was preoccupied with these thoughts that night and knew instinctively I would return to the Golden Lion the next day without fail. I spent most of the following morning looking at the clock behind me as I struggled to read a long tome on Victoria criminal theory. Fretfully, I watched the hands of the clock crawl toward one o'clock, the usual time I took my break. That morning, I came to appreciate what Einstein had meant by relativity. I forced myself to remain in the library until exactly one o'clock, but the last half hour, I accomplished nothing, scanning the same page time and again. Finally grabbing my coat, I rushed out into Great Russell Street and down the familiar back alleys toward the Golden Lion. I only thought of my determination to meet Audley.

As I approached the pub, however, the familiar fears began to enter my head. What if I contracted some disease from Audley? What if I unwittingly transmitted gonorrhea to Ann as a result? Would I lie and tell her that I was having a relationship with another woman or confess the truth? I couldn't imagine Ann accepting either one, although she might take the former more readily than the latter explanation. Yet a simple injection easily treated gonorrhea. What if I were to get something much more serious? I had read a good deal recently about AIDS, which had become an alarming problem in Britain as it had in America. I hadn't really given it serious thought until the prospect of sexual relationships with Audley seemed a real possibility. Now that mysterious ailment with its dire consequences became a reality. These thoughts loomed ever larger in my head. I felt myself chill as the implications began to fall logically into place. Yet I did not turn back because my desire for Audley seemed to push these other considerations roughly aside. By the time I reached Cambridge Circus, however, I had successfully compartmentalized them as unthinkably absurd. They did not stop me from wending my way toward the Golden Lion.

When I entered the pub, I looked around almost frantically to see if Audley was in. Sure enough, I saw him standing near the Panoram, talking with an older man. I walked over to the bar to get a beer and then turned toward him. My big moment had arrived. Today I would consummate my fantasies, but again, it was not to be. The older man talking to Audley walked away, and Audley downed his beer quickly in preparation for leaving.

"How ya doing?" I hoped the sense of nervousness in my voice was not too obvious.

"Super. Glad to see you here again. I think you spend more time here than I do," he laughed.

"I was hoping we could talk," I began.

"Gee, I'm sorry. I have to leave now. I wanted to talk with you too." At that point, he put his hand inside my unzipped jacket and ran his index finger underneath my left nipple. "I want to get to know you better." I tried to say something, but the sensations distracted me.

"Do you ever get here at night?" he asked, taking his hand away.

"No, that's difficult," I stammered. "I really can only get here in the afternoons."

"That's a shame." He smiled broadly at me. "Well, maybe I'll see you tomorrow. Sorry I can't stay and talk now." He winked at me and then walked away quickly. I watched as he departed with the older man. I felt tremendously disheartened after he left. I had been so close; he clearly had an interest in me—if only I could work out something suitable. Finishing my beer, I started back to the British Library but found that I just could not gather the inspiration to return to work. My nerves were too shattered for that. Instead, I spent the next two hours walking through the streets of London, not going anywhere in particular, just exploring. My thoughts, however, were entirely on Audley and the sensation of his hand on my chest. I marveled at how a simple touch could have such an electrifying impact.

I think that night, for the first time, I sensed my imprisonment. Even worse, I recognized Ann as my warder, and I began to resent her. I knew intellectually and rationally that the fault did not belong to her. I had constructed my own prison; she had only inadvertently become part of the mortar and bricks that held me. Nevertheless, I began looking at her in a new light. Without Ann, I could easily meet Audley at the Golden Lion. I could spend the night with him, sleep naked with him, holding him in my arms. The thoughts were delicious, but they made the anxiety greater. She had gotten a letter from her parents that day and seemed to be somewhat homesick. Perhaps she felt the same resentment toward me because I had brought her to this foreign place. Whatever the cause, we distanced ourselves. Regretting my feelings, I tried later to make up to her, but she received it coolly. Her rejection of my sexual advances only served to renew and intensify my earlier frustration.

Happily, the next day was Friday, and I had the weekend to anticipate. We planned to drive to Stonehenge and Salisbury on Saturday, which I had looked forward to despite the raw weather. I found that I got a great deal accomplished that day. I guessed I was more sanguine about the possibility of missing Audley. I walked to the Golden Lion without the same sense of trepidation I had felt the previous day. I had a certain amount of confidence in my step. The Greeks would instantly have recognized it as hubris. When I got to the Golden Lion, Audley was not in sight. Although disappointed, I had prepared myself for the possibility that he would not show up. Having missed him many times before, I would not have been surprised if he did not appear today. I had, after all, seen him several days in a row. I felt a good deal of pleasure then when I saw him enter. He looked around quickly, obviously seeing who was there, and smiled when he saw me. He ordered a pint and walked immediately over to me. "How ya doing?" He grinned broadly.

"I didn't expect to see you today. Glad you came."

We both took awkward sips from our beers.

"Listen," I said, observing the nervous tremor returning to my voice, "I was hoping that we could get together some time. Do you think that's possible?"

"Of course." I wondered if he meant the same thing that I did. "When do you have a day off?"

"My time's my own. I can work any time that I want to." I paused for a moment. "I don't really have to go back this afternoon."

Audley smiled. He allowed his free hand to rub against the back of my hand. "I've been hoping that we could see more of each other. This afternoon sounds fine." He took a deep drink of his beer. By this point, I was shaking like a leaf, and Audley noted it. "Are you shaking?"

"Yes," I admitted. "It's not often that I pick up someone in a bar."

"I would have thought you would do it all the time. Guys must throw themselves at you constantly. You're quite a looker."

Audley's remark flattered me, although I hardly believed he was serious. How could he be so attracted to a man almost twice his age? "Like another beer?" I asked.

"Won't say no. Where would you like to go this afternoon?"

I ordered the beers and then replied, "Well, I have no place in mind." We seemed to be dancing a rather graceless ballet to work out this arrangement.

"You could come to my place. My roommate's not there. We could be alone, ah . . . talk and get to know each other, if you get my drift." The butterflies in my stomach had, by now, become pterodactyls flapping their scaly wings.

"Sounds fine to me." *This is it*, I thought. I was finally going to do it and hadn't yet run screaming from the bar.

Audley helped a great deal by being so reassuring. "Don't worry about a thing," he had said as he finished his beer. "Ready to go now?"

"Anytime you are," I replied, anxious to get out of the Golden Lion and start toward the goal.

"There's one thing we had better settle first. Guys usually like to give me thirty pounds as a present, but seeing as I like you, twenty would be much appreciated."

At first, I did not know what he meant. Then slowly, it began to dawn. "You mean you want money?"

"You don't think you get it free, do you?" he said with a laugh.

I started to go cold all over. How could I have missed it? Why had I not suspected Audley was like the other young men here? He was nothing but a hustler. I tried to recover my stability. "But I thought you wanted to get to know me," I said rather foolishly.

"Sure, I like you. American blokes are interesting characters. But it's still going to cost you twenty pounds, like anyone else."

I wasn't sure what to say. I had built a tremendous illusion about him; I felt a strong, passionate attraction for him. That image, however, quickly slipped away. I had been totally fooled and started to get angry, not so much at Audley but at myself for not sensing it. Finally, I stammered, "But I don't use hustlers. And I didn't think that you were. . . ."

"Oh shit," he interrupted. "What did you think I was here for? My health?"

I paused briefly before I finally said, "I guess we have nothing else to talk about. I'm just not interested."

Now Audley seemed mad. "Then why did you carry on with me for so long if you didn't want to get off?"

"I never thought you were a hustler," I said again. Our voices got louder, and some standing near us began to watch.

"What a bloody arse you are!" he exclaimed. "Well, I guess we have nothing more to say to each other. See you around, chappy." He drank down the rest of his beer and walked off. I didn't even bother to finish mine. I put it down, half full on the bar, and rushed out. But unlike the first time I saw Audley in the Golden Lion, I did not look back.

I returned to the British Library, collected my belongings, and went home. The train ride was the longest I had ever experienced. Totally depressed, I cared little when Ann—somewhat startled by my early arrival home—tried to pry out of me what was wrong. I made some noncommittal statement about a headache and sat in the lounge sulking. The next day, we drove to Stonehenge as planned. Although my heart was not in the trip, I had to build a facade for Ann to hide my hurt. Nevertheless, my soul felt as bleak as Salisbury Plain.

Chapter VIII

Homily

After that afternoon, I did not return to the Golden Lion for several weeks. In fact, I felt that my entire plan to seek fulfillment had been dashed permanently. It seemed the possibility of achieving my desires no longer existed. The Golden Lion, the only place in which I felt comfortable, turned out to be a den of rent boys who had no interest in me, only my money. I emphatically rejected that solution to my problem. The other gay retreats did not hold the same allure. Being much too shy to go up to these strangers and begin a conversation, I could not get involved. That, of course, had not been a difficulty in the Golden Lion since everyone there eagerly talked to me. Undoubtedly, the principal attraction involved the money that might come their way if they did get to know me. The whole situation appeared hopeless. On the one hand, I felt a debilitating unease in the Salisbury or the Kings Arms. On the other, the Golden Lion apparently held no prospects either.

The first night, a terrible depression overcame me. My entire life seemed empty and aimless. I could not even make myself into a good adulterer. I watched Ann sleeping next to me. *How*, I wondered, *had I gotten myself into this mess? Why had I been so convinced that I could control my true nature? What had ever possessed me into believing that I could alter myself by getting married? Why would I have thought that Ann could turn me into a raging heterosexual?* Perhaps I should have married some voluptuous femme fatale who would have encouraged me to forget boys. I loved Ann but certainly not because of the passion within me. I had known that from the very beginning; I should have been aware of the consequences. I lay awake the entire night, thinking about my future. By dawn, I had determined once more to shove my desires back where they had come from in hopes that they might remain dormant again. The prospect of success seemed slim, but I saw no alternative. Audley was an unacceptable pipe dream. His looks and his attention had been based on nothing but falsehood. The more I thought about it, the angrier I became. Why had I been so deluded?

The next morning, Ann commented on my restlessness. "Is anything bothering you? I heard you stirring all night long."

"Oh, nothing really," I lied. "I couldn't sleep very well. I don't really know what the problem was."

"Do you think you'll be able to get any work done today if you haven't slept?"

"I guess I'll just have to try," I said dismissively.

In fact, I did not accomplish very much at all, not only from tiredness but also from preoccupation. I kept turning over in my mind the path by which I had gotten to this point in my life. I felt totally frustrated since I could not envision an escape. *Perhaps*, I thought, *I should take up Audley's offer. I could afford the twenty pounds.* Yet the more I thought, the more my conviction rose that I had made the correct decision. I could not stoop to prostitution. What I planned to do was sufficiently evil; I felt enough guilt about that. To pay for it was beyond the pale. Just as these pious thoughts passed through my mind, I recognized the hypocrisy.

I wondered how I could get my life back to that of a normal married male, how I could reestablish a meaningful relationship with my wife, how I could be a father to a daughter I hardly knew. I recognized I had become so preoccupied in recent months with my problem that I had rather neglected Sarah as well as Ann. Perhaps with this nonsense ended, I could build bridges to my family and restore everything to the way they had been before. But before what? Before Tommy's death? That was impossible. Could anything really be restored to their previous condition considering what we all had been through? As I mulled these things over, a nice-looking young man walked past my desk, and I looked up. My eyes explored the contours of his body. I admired his good looks. Then I realized that, in fact, nothing could be normal since I was not normal.

I did stay away from the Golden Lion and other gay hangouts for several weeks, although I thought often about Audley. I felt like a reformed drunk. At times, resentment filled my thoughts; at others, I grew increasingly curious about him. He did not seem to be a tough like Ed. He actually seemed to have a certain amount of refinement despite the lack of an educated tongue. Would he talk with me about his life and inner thoughts even though I was not a paying customer? By the beginning of March, I had decided that I would return once again to the Golden Lion. I kept warning myself that this might be my last opportunity. I needed to give it all one more chance. My resolve to stay on the wagon had silently slipped away.

When I entered the Golden Lion again, it had been after a fairly long absence, and I had to acclimate myself to the surroundings again. I quickly recognized that the same group of men I had seen on my first and subsequent visits was still in their accustomed places. I looked around for Audley but did not see him. Procuring my usual pint of lager, I stood by the bar next to a very tall man about my age, if not older. He spoke to a younger man with a detectably Scottish accent. The taller man had obviously consumed too much, and his voice became louder with each swallow of beer. I became aware that, although he talked to the other young man, he looked directly at me. Finally, he raised his voice even higher and moved closer to me. "Now take this one. I can tell he's a phony."

"You can't be sure of that," said the young Scottish lad.

"Oh yes, I can," slurred the older one. "Why, he's been coming in here lots of times, and I haven't seen him spend one penny on anyone but himself. He's a phony, I tell you."

I became extremely self-conscious about the entire scene. The older man talked so loudly that others around us turned to look. I wasn't quite sure what to do. At first, I thought of joining the conversation so pointedly aimed in my direction. Alternatively, I considered making a quick exit from the bar, abandoning a chance to talk to Audley should he come in later. I decided that perhaps the best thing was to ignore the whole scene; I slowly began turning my back on the pair.

"You know I'm talking about you, don't you?"

"I beg your pardon?"

"No begging my pardon. You're a phony." He pushed his rather unattractive face closer to mine, and I could distinctly smell the cause of his aggressiveness. I had seen the man in the pub at other times, but he had stood rather quietly to the side as I had on most occasions. His behavior now was quite out of keeping with past observations.

"I'm not quite sure what you mean," I responded, trying to move back as subtly as possible and becoming distinctly aware of the possibility that this man might be violent. Not being particularly brave, I wanted to avoid physical harm at all costs. The whole affair made me increasingly nervous, and I wished that I had taken my choice of abandoning the pub at the very first opportunity.

"Of course, you do. You come in here practically every day and don't spend a penny on anyone but yourself." The accusation was not true since I had bought Ed a beer several weeks before, although not out of choice. "You can't come into a place like this and expect just to drink by yourself. There are other people here to consider."

"Now, George, perhaps you're being unfair to the man," interjected the Scotsman.

"No. I know what my eyes tell me. And they tell me this man's a phony. He's here under false pretenses."

"False pretenses?" I repeated.

"Yes. You think that you can get something for nothing. And in this place, you can't do that." What he alluded to now became clear, and the anxiety of recognition now intensified as the fog lifted. "When you meet a young man that strikes your fancy, you're supposed to buy him a drink. Take Haggis here. Does he strike your fancy?"

"I haven't given it much thought," I replied.

"Does he strike your fancy?" George repeated with even greater urgency. I began to feel real panic until the young man whom George called Haggis—probably George's designation and probably not complimentary—interrupted.

"I don't think you should put him on the spot like that."

"All I want to know is if he fancies you."

If I made light of the conversation, I thought, *it might smooth things over.* Otherwise, I feared it would be impossible to extricate myself gracefully. Every time I backed up a little, George would follow in hot pursuit.

Finally, out of desperation, I said, "Yes, I find him rather attractive." On the whole, I didn't, but I thought that discretion was the better part of valor at this point.

"Then why don't you buy him a pint?"

"Now, George," interjected Haggis, "don't put him on the spot like that."

"Well, if he fancies you, he should buy you a drink."

"But I have a drink here. I don't need another just yet." Haggis then paused a moment to think. "But of course, I won't say no if he offered me one when I finish."

George smiled triumphantly. "So then you'll buy him a drink?"

Completely intimidated by this entire routine, I agreed to purchase a pint of bitter for Haggis when he had completed the first. I began to feel some sort of comradery with Haggis not only because I was now the source of his next drink but also because he seemed somewhat nervous about George's behavior. When George turned away for a second to talk with another friend, I leaned closer to Haggis. "Is he always this way?"

"I've never seen him so drunk before." I had already begun to admire the softness of his accent. "Really, you don't have to buy me a beer if you don't want to. I don't need another."

"No, I said I would," I replied with a certain self-sacrificing air. "I'll have another with you." That meant very little would get done that afternoon in the rarified atmosphere of the British Library.

"It probably is a good idea to humor George. I never have seen him this drunk before," he repeated.

I walked over to the bar and ordered a round of drinks for the two of us. George smiled contentedly when I walked back and handed Haggis his drink. Since he was now somewhat indebted to me, Haggis began to strike up a conversation. "You're an American?"

"Yes. I'm over here doing research. You're from Scotland, aren't you? What brought you to London?" The conversation had all the brilliance of most pub fare.

"I couldn't get a job in Glasgow, so I decided to try London. But I haven't had much luck here either."

"I guess the Thatcher administration hasn't helped much."

"Old Maggie hasn't been too kind to me. I haven't been able to hold a job on account of my eyesight. I used to be a cook but was made redundant because of my eyes." Apparently, he was going progressively blind, although he received shots regularly to retard the deterioration. But he could not hold a job, and state assistance was, in some way, withheld from him. He therefore found his way into the Golden Lion as a means of support.

At one point, he asked me, "Do you ever use any of the guys here?"

"You mean have I ever paid for it? No, I haven't." I was quite firm in what I said.

Haggis smiled at me. "I was just wondering." Clearly, he hoped I would perhaps make an exception in his case. His tale of woe so touched me that I would have been almost willing to forgo my principles in this case but decided against such a course. We had talked for about ten minutes when George rejoined us.

"You have been nice to Haggis. Don't you think it would be friendly to buy me a drink? You and I might become friends."

Before I could think about it, I replied, "I highly doubt that." I could hear Haggis sniff when I said it.

"Don't get smart with me. Listen, I probably would be the best fuck you've ever had. You couldn't handle me. I bet you've never had anyone like me before. I'd drive you right out of the bed." The more he spoke, the louder he became again. He then returned to his old refrain. "Do you fancy me?"

"Come on, George," Haggis interrupted. "Don't get started on that again."

"You shut up. I want to know if he fancies me."

"I think you had better humor him," Haggis whispered to me hoarsely. But I was now in no mood to honor his request.

"Do you fancy me?" He pushed his face ever closer to mine so that the smell of his breath overwhelmed me.

"Not particularly." I waited for his response, which I felt might be violent. I looked carefully at the exits to find a clear path to beat a hasty retreat. Much to my surprise, he just laughed.

"The least you could do is buy me a drink."

Not wishing to cause further trouble, I asked him what he wanted. I was thankful that he just wanted another pint of bitter, like the one he had only half-finished, rather than something more exotic. The cost of this visit to the Golden Lion rose quickly. I walked over to the bar, purchased another pint, and handed it to George. He stood grinning at me, holding the two pints for quite some time. Finally, he walked over to his friend and handed him the pint I had just bought. "I can't drink this, Henry. Would you like it? That nice gentleman bought it for me." Henry looked rather astounded. I was not sure if it was because of the offer of the pint or the fact that someone had actually given it to George.

George had succeeded in doing what he had set out to do, humiliate me. Why he wanted to do so, I could never figure out. I guessed I was supposed to be like the other men who came into the Golden Lion. I should have had a quick drink while I looked over the stable and made my selection. Yet I had been coming in here all these weeks and never walked out with any of the young men. Moreover, I had never provided any of them with a drink. George was right on that score; it was the usual tradition to offer such libations before serious business negotiations. I must have stood out more than I realized. Yet I could not, at the same time, wonder why George hung around here every day. Certainly, no one would buy his services, despite his boasts of sexual prowess. Nor had I ever seen George approach any of the young men. It seemed to me that he was not much different from me in that respect, but he clearly belonged in the Golden Lion, and I did not.

Haggis apologized again for George's conduct, but I waved it aside, attributing it to an excess of drink. In fact, George never bothered me again, although he would from time to time leer at me from across the room. On the contrary, he never seemed concerned whether I fancied him or not. Haggis and I continued to talk mostly about his various efforts to find gainful employment until I finished my beer. I bid him goodbye and returned to my work. But the experience had shaken me. It was another week before I returned to my favorite pub.

No matter how hard I tried, I kept getting drawn back into the Golden Lion as if some force or deity lured me into the clutches of this snare. I just could not keep away. On my next visit, I did not see Audley. Instead, I struck up a conversation with Haggis again. I also bought him a pint without pressure from George, who, I was glad to see, did not make an appearance.

"Be sure to tell George that I got you a beer next time you see him."

"I don't think he really was worried about it. I've never seen him that way before. Something must have gotten into him."

We talked idly for a few minutes until I decided to get more serious. "Do you really have to do what you do to get by?"

"Well, I have a regular job once in a while, generally a short-order cook or a salad man. But then they discover that my eyes play tricks on me, and I'm back here again."

"Where do you live?"

"Right now, with a friend. He's letting me sleep on his sofa. But I can't stay there very long."

"Have you thought about going home?"

"No, I couldn't do that."

I decided not to push that line of inquiry since he clearly seemed uncomfortable. Instead, I asked him about the going rate and if he had run into any unusual sorts.

"Well, I do remember this one bugger who was into yellow fountains. I really don't like that sort of thing myself."

"Yellow fountains?"

"Yeah, you know, urine."

I confessed that my limited experiences had not progressed to that one. I started to ask him for amplification but decided that my imagination could suffice.

"When I said that I wouldn't, he kicked me out. Didn't give me a farthing either. I was bloody mad, but he was bigger than me. I think he was also the best-looking one that I ever knew. It's a shame he had such odd ideas."

The more I talked with Haggis, the more I got to like him. I also felt quite sorry for him and thought again about spending the money on him. I did not find him physically attractive. He was rather short, and his face was not appealing. He squinted so badly at times that he screwed up his entire face, making him look almost hideous. But his sincerity and warmth more than made up for it. I looked on the twenty-pound investment as a form of charity. Of course, it would cost much more than twenty since I would also have to rent a room somewhere. Obviously, we could not use his friend's sofa. No more came of these thoughts since Haggis had an eye examination that afternoon, and I never got to raise the possibility. We parted with a friendly goodbye and no definite plans for the future.

That night, I began mulling over the possibility of hiring Haggis, and my previous objections forced their way to the forefront again. It was just something that I could not do, no matter how good the cause. I sat in the lounge reading *Private Eye*, watching Ann rock Sarah to sleep. The level of my perversity would not descend to those depths. Simple adultery was enough for me to handle.

The next day, I returned to the Golden Lion firmly resolved that if I encountered Haggis, I would continue on our simple conversation, and that would be the end of it. But instead of Haggis, I first saw George when I entered. He gave me his usual leer as I ordered my pint. I felt his eyes on me as I walked to the corner, my prospect to survey the room. He made me so uncomfortable that I decided to climb the stairs to the lounge bar to escape his presence. At the top of the stairs, I at once saw Audley sitting with one of the other regulars. He looked up, but when he recognized me, he returned quickly to his conversation, ignoring my arrival. What a change had occurred since the last time we met. I wanted to retreat down the stairs again but determined not to allow him to chase me out. Besides, George lurked below. Instead, I settled two tables away and quietly drank my beer. I purposely sat with my back to him so that I would not have to look in his direction, although my desire to feast on his beautiful face was quite strong.

The two continued to talk for a few minutes until the other man departed. Audley and I were the only ones remaining in the lounge bar. I heard his chair scrape across the floor, and I breathed a sigh a relief, thinking that he was on his way out also. Instead, he walked over to my table. He looked at me seriously, with none of the penetrating eye that I had become so accustomed to, which I really liked. "How're you doing?"

"Fine. And yourself?"

He did not bother to continue with the pleasantries. "Just remember, if you change your mind, I'm usually here. I've taken a fancy to you and would certainly be willing to oblige." I instantly thought of George's question to me the previous week.

"No, I highly doubt that. If you wait for me to kick in your rent money, you'll find yourself on the street." The tone of my response even surprised me. I was sure Audley had not expected the vehemence.

After pausing for a moment, he said, "Sim, you don't have to worry about me. I get plenty of takers who pay real money. There aren't too many freeloaders around here." He turned and started to walk toward the exit but hesitated when he got to the top of the stairs. He thought for a moment, a serious look clouding his unusually untroubled continence, and then walked back over to me. "What have you got against paying for it? You're an American. You've got lots of money."

"On that second point, you're sadly mistaken. I'm a college professor, underpaid and overworked. Don't get the idea that all Americans are rich because they aren't. You just happen to get that impression from the ones you see wandering around London with their minks and loud voices."

"But, Sim, you can't tell me that you can't afford twenty pounds."

"It's not the affording. It's the principle. I won't pay for sex."

"But a man in your condition hasn't got much choice."

"What do you mean by that?"

"Well, you are married. That's about the only safe way of getting it."

"How did you know I was married?"

"Oh, I've seen enough guys come in here with the left hand always thrust into the pocket. You didn't think you could fool anyone here?"

"I wasn't trying to fool anyone," I countered sheepishly.

"Don't try to kid me. But you still haven't explained why you won't pay for some love."

"You just explained it yourself."

"I did."

"Sure, it's called making love between a man and a woman or between two men for that matter. I just don't believe that an exchange of cash can really make it happen."

"Well, I've done it for free with a friend or for cash with a stranger, and it feels exactly the same to me."

"Does it now? Perhaps you're right since I haven't tried it the second way." I did not want to admit that I hadn't tried it the first way either for almost twenty-five years. "But I'd wager that there is an intensity of feeling that comes with the first that is rarely present in the other."

"But the money gives it an added feeling."

"You spend the money in a day. It has no lasting power."

"Cuming only lasts a few seconds. That's all the feeling I know. But the twenty pounds will go much further."

"Memories last a good deal more than either cuming or money. They last a lifetime." My philosophical nature rose to the fore. "Love is something that will keep us sane. Without it, this would be a pretty sorry world."

"Then why don't you get love from your wife?" Although a fair question, I resented the implications.

"I guess because I was created differently from other men. I do love my wife very much, but I have an inner longing that I can't suppress, which it seems only the love of another man can fulfill. I assume you have that same need as well?"

"All I know is what I like."

"But it's more than the money."

"Yeah, I suppose you're right there."

"You have the same basic drive that I do. But to me, it's more than physical pleasure. You're right on that. The sensation does only last a second. But the closeness and the affirmation of life are things that will continue long afterward." It was amazing that I could speak with such authority considering the fact that I had not engaged in any of these activities since I was a teenager, other than in my rather robust fantasies.

"That's nonsense. We have sex because it feels good. It's as simple as that. And to me, because it pays good money." Audley was clearly getting tired of my flights of sophistry and started to get up. "I've had enough of a sermon for today. I better look downstairs, or it will be too late for me to get anything this afternoon."

"I wasn't trying to preach to you. You wanted to know why I won't pay for it. I was just explaining it to you. You don't have to accept it. You have the right to your opinion, but allow me mine."

"You mean you've never paid for it? I just can't believe it. A guy your age just can't walk into Heaven and pick something up. Even the crowd at the Salisbury is younger." He was trying to get my goat now. He seemed to enjoy playing with me.

"Listen, there is plenty of life left in me. I could hold my own with you." I wondered about the source of this bravado. Certainly, my lack of sexual experience with males did not warrant such a claim, and my marital experiences were practically as limited.

"Well, you're going to have to pay for it if you want to find out." At this, Audley got up from the table. "Listen, I like talking to you, but I've business to do. Need a little extra cash to see me through the week, if you know what I mean. If I spend all my time up here talking with you, I won't get anywhere. Cheers." And off he went down the stairs. I sat there for a few moments, fuming. Why had I allowed myself to get bested by him? He had dragged me into proclaiming those sanctimonious decrees and then made me the butt of his humor. Yet I could not help liking him. He had a freshness I did not find in the other hustlers downstairs. Somehow he had been protected from the callousness that infected the others. That was why I did not recognize him as a hustler when I first saw him and even after I talked with him a few times. Something about him, something vital and alive, made him different. I felt driven to get to learn more about him, to discover the source of those qualities. But I doubted if I would ever have another chance to sit down and talk as we had this afternoon.

I finished my beer and descended the steps. I could see Audley talking to an older man in the corner. The older man walked over to the bar, purchased two drinks, and returned to hand one to Audley. Aud did not have his usual pint of lager; instead, he had ordered a mixed drink, probably a gin and tonic. Obviously, the older man had reason to impress the younger. Nevertheless, I questioned Audley's taste in men. The gentleman was rather heavyset and, despite the coldness of the day, was sweating profusely. His face, covered with pockmarks, was fundamentally unattractive. As I walked past them, the older man almost whispered in Audley's ear. With his back to me, the heavyset gentleman could not see me give Audley a wry look and gesture in his direction. Audley merely raised his eyebrows as if to say it was all in good cause and returned his attentions to the secret communication. I pushed the door open with my back so that I could take one more look at the couple. They shook hands, apparently consummating the business transaction. That certainly was not love, but I doubted if Audley would get any pleasure from it either. It must have been all in a day's work. I wanted to remember to ask Audley, if I saw him again, about the experience.

I returned to the British Library in a better frame of mind than I had had for several weeks. For some reason, talking with Audley had raised my spirits, but for what reason I really cannot clearly explain. With the end of March fast approaching, I certainly stood no closer than previously to fulfilling my desires for male contact. In fact, talking with Audley allowed me to avoid taking the steps needed to complete that task. Yes, I knew quite a few gay men now, but none of them appeared satisfactory partners. I buried myself in my work for the remainder of the afternoon and tried not to think about it.

At five o'clock, I decided to wander the streets before getting the tube back to Amersham. I wanted to sort things out in my own mind. Would I continue to hang around the Golden Lion, wasting my time talking with Audley, or should I go to some other pub—the Salisbury or the Kings Arms in Poland Street—to see if I could pick up something? Crossing Bedford Square rather than my usual route up Gower Street to the Euston Square station, I passed the Russell Hotel and took a side street going I did not know where. Turning into Marchmont Street, I looked into the shop windows I passed. I happened on a bookstore called Gay's the Word and, intrigued by the name, decided to enter it. I had come on this bookstore as if drawn by fate, for it carried material for gays and lesbians, not the pornography of the Zipper but serious literature and nonfiction materials. It also handled pamphlets dealing with a variety of subjects, including problems of adjustment and more somber discussions about AIDS. I explored the shelves briefly and scanned a bulletin board with listings of counselors who deal with gays and requests for roommates. The back of the shop contained a small sitting room where a group of men sat around drinking coffee and chatting. Although I wanted to sit down and talk with them myself, time had slipped by, and I feared Ann would wonder about my tardiness. I decided that I would return someday perhaps to talk, perhaps to meet someone. As I left the store, I laughed at the irony of discovering that place. I seemed incapable of escaping my fate. Even when I innocently strolled the streets of London, I seemed drawn to these situations.

I decided to wend my way to King's Cross station to catch the Metropolitan Line. Cutting through a number of small streets, I reached Judd Street, which led to Euston Road. Halfway up the block, I came across again by chance—or was it fate?—a small Lutheran church. I did not even realize that London had Lutheran churches. Other than the Church of England, I thought one would find only Baptists or Independents. I tried the door to look inside but found it locked. I scanned the signboard outside and noted that services were held every Sunday morning at ten. The building was in immaculate condition, and the board had been recently painted. *How like the Germans*, I thought, *to be so neat.*

I finally caught a train to Amersham, and after the long walk down the hill from the station, I arrived at our door almost an hour later than usual. "What took you so long?" Ann greeted me when I unlatched the door.

"I stopped at a bookstore on the way home."

"That will get you every time. Make any grand purchases?"

None that I could show you, I thought.

"No. I was looking for a new book on Dickens," I lied. "But apparently, it had not come in yet." I thought to let it go at that but then decided to mention my other discovery. "I happened to pass a Lutheran church on the way to the station. I never knew that there was one in London."

Ann seemed only mildly interested. "Next, you'll be telling me that you want to go."

"As a matter of fact, I had considered the possibility. I was curious if a Lutheran church in England would look anything like one in Selinsgrove. I thought maybe we could go next Sunday and then take Sarah to Speakers' Corner afterward."

"What nonsense. We haven't been to church in years. Why the sudden interest now?"

"I'm really not sure. I just have this strange urge." I laughed when I said this, but Ann apparently did not recognize its humor.

"You may go to church if you wish, but Sarah and I will stay right here. I don't want to take her into those crowds anyhow. Lots of nasty people are there, and Sarah shouldn't be exposed to that."

I tried to suppress the discomfort I felt toward Ann. I was not really sure why I should have felt it at all; nevertheless, the prison walls became more apparent. Obviously, my own deceitfulness troubled me, but her out-of-hand rejection of my proposal also rankled me. In an uncharacteristic expression of independence, I announced the next morning that I intended to go to church on Sunday and planned to take Sarah with me. I usually went along with whatever Ann wanted to do on the weekends, especially after Tom's death. My pronouncement obviously startled Ann, who showed more anger than I had seen in quite some time. The argument over whether I was taking Sarah with me—clearly, Ann could not stop me from going—raged for most of the day. Sarah seemed pleased that I wanted to take her with me and did not seem aware that it caused a division between her parents. I insisted on my perfect right to take my daughter to church if I wanted, and Ann retorted that she would not permit her daughter to be involved in such hypocrisy. Some time that afternoon, Ann must have sequestered Sarah because, the next morning when I went to get her dressed to go with me, Sarah announced her decision to remain at home with Mother. "Daddy, I really don't want to go to church. It's boring." I could hear the voice of her mother speaking.

"But we're taking the underground into London, and you love to do that. Then we'll do some neat things after church is over."

She thought for a moment but shook her head. Obviously, Ann had been particularly persuasive and graphic about the horrors of church. To no avail did I try to assure her of the fun we would have. I left the flat alone, resentful of Ann's interference. She had almost a look of triumph on her face as I walked out.

During the train ride to London, I reflected on my relationship with Ann and the coldness that had crept into it. Yet seeking affection from Audley seemed about as senseless as hoping for it from Ann. I fantasized about how things might be reversed, how Ann might fight with Audley over possession of me. How delightful it would be to see the two of them throwing themselves passionately in my direction. How fitting it would be to push them both aside. Each had their chance and muffed it. Then I mused about the possibility of Audley moving in with Ann and me. What joy I would have in choosing each night where I would spread my affection. Both would eagerly solicit my favor, and I would delay until the last moment before making my choice each night. I saw myself as some latter-day Caligula, satisfying my wanton lusts with abandon. I even envisioned myself wearing a toga. My reverie was finally broken when the train pulled into Baker Street, and I had to rush to catch a Circle Line train going to King's Cross.

I didn't know what I expected to find at church. Perhaps I wanted divine revelation to help me resolve my dilemmas. Maybe God would speak to me, tell me which pub I should frequent to find suitable companionship. Or he might signal me that I should give in to Audley's proposition, even lend me the money. Possibly, I had a deep sense of sin about my desires and activities. I might seek repentance and absolution. Whatever the goal, I did not accomplish it at the Lutheran church in London. The people seemed friendly enough and were glad to see a new face; they solicited my return. Yet the experience left me empty. I desperately needed something to pull my life together, but this group—mostly a graying set—could not provide it. I did not reach the depths of spiritual solitude that I had that twilight at Saint Thomas's. I had come to reject the traditional creeds of the church. I had become a cynic. The virgin birth and the miracles contained no inspiration for me. Doctrinal beliefs had vanished in college, and they remained that way now. Nevertheless, I found something that day in New York, which I sought again. I had come very briefly into contact with some spiritual force that I knew I needed but had eluded me. That Sunday in London, I sought it again but failed to come close to it. Yet I realized I had been driven to find that feeling again. Some divine spark had made me go that Sunday, to do so in an act of defiance of Ann's mocking. But I knew I had to search beyond this first step. I also sensed that this was not a substitute for my sexual desires but a complement to it. At the end of the service, the organist had played the Bach fugue known as the "Gigue," one of Bach's most joyous works for the organ. It had lifted my spirits significantly. The service itself had not contributed to my sense of well-being, but the music had. Somehow my homosexuality didn't seem quite so bad, at least for the short time that the emotion of the music stayed with me. I walked out of the church, my emotions in shreds. My search had not ended; it must continue if I were to find some sort of inner peace.

To lift my spirits, I went to Speakers' Corner to witness the carnival atmosphere. I saw other fathers there sauntering through the park with their children, and I resented even more the fact that Sarah had remained at home. The weather had turned for the better that afternoon, and many people ventured out to take advantage of the balmy weather. The bulbs had begun to bloom, decorating Hyde Park with all the festive atmosphere that nature could provide. I listened to the speakers for a short time. The inevitable critic of the United States stood there condemning my country for its imperialism. I was amused to find that I agreed with much of his attack. Another fascist demanded that all wogs should be expelled from Britain to restore its pristine Anglo-Saxon quality. I observed the placard proclaiming that the end of the world was at hand and, on the reverse, my need to repent in a hurry. I wasn't sure if I would have enough time to repent if things were coming to a close that quickly. Meanwhile, I listened to another savant denouncing Christianity as the world's greatest evil and spouting the religion of Madalyn Murray O'Hair. I recognized O'Hairism as much of a religion as Christianity was. It just depended which faith one would ultimately decide to follow. For the moment, I had suspended judgment.

I spent about an hour listening to the speakers and wandering through the park. My resentment toward Ann mellowed as I recognized that I really had no right to condemn her. I had stooped so low myself that I could not stand in judgment of her. During the train back to Amersham and the walk to our home, I pondered these thoughts. I found that Ann had also thought about the way she had acted and repented. While we said nothing overtly, we both recognized the foolishness of the struggle between us. Finally, I suggested that, on such a lovely day, we should walk through the village and have tea at the Willow Tree Restaurant. As we enjoyed the scones and clotted cream, we chatted with the young proprietor who beamed when we praised his establishment. On the way home, I mentioned the fact that I intended to go to church again next Sunday, to Westminster Abbey to hear the choir sing. For some reason, that suggestion sounded more legitimate to Ann than others might. I also suggested that Sarah could accompany me this time since I planned to visit the zoo afterward. It was an offer that, as it turned out, Sarah could not refuse.

Chapter IX

Credo

Almost antiphonically, I seemed to go from gay hangouts to church and from church to the lairs of queers. The next Monday, I dutifully returned to the Golden Lion, seeking the perfect man to satisfy my wants or at least to talk to Audley again. The previous day, I had not prayed fervently to remove the stain of faggotry from my soul the way I had in Saint Thomas'. The setting just did not seem appropriate in the Judd Street church. Or perhaps I did not feel as dirty as I did after leaving the Adonis Theatre. After all, I had come to know Audley and Haggis and Ed as human beings and not sex objects in a darkened theater. They had faces and personalities, not just erect cocks. I realized that I had slowly come to identify myself with them, although with difficulty since their life experience and mine differed so completely. Yet I recognized a sense of community with them. Despite Audley's bravado, he demonstrated at least some of the unease I felt. He had to justify his actions too strenuously to be completely secure. Or at least I hoped that he understood something about what I had said to him about my own beliefs. I decided I might have returned to the Golden Lion to explore that possibility further.

Yet Audley did not appear that day. I stood quietly at the bar alone, drinking my beer without making any effort to examine the others there. From time to time, George eyed me from the corner; but thankfully, he did not approach me. He remained rather sober today and did not have the glassy stare that had attempted to penetrate my secrets the other week. I actually mustered the nerve to smile at him and nod a form of greeting, which he acknowledged peremptorily. But when George came over to the bar to refresh his beer, I thought it wise to move away and stand next to the Panoram. I really didn't want to take any chances.

Shortly, a young man—I would judge that he could not have been much older than eighteen—moved to the bar near me. I had seen him on several occasions conversing with the gang at the far end of the bar, and I assumed him to be a regular. I also guessed how he made his living and had never seriously engaged him in any way. Now he took this opportunity to approach me. He took his beer, turned with his back to the bar, and began looking in my direction. At first, I kept my eyes downcast so as not to link with his, but he gazed so insistently that I could not help but look up and encounter his glance. He then proceeded to look from my face slowly down the contours of my body. The meaning could not have been more obvious. He then stared me in the eye again, and in a gentle small voice, which I recognized instantly as a gay signal, he said, "Hi." I nodded a reply and smiled. He was rather cute, and the thought crossed my mind that, in fact, my initial suspicions might be in error. He could have a serious interest in me as a mature, good-looking man. Perhaps he found blond hair and brown eyes attractive.

I decided that I would never know if I did not follow through. Gulping the rest of my beer, I came up next to him to order another. Although I had planned on only one that day, I had to explore this opportunity fully. As I stood there waiting for my beer, he moved closer to me so that our bodies almost touched. I did not respond in quite the way I had when Audley caught hold of my hand in the men's room downstairs, but still I felt the surge. I paid for my beer and turned around, purposely brushing my hand against his.

"I've seen you here quite often, now haven't I?"

"Yes, I usually come in here a couple of times a week," I replied.

We stood silently sipping our beers and looking at each other for a moment. Finally, he added, "Are you in the market for a nice young man?" I immediately understood the drift of his question, and my response was as immediate.

"I'm not interested in paying for it, if that's what you mean."

My vehemence obviously took him aback. At first, he did not know how to respond. After a pause, he shifted his tactic. "You married?" he queried.

"Yep. Got kids too."

"I could never do that."

"What do you mean?"

"Have kids."

"Why not? Have you ever done it with a woman before?"

"I tried once but just couldn't get myself to do it. The thought of it makes me sick." His confession quite surprised me. He was a very attractive young man with boyish good looks. He appeared quite masculine without any traces of effeminacy. Had I met him under any other circumstances, I would never have taken him for gay. I found myself very drawn to him with none of the hesitancy that I felt with Ed. Ed had a rough-trade quality that immediately put me on my guard. I felt sure that if I engaged in sex with him, I would either get beaten up or robbed. This young man had a reassuring softness. He did not raise any of those kinds of fears. His aversion to heterosexual relations did amaze me, however. I really don't think he said it just for my benefit.

"I guess I've never had that sort of trouble," I replied. "But I have a powerful attraction to men also."

"I would think that you would want to work out something with me in that case. It's much safer that way."

I thought, in fact, it was probably quite to the contrary. He seemed harmless enough from his exterior, but the more I talked with him, the more uncomfortable I became. Something peculiar about him made me increasingly cautious. Perhaps it was the intensity of his soft-spoken calmness. The small circle that he had tattooed on the back of each finger in particular sparked my curiosity. I had seen them on some of the other men in the pub and wondered if they symbolized something having to do with homosexuality. I had never come across anything like it elsewhere. The thought crossed my mind to launch into the sermon that I had presented to Audley a few weeks before but saw that I would waste it as much now as I had on Audley. Moreover, I certainly did not have the same physical and emotional attraction to this nameless young man as I had developed for Audley in the weeks before we actually understood each other.

"I'm just not interested in that sort of thing."

"But a lot of men in your position are willing to pay for it."

"Sorry, I'm not." I finally got it across to him that I did not engage in a subtle negotiation over price but was dead serious about what I had said.

"Well then, you're hanging around the wrong place. This is a hustler's pub...."

"Oh, I know that."

"You probably should go to the Salisbury or somewhere like that where it's free."

I started to tell him that I had already been there, but he did not give me the opportunity. He picked up his beer and walked back to his friends. He entered into a secret conversation with his buddies at the end of the bar, obviously telling them my amazing story. They turned several times to look at this strange American who frequented the Golden Lion without any intention of purchasing. I purposely sipped my second beer slowly so that it would not appear that their glances had driven me from the pub. Nevertheless, I was quite happy when I had finished and retreated to the safety of the British Library again. The whole episode had embarrassed me, but I hoped they had not perceived it.

That evening came the news that upset me even more. A letter from my mother awaited my return. Ann had already read it; and from the look on her face, I knew it contained bad news. "Aren't you going to tell me what's in it?"

"No, you'd better read it yourself."

I scanned the letter and saw at once that it contained a definitive plan for her visit to us. We had made it very clear that no room existed for her in our almshouse, thinking that she would not come if she had to take lodgings elsewhere. In response, she asked us to pay for a room near us, but I had informed her we just could not afford it. We had also put off her requests for appropriate dates for her visit as we had done at Christmas. That seemed to set the matter to rest, and she had not mentioned a visit since December. Now she announced that she had made reservations to fly over in June and wanted us to make a booking for her at a nearby lodging house. It seemed that my sabbatical had ended. Even Ann's parents had not ventured to make the trip over since they told me privately that they thought we needed time to ourselves. If they only knew how useless it had been. Now Mother announced her intention of intruding herself on us.

Ann seemed to take the idea somewhat more casually than I did. "Perhaps it is the gods punishing you for your hypocrisy for going to church Sunday."

I resented the remark but did not acknowledge it. "We have got to think of some way to forestall her."

"She plans to come for only two weeks. Perhaps we could survive that since she won't be living with us."

"But she'll be here all the time and will expect me to stay home and take her around. I just won't do that." For a brief moment, the wicked idea of taking her to the Golden Lion for a pint entered my mind. Perhaps the ultimate punishment for imposing herself on me was to reveal that her son was a faggot. "Maybe I'll pray for cancer." The remark hardly left my mouth when I realized its callousness. Ann stiffened, and I hurried on. "Perhaps I'll write my brother and tell him that he has to keep her home. He knows what I think about her. Maybe he'll help."

Ann remained mute to this suggestion, the hurt of my earlier remark still smarting. It amazed me, when I thought about the exchange later, how we could unintentionally hurt each other in such subtle ways.

I mulled the whole matter over the next day. It caused me as much emotional distress as discovering that Audley was a hustler. It was a dreary rainy day, and I did not bother to walk down to my favorite hangout. Instead, I wandered through an exhibit of Roman statues in the British Museum that had recently opened. I did not find the marble penises particularly stimulating.

That night, Ann and I again failed to resolve the question of what to do about my mother. Overnight, Ann had come to sense what I knew, that Mother designed her visit to increase our problems. There seemed something pathological about her, and I wondered if she did not delight in the thought of the discomfort her letter obviously brought us. In my darkest moments, I even wondered if she did not relish Tommy's death because of the resulting unhappiness. The more Ann and I considered the matter, the greater my hatred for the woman grew. She had destroyed my childhood; now she wanted to bring me to grief again. *Wasn't it her doing*, I thought, *that drove me to seek sexual releases that haunted me? Hadn't she driven me to the Adonis Theatre and to the Golden Lion?* I tended to make her loom larger in my problem the more I thought about it. In any case, Ann and I felt the challenge, and it seemed to bring us closer together in our efforts to resolve it.

"Why don't we just write her and say that we plan to take a research trip at that time?" Ann suggested.

"Because her travel plans will then become completely flexible. She set those dates, but nothing prevents her from coming at another time. She just wanted to make us uncomfortable, and the exact timing of the plague is irrelevant."

"Don't you think you might be a little too harsh on her?"

"Not in the slightest," I retorted. "She has no interest in coming to England. She only wants to disrupt our lives. She wasn't free to do it before because of her work. Now that she's retired, I expect to see her descend on us with regularity and not because she likes either one of us."

Ann looked disturbed at the vehemence of my feelings. "I didn't realize that you felt that strongly about your mother."

"She's responsible for a lot of misery in my life. I can never forgive her for it."

"Don't you think you are being a little too harsh on her? You know I'm not that fond of her either, but you seem to carry that feeling too far."

"You just don't understand the extent of the damage she has done to me," I said cryptically. Ann tried to press me, but I refused to comment further. That night, I sat down and wrote Mother a straightforward letter telling her that she was not welcome. I didn't even try to disguise the reason. I bluntly told her that we would see her when we returned to America but that we wanted to be left alone here.

Dear Mother,

[I thought about thanking her for the letter but decided that I won't descend into hypocrisy.]

We received your note about your proposed visit to us. Unfortunately [I didn't really feel the least unfortunate that I won't see her; perhaps this hypocrisy could be tolerated though], you will not be able to come at that time. I have thought about this a long time and have concluded that perhaps the less we see of each other, the better. You don't seem very happy about our visits to Selinsgrove [actually, I think she received a great deal of pleasure in making us all miserable], and I certainly have not enjoyed them. While I want to see you from time to time, I think it is best to restrict those visits to Selinsgrove. We would be in each other's way too much over here since you would be quite dependent on us. Under these circumstances, I just don't care to see you.

I did not dwell further on her visit; it should have been abundantly clear to her how I felt. I then discussed some of the things I had been doing and the trips we had undertaken. My closing was pleasant enough for any dutiful son.

I felt the greatest sense of release after I posted the letter. The tie had been broken. I no longer pretended to be the loving son I had always protested to be. I had severed the umbilical cord in an abrupt manner. A sense of independence swept over me; I felt as if I could be more myself, that I no longer hid from her as I had concealed my erection behind the door. I felt a sense of pride, like the pride of my manhood. It was an exhilarating feeling.

I did not tell Ann about the letter until after I had mailed it. She was very angry with me for speaking so bluntly. "We probably could have tolerated her for a week or two."

"I'm sorry, Ann, but I couldn't even stand her for a day."

Ann continued to wonder why I held such strong opinions about my mother, but I refused to elaborate. Mother evidentially did not seem to mind the insult too much since she wrote back that she had decided to go to Hawaii with a friend instead. Her casualness infuriated me so much that I wanted to inform her about my perversity and say, "Look what you have done to me." But then I was sure she would have only enjoyed the fact that I was a queer. It would only confirm all the ugly things she thought about me already.

I had posted the letter to Mother at High Holborn and then walked down to the Golden Lion on my one o'clock break. I looked for Audley as usual, but again, he was not there. *Had he decided to move his hustling to some other location?* I wondered. I did not really know of another hustler's pub in London, although I recognized that others must exist. I ordered a beer and saw that Haggis sat deep in conversation with a group of older men at one of the tables. I smiled at him, but he did not notice me, I guessed, because of his dimmed eyesight. Finally, he got up to fetch some beers and stood next to me.

"How are you today?" I inquired.

"Oh, it's you. Didn't recognize you at first." He ordered the pints. "I'm doing pretty fair. Went to a job interview yesterday and have to be back tomorrow to see if I got it."

"What sort of job is it?"

"Short-order cook." He carried the beers over to the older men and returned to continue our conversation. I wondered if he still thought he might make some financial arrangement. "I'd be making hamburgers in a place on Leicester Square."

"You don't mean at the Burger King?"

"Yes, that's the place."

"Where you can have it your way," I quipped. Haggis only gave me a puzzled look.

"They seemed a little worried about my eyesight, but I told them that I could do just fine. I told them that I was in pretty desperate need of a job. I hope they will take that into consideration."

They probably wouldn't, but I didn't tell Haggis that. I also thought about slipping him the twenty pounds without any sexual compensation since I grew more sorry for him each time I saw him. He was a very decent person who had fallen onto hard times. He had been forced to utilize sex as a means to get by. The tattooed young man who approached me two days before was obviously able bodied and quite capable of fending for himself. But Haggis was a different situation. He clearly did not hustle for the quick cash; the circumstances really did not give him much of an alternative.

"What will you do if you don't get the job?"

"I'm not sure. I'm running out of money. I might just have to return home. Of course, there is no guarantee that they'll take me back."

"Do they"—I assumed he meant his parents—"know how you support yourself?"

"They don't know very much at all about me. I just packed up one day and left. I went home once but didn't talk about what I had been doing."

I did not pursue this further because the young man who solicited me the other day walked in the door and over to his friends at the end of the bar, catching my attention. He kissed the gold-braceleted man, who seemed to be their ringleader. "That guy tried to accost me Monday," I told Haggis.

"Which one?"

"The young guy who just walked in the door. He's sitting next to the man in the blue suit at the end of the bar."

"I can't see that far. What did you say he did to you?"

Haggis probably didn't have much education and did not understand what I meant.

"He tried to hustle me," I explained. "He's been in here lots of times. You probably know who he is. He looks very young, about eighteen, with short dark hair. He didn't tell me his name. I noticed that he has small circles tattooed on his fingers."

"Yeah, I know what you mean. Must have gotten out of prison not too long ago."

"How do you know that?"

"The ring tattoos. They aren't allowed to get tattoos in prison, so they often do it to themselves on the fingers like that."

I wondered how I had misjudged that young man so much. "Is that sort dangerous to fool around with?"

"Not unless you try something stupid. Most of the guys here are like me, having a hard time. Once in a while, you'll run into a tough character. Most of 'em aren't like that."

"It really doesn't matter much anyhow since I don't plan to use their services."

Haggis looked somewhat saddened by my remark but continued the conversation for a few more minutes. Finally, I finished my beer and excused myself. Although Haggis made another no sale from me, he said he hoped to see me again. I wondered, though, if I would return. Despite Haggis's reassurance, I was uncomfortable about hanging around a place frequented by that type of person. I worried that I wasn't a good enough judge of personality to make a distinction between a dangerous and benign character. For all I knew, Haggis or Audley might have a criminal record; I certainly did not know Haggis's real name and thought perhaps Audley was made up as well. But the more I thought about it, the more I recognized the bond that held us all together. Even though I felt particularly threatened by George, I could not deny that we belonged to the same fraternity, brothers of the flesh as it were. Ed, Haggis, George, the tattooed young man, Audley, and I were all homosexuals, in a sense all outcasts from society, although their condition was perhaps more obvious than mine since I had a cover. Nevertheless, we were all comrades. I thought of how the Dr. Pepper song might apply to those of us who gathered at the Golden Lion. "I'm a faggot. He's a faggot. Everyone here's a faggot. Wouldn't you like to be a faggot too? Dr. Faggot, drink Dr. Faggot." Ann thought it quite peculiar when I came home humming that jingle.

I remembered Dr. Pepper the following Friday when I entered the Golden Lion. I stayed away on Thursday but could not resist the temptation to return again before the weekend. A number of people I did not recognize along with the regulars crowded the pub that day. Ed came in just after I did with his pool cue, and George stood staring at me from his corner. As I bought my beer, I even thought about walking over to my bud George and striking up a conversation. That thought vanished when Audley came up to me.

"Hi, Sim. Ignoring me?"

I looked up in surprise. After I greeted him, I said, "I didn't even see you."

"You've found someone else?" he said with a mocking pout on his face. "You used to have eyes only for me."

"No, honestly, I didn't see you." I would have continued to excuse myself had his laughter not awakened me to the fact that I was being unduly defensive. "How's business?"

"Not so good. Want to help out?"

"Not today. Thanks all the same."

Audley started to walk away with his beer but then turned back. "Why do you keep coming here?" His gaze was steady and serious.

"To see you," I only half-joked.

"You know how you could see a lot more of me."

"You needn't explain."

"Seriously, I don't understand why you hang around. This place really isn't for someone like you."

"I guess I'm just comfortable here."

"I can't figure you out. Are you really gay?"

"I told you so before, just as much as you are."

"Did you fool around much with guys when you were in the States?"

"If you want to know the truth, I've never fooled around at all. Well, when I was a teenager—you know, you pull mine, and I pull yours. That sort of thing."

A look of disbelief crept across Audley's face. "Let me get this straight." His Yorkshire accent seemed to broaden as he spoke. "You've never had sex with a guy since you were young."

"That's right," I confessed. "I'm a complete novice. My sex life with men has been restricted to my fantasies."

"You've got to be joking. Then how do you know you'll like it?"

"Well, I knew I liked it as a kid, and I'm sure I'll like it just as much, if not more, as a man. Of course, there is no guarantee. I might just find that I'm not homosexual and that sex with a guy is repulsive, but I doubt it."

Audley seemed intrigued by my confession. He asked me to sit down at one of the tables so that we could continue. "Won't that interfere with your search for customers?"

"No, I can always get something tonight. Now answer my question. How do you know you'd like it if you've never really tried it?"

"I confess it's just a feeling. But I know deep down inside me that I function with men."

"You mean you don't have sex with your wife?"

I almost said "not very often" but thought that would be unkind to Ann. "Sure, I've fathered two kids. But I know that sex with my—a woman is not as fulfilling to me as it would be with a man."

"That sounds like a bunch of shite. How can you know that unless you tried it?"

I tried to turn the tables on Audley but without much success. "How did you discover your homosexuality? Did you have to try it before you found out?"

"Well, I just started fooling around with other guys. But I seemed to enjoy it more than they did. When they stopped, I kept on going, that's all."

"Have you had sex with women?"

"Sure, a couple of times, but I didn't enjoy it very much."

"But you don't have any inner sense that you were homosexual?"

"Never thought about it. I just do what I enjoy. It's as simple as that."

Obviously, Audley had never agonized over it the way I had. I wondered if any of these people had. Perhaps they just accepted their condition without reservation. They were what they were, and introspection was not requisite. I just wasn't that sort of person. I had to try to understand why I was that way. I had not come to terms with myself, had not fully accepted my condition as natural. To me, it was quite abnormal, something therefore that had to be rationalized. I needed to find an excuse for being queer; Audley did not. I envied that.

Finishing my beer, I decided to have another. It was Friday, and I had accomplished a great deal that week. I deserved a rest. As I got up, I asked Audley, "Would you like another?"

He looked surprised. I supposed the only time anyone else offered him a drink was as a prelude to a proposition. Since he knew that was not the present case, he seemed flattered. "Sure, Sim. I wouldn't say no." I returned with the two pints and slipped into the seat next to him. I had been sitting across from him but felt uncomfortable about other men listening to our conversation. I had felt much more at ease when we had been sitting in the lounge bar upstairs.

I decided to test some of my pet theories about our predilection. I had read a good deal about homosexuality on those Friday afternoons in the Dickinson Library, and much of the "scientific" conjecture seemed to fit my situation, but I had not had an opportunity to verify it with anyone else. I had never had a serious conversation with another gay before, and I wanted to take advantage of Audley's seeming willingness to talk. "Do your parents know you're gay?"

He looked uncomfortable at first. Obviously, his clientele did not bother to ask him personal questions, and the English in general tend to be more reserved than Americans. I tried not to appear prying where I did not belong, that it was idle curiosity. As time went on, Audley became much more forthcoming. Now he remained diffident.

"I think my mom knows, but she never says anything about it. They say that the mother is always the first to know." He seemed to warm slightly. "My guv's called me a queer a couple of times, but I think he was only trying to get at me."

"What do you mean?"

"Well, we don't get on much, him and me. Whenever I do something he don't take to, he calls me something. *Queer* just happens to be on his list."

"But you get along with your mother?"

"Oh, she's super. She'd spoil me rotten if he'd give her half the bloody chance. She sometimes smothers me with love. I guess she tries to compensate for him."

"Looks like you fit the profile like I do?"

"What are you getting at?" He became reserved again.

"Oh, a couple of years ago, I read some books on homosexuality, trying to find out more about it. There was this one book by a guy named Bieber, I think, which argued that homosexuality resulted from the types of parents we had. It usually arises when a boy has an absent or unaffectionate father and an overbearing or overprotective mother. It sounds like you win on both counts."

"How do you mean?"

"Well, you don't seem to get on with your father, and your mother is an especially loving person." I did not use Bieber's much harsher terminology to describe these types.

"I guess you're right." He took a long draft of his beer. "Is your father a bastard like mine?"

"No, actually, my father was killed in the war. I didn't really know him." Audley seemed uncomfortable, and I continued quickly. He often seemed to have problems dealing with reality. "Because I didn't have a loving male parent, it probably triggered something in me. But I think my real problem was my mother. She tried to dictate my every thought and deed. She isn't loving like your mother. She just tried to control me."

"And so that made you gay?" Audley seemed amused.

"Well, that's what Bieber says."

"Myself, I don't try to figure it out. I just know what I like," he repeated.

"But don't you sometimes wonder why you like men instead of women?"

"Not really."

I supposed that it could be true that he avoided worrying about these things. I sat quietly for a moment thinking about his nonchalance. Perhaps I was more self-analytical than most. My failure to accept myself drove me to find answer. Audley seemed comfortable about himself.

Audley took another long drink of his beer and then broke the silence. "Does your wife know you hang around here?" he asked.

"Are you kidding? If she found out about me, she'd probably kill me."

"Well, then why did you get married?"

I started to say that I loved her but caught myself. It sounded too self-serving and, in reality, only represented part of the truth. That became clearer to me every time I thought about it. "I grew up in a small town. Every one there got married and had kids. Even though I might have felt myself to be different, I had to go along. When the other guys got dates and went to the dances, so did I. I couldn't appear to be a queer."

"But you knew you liked guys better?"

"I know now that I did. But then it was difficult, even impossible, for me to admit that to myself. I always thought that it would go away someday. I knew I liked to look at guys and to see them in the shower, but I didn't connect that with being homosexual. I only fooled around with a couple of guys when I was in school and eventually stopped doing that altogether."

"So you really haven't had any real experience?"

"I suppressed it for twenty years. But I got to the point where I couldn't hold it in any longer. I had to try it—but only under the proper conditions." I felt that I had to add the last statement for Audley's sake.

"Didn't you tell me that you taught at university?"

"Well, it's a small liberal arts college in Pennsylvania. You don't have anything quite like it in this country."

"Couldn't you fool around with some of your students?"

"Not really. I could get fired if I were caught. Anyway, I really didn't want anyone to know. Would you want your parents to find out?"

"I haven't really tried to hide it from them. They haven't asked, and I haven't said. But I don't really try to hide it."

"Well, I can't let anyone find out about me because I'm married."

"And you have kids," he added.

"Yes, two. Ah, or at least I had two. My son died two years ago." I told Audley briefly about Tom and how he died. Again, news of the real world visibly unnerved Audley, but he nevertheless seemed genuinely interested and did not constantly keep a lookout for potential customers the way he had at other times. "I have a daughter, Sarah," I concluded. "She's five."

"I've always wondered what it would be like to have a kid. I guess I'll never know. I don't intend to ever get married."

"For God's sake, don't. It's not that I don't enjoy marriage in a lot of ways, and I'm certainly happy that I had children. But if I knew when I married what I would feel now, I'm sure I won't go through it again. I'm not the marrying kind as they say."

"My dad's been after me to get married. Thinks that it will settle me down. He can't figure out why I don't hang around girls more often. That's the main reason I moved to London, to get away from his prying."

"In a sense, that's why I'm here too." I thought with some relief that it would be almost another year before I would see my mother again. "Mother never approved of anything that I ever did. We fought constantly when I was growing up, and I've tried to avoid her as much as possible ever since."

My vehemence did not seem to bother Audley. "I can certainly sympathize. Me god, it's getting late. I'm supposed to meet someone at Jonathan's in a few minutes, so I need to run along. Do you think you'll be in this weekend?"

"Probably not. I plan to bring my daughter into town to go to Westminster Abbey for church, and then I thought I'd take her to the zoo."

"You go to church?"

"Yes, occasionally. I used to go all the time when I was a kid but stopped when I left home. I guess I associated church with all the things I didn't like about my childhood. But for some reason, I've been drawn back to it. Perhaps it was the death of my son." It startled me just how open I became with Audley. Normally, I was very reticent.

Audley looked rather bemused that anyone would go to church but didn't say anything about it. "Which zoo will you go to?"

"Oh, I guess Regent's Park."

"I haven't ever been there. Maybe I'll run into you." Audley got up from the table, swilled the rest of his beer, and walked out. Before he was outside, he turned toward me and said, "Cheers, Sim."

I didn't quite know what to make of his last comment. The fact that he had talked with me so long also puzzled me. Why would he bother to spend so much time with someone he knew was not interested in his trade? Perhaps flush with cash, he didn't need to pursue a commercial prospect. Or maybe he had a business appointment at Jonathan's. Probably Jonathan's was another gay pub that I had not heard of yet. I wanted to ask Audley next time I saw him.

We spent Saturday at home. It rained all day and spoiled any plans for a drive. Although I was willing to venture out, Ann was uncomfortable driving in the rain and preferred to stay put. "If it's clear tomorrow," I asked Ann, "will you come into London with Sarah and me to see the zoo?"

"I suppose you'll want me to come to church with you?"

"No, I thought you might just meet us at the zoo." I tried not to react to the implications of her tone.

"You're still determined to take Sarah to church, aren't you?"

"Yes, I am. I think she'll enjoy the spectacle, if nothing else."

"You know it's a boring long service and that she'll not be able to sit through it."

"It only lasts an hour, and I intend to take things for her to look at if she gets itchy. And the prospect of the zoo should encourage good behavior."

Ann didn't say anything more about my plans, but I could tell they upset her. I wanted to inquire about the source of her discomfort but decided not to press the issue for fear of irritating matters further. I did ask her again to meet us at the zoo, but she said that she wanted to write to her parents instead. I knew that was just an excuse.

The next day was gloriously sunny and warmer than it had been in months. Easter was approaching, and the weather accommodated itself to the coming of spring. Good weather had blessed our entire visit, and the winter had been much milder than we would have experienced in Pennsylvania. Sarah seemed very excited about taking the train into London and going to the zoo. I had even managed to convince her that she would have a good time at church despite her mother's efforts to persuade her to the contrary. We arrived at the abbey a few minutes before ten thirty, when the service began, and found seats in the north transept toward the back, where Sarah would not bother too many people.

When I consulted the *Times* about the services, I noted that Matins were followed by a communion service. Since I wasn't quite sure what Matins were, I decided to investigate, especially since they could not last longer than an hour. It turned out to be very much like the service I didn't understand at Saint Thomas' Church in New York. We sat, stood, and knelt alternatively and listened to the choir sing various anthems. The music was absolutely magnificent, and I did not mind so much that I really didn't comprehend why we did the things we did. The dean focused his sermon on the miners' strike ushered into its second month by increasingly strident statements by Scargill and MacGregor and intensifying violence at the collieries. He called for tolerance and a search for accommodation. As Sarah sat quietly coloring her book, I heard that Christ loved all men, coal miner and coal owner alike. *Could Christ love a queer?* I wondered. From what I had been taught in Sunday school, he could not. One earnest teacher, quoting 1 Corinthians 6:9–10, once told my class that "here, God makes it quite plain that even being an effeminate boy is sin in His sight."

But the dean quoted, "Come unto me, all ye that are heavy laden and I will refresh you."

What nice sentiments, I thought. But would he accept my burden? The dean called on both sides of the conflict to try to understand the position of their adversaries, making compromise possible. Perhaps that was what I was trying to do, compromise between the straight world and my gay inclinations.

"We are a Christian nation," the dean urged. "And Christian solutions needed to be the basis for this crisis." What was the Christian solution to my dilemma?

Religion, I thought, *could not help me in my situation, yet I was am caught up with the beauty of the setting and the music as I had been in New York.* After the service, I had an inner calm that I had not known for a while. I wanted to remain for the communion service and regretted that Sarah's presence prevented me. At the conclusion of the service, we sang "O God, Our Help in Ages Past" as the final hymn, and then I walked slowly down the center aisle, holding hands with Sarah, while the organist played the Bach prelude and fugue based on that hymn tune. The sound swelled through the church and swelled my heart.

How could religion inspire such grandeur in the mind of that genius? I marveled.

That fugue had special meaning as well because the tune on which Bach based it was called Saint Anne. Ann and I had often referred to it as our song when we were first dating and attending the chapel at Susquehanna. Then the words of the hymn did not have the same profound meaning as they did today. "Under the shadow of Thy throne, Thy saints have dwelt secure," we had sung. "Sufficient is thine arm alone, and our defense is sure." Now the hymn became like a prayer that I yet could not utter with my own lips.

The warmth of the sun outside the abbey quickly cheered me. Sarah had been quite well behaved during the service, and I felt like going home and bragging to Ann about how wrong she had been. But under the circumstances, that would have been a very bad idea. I did intend to let her know that Sarah had survived the experience. We took the underground to the Regent's Park station and walked through the park toward the zoo. The spring bulbs, even more in their glory this week, lined the path with their yellow and purple flowers brilliantly intensified by the sunshine.

Just outside the main entrance of the zoo, there sat Audley on a park bench. At first, I didn't know whether to recognize him. He gave me a few quick glances but was not obviously expecting me to acknowledge him. Since Sarah probably would not have any understanding of what was happening, I decided to speak to him. "What are you doing here?"

At first, he hesitated. Finally, when he saw that I wanted an answer and was not angry, he replied, "Just thought I'd come to the zoo today. You gave me the idea. Never seen the pandas."

"Are you kidding?"

"Actually," he confessed, "I just wanted to see your family, to see if you really had one. I didn't think you would say anything to me. I had an hour to kill before the Golden Lion opens."

On an impulse, I said, "Do you want to see any of the zoo first? I'm sure Sarah would like you to join us." Only later did I think that Sarah might tell her mother about this chance meeting. Audley agreed that he would like to accompany us. We spent some time exploring the big cats before we walked past the birds toward the pandas. Audley seemed like a child as he watched the couple play in their separate cages. He solemnly told Sarah that they also came in pink and green and originally came from darkest Africa. I did not bother to correct him, although I was not sure whether he knew the truth. We then walked up toward the central green and ate the most wretched hot dogs I had ever tasted in my life.

"You look very smart today," Audley commented as he devoured the last of his hot dog. I had worn a blue blazer and forgot that Audley had rarely seen me in a coat and tie. "Where's your red carnation?" He ran his hand up my lapel to the buttonhole.

"It's only Baptists that wear them," I observed half seriously. "Anglicans don't wear flowers, although in my case I guess a pansy would be in order." Audley didn't seem to understand the reference, and I chalked it up to another linguistic difference between our two cultures.

At one o'clock, Audley excused himself. I was genuinely disappointed to see him depart, having witnessed a side of him that I had not seen in a long time. He tended to be rather serious since that day when I had turned down his business proposition. Now he seemed to have some of his youthfulness back again. His mercantile transactions aged him considerably. As we left, he said goodbye to Sarah and winked at me.

When he was out of earshot, Sarah asked, "Who was that man, Daddy?"

I then realized that I had never actually introduced her to him formally. "Oh, just some guy I know," I said noncommittally. Of course, as soon as Sarah arrived home, she told her mother of the friend we had met at the zoo, and I had to explain to Ann that it was a fellow researcher at the British Library. I was, in some ways, glad that he was a male friend since I might have found a woman more difficult to justify.

Chapter X

Intercession

The vision of Audley—and that was the correct term—remained with me for the rest of the day. Why had he made that effort? What had been his motivation? Certainly, he did not think that I had altered my resolve just because we had talked? The whole affair did not make sense. I was only thankful that Sarah's chatter had not raised Ann's curiosity about the person we had met at the zoo. It saved me from some awkward explanations.

On Monday, I determined to ask Audley what prompted him to appear the day before. I retraced the path I had traversed so often seemingly more each week. I now walked into the Golden Lion with the boldness of a regular. I almost mustered enough nerve to go over and kiss the men at the end of the bar as if I belonged with them. How I had slipped into this lifestyle without much effort and with only some initial anxiety. The early pain had actually been greater than I now recalled. My original shyness now seemed a remote and senseless emotion. But those feelings represented only half of me; the other half still recoiled from the life that now engrossed me with greater regularity. Part of me, perhaps still the major portion, still remained horrified by the prospect of it all.

I stood there among my friends, although I really didn't know them. I had grown comfortable with them; they had become an integral part of me. They had opened up inner recesses of my being that I had not realized existed. I was free, at least in the Golden Lion, from the charade and the masks. I could be myself in a way that I could not be in the world beyond those doors. There, I had to play the straight college professor, arrogantly condemning the world of perversion and filth that existed inside. Once I entered these portals, the pretense slipped away, liberating me.

Nevertheless, the pain always resided just beneath the surface. My freedom came at a cost. I could not accept my homosexuality. I had yet really to come to terms with it. Yes, I felt comfortable with my brothers, but something deep within me cried out against its unnaturalness. Society did not approve. What if Ann knew? What if my friends and colleagues discovered my secret? These fears haunted me. Inside the Golden Lion, they receded into the mist; but once on the street again, when I associated with "normal" people, they returned to me. I despised my mother for bringing this plague on me. I even hated my father for dying and depriving me of the affection that would have cured me. All these thoughts raced through my head.

Each time Ann denied my marital rights, my sense of frustration grew. Increasingly, she became the jailer. What if the lack of heterosexual stimulation had converted me from a latent homosexual into one who wanted increasingly to be active, to come out of the closet, to experience in the flesh the joys that I had only formulated in my fantasies? Each time she refused, my anguish grew; but something deep within quietly repeated that no matter what she did, the compulsion would not abate, that it grew like a cancer each day until it would consume me. The need for release became more than I could tolerate. It lured me repeatedly to the Golden Lion, where I hoped to gain my freedom at last. What I could not understand was why Audley and I continued to be drawn together. I knew that I should be looking elsewhere, that the conditions Audley set, even with my debilitating need for fulfillment, remained too high. Yet each time I saw him, I returned to his side. Whenever I contemplated going to a new spot, the attraction of the Golden Lion became too strong to resist because I knew I might encounter Audley there.

I entered the pub again that day and, at once, spotted him standing by the bar. He almost seemed on the lookout for me because, as soon as I walked in the door, a smile crossed his face, and he started toward me. As I ordered my pint, he came up to me and put his arm around me. The thrill that ran through me overpowered me, and I shut my eyes and gulped in air, feeling every nerve of my body come alive.

"Glad to see you made it today."

"Me too," I stammered. The feel of his touch still lingered, even though he had removed his hand from my shoulder. Trying to calm my nerves, I asked him about yesterday.

"I was glad I ran into you yesterday. I enjoyed meeting your daughter. What was her name again? I'm sorry, I've forgotten."

"Sarah." I paused as I sipped my beer. "I was happy to see you also. But I wondered why you were there. You could see the zoo anytime you wanted."

"You were as good an excuse as any. Anyhow, I'm starting to take a fancy to you. I've never met anyone quite like you before. I've taken you on as my research. You do yours every day at the library. I'll do mine here and at the zoo. You see a lot of strange blokes in both places." He laughed softly, his teeth sparkling through his partially opened lips.

"That isn't a very good explanation, you know. I think you just hope that someday I'll break down and pay your price."

"Listen, mate, I've given up on that notion a long time ago. You're clearly determined to stick to your original idea, even if it does leave you completely bonkers," he said. I smiled and nodded. "Either you're crazy or have a tremendous amount of willpower."

"Probably a little bit of both. What did you do the rest of Sunday?"

"Actually, I went home and had a lie-down. I had been out late on Saturday and was tired out."

"Business engagement?"

"Of course, are there any other?"

"I thought perhaps you had fallen in love and were consummating it."

"No, just doing the trick for a few quid." He laughed more broadly now, his mouth opening even further. Somehow this laugh seemed more forced than the first.

"So you're set for cash for the rest of the week after Saturday's efforts?"

"Actually, I've got to conjure up some cash quickly. The rent comes due tomorrow, and I have to pay up or get out. Don't have a few tanners you could lend me until next week, do you?"

"Sorry, this branch of Barclays is out of cash for the moment."

"Guess I'll have to pick up someone this afternoon."

"Like the guy you picked up last week?"

"Which one?"

"You know, the older man, slightly overweight and sweaty, the really handsome one."

"Oh, I remember now. Yeah, he was quite disgusting, wasn't he? But he paid good cash. Can't complain about that." But Audley wasn't smiling now. As we talked, Audley continued looking around the pub, carefully examining each new patron who walked through the door. I could tell that he constantly surveyed the room to locate any potential customers. Over the weeks that we had talked, I had grown accustomed to his cruising. But mostly, regulars not really interested in his services entered the pub. He sought the tourist or the out-of-town businessman seeking release. They came in occasionally, but a rather large choice in the stable from which to pick awaited them. Audley had to stay alert just in case a prospect appeared so that he could be out on the paddock for show. With his good looks, however, he had little difficulty attracting potential riders.

As we talked, one such prospect did enter the Golden Lion. Aud quickly put down his beer and excused himself. I watched intrigued as he moved across the room to be within eyeshot of the stranger. I saw him catch the man's eye and begin the same penetrating stare that had captured me. This man seemed more aware of what was going on and responded quickly. Within a few moments, Audley and the man in the business suit were in conversation.

I drank my beer and admired the technique. A few minutes later, another stranger joined us, a younger man, obviously American and clearly very nervous. I noticed at once his haircut that suggested that he was in the military. He moved to the bar and ordered a pint of bitter; he must have been in Britain for some time to develop such taste. He turned around and leaned against the bar next to me, in the same position I had assumed. Seeing the young man, nervously watching his drink, was probably quite married (the left hand thrust in a telltale fashion in his pocket), I decided to strike up a conversation. "You an American?" I queried.

He glanced quickly down at his shoes as if he had been just caught stealing. "Yes" was all the response I got.

"What part of the States?" I continued.

"From Wisconsin." I feared this chat was going nowhere.

"What brings you here?"

At first, he did not want to answer me, but I tried to be as reassuring as possible. Perhaps he thought I was military police, but my longish hair probably belied that fear. "I'm in the U.S. military, the Air Force. I'm stationed at Lakenheath near Cambridge." He was rather tall and somewhat stocky in build. He wore thick horn-rimmed glasses, which called too much attention to his face. He seemed a likable person, although I did not find him sexually attractive. "Came down to London to pick up some papers from the embassy and thought I would look around the city before I had to return."

"What brought you to the Golden Lion?" I knew the question was unfair and that I had only increased his unease.

"I was just walking past." His voice hesitated between clauses. "It looked like a nice place." I knew at once that he lied. No one would enter the Golden Lion because it was an attractive pub. Others in Soho might fit that bill but certainly not the Golden Lion. He had come on the same mission that had brought me here.

"Hi, my name's Frank." I got it right this time. At least this American would not know my real name. "What's yours?"

"Tim," he said almost apologetically. It was quite clear that whatever he came looking for, it was not another American.

"How long have you been stationed here?"

"A few months." He looked around the pub almost frantically. I felt sorry for the uncomfortable position that I had put him in and thought that I should try to get him out of it.

"Listen, you might not want to hang around this pub. The men here are mostly gay, and there are quite a few hustlers." Almost as an afterthought, I added, "I'm gay and spend a good deal of time here." It was really the first time that I had ever really spoken those words, that I had ever made that confession to anyone.

My words, however, seemed to disarm him. At first, he didn't say anything but then finally made his own confession. "Actually, that's why I'm here. I saw it listed in *Gay News*."

"That's exactly how I discovered the place myself. I've been coming in here for a couple of months now. But unless you're willing to pay for it, there really isn't much action." I sounded more and more like an old pro.

"But that's why I found this pub. I don't have much time, and I figured that the only way I could get something was to pay for it."

I started to deliver my sermon again but decided to spare poor Tim of my wrath. "Well, there's lots to choose from" was my only observation.

Tim now seemed to want to justify himself. "You see, I'm married."

"Join the club." I held up my left hand to show him the telltale gold ring.

"Then I guess you understand." I nodded. "My wife's living with me on the base, and anyhow, there really is nowhere to go around there to meet anyone except into Cambridge, and I really don't have much of an excuse to do that." I felt like Pat O'Brien hearing confessions in an old B movie. "I thought I could control it once I got over here, but the urges have been overwhelming." I sympathized, although I felt that he had real experiences to look toward rather than the fantasies that had been my only solace. "I haven't been able to talk to anyone about it over here either. I can't say anything to a military doctor or chaplain. I don't trust them. I bet they would turn me in as a faggot, and I'd be out of the Air Force tomorrow."

"I bet you're right." But I didn't think he heard my comment. He continued talking in a torrent.

"I went to a psychiatrist back in the States for a while, but it didn't really help. He told me that I would have to live with it the rest of my life, that there was no cure. I am gay and will just have to get used to that fact." By this point, he seemed on the verge of tears. "I've been going wild over here. I even thought about suicide at one point because the pressures were getting too much for me to bear. I've just got to be with a man to relieve these tensions."

"I thought I was in bad shape," I commented. "Listen, I have a friend here in the business of dealing with these sorts of problems. I'd bet he'd be able to take care of you this afternoon." I looked toward Audley talking to the man in the business suit; obviously, they had concluded the transaction and were about to leave. "Just wait here a moment."

I rushed over to where Audley stood. I pulled him to the side and began to implore him about Tim. "See the guy standing over by the bar? I've been talking to him while you were negotiating. He's really in a bad way." I talked very rapidly now, and Audley seemed to be having trouble keeping up. "He's here only this afternoon. He's like me, with a wife. He needs it really bad. He's a very nice kid, and I thought maybe you could help him."

"But I've already worked out something with the chap over there." He pointed to the banker. "I can't just abandon him like that."

"But this is an emergency. I think the guy will go crazy if he doesn't have some release, and I don't want him to get mixed up with some of the other characters in this place." Audley seemed flattered that I regarded him in a higher light than the others in the Golden Lion. "Please help him."

"Let me talk to him. I guess that's the least I can do." Audley approached his business partner and exchanged a few words. Then he walked over to Tim and began talking with him. After they conferred, Audley returned to the banker. I thought the negotiations had been futile and that Audley was about to carry out his previous commitment.

I intended to console Tim but could tell instantly by the look on his face that, in fact, an arrangement had been reached. I could also hear raised voices coming from the corner where Audley stood with his erstwhile friend. Obviously, the banker did not take rejection well, especially after they had already struck a deal.

"He told me that he would take me to his apartment!" Tim exclaimed excitedly. The transformation seemed complete. "He's a really nice guy. What did you say his name was again?"

Here was someone about to engage in one of life's most intimate acts, and he did not even know the person's name with whom he was going to share it. There seemed something strange about the entire proceedings, but I knew that, given the proper circumstances, I would do exactly the same. "Audley," I informed him. I tried to prevent myself from envisioning what the next few hours would hold for Tim, how they would go to Audley's apartment, would hold each other, would remove their clothes. The thought of it brought too much pain to me, yet I had been responsible for arranging the whole affair. I had become Audley's pimp yet would receive no compensation.

Audley walked back over to us and said simply, "Ready?"

Tim swallowed the remainder of his beer, in his haste allowing some of it to run ungracefully down his chin. "Let's go," he said with a grin. "See you later, Frank. Thanks a lot."

Audley gave me a puzzled look. "Frank," he repeated softly.

"I'll explain later," I said, brushing him off quickly.

Audley just smiled. He obviously understood. "Thanks for the business. I'll return the favor someday." And out the two of them went. I returned to the library but had difficulty driving visions from my head.

Ann and I had, by now, begun discussions about the fast-approaching Easter holidays. We had long talked about the possibility of a trip to Paris during April if for no other reason than the old popular song. We now got serious about the arrangements. Ann had consulted a travel agent and obtained information about cheap fares while I had learned the name of an inexpensive hotel from an acquaintance at the library. I looked forward to the trip as a means of getting my mind off its preoccupation with Audley and things gay. Ann just wanted a change. I thought the confines of our small flat had finally become oppressive. She talked more frequently about our house in Carlisle and about her parents. She seemed disturbed that neither Sarah nor I shared her sense of loss.

Because the British Library would be closed on Good Friday, we decided to leave the Wednesday before and return the Sunday after Easter. We located our hotel on the Left Bank without difficulty, and I quickly discovered how to use the Métro, my experience with the London Underground providing excellent training. Soon we traveled around the city with ease, although Ann always had a perplexed look on her face when we actually arrived at our destination. Fearing that the Louvre would be closed on Good Friday, we went there first. Sarah turned out to be more prepared to sit through a church service than to study a long line of Renaissance painting despite their significance. The *Mona Lisa* turned out to be, in some respects, a disappointment. Rather smaller than I had imagined, it remained partially obscured by the sea of heads that pressed around. I made certain that Sarah got a look at the painting, hoping that someday she might recall the event. The fact that Leonardo and I shared something fundamental about our natures also prompted me; it actually raised within me a sense of pride.

On Friday, we went to some of the other sights. I knew that the churches would be open and recommended that we see Notre Dame. Tourists and worshippers milled around the outside of the cathedral. The sight of the edifice, which I had studied so often in pictures, electrified me. *I am actually here*, I thought in awe. When we entered the partial gloom of the interior, the mixture of gawkers—pushing and shoving their way through the aisles to see the sights—and the devout—obviously touched to be in that place on the most solemn day of the year—struck me. We circumnavigated the cathedral once, and as we passed the high altar, I noticed a line of people in the center aisle waiting to kneel before three priests apparently holding some sacred relics. Each worshipper kissed the object held out to him by the priest, who then wiped it with a white cloth. The worshipper then moved off to the side. I stopped and watched this ritual for a moment, until I felt Ann tugging at my arm.

"Come on, we need to get going," she whispered.

"What do you suppose they are doing there?" I nodded in the direction of the line.

"How should I know? Probably some superstitious nonsense."

"I'm curious. Wait a minute while I try to get a closer look."

"For pity's sake, let's get out of here before you get involved in some Catholic silliness." Like many small-town Americans, Ann had a deeply ingrained prejudice against Catholics despite her parents' liberalism, which did not acknowledge such notions openly. To be religious in her eyes had only recently become suspect; to be Catholic had always stood beyond the pale.

"It will just take a moment," I replied and walked over toward the gathering. I could not get close, however, because an usher blocked the side entrance and directed me to the end of the line. He also handed me a sheet written in French every worshipper received as they left the enclosed area. I did not look in Ann's direction to avoid the look of disapproval I would find on her face. Instead, I walked to the center aisle and joined the line, my curiosity much too excited to leave without further investigation. The queue moved ahead quickly; the ushers did not allow anyone to tarry. I read the sheet with difficulty, translating the French in the semidarkness of the cathedral. I would venerate, I learned, the crown of thorns placed on Christ's head at the time of the Crucifixion. I would also see a piece of cross on which he hung. I did not have time to decipher the nature of the third relic by the time I got to the head of the line. Ann stood to the side observing me for a few moments but eventually took Sarah by the hand and marched out. Sarah had been watching me also and had waved several times. She waved again as her mother escorted her out.

I studied what the worshippers did so that I would not appear the fool. They knelt down and kissed each relic, first the crown of thorns encased in a doughnut-shaped glass decorated with a spiral of gold filigree, then the piece of the true cross similarly protected, and finally the third relic, which I later learned was one of the nails. I had little time to scrutinize when I reached my destination. Kneeling down, I was presented with each relic in turn, which I reverently kissed. I tried to get a glimpse of each but found that the whole scene unfolded so quickly that I had little time. I did remember thinking, *Let this pass from me*, as I kissed the crown of thorns.

I left the cathedral immediately when I had finished and found Ann and Sarah sitting on a wall outside. Sarah excitedly asked me what I had seen, and I tried to explain it to her. Ann remained in stony silence the rest of the day. That night, we argued. Ann was furious that I had wasted her time carrying out that ridiculous ritual. "You consider yourself an intellectual, yet you could do something as irrational as that."

"Ann, I was just curious. It was the only way I could get close."

Ann scoffed and repeated her condemnation. "I just don't understand how you are getting yourself involved in all that religious stuff."

I tried to assure her that I was not going through any sort of religious conversion and that she had little to worry about. During the night, however, I turned a great many things over in my mind. I remembered the prayer that had darted through my mind as I kissed the crown of thorns. Did I think that sign of reverence might wipe away the stain on my soul? Would God, for such simple compensation, provide a miracle for me? I did not even believe what the little sheet in French had told me about the objects I had venerated. Nothing in my rational being could accept that business as fact. Yet the others in the line had undoubtedly thought the dark object inside the glass tube was a truly holy relic. Surely, they expected their own miracle as a reward for their piety. While I wanted my prayer fulfilled, I really could not believe that it would happen. Where was the loving God about whom the Christians spoke? Where was the God who had hung from a tree for the sins of the whole world? He was nowhere to be found when I needed help. If God existed at all, he was a cruel god who played with mortals, like one envisioned by Thomas Hardy. Yet the piety had lasted; the hope of miracles persisted. Was that merely part of human weakness?

I then envisioned my problem in terms of the crown of thorns. My homosexuality seemed like that crown, pressing into my brow, drawing invisible blood, which only I could perceive running down my cheeks. I could feel that pain, detect the warm liquid streaming down my face; no one else was aware of the torment. What I had done that morning, in fact, by kissing the crown was to reverence my own pain. I had knelt down to it, had glorified it. I had worshipped the very thing that tortured me, my own crown of thorns. Was I to be crucified also? My suffering had persisted for a long time; it intensified every time I thought about the hopelessness of my situation. If there was a God, he had abandoned me as much as he had his own Son.

I suddenly recoiled from these thoughts, and for the first time since I was a child, I prayed in earnest. Tears even filled my eyes. *Please, God*, I pleaded, *take this stain away from me. Make me whole. Perform a miracle and turn me into a normal heterosexual.* My sense of confusion and bewilderment overwhelmed me. My prayers welled from more sincerity than they had in Saint Thomas'. I actually felt a presence responding to my outcry. I knew for a brief moment that a God existed who cared, who would cure me. My rational self, however, kept intruding to tell me that I was on a fool's errand.

The next morning, we strolled around Montmartre, passing the Moulin Rouge and the various strip joints that lined the street. At one point, I dropped behind to buy some film for my camera. As I caught up with Ann and Sarah, a Frenchman attempted to lure me into one of the shops to view the wonders. His English was quite good, although he probably didn't need much knowledge of the language to describe the various delights I would encounter inside. Extremely embarrassed by the whole situation, I pulled away from him. "Sorry, not interested."

I must have turned bright red when he shot back, "What's wrong? You a queer." Undoubtedly, he knew how to get the goat of an American male.

I practically ran down the street toward Ann. "What's wrong with you? Did that man try to get you to go into the shop?" She had observed the incident.

As I told her what happened, I noted that we stood in front of a gay theater. Ann expressed her disapproval of that section of Paris. "I wish you hadn't brought me up here. It's disgusting. I didn't think that such an open display"—she had lowered her voice so that Sarah would not hear—"of sex was allowed. But I suppose anything can happen in Paris. It's just a good thing that Sarah can't read yet."

I listened to her but looked at the pictures outside the theater advertising the American-made films. My prayers obviously had not been answered because the desire to see these films was as strong as ever. I watched a handsome young man enter the theater, and instantly, I wanted to follow him. My attraction to men had not abated in the slightest. I felt drawn to him, drawn to the whole situation. God had failed me. My crown of thorns, I concluded in despair, rested firmly on my brow.

It was more than a week after our return to London that I went again to the Golden Lion, not that I had tried to avoid it. My conviction had grown stronger than ever that nothing would take away my homosexuality, neither prayer nor rational determination. It seemed there to stay. Instead, I had spent some time shopping at Hamleys for Sarah's birthday and trying to get our finances back in order after our spending spree in Paris. But all along, I knew I must go back to the Golden Lion. I belonged there or some such place, and I recognized more than ever that I would have to fulfill my nature. I hoped to talk with Audley about other locations in London where I might meet men like me. He owed me a favor after I had arranged some business for him.

Audley stood by the bar when I entered my familiar haunt. He smiled when he saw me and walked over. "Haven't seen you for ever so long. Where have you been?"

I explained that I had gone to Paris with my family for Easter. "But you knew I couldn't keep myself away from you long."

"Don't get cheeky with me. I'm sure you picked up lots of blokes in Paris. They say there are lots of them there." Although Audley seemed very friendly, I could tell that something bothered him.

"I only wish I had. No, it was a very straight vacation. Absolutely nothing exciting happened to me there."

"It's been pretty dull around here also. Business has really been off."

"How did your trick with Tim go?"

"Tim?"

"The American I introduced you to a few weeks ago."

"Oh, him. It went fine. We had a good time together, and I arranged to see him a few days later before he left. He certainly was in bad shape. I've never seen such a bundle of nerves in all my life."

"You haven't seen me then," I quipped.

Audley laughed. "No, this guy was a nervous wreck the entire time. I don't see how he got any enjoyment out of it. He seemed almost desperate."

"I know the feeling."

"Listen, Sim, I really can't have much sympathy for you. You could deal with it in the same way that guy did."

"No, I can't. Believe me, I just can't."

"I don't think I'll ever come to understand you. You seem to live in your own fantasy world." He paused for a moment and then laughed again. "Of course, that's what my guv used to say to me all the time."

"You really don't get on with your father, do you?"

Audley did not bother to answer me. He just took a long draft of his beer and looked into emptiness. He clearly was not in the mood for my probing.

I was at a loss about how to continue the conversation. "You seem very quiet today," I commented. "Anything troubling you?"

At first reluctant to answer, he finally said, "I'm supposed to meet someone at Jonathan's, and I'm not very keen about it."

Here, I saw my opportunity to change the subject from personal inquiries about Audley. "I've heard you mention Jonathan's before. What is it?"

"It's an after-hours club," he explained. "It is a place where men could go after regular pub hours for a drink."

"Can anyone go there?" I asked.

"No, you have to be a member or go with someone who is."

"Where is it located?" I could sense that Audley was not prepared for so many questions.

"Irving Street" was all the reply I received.

"Listen, do you want me to stop bothering you?" I asked.

Audley paused a moment and then apologized. "I'm sorry. It has nothing to do with you. I'm just not very jolly today."

"What's the problem? I don't mean to be nosy," I added.

"It's the guy I'm meeting at Jonathan's. I'm quite uncomfortable about getting involved with him."

"How come?"

"He's from a pretty rough crowd. He's anxious to get to know me. He's taken a fancy to me and is willing to pay plenty for the privilege. But I just don't like the arrangement."

"Why get involved then?"

"I really need the money. Things have been slow recently."

I almost wanted to muster my best pontificating manner, the tone I used when students turned in their papers late because of too many fraternity parties. *Why don't you get a regular job?* almost slipped from my Puritan lips, but I refrained. "I'll lend you ten or twenty pounds if that would see you through." I surprised myself by the offer.

"That's kind of you, but I can take care of myself." Then Audley seemed to want to change the subject. "Jonathan's is on Irving Street just off Leicester Square."

"Is it like the Golden Lion?"

"If you mean, is it a hustler's bar, not really. Some do hang out there, but most just go to meet other guys. I can take you there sometime if you want."

"Yes, I'd like to see it. Open up new vistas."

"You might meet someone to your liking." We both laughed. "You really could come with me today. I need to be there when you enter and pay for any drinks at the bar. You might even consider buying me one."

Although it meant giving up my afternoon to dissipation, I did not want to miss the opportunity and agreed to accompany him to Jonathan's.

He warned me that I could not be near him when he engaged in his discussions. I intended to have a look around and then leave on my own.

We finished our drinks and had another; Audley's appointment was not until three o'clock. When the bartender rang for last orders, we departed down Dean Street. For the first time, I left the pub with Audley. I wondered if George and the others thought I had agreed to purchase his services. I had fun speculating about it. We wended our way through Chinatown and into Leicester Square. The line for the half-priced theater tickets still stretched down one side of the square next to the Midland Bank. We passed the Odeon, where a small group clustered outside to watch the video previews. We then entered Irving Street and passed a Temple record store where I had recently purchased a recording of Mahler's *Fifth Symphony* and across the street to an unmarked flight of stairs next to a restaurant. We ascended to a second-storey door. Audley pushed open the door and, with much authority, gained entry.

The small lounge bar was practically empty. Only the bartender and one customer stood by the bar. The bartender asked Audley something in low tones, and Audley then directed me to sign the guest book. The need to give my name and address disturbed me. I used my correct name but gave the University of London as an address. The thought of a solicitation or a visit from the police scared me. Audley struck up a familiar conversation with the bartender and eventually introduced me as a friend. We both ordered a gin and tonic, Audley subtly making it apparent that he expected me to pay. I slipped him two pounds, and he handed me my drink.

"When that guy gets here, I'll talk with him alone. You'll have to take care of yourself. Who knows? You might meet your future lover." Audley laughed but then quieted down when the door opened. His upcoming appointment clearly made him anxious. But the men who set foot through the door came from the Golden Lion. The man with the gold bracelets led his entourage into the club, including the young man with the tattoos. They looked in our direction but ignored us.

As we sat in a corner of the club finishing our drinks, Audley continued to tell me what he had begun on our walk over to Jonathan's. A stranger had approached him one afternoon in the Golden Lion about a potential long-term business arrangement. The gentleman in question had seen Audley in the Golden Lion on a previous occasion and, attracted by his looks, wanted to get to know him more intimately. The sum of money involved was quite large, but the commitment was also. Audley had quickly come to a realization that the prospect was not just any john off the street. "He made it obvious to me that this guy interested in making a date would demand the utmost secrecy in our relations and that I had better not talk about it to anyone else. There was a clear threat in his tones, and I really didn't feel very comfortable about it."

"Why did you agree to meet him in the first place?"

"The offer was very attractive. I'm not in a condition to pass up that sort of money. Listen, Sim, don't start preaching at me." Audley's tone was sharp; I sensed that he was uneasy enough about the arrangement and didn't want me to add to it. I knew it would do no good to say anything further since he seemed determined to go ahead with his meeting.

"Just be careful," I ventured. "I like you very much and don't want to see you get hurt." He seemed to appreciate my confession.

By this time, a large crowd had filled Jonathan's. Others from the Golden Lion entered, but a number of new and interesting faces also appeared. Much to my surprise, one of the last was a man in clerical dress. He was young and very attractive. A number of the other patrons who obviously recognized him smiled and chatted with him. Although at first I thought he might be there to convert these sinners, his behavior and familiarity with these gay men demonstrated his kinship with us. As he continued to cross the room, I studied him carefully. He was indeed very appealing. Audley noted my interest and interrupted my thoughts. "Would you like to meet Father John?"

"Certainly," I replied quickly. "He's really cute."

"Isn't he now? Hello, John, how's the salvation business?"

John looked over in our direction and smiled when he recognized Audley. He took his sherry from the bar and approached us. "Audley, haven't seen you for ever so long. You've been keeping out of trouble?"

"Of course not. I want to introduce you to a good friend of mine." He turned in my direction. The priest and I shook hands, and he joined us at our table.

"You're not one of Audley's business prospects, are you?"

"Not this guy," Audley answered for me. "He has many stuffy ideas about my profession." Audley laughed, but John didn't.

"I'd probably agree with him. You're too nice a person to be involved in that occupation." The disapproving tone in his voice was quite evident, and I noticed that Audley winced ever so slightly.

"You are beginning to sound like Sim here. He keeps preaching at me as well."

"Obviously an intelligent gentleman." Father John turned and raised his glass approvingly.

He certainly is cute, I thought. Audley started to say something further when he noticed a new gentleman enter the room. Obviously, this was the expected appointment. Audley rather hurriedly and, I thought, nervously excused himself, walked to the other side of Jonathan's, and sat down. Soon the two engaged in deep conversation.

"I don't like the looks of that character Audley is talking to," John observed. I described briefly what Audley had told me about his engagement, and the priest shook his head in disbelief. "He's too decent a young man to get mixed up in something like that. He's going to get himself hurt. But how do you know Audley?"

I told him how we had met at the Golden Lion. I explained that I wanted to meet friends while I was in London but felt embarrassed about discussing why I wanted to meet them. After all, John was a priest. But there really wasn't any need to fill in these details for him.

"All you're going to meet at the Golden Lion are hustlers. There are many other places in London to meet gay men. I'm sure you could meet some very nice ones at the Lambeth, for instance. It usually gets quite crowded around nine o'clock." He then added by way of explanation, "In my position, I avoid going into public places for very obvious reasons."

I laughed and then added, "So do I for the most part." He turned as if to ask a question.

"You see," I continued, mustering the nerve to make my confession, "I'm married."

"For some reason, I almost guessed that you were." His smile reassured me that he was not about to condemn me. "Yes, we really are in somewhat analogous positions. I'm sure it is no more comfortable for you than it is for me."

I hesitated to ask but then decided to get everything out. "Then you're gay also?"

"Of course." Again, he smiled reassuringly. He was perhaps ten years my junior but had a carriage that made him seem much older. I felt somehow comforted by his presence. His manner suggested that, unlike Audley who always resisted questions at the beginning, he quite accepted them.

"Then you don't mind talking about it."

"To the right people. I'm not about to make the grand pronouncement to the folks at High Mass next Sunday."

"You're an Anglican priest?"

"Yes. I'm an associate at All Saints Margaret Street, the church of the queers, so to speak."

"Many gays go there?"

"At times, it seems that half the congregation is in drag," he laughed. "Actually, it is a fairly fashionable church with a good many important Americans showing up. But it also attracts a good many of the brethren. At one time, even the rector was a camp follower. The current rector is not but doesn't seem too uncomfortable about the situation there."

"Does he know you're gay?"

"We've never actually talked about it, but I think he understands. Again, it's just something we don't discuss. I keep my private life very much to myself. I never bring anyone back to my digs—for one thing, it is just across the street from the church—and don't hang out in public places. I come here once in a while and have a group of friends that satisfy my needs."

I asked him if that included physical needs, but he only smiled, which I took to be an affirmative. Nothing more needed to be said.

"And yourself? What brings you to Jonathan's as if I needed to ask?"

"Audley brought me here to broaden my horizons. I guess I've been looking for the perfect man with whom to fulfill my fantasies."

"Your fantasies are not yet fulfilled?"

"Not at all. I've kept things very carefully under wraps."

"Your wife doesn't know."

"Good God, no. She'd never understand."

"No, they usually don't. Then how do you get by?"

"I don't. That's the whole problem. I've just repressed all my life. I've pretended to be heterosexual for so long that I've almost come to believe it."

"That's not particularly healthy."

"I've slowly come to that realization. That's why I'm trying to do something about it."

"So you've taken up with rent boys like Audley." Father John's tone was not approving.

"That hasn't worked out. I just have not been able to bring myself to buy the services of some guy to satisfy my needs because it wouldn't."

"Well, that's a relief to hear at least. But how have you gotten so close to Audley then? You two seem pretty chummy."

I explained how we had grown together in that strange, surreal world of the Golden Lion. "I just haven't met anyone else I feel really comfortable with. I think Audley brought me here in hopes that I would run into someone. But all I've done is bother you."

"You're no bother. You're a very good-looking man. I've always found blond hair and brown eyes attractive." His compliment caused the warmth to crawl up my neck. A man had never said anything like that to me before, and I reacted uncomfortably. It was only months later when I emerged from my naiveté and realized that Audley had introduced John to me for a particular purpose. But the thought of a relationship with a priest was more than my mind could comprehend at that time.

"I guess I'm also having difficulties coming to grips with what I am. I've pretty much admitted to myself that I'm gay, but it still doesn't remove the guilt associated with it."

"What guilt?" John responded with some vehemence.

"Why, about being gay. I'm not a religious person, but I've even prayed to try to get God to remove it."

"And he didn't." John said this in such a way that he seemed to anticipate my answer.

"No, I'm as gay now as I was before, perhaps even more so."

"Then perhaps God wants you to be that way."

"How can that be? All I was ever told when I was growing up was that being a homosexual was an abomination in the sight of God, that God could not love a queer."

"The position of the Church of England is really quite different from that. Although it has not actually fully accepted homosexual behavior, it does not condemn it either. And how could it when a good many of the clergy are gay?"

"You're joking?"

"Of course not. There are gays among both the priests and the bishops. I've run into a good many older clergy who had somehow sublimated it, have played the married act fairly well but internally have been driven mad by fantasies. And there are plenty of others who are acting out those fantasies regularly. I'm instantly on my guard when I run into any priest or organist, unmarried or married."

We both laughed at this. "Then you have no difficulty reconciling your sexual preference with your vocation?"

"Of course not. Why should I?" His tone was not defensive. "God made me the way I am. I didn't choose to be gay. I just am. It is part of my fundamental nature. He also called me to be a priest. I do not see the two as being contradictory."

"But you could be celibate."

"God didn't call me to that," he replied emphatically. "And I'm not rationalizing my sexual activity. I am fully convinced that God blesses my relationships with men because they are carried out in love. I don't hang around school grounds picking up little boys or anything of that nature. I have close, intimate friends with whom I share my life and my sexual expression. To do otherwise would destroy me mentally and make me of no use to anyone."

"I thought we were to cleave to one woman."

"Yes, the majority probably does. But quite clearly, I am not part of that majority. I did have a long-term relationship at one point—lasted almost four years—but since it has ended, I have wanted to be more careful about making such a commitment under my circumstances. I got too hurt the last time. What I am doing now, I consider to be just as righteous as the guy who dutifully goes home to wife and children every evening."

I could not help but believe that much of what he said was a rationalization, but it seemed to work for him just fine. What I had going for me didn't. "When I used to go to church, I was always told that the queers would go to hell. It was as simple as that."

"Even admitting that homosexuality is a weakness—and I regard that as so much rubbish—nevertheless, Christ loves all sinners. According to Saint John, 'God so loved the world, that he gave his only begotten Son, to the end that all that believe in him should not perish, but have everlasting life.' That's all that believe in him, not everyone except gays. He does not single out some for salvation and others for condemnation just because of the types of sins they have committed. And since I don't even consider homosexuality a sin, well, there you have it." He said the last with some note of triumph. "What you have yet to overcome is the sense of guilt that you carry with you. You are gay and should be proud of it. You are different from ordinary men. That is a point of honor, not shame."

"Well, you are correct about one thing. It is a point of shame for me. I only wish I could have your sense of it."

"It takes time, but someday you will. I didn't always harbor such pleasant thoughts about it myself. I had my road of struggle just as you have. From what you said before, you have really only just now come to acknowledge you are gay. Self-confession of that nature is quite difficult. The rest will come along in due course and with a good deal less strain. Mark my word."

We had become so engrossed in our conversation that I had paid very little attention to what Audley had been doing. I saw that he was engaged in deep conversation with his business associate. At times, the conversation seemed animated. The stranger appeared to be an unsavory character, someone with whom I did not expect Audley to associate. But then I couldn't always monitor his business dealings. Finally, the conversation grew considerably heated, causing some in their vicinity to stare in their direction. Audley, at one point, started to rise as if to leave, and his companion restrained him. Audley struggled free and rushed out. I felt a sudden protective urge compelling me to intervene.

"I think Audley's having some trouble. Perhaps I should follow him."

"Audley probably can take care of himself," John said reassuringly. "He's been in this business a long time and has been involved with rough characters before. It tends to toughen one rather quickly. But suit yourself."

"You've been very helpful to talk with."

"My pleasure, handsome man. Remember, if you want spiritual guidance, come see me at All Saints Margaret Street." The proposition passed me by totally unheeded. I hurried down the stairs to Irving Street but failed to spot Audley. Crossing Leicester Square, I retraced the steps I had earlier walked with Audley to the Golden Lion, now tightly shut. It began to drizzle as I abandoned hope of finding Audley and walked back to the British Library, the afternoon now almost completely gone.

Chapter XI

Confession

I did not see Audley again for several weeks, not until late May. The spring flowers decorated London profusely, and the previous Saturday, Ann, Sarah, and I made a return visit to Regent's Park to witness the cherry blossoms in full bloom. The continued thought that we did not have much time left for our stay in London troubled me. Within a few weeks, we would return to Carlisle, and I would be leashed to my old routine. *Perhaps*, I thought, *it is for the best since I could not continue to exist in this dreamworld forever.* Yet panic began to grow within me; I knew the time was running short to complete my business here. The sense of urgency swelled as I went with greater regularity to the Golden Lion and the other gay pubs. On some occasions, I would rush through two pubs seeking an intriguing prospect, but the strangers seemed to take little interest in me. They must all know that I was married and unavailable. Only Audley treated me as a true friend, although I knew physical fulfillment was impossible.

Audley had not ventured into the Golden Lion for quite some time. I frequently waited in vain to see him. For many days, I stood quietly in the corner of the pub, drinking my beer, cautiously eyeing the other patrons in the establishment. Once or twice, I talked with Haggis, who continued to suffer from a series of calamities. He failed to get the job at Burger King and held another position only a few weeks until his eyesight became a hindrance. Each time we talked, I made it a point to buy him a drink; with exaggerated gestures, I presented him with his drink in full view of George, who continued to watch me suspiciously from his vantage on the opposite side of the pub. Yet the true object of my visits to the Golden Lion, to see Audley again, had to wait.

About three weeks after the incident at Jonathan's, Audley finally made an appearance. Instantly, I realized what had kept him away. The signs of a serious beating clearly marked Audley's face. His cheeks bore bruises, and he sported a serious cut over his left eye partially concealed by a bandage. As soon as he saw me, he walked over. "Don't say a word," he proclaimed immediately. "I don't need any more lectures from you."

I really didn't need to ask him what had happened. His tone and his physical appearance clearly revealed the problem. But I could not resist the urge to press him on the matter. "What happened to you? Run into a sadomasochist?" I had to work hard at suppressing a smile.

"A what?"

"Who beat you up?"

"As if you couldn't figure that out yourself. I had second thoughts about the business transaction I had made, and I received payment for it, that's all. I don't need one of your sermons again to remind me that I made a mistake."

"Aud, I really am concerned about you. I'm not interested in scoring points because of your pain. I feel very sorry for you." Audley perhaps sensed a hint of moral superiority, which I really did not intend.

"You needn't bother." Audley's tone remained quite sharp and defensive.

When it became apparent that I did not intend to lecture him, Audley calmed down. We stood silently for a moment until I offered to buy him a beer. He agreed, perhaps somewhat reluctantly, thinking that I might demand his attention to my preaching as compensation. Instead, I began talking about some of the places I had been the last few weeks. I also told him that I planned to go to the abbey for Evensong at five o'clock. My small talk seemed to allay Audley's fears that I planned to criticize him. Finally, he brought up the injuries himself.

"I was really in bad shape for a few days."

"Where did it happen?"

"Some blokes came to my flat one morning before I had gotten out of bed. The guy I share with had already left. They simply beat the feathers out of me. Neither said a word the entire time. I lost consciousness and woke up when Derek tried to help me."

"Derek?"

"He's my flatmate. He had come home at noon, so I was out for over an hour. I was in such bad shape that I couldn't go out for a week. This is the first time I felt pretty enough to try to get some work." He smiled for the first time.

"I know I wouldn't hire you in that condition."

"That isn't saying much since you wouldn't pay me under any circumstance."

"You know what I mean," I said with some exasperation. "Isn't there something that you could do to hold you over until you're in better condition? I really don't think many men are going to take a second look at you in that shape."

"Derek's been pretty decent about helping out. But I owe him a few bob, and I have to get something soon. I just don't have much training other than hustling."

"And there's nothing else you can do?"

"I always thought I would try out for a show to see if I could handle it, but my pretty face isn't going to help there either."

"A show? Are you an actor?" Here was a side of Audley about which I had no comprehension.

"No, I've done a lot of dancing but only in Manchester. I've never tried to get anything in London. Never felt that I was good enough."

For the first time, I recognized that Audley's physique was that of a dancer. His tall, thin frame supported lean muscles. Obviously, he remained in good physical condition despite the number of beers he consumed at the Golden Lion. "A dancer? Well, I am impressed. What type?"

"Most of my training when I was young was in ballet, but I know I'm not good enough for that. I probably could do show dancing with some practice though. But it is all too ridiculous to think about. No one is going to hire me." He seemed to want to dismiss the subject, something he now regretted raising. He nervously fidgeted with his drink.

"How can you be so sure? Have you ever tried?" This new and intriguing face of Audley excited me, and I pushed on.

"Not really. I never took the whole thing seriously anyhow. Listen, I'd rather not talk about it now." Audley remained silent for a moment or two and then returned to our original topic. "I should be able to pick something up, especially at night. It's pretty easy to sell sex."

"From the looks of your face, it isn't always that easy," I said sarcastically.

"I knew you would take any opportunity to rub it in." His face began to cloud over once again, and the muscles of his neck tightened.

"I'm sorry, Aud. I didn't mean to offend you. I thought you ceased paying attention to my sermons long ago."

"You're right, guv, I have."

The reference to me as a father bothered me somewhat, but I let it pass. "I really must be going now. I'd like to stay longer and chat, but I plan to go to the Evensong. I need to get some work done first."

"You certainly are wrapped up in religion these days. I gave that all up years ago. My father forced me to go to chapel every Sunday. He reckoned it would fix me up. Just to make sure it won't, I stopped going as soon as I left home."

"I'm really just interested in the music. I love the sound of a men and boys' choir." For some reason, Audley asked me the time of the service before we bid goodbye to each other. I left, regretting that I had put Audley into a sour mood.

Returning to the British Library, I pored over an evangelical tract dealing with the need for a religious revival to curb the crime wave sweeping London. The writer published a similar pamphlet just two years later, calling forlornly for another renewal. *Religious piety did not help reduce crime*, I thought, *any more than it had ended my homosexuality.* At four thirty, I put my books back on the shelf and hurried to the Tottenham Court Road station to catch a train on the Northern Line. The underground was hot and particularly smelly that day, and I happily reached Westminster and fresh air. The days were now very long, and the sun still shone brightly as I walked past Parliament and crossed the street to the abbey. With only a few minutes left, I rushed, not knowing where to go once I reached the church.

Seeing Audley squatting down at the entrance to the abbey in front of a signboard announcing the services and the availability of a super tour shocked me tremendously. He stood up when he saw me coming toward him. "You'd best hurry. The service starts in five minutes."

"What are you doing here?" I asked in amazement.

"No time to explain now. We've got to get our seats."

He guided me by the arm through the entrance of the church. "I asked one of the vergers where we should go."

We sped down the side aisle and through some rope barriers, ignoring an usher who asked if we had come for the service. We entered the ornate quire and looked quickly where to sit. Special music stands and lights clearly marked the area for the choir. To the right and left of the aisle, a small congregation had gathered, some kneeling in preparation and others gazing around them. I spotted two seats in the top row close to the choir, and we climbed to them. Once we had settled ourselves, I looked at Audley and started to ask him what it all meant. He merely smiled at me as the organ began its prelude. I looked in front of me and found a plastic card outlining the order of service, which made it easier to follow than at Saint Thomas'.

The organist had almost completed his piece when the choir appeared, preceded by an elaborate gold cross. They filed into their places, and the clergy entered their stalls. The service, especially the music, was beautiful, perhaps more so because every once in a while Audley and I looked at each other and smiled. I thought he actually paid more attention to me than to the liturgy; I made a valiant effort to concentrate on both. When we stood for the choir to sing the Nunc Dimittis, I let my eyes scan the decorations around me. I examined the Gothic carved and gilded wood. The gold stars painted on the blue background in the ceiling of the alcove in which we sat particularly struck me. The combination of music, architectonics, and serenity overwhelmed me. I felt in the presence of the divine.

The choir sang the vesicles, and the officiating clergyman intoned the collects. We then sat to hear the choir sing the anthem. I turned to Audley and smiled, but the music instantly brought me up. The organ began to play a melody that had remained in my head since the day we had buried Tommy. The tune reminded me of pipes played by a shepherd in the fields minding his flock. The choir then began to sing the too familiar words of "Sheep May Safely Graze." Emotion overcame me. I could feel the tears welling in my eyes, ready to spill down my cheeks. Audley must have noticed since he leaned over and asked if I were all right. I merely shook my head and continued to be caught in the music. I first thought of Tommy and then of Audley next to me. I considered my predicament. It all became a whirl over which I had no control. Yet when the music ended, peace silently slipped over me. Strangely, I knew that Tommy was safe. But I also sensed that I was also. And near me sat Audley.

The officiant completed the service with prayers for the royal family and the Order of the Bath and dismissed us with his blessing. The organ began to play a triumphal voluntary as the choir exited. At the conclusion of the service, I knelt down like other members of the congregation but did not have any particular prayer. I just listened. I looked to my left and found that Audley too knelt. I could not tell if he were actually praying, but he did have his head bowed and his eyes closed. *How beautiful he looks*, I thought.

We both stood up and returned to the center aisle while the organ continued to sing its praise, like the day that Sarah and I had attended the service, but now I walked toward the back of the abbey with Audley. The confusion of emotions I felt on the first occasion was absent now. I could not explain it, but I had an inner calm. Through the rest of the day, the sound of the Bach piece haunted me, eliciting memories of Tommy and of Audley.

The sun still shone brightly, giving a more brilliant prospect to the world than when I had exited from Saint Thomas'. When we got outside the abbey, I pressed Audley to explain why he had come to the service.

"I really wanted to find out what attracted you to it," Audley responded to my query. "It was actually quite beautiful. My parents didn't approve of the church. They were strictly nonconformists. They said it was too much like popery. But I thought this service was very nice indeed."

"I'm glad you came. It gives me an opportunity to see you again outside the Golden Lion. You seem a different person when you are away from that place."

"Don't think you're going to get me to church every day now. This was a onetime event." He laughed. "I might reform, and I mustn't do that, now can I?"

"No, I don't think there is anything that will get you to repent."

"Nor do I really think I have anything to repent for."

"I wonder if your father would agree to that," I asked wryly.

"Let's not ruin a beautiful evening by bringing him into it."

By this point, we had reached the tube station. We caught a Circle Line train and headed toward Charing Cross. "I guess it's too early to go to Heaven," Audley had observed. "Guess I'll go home first and get ready for the night's work. Perhaps if it is dark enough there, no one will notice the scars."

"Please be more careful. I don't want to see you deformed any more than you are already." But in fact, Audley seemed as handsome as ever, despite his bruises.

"I'll be cautious." He paused for a moment and then added, "I'll be in the Golden Lion on Tuesday. Will I see you there?"

Although somewhat surprised by the offer, I quickly responded, "Sure. Love to see you." At this point, the train pulled into Charing Cross. I got off and watched it pull out, carrying Audley to his mysterious dwelling. No matter how hard I tried, I could not satisfactorily visualize how he lived. He seemed to live in the Golden Lion and have no other place for his home. To imagine Audley in some domestic setting was almost impossible.

I arrived home late, which perturbed Ann. I explained that I had attended an Evensong, annoying her further. We spent an uncomfortable evening together, Ann sitting in stony silence in the high-back chair rather than next to me on the sofa, her usual spot. I finished the *Times* and began the novel by Barbara Pym I had been meaning to read for some time. Ann retired early, and I continued my reading until one o'clock. I would not enjoy my marital privileges that evening, I knew; I did not even bother to pursue them.

When I did climb into bed, Ann's heavy and regular breathing suggested that she slept soundly. I did not sleep for a long time. I continued to think with pleasure about Audley sitting next to me in church, our eyes meeting from time to time during the service. I also thought of the sleeping figure next to me, cold and frigid, slowly growing more distant from me each day. I knew my escapades helped build the walls that grew between us. I also recognized that, for some reason, she had been wall building as well ever since the death of our son. I could rationalize my own construction efforts; I could not understand hers since she never articulated the reason. Perhaps I should tell her about my attraction for men. The thought popped into my head, not inspired by anything that I had been thinking. *Why would I even consider that step?* I wondered. To consider I would ever tell her was ridiculous nonsense. No need existed, especially since it did not appear that I would ever do anything about it. Yet I continued to ponder the words of revelation. It almost seemed my means of getting even with her, although I was not quite sure why I was getting even.

She would be lying in bed, filing her nails—she never filed her nails in bed, but it made a convincing picture—when I would climb in next to her. I would begin amorous advances toward her, and she, as usual, would complain of headache—again, Ann never used that as an excuse, being much more direct and honest than that. The anger would swell within me until I could no longer tolerate it. I had to have it out once and for all.

Well, I don't really need to anyhow, I would say. *I'll just pick something up tomorrow to get it off.* That would be the first shot across the bow.

And where do you plan to do that? she would ask in astonishment.

At the Golden Lion would be my simple reply. The second shot across the bow was so close that it scorched the masthead; the next would be aimed directly at the main mast itself.

What is the Golden Lion? she would demand, her voice booming in my ears—actually, even when she was angry, Ann barely spoke above a whisper.

It's a gay bar I hang out in, I would reply.

You hang out in a gay bar! she would shriek.

Yes, Ann. You see, Ann, I am gay, always have been. The fatal shot had been fired. She reeled in pain as the cannonball ripped through her flesh, tearing her apart before my eyes. It would be the ultimate victory.

Ann stirred quietly next to me. *Unfortunately,* I thought, *I could only use the shot once. Once fired, it could never be retrieved. What would it profit me?* I would lose everything that I had worked so hard to gain. Of course, Ann would never want to remain with me. No matter how open minded she might be in many ways, I knew that she could not accept the fact that she had married a queer. That, of course, would mean separation and eventually divorce. I would have to abandon my home and my position in society. What if she told the world, or one person in Carlisle for that matter, that I was gay? My place in that community and in the community of my work would be altered irretrievably. It would also mean that I would have to give up my daughter. I had already relinquished one of my children. I did not think that I could separate from another without self-destruction. No, it would have to remain my dark secret. It could never come to light. My anger would have to be kept within bounds so that it would never burst forth.

When Tuesday came, I anxiously entered the Golden Lion to keep my date with Audley. At least I hoped I had a date. Not seeing Audley there would not have surprised me. The realization had not dawned on me yet that Audley liked seeing me as much as I enjoyed his company. Now I just waited with anticipation for his arrival. I purchased my lager and fiddled with the glass. At first, I did not see him as I scanned the room. Not more than five minutes passed, however, before I saw someone coming down the stairs from the lounge bar. A smile crossed my face as I beheld Audley again. The smile that also brightened his face gave me a warm feeling.

He did not cruise me any longer; the expression appeared to be a genuine indication that he was as glad to see me as I was him.

"I sat upstairs. Thought we could talk better there." The air of excitement about Audley surprised me. I followed him up the stairs and sat at the table he had reserved for us.

"Something happened?" I asked. "You seem pretty excited."

"I got a job!" he exclaimed, a look of deep satisfaction on his face.

"Honest labor. I can't believe it."

"It's just part time, mind you. And the pay's not very much. But it's something."

"What is it?" I began to share his enthusiasm.

"The guy I live with works in a warehouse. They needed someone to help with the loading on a part-time basis. Derek said that I could do the job, and they hired me. It's only three days a week and probably will be over in a month, but at least it's work." He then added an afterthought. "It will also leave my nights free."

I could feel my face begin to tighten and worked hard to keep from showing my discomfort at the last statement. "That's great news." I beamed as much as possible, but Audley had caught my change of mood.

"You thought I might give up my evil ways? Unfortunately, this job does not pay enough to do that. Besides, it is only temporary."

"No, I'm just glad you found something. I don't expect you to become the reformed drunk overnight." Still, the hopes lingered that he would move away from the lifestyle that so offended me.

"I'm not so sure that the job will work out at all. It requires a good deal of strength to cart around those boxes."

"But you are certainly strong enough. Just look at those muscles." I looked admiringly at the clearly defined arm muscles appearing from beneath his sleeve. He wore the same open mesh shirt I had seen him in that first time. I could see his beautiful pecs through the red mesh. "With a build like yours, you shouldn't have any real problem."

"These muscles were meant for dancing, not for lifting weights. Besides, I'm so out of shape that I probably couldn't dance anymore either."

I had wanted to ask him more about his interest in dancing but had not found the appropriate opening. His veiled comments of a few weeks before had intrigued me. Now, I thought, was the time to explore further this unknown area of Audley's life, something seemingly so out of keeping with the rest of him. "When was the last time you did any dancing?"

"I guess about three years ago. I had a small part in a local production of *Swan Lake* in Manchester. My guv found out about it and pulled me out of the production."

"How could he force you to quit? You must have been over eighteen."

"Actually, he took it out on my Mum. He blamed her for getting me involved in ballet. He could never understand that I enjoyed it and had never been pushed into it. The night he found out I wasn't really hanging out with my mates at the local, he beat up Mum. The next day, I packed my bags and moved to London. I tried to get her to come with me, but she feels that she must stay with him no matter what the wanker does to her."

The anger swelled within Audley and became physically apparent in his growing redness and the heaviness of his breathing. "If it bothers you too much," I interjected, "we don't have to talk about it."

"No, I get pleasure out of thinking about the sock I gave him before I left. I had wanted to do it all my life. I got back at him for all the pain he had given my mother. And he didn't dare call the constable since he had brushed her pretty badly."

"So you came to London. . . ."

"And became a rent boy," he completed the sentence.

"Why did your father hate your dancing so much?"

"He said only puffs did that. I never became a real dancer, but I certainly am a puff." He laughed ironically. "He owns an ironmongery in Manchester. They live very comfortably, and he expected me to follow in the business. But I was not the cooperative son he wanted. I liked dance and music and had no interest in spanners and saws. Mum arranged dance lessons for me after school and didn't tell him about it. I took lessons for ten years before he discovered it. She saved out of her house money to pay for it. When he finally did find out about it, he made me drop them. But within two months, I was back again."

"Well, you must have been pretty good if you danced publicly in Manchester."

"Not really. My instructor finally concluded that I was not quite good enough to go professional. He did help me get some small dancing parts in local theaters. But then my father found out about it."

"I don't see how you were able to get away with it."

"It wasn't easy. But he never paid much attention to what I was doing. My Mum covered up pretty well for me. And the shows only lasted a week or so. They weren't like London shows, which run several months or more."

"Was your role in *Swan Lake* your first?"

"Actually, I had danced in several parts before that. We always managed from him learning about it. He finally found out when a neighbor mentioned my dancing to my father. Then he beat up my Mum. Didn't even bother to talk to me about it first."

"Why did your mother put up with it?"

"She was always afraid of him. She also felt helpless and alone. She hated where we lived and always wanted to go home again to North Walden, but he always kept her trapped."

"You moved from North Walden?"

"No, I was born in Manchester. My guv had his shop there, and Mum moved there before I was born. They were cousins, and he would come to North Walden to visit. My grandmother convinced my mother that if she did not accept his offer, she would never find another suitor. She didn't like him but accepted anyhow. She was twenty-two, and everyone felt that if she didn't get married soon, she never would. I think she feels she would have been better off if she had remained a spinster."

He paused, taking a deep draft of his beer, but seemed willing to continue talking with some prompting. "Audley End is just outside North Walden. That's where Mum got the idea for my name. I could never understand that one. It's just a big old house. I used to go visit my grandmother, and she would take me over there to run around the grounds. They had peacocks and a big hill in the back I could run down. I disliked visiting my grandparents since there was little else to do. But Mum kept dragging me there because she wanted to get away from her husband. She hated Manchester, and he hated North Walden. And I was torn between the two of them."

"You never got on with your father?"

"I always hated him, and he returned the favor. He didn't like me because I was not the child he wanted. I didn't instantly get excited about his business. He wanted me to work around the shop all the time, and I despised it. I was always a different kid from the others. I didn't much enjoy football. He would always drag me to the Manchester United games, and I hated every minute of it. The kids there were rough and liked to fight. I would have preferred to stay at home and read or listen to music."

"So you snuck off and took ballet rather than kicked the ball around with your mates."

"That's right. When he found out, he called me all sorts of names."

"Most of them true?"

"I suppose so. It only drove me to rebel more against him and what he liked. I picked up the dancing again as soon as I could and began to fool around with guys more than ever. Word of that began to get to him also. Although I denied it, he beat me up anyhow. Told me that if I didn't hang around dancers, I wouldn't get such a reputation. He never could bring himself to believe that I was bent though. Always believed me when I said it was just guys trying to get back at me for something or other."

"Even now, he doesn't believe it?"

"He doesn't know anything about what I am doing with myself here. I've only been back once to see my Mum, but it was so bad I left again as soon as possible. He has no idea how I support myself. I'd love to tell him, but it would probably kill her. I don't want to hurt her if I can help it."

He sat for a few moments in silence, contemplating his beer and his life. I didn't press him further, thinking that he would get resistant if I pushed him too far. As it was, he had revealed more about himself in a few minutes than the entire time I had known him. He seemed to undergo some sort of catharsis as if the retelling of his myth had restored some of the vigor lost after the beating. When he spoke of his father, an air of defiance crept into his voice. When his silent meditation had finished, he changed the subject to me and my work. Although he clearly did not understand what I did in all those hours in the British Museum, he tried to show some interest as I described briefly my latest discoveries. His talk of my work reminded me of my resolution to spend less time in the Golden Lion and more at my desk. It was now June, and I only had a few weeks left before I had to return to teaching. I had resigned myself to the probability of not finding anyone to fulfill my fantasies. Nevertheless, I would continue to visit the Golden Lion and talk with Audley since nothing else was likely to happen. We finished our drinks, and I excused myself. As I stood to leave, Audley stood up and gave me a hug. A chill ran through me that I felt everywhere but especially in the groin.

"Thanks for letting me talk, Sim. I need to get that off my chest sometimes."

The physical contact with Audley agitated me a great deal. I found that I was shaking when I descended the stairs. At the bottom, I ran into Haggis. I intended to greet him as I passed but paused to say something further. He looked very low.

"How are things going?" I asked.

"Not so well. I still have not been able to find a job. I had one for a short time but then lost it on account of my eyesight. They were afraid I might put the wrong things in the salad." I tried to cheer him with a few words of encouragement, but my efforts did not seem to have much effect. As I returned to the British Museum, I realized that the predicaments of some were far worse than my own. I became angry at myself for the sin of self-pity. At least I had gotten a hug. What more could I ask for?

As usual, I had trouble getting much more done that afternoon and left a half hour early to walk through Russell Square. The park was now crowded with people taking advantage of the long warm days. The lack of rain and the extraordinarily warm weather for London brought people out. Some lay about on blankets; a few men had removed their shirts while the women had taken off their shoes and pulled their stockings down to their ankles. I began retracing my steps the day I had discovered the Lutheran church, passing by Gay's the Word Bookstore. Slipping my left hand into my pocket, I entered to do some browsing. I looked at a few books and then moved toward the back to examine the notices on the bulletin board and listen to the conversation of the men gathered around a table, drinking tea. They seemed to be talking about the problems of being gay and developing relationships that lasted more than a few months. The self-pity began to emerge again because I thought of my own position in which I could not even achieve an afternoon's tryst. Fearing that they might suspect that I was eavesdropping, I retreated to the bookshelves again, hoping to find something that would satisfy my longing to gaze at male genitals, but this establishment did not cater to the same clientele as the Zipper. I did, however, come across a book entitled *Sexual Preference* produced by the Kinsey Institute. It had been completed just a few years before and purported to test the validity of various explanations for the existence of homosexuality. I glanced through several pages and found the chapter headings intriguing. Although pricey, the book left the shop with me. It was all very impetuous since I realized when I got to the street that I could not take home the brown paper bag stuffed firmly under my arm. There seemed only two solutions, either toss the book away or leave it on my shelf at the British Library. I did not have the nerve to attempt to return it. I retraced my steps to the library. Thankfully, it was a Tuesday evening, and the library remained open until nine. Great horror swept through me when the guards insisted on examining my parcels at the door. I was grateful when they did not insist on looking at the title. I walked quickly back to the North Library and went to my shelf. Slipping the book out of its concealment, I placed it behind all the other books on my shelf. I left it sitting there, screaming to be discovered by one of the librarians, and hurried out again. I remembered this later as the first time I had gone public to the straight world that I was gay.

The next day, I removed the book from its concealment and, carefully discarding the dust jacket, opened it on my desk. I kept another book handy to cover it in case anyone came too close. Because the library remained relatively empty that morning and no one sat at the same table, I could skim the book undisturbed. I rushed through half the book, which dealt with lesbianism, and got right to the heart of the matter. The authors had conducted surveys to determine if basic similarities in the background of gay men caused them to be gay. They presented and tested all the stereotypes. All seemed to be found wanting. The close, confining mother, the distant father, all the things I had heard all my life as the cause of homosexuality seemed not to have any statistical basis. I had never been one to put much faith in statistics, but these seemed convincing. Only two factors appeared to be related to homosexuality but resulted from rather than caused the problem, an inability of a gay male to relate to his father and the lack of gender identification. In the first case, I did not find any connection because I had never known my father to fight with him. I had always argued with my mother, but that seemed not a problem. With the second, I could more easily identify. I was always the one whom the boys picking sides for baseball fought over not to have. The book concluded with the observation that homosexuality seemed best explained through genetics or factors that happened so early in life that they cannot be pinpointed.

With great excitement, I rushed to the Golden Lion to report the findings to Audley. He did not have to blame his father any longer. It was no one's fault; we were just born that way. Moreover, it seemed to take a great burden off my shoulders. It was nothing that I had done. I felt free.

I was glad to see Audley standing by the bar when I entered. He seemed to notice my excitement as I walked over to him. "Looks like something good has happened to you."

"It sure has. I've discovered that I have nothing to be ashamed of." It later amazed me how that initial exuberance had swept away all my previous fears. Of course, they all returned to haunt me again but never with the same ferocity that I had once endured. My generosity got the best of me, and I bought Audley a beer and asked him to retire to the lounge bar so that we could talk more intimately. There, I explained what I had read in the book, about the great discovery I had made about us. "So you see, your problems with your father just come with the territory. He did not make you gay. He just reacts to you because you are gay, and presumably, he is not." I had very quickly become the expert. The absolution of his father rushed from my lips. I hoped that it would make him look differently not only at his father but also at himself. I wanted him to take true pride in himself. His nonchalance about being gay was superficial. I was convinced that his degrading profession was not just a means to get by. He was intelligent, talented, and articulate. He could certainly do more with his life than he had so far accomplished. Prostitution was a deliberate attack on his father and degrading to himself.

Audley, of course, thought it all nonsense and dismissed my research as fuzzy-headed intellectualism. He did not put it in those terms. It seemed the expression was "bosh," but it meant the same thing. I tried to continue the line of conversation, but he did not want to communicate that day. Instead, he turned the discussion back to me, asking me about things in which he had no real interest, such as my writing. Then he asked me about church. "When are you going to church again? I might just go with you."

"Actually, I was considering going to see your friend John at All Saints Margaret Street next Sunday morning. I thought it would be fun to hear him preach." A few days before, I had located the church in the maze of roads north of Oxford Street. I started to enter the church but heard a service in progress and moved away. But I stopped to examine a notice board near the gate with its list of services and saw when John was set to preach. "You wouldn't want to come with me?" I asked, half-kidding.

"Might do. What time does it begin?"

When I told him ten thirty, I saw his face cloud. Saturday was always a work night, he informed me; and he generally slept until the afternoon on Sunday. He had hoped it would be like the Evensong, at the respectable hour of five. Although he did not hold out any promise that he would meet me there, I left with the sense that he might indeed make an appearance.

Audley did not disappointment me, although he did not arrive until the service had just about started. I stood in the courtyard, beginning to despair for him since he had suggested that he would sleep all day. I waited hopefully anyhow, watching people stream into the church. Women, many of them colorlessly appareled in black coats and gray felt hats, outnumbered the men. But some smartly dressed Englishwomen and several stylish Americans attended the service, adding glitter to an otherwise drab congregation. As I stood observing the people enter, I could feel eyes penetrating into me. Apparently, I had become sensitized by hanging around gay pubs too often. I casually glanced around and discovered a man perhaps a few years younger than I was watching me very keenly. I turned away, looked back again, and found him still staring at me. I looked the other way again, but the third time, I allowed our eyes to lock. A smile crept over his face, a smile of recognition.

Audley's approach interrupted our rendezvous. "Can't trust you alone, can I?" he greeted me.

"What do you mean?" I replied.

"I saw you cruising that bloke over there—and in church at that."

"Just an innocent encounter," I insisted. Obviously, Audley enjoyed my discomfort of being caught.

"We had better find a seat before the parade begins," I urged, changing the subject.

We made our way into the garishly decorated church. I found myself swept into a Byzantine splendor, the interior of the church richly, almost obscenely adorned with mosaics and gilt. The elaborately and magnificently festooned altar and the whole interior shimmered from the light of the many candles that burned in every conceivable location. The church had become quite crowded, much more so than others I had attended on my other infrequent forays into church. With difficulty, we found two seats together on the side near the back. We had no sooner taken them than the organ broke into triumphal sound, playing the processional hymn. The spectacle that followed inspired me. First came a thurifer swinging the incense, sending clouds of smoke billowing up toward heaven or at least the heavenly host depicted in the mosaics. Two candle bearers and the crucifer followed, preceding the choir into the sanctuary. Finally, more clergy than I could imagine necessary in a neighborhood church came in procession. Father John, richly outfitted in brocade and tassels, trooped at the end. The clergy moved to their places, and John, standing in the middle, bent to kiss the high altar. Turning to the congregation, he welcomed us to this special celebration of Whitsunday, a term that I did not recognize. He apologized for the lack of clergy in the Mass but explained that the rector attended a conference in America, and the other associate had been taken ill. "Therefore, you have the fortune or misfortune to have me as your celebrant and preacher." It seemed to me that plenty of clergy inhabited the *sanctum sanctorum* already and required no apology. Of course, I did not understand yet the intricacies of the Anglican ecclesiastical hierarchy.

With some difficulty, Audley and I tried to follow the liturgy in the small green books we had been handed upon entering. I noted a great deal more movement in this service than I had observed at the abbey. Everything was done with an almost military precision with bowings, tipping of hats, and genuflections that I did not comprehend and found almost comical. Clearly, John took it all very seriously, and I tried to see it in a positive light. Although I had only talked with him for a short time, I had been impressed by his obvious intelligence. I assumed that if he thought it was not ridiculous, then I should give it a chance as well.

After several readings from scripture, one about the coming of the Holy Spirit to the disciples following the ascension of Christ, Father John entered the high pulpit to begin his sermon. "Today," he began, "we celebrate the birthday of the church. This is the day when the disciples received the power to enter into the grand commission to baptize in Christ's name, to heal the sick and feed the poor, to bring Jew and Gentile alike to our Lord's Table." Whitsunday, I concluded, must be what we Lutherans called Pentecost. As John continued to discuss the significance of the day, I allowed my eyes to circle the congregation. In addition to the people I observed entering the church, I noticed quite a few men who I supposed were gay. Along with the man who had exchanged glances with me, several pairs of men and an odd assortment (no pun intended) of singles who I sensed had much in common with me were scattered throughout the congregation. Had I overlooked these signs before, or were the number of gays gathered here more than usual in a church? There seemed almost as large a collection as one would find on an ordinary day at the Golden Lion. Here, gay men like myself worshipped openly in church. Most churches I knew denounced us, but here, we seemed accepted without condemnation.

As if by divine inspiration, John answered my questioning in his sermon. He could, of course, have been accused of special pleading, but I saw no discomfort on the part of this gathering to suggest that they felt so. "What then is the church whose birthday we celebrate? Many people think of the church in terms of bricks and mortar. In fact, the church building only houses the Church. This grand edifice could burn down tomorrow, and the Church would still be here. We are the Church, the children of God. Those who come to see the ornate buildings and ornate services and fail to understand that point are sadly misled. We need none of these things to be the Church. Men and women are the Church, the body of Christ. We act as His hands and feet on the earth to continue His work, which He began during His earthly ministry. The first apostles made it very clear that the Church was open to all, Jew and Gentile alike. If you believe that the Church is only those who attend this particular parish, who follow our form of worship, then there is a great error there as well. Our service to God is in a way that suits us, and which must be pleasing to the Father. But that does not mean that other forms of religious expressions are not acceptable in the sight of God. Whenever we get the itch to believe that ours is the only form of worship suitable to God, we become seriously in danger of idolatry, since we worship the form of worship rather than the God to whom it is directed."

"We also get ourselves into serious problems when we believe only certain types are part of the church. Being an Englishman is not a prerequisite to getting into heaven, despite what you might have been told to the contrary. God does not incorporate us as members of Christ's body on the basis of nationality, race, or color. We are all created in God's image, whether we are white or black, male or female, Labour or Tory, gay or straight, English or Chinese. It is all the same in the sight of God." At the mention of gays, I felt cold run through me. Although John had said essentially the same thing at Jonathan's, his public profession from the pulpit had a greater impact on me. "If you can look to the right or left and see someone you believe ought not to be occupying that seat, then it is you who are misplaced. If you condemn anyone because he or she is different from you, holds different political views or a different lifestyle, then you are not following Christ's command that the church is open to all who seek him. God determines who His children are. We do not. We therefore celebrate the birthday of the Church, which is our birthday as well. When we were baptized, we became a part of that Church. And nothing can separate us from the love of God. And to God the Father, God the Son, and God the Holy Spirit be all might, majesty, and dominion this day and forevermore. Amen." I suddenly became aware that Audley had sat next to me throughout the discourse.

After the creed, the offertory was taken, and the Communion service began. The incense filled the air again, and the pageantry reached a new peak. As the congregation began to move forward to receive Communion, Audley—who had been silent and rather wide eyed during all these proceedings—leaned over to me. "What do we do now? I haven't been in church in so long I have forgotten. We did not have anything of this sort in our Methodist church that I can remember."

"We just go up to the altar and kneel," I explained. "Watch what others do as the priest comes down the line and do what they do. He'll give you a small wafer and then some wine." I tried to sound the expert but had really only received Communion once since college, that Sunday at the abbey.

No sooner had I finished my instruction than our turn came to move to the altar. Audley followed me out of the aisle and toward the front. I studied the details of the church as we proceeded forward. The elaborate side altar to the left of the church was particularly striking. On the other hand, the statue of the Virgin Mary surrounded with rings of candles to our right bothered me. Large numbers, especially the older women, moved to the image to light a candle after communicating. We finally reached the altar rail, and with some squeezing, Audley knelt next to me. The usher had attempted to separate us, but Audley had insisted that he go with me. Father John came first with the bread. Most communicants stuck out their tongues, and he placed the wafer on it. Audley and I followed suit as John said to each, "The Body of Christ."

Another clergyman came with the chalice from which Audley and I both partook as he said, "The Blood of Christ." Throughout, I was aware that Audley's leg pressed against mine. The electricity almost overpowered me.

We returned to our seats and knelt as John pronounced his benediction. I felt a quiet descend on me as I watched him make the sign of the cross over us and allowed my eyes to drift upward to look on the face of Christ looking benevolently on us. John turned to kiss the altar once again as the organ burst into the recessional hymn. "Christ is made the sure foundation, Christ the head and cornerstone, chosen of the Lord and precious, binding all the church in one, holy Zion's help forever, and her confidence alone." The choir began to move out of their stalls, followed by the clergy. Audley and I both sang, and at one point, he turned toward me and smiled. I felt the presence of God. "To this temple, where we call thee, come, O Lord of hosts, today. With thy wonted loving-kindness, hear thy servants as they pray, and thy fullest benediction shed within its walls alway." Thanks to Father John, I knew the church was the people of God and not the gaudy edifice within which we sang these words. "Here vouchsafe to all thy servants what they ask of thee to gain, what they gain from thee forever with the blessed to retain, and hereafter in thy glory evermore with thee to reign."

I thought about what I was asking God to gain. Was it not to be gay? Somehow that did not seem to be what I was going to get, no matter how fervent my prayers. Perhaps all I could ask was freedom—freedom from guilt and freedom to be myself. That became my prayer as I knelt at the conclusion of the service.

Afterward, Audley and I walked out into the courtyard of the church. By now, the sun shone gloriously, and the temperature had risen noticeably. Father John walked over to us and greeted us warmly. "I'm so glad to see that you were able to get Aud to church," he said to me.

"You don't think I could have gotten here myself?" Audley retorted.

"That seems quite out of the question," the priest said dryly, and we all laughed. "I need to greet some of the others here. Why don't you stop by my flat for a cup of tea if you have time? I'm just across the way."

We both agreed, although Audley seemed somewhat uneasy at first. I wondered if he had a business engagement for later in the afternoon when the pubs opened. We waited until John had completed his ecclesiastical duties and then crossed the street to a red brick building with a small brass plaque revealing that it was the Institute for Christian Studies and had been dedicated by Archbishop Ramsey. We climbed to the second floor, and John let us into a small but beautifully furnished flat. He asked us to make ourselves comfortable while he put on the kettle.

The conversation over tea was not profound. Much of it consisted in sparring between Audley and John over Audley's profession. I wanted to discuss some of the things in his sermon; but when I started to raise it, John suggested that I should ring him up later in the week, and we could have lunch. I said that I would, and we took our departure. On the way home, I thought of the irony of the entire setting. We were three men with almost totally different backgrounds and experiences, yet one common thread held us together in bonds of steel. It also struck me that this was the first occasion when I had been with a group of gay men in a setting other than a bar or porno theater. There was something very pleasant about that experience.

Chapter XII

Sursum Corda

On the following Wednesday, I finally reached Father John at the church office. We arranged to have lunch the next day; and on Thursday, I went to All Saints Margaret Street for our meeting. He ushered me into his book-lined office, where we chatted for several minutes before he suggested we adjourn to an Italian restaurant around the corner on Goodge Street. As we passed through the reception area, he told the secretary that he would take a long lunch. We walked along the busy midday streets toward the restaurant, exchanging small talk until we reached our destination. As we waited to be seated, I could not help but admire his youthful, good looks. He stood an inch shorter than I did, with hair just a shade or two darker but still on the blond side. His mustache was a slightly darker shade while his dark brown eyes contrasted nicely with his hair. I thought it a shame that from the white clerical color down, his appearance was totally drab. Someone as striking as he should not have to hide his natural attractiveness under clerical black.

Once we had been seated and given our order, John began the discussion. What started as a friendly conversation evolved slowly into a pastoral counseling session. I soon became aware that he did not intend just an idle chat but to help me deal with my crisis. The initial recognition was somewhat off putting, but I soon warmed to the sincerity of his effort. In the end, it proved a most helpful discussion, although the positive results were long in coming.

"What intrigues me," he began after the waiter had left and we discussed the likelihood that we shared his sexual orientation, "is your relationship with Audley. You said before that you had no dealings with hustlers, but you still see a lot of him."

I explained with some embarrassment, considering John's vocation, that I had gone to the Golden Lion to meet men; and although I discovered that most of them there did hustle, I grew to enjoy my sparring with Audley. He was the only one whom I had really come to know; perhaps out of laziness or shyness, I just could not get comfortable in the other gay pubs.

"It's a pity that you haven't been in town at night. You certainly could meet someone at Heaven or the Vauxhall. During working hours, the only ones available are generally those who do it for a living."

"That's pretty hard considering my wife. I hadn't really thought of a good excuse to come down here in the evening. She is pretty insistent that we should do family things at night. I never was one to go out with the guys when we were in America. It might appear strange to begin it here."

"Well, that really is about the only place you will meet anyone decent, unless of course you want to try the loo at Victoria station." He laughed at his last comment, although I did not entirely understand the humor. "But what is really more mystifying is Audley's interest in you. He's told me of other visits to churches and a number of afternoon talks. I'm really surprised that he would take the time. He usually sticks to his business."

"You don't imagine that he thinks I will eventually agree to pay him?"

"Not at all. I think I can guess the reason, but it seems somewhat far fetched."

"And what's that?"

"I'm not sure I should tell you." He paused for a moment as the waiter brought our lunch. Breaking off a piece of bread, he finally continued, "I think Audley loves you."

"What?" The thought seemed almost laughable.

"I'm quite serious. I don't mean that in the sense of a lover. At least I don't think it has gone to that extent, no. I think he has been really taken with you because you are probably the first male who has ever taken him seriously, who has shown a sincere interest in him as a person and not just a trick."

I was at a loss about how to respond, and John saved me the trouble by continuing the flow of the conversation. "His father apparently always treated him like dirt. While his stories might be somewhat exaggerated, there certainly wasn't any love between them. All the other men that he has dealt with except you have just used him. He has come to respect you."

"How can you tell all this?"

"He's told me about some of your conversations and the things you had to say. I've said some of the same things, but he never heard them. But from you, he seems to listen. Perhaps you appear to be vulnerable like he is and not hiding behind a collar."

"I thought all I ever did was criticize his hustling."

"But you've taken an interest in his well-being in a sincere way because you like him."

"But I'd love to go beyond mere conversation. I wanted to use him just like everyone else. I just wasn't willing to pay for it. I don't see how he could respect that."

"You say that, but it is clear from the impression you left with him that you wanted to go beyond mere jumping into bed and getting it off. You talked about relationship that is not something he meets up with every day. All I can say is that you made a big impression on him. Otherwise, he wouldn't be showing up with you at church."

We ate our lunch in silence for a few minutes. I really did not have a reply or observation. What he said seemed too ridiculous to give credence. Yet I could not explain the sense of friendship developing between us. I certainly knew that I wanted to see Audley, even though I knew that it probably would lead to nothing physical. I had almost given up the idea of having sex with a man while I was still in England. I had already begun plans for a trip to New York.

"How are you doing in your own life?" John asked after a gulp of wine.

"What do you mean?"

"You know what I mean. How are you confronting the fact that you are finally admitting to yourself that you're gay?"

"I guess I'm not doing very well. At times, I think that I have accepted it by appearing in public places associated with homosexuals. But then they seemed just as closeted as I am."

"I'm not saying you have to make a public pronouncement. Certainly, I haven't."

"You came very close in that sermon."

"Not at all. I carefully concealed my statement about gays among a group of other undesirables. You heard it prominently because that is what is on your mind. The rest of the congregation probably didn't hear it at all."

The waiter came with more of our order, and John quickly changed the subject to a concert he had recently attended. He clearly did not want even this stranger to know his private affairs. After he had left, we resumed our discussion. "What you really have to do is come out to yourself. You have begun that process, but it clearly is not completed yet. The biggest thing we gays must confront is our own homophobia."

"How do you mean?"

"We have all formed stereotypes in our own mind, and if we do not recognize ourselves in any of those stereotypes, then we have difficulty coming to terms with ourselves."

"Oh, it took a long time admitting to myself that I was actually gay."

"And you still haven't completed the process. You still stand at the outside looking in. You have yet to be gay in the fullest sense. Once you have done that, your entire perspective will be different."

"Should I not experience it physically?"

"You couldn't stop it, even if you wanted to with all your might. You don't strike me as the monkish type. You have come too close to the fulfillment of your gayness. Whether it will be here or somewhere else, the consummation is not far off unless I miss my bet."

"I haven't succeeded here despite many visits to the Golden Lion."

"You're still very much afraid of it. You are still toying with the idea. When you're ready, the time and opportunity will present itself."

"I don't see how I could be more ready."

John just smiled. "We've all been there. Just remember, you are not alone. There are countless of us out there all going through the same process of self-examination and self-doubt. Most of us are eventually able to come to terms with it." He paused and ate a few more mouthfuls. "But once you have come out, what will you tell your wife?"

"My wife? I really didn't think it was her problem."

"Unfortunately, it is not just your problem as you call it. It belongs to both of you. You may be the person who's gay and going through a traumatic period, but your wife is also involved in this whether she likes it or not." I did not like the direction of our discussion and looked cautiously at my watch to see if I had to leave soon.

"You don't think I could keep it from her? I have so far."

"Perhaps in the short run, you should. You really need to understand yourself fully before you do anything rash. But in the long run, honesty is probably the best policy. When you understand what you must do, then you need to work it out together."

"You mean I should lead a gay lifestyle?"

"Not at all. You could perfectly well decide to remain married. Don't get the notion that I am trying to lure you into the gay life. You needn't look at your watch and fidget. The last thing you should do is rush into a decision. You should put it off as long as possible, until you are really comfortable with yourself. Sometimes the best decision is to make no decision at all. Who knows? You or your wife could be dead tomorrow. That would put an entirely different complexion on the matter, wouldn't it?"

"But you said I needed to tell my wife."

"No, what I meant was that your actions involve more than just yourself. It is a consideration and, in the long run, probably a step you will have to take. But that is a long way off. You need first to know what you need to do with the rest of your life, and that is the decision that needs careful attention."

"But I return to my earlier question, should I avoid any contacts with gays and try to live a straight life?"

"You need to be true to yourself. If you are gay, then you have to be that way. Trying to repress it will, in the end, destroy you. My guess is that you are gay and will discover the full dimensions of that shortly. But in the last analysis, only you can answer that."

John asked me about the nature of my previous exposure to the gay lifestyle; I told him about some of my adventures in bookstores and movie houses. "What you really need, I suppose, is a truly loving friendship. Too many gay relationships begin as anonymous sex, followed by a morning of reintroductions. It's pretty bad when you don't even remember the name of the man who slept next to you all night."

"I doubt that anything like a relationship is possible for me. I have a feeling that all I will ever experience is the sleazy side of it."

"Don't get discouraged. Unfortunately, you have only seen the dark side of the lifestyle. There is a great deal that is beautiful about it. You just need to give it time."

Our conversation lasted almost two hours. I left him at the church probably more confused than when I had arrived. Yet it seemed reassuring in a number of ways. That evening, I thought a great deal about what John had said. I utterly dismissed the notion that I would ever tell Ann about my homosexuality. Such a thought was too absurd to contemplate seriously. I also considered what he said about Audley's feelings toward me. It did strike me as rather odd that Aud should spend so much time with me. I had puzzled about that myself, yet it seemed a ridiculous explanation. I was almost twice his age, and we had little in common other than our sexual preference. In the end, I dismissed the entire matter.

It was another week before I saw Audley again. I had avoided the Golden Lion, trying to complete my work. Three lunches in the museum coffee shop were more than I could bear, however; and I ignored my resolution and found myself again in my favorite haunt. When Audley did not show up for two days after my triumphal return, I stood around glowering at George or exchanging pleasantries with Haggis or Ed. Ed, like Audley, came to realize that I was not in the market and began treating me like a regular rather than potential customer.

Finally, Audley reappeared on a Friday afternoon, perhaps fortuitously so. That evening, Ann and I had tickets to attend a concert at the Barbican. The London Symphony was doing a cycle of Tchaikovsky symphonies, and I particularly liked the fourth. Therefore, I had purchased two tickets as a treat to celebrate the coming of summer. Unfortunately, that day, Sarah came down with the flu, and I was given the task of disposing of the tickets. I had worn my good clothes just in case I could not find someone interested in buying them.

Audley immediately commented on my attire when he saw me. He made the same comment about being a banker that he had several months before when I had shown up at the Golden Lion similarly dressed. I explained about the concert tickets and the possibility that I might attend. We talked for a while about our respective activities since we had last seen each other, although I did not mention my lunch with Father John. The notion of inviting Audley to attend the concert with me only came as I was about to leave.

"I know you said you like music," I began. "If you aren't doing anything tonight, would you like to come with me?"

He hesitated for a moment before he answered, "I certainly would like to go. Haven't been to a proper concert in a long time. But I really need to do some things tonight. Thanks for the offer."

I really hadn't expected any other response. I bid him goodbye, expressing my hope that I would see him again next week. I went out the door and walked down Romilly Street until I heard Audley's voice calling from behind. "Ho, Sim." He ran up beside me. "On second thought, I'd like to go tonight. What time should we meet?"

I really didn't have much time to think about what to say. "Would you like to have dinner first?"

"I'd better not do that, thanks. Could I meet you at the Barbican?"

"The concert begins at eight. Shall we say a quarter to?"

"That would be fine. See you then."

He didn't even give me time to say anything else. He rushed back to the Golden Lion. I realized that he was going to try to work up some business this afternoon and meet me afterward. The thought of attending the symphony with a man who had just had sex with another did bother me. But then I concluded that to be with Audley that evening far outweighed the negative aspect of the arrangement.

I did not telephone Ann about staying since she would then know that I had not attempted to sell the tickets. I wasted some time after the library closed at four forty-five and then had a light dinner at a Greek restaurant near the Barbican. I got to the hall at around seven thirty and discovered any number of people trying to buy tickets. I hoped that I could be convincing when I told Ann that no one had any interest in our tickets. The rain, which had fallen all day, continued to dampen the crowd milling outside. Promptly at the appointed time, Audley showed up dressed in his best clothing, the same slightly small jacket that he had on the Sunday we went to All Saints. He still had the worn tan Burberry that he carried every rainy day. He had obviously rushed to make it on time, and he was quite out of breath. We entered the hall and found our seats on the left side of the auditorium. I couldn't help telling him how glad I was he had decided to accompany me.

The first half of the concert consisted of the *Marche Slave* and the *Romeo and Juliet Fantasy Overture.* The intensely romantic music filled the hall, rushing over me and impregnated me emotionally. Even though intellectually I preferred baroque music, the grandeur of this music overwhelmed me. Moreover, every once in a while, Audley's leg would touch mine. By the end of the first half, it rested firmly against me. This physical touch and the spirit of the music joined us. The combination of tactile and sensual articulation was profound. Audley seemed as caught up by it as I was. During the interval, we walked out silently to the lobby to have a drink. I bought a sherry for myself, a gin and tonic for Audley.

"It has been a long time since I heard an orchestra play," he observed after a time. "I really have missed it."

"Did you go often in Manchester?"

"Every once in a while, Mum would take me. But my father did not really approve of that either."

"It doesn't sound as if he approved of anything you did."

"I really can't think of anything." He looked around for a moment and then said, "I don't want to talk about him anymore. I just want to forget."

"Perhaps that's best. I try not to think about my mother either."

"What will you tell your wife about trying to sell the tickets?"

"I guess I'll just lie. It wouldn't be the first time."

"Then you'll not mention me?"

"Certainly not. I'm not ready for any major explanations yet—or ever for that matter," I added, remembering John's advice.

The bell announced the time had come to return to our seats. Once we got settled, Audley put his leg against mine as the performance started. The *Fourth Symphony* was perhaps my favorite Tchaikovsky piece. The irony struck me that the symphony was written in response to Tchaikovsky's own confrontation with his homosexuality. The program notes imparted that he had entered into a marriage much against his better judgment. The year before he composed the symphony, he had written to his brother, "What a dreadful thought that people close to me may be ashamed of me! In a word, I am determined by means of marriage or public connection with a woman to shut the mouths of sundry despicable creatures whose opinions I despise but who may cause pain to people I love." The marriage ended in disaster a few weeks after it began, and Tchaikovsky immersed himself in the composition of this symphony.

The music that I heard, therefore, came from the same torment that I felt. He confronted his homosexuality and recoiled. I was still doing the same. I don't think I married out of the same conscious sense of trying to cover my shame, yet the result was identical. I hid behind respectability. I could not yet step forth into the light.

The fanfare of the French horns answered by the trumpets proclaimed the opening movement of the symphony. It began in a somber mood, touching my own emotions, intensifying and honing them. Acting almost like marijuana, the music magnified the feelings already deep inside me, striving to be free. The music soured with my spirit, entrapped too long in its prison. *How suffering could produce such a creative urge*, I marveled, wondering if my own suffering would bring a similar burst. The plaintive sound of the oboe, in particular, haunted me as if the composer felt my pain and answered it with his own. We became one through his music. I knew that I could understand it perhaps better than anyone else in that hall since his malaise was uniquely mine as well. I did not stop to think that perhaps other men in my own predicament shared my feelings and a seat in the Barbican.

I became aware that Audley was looking at me. Perhaps he sensed my inner strife. When I returned his glance, he did not smile his usual smile of recognition. Instead, his face showed a depth of emotion that I had never seen. The music seemed to have the same impact on him as it had on me. No smile crossed his face; he just looked at me deeply.

Audley appeared to turn his attention to the music again. But suddenly, he picked up his raincoat, which he had kept folded on his lap, and opened the coat so that it draped not only his left leg but also my right leg. He then slipped his left hand under the coat and took hold of my right hand. The action startled me too much to do anything. My first impulse had been to pull my hand away. Yet it was as if the contact between our hands had completed an electric circuit, one so strong that like a prisoner trying to climb an electrified fence, my hand became fast to his. The electricity rushed through my body. At that movement, the music hit an emotional crescendo, matching the upsurge of my feelings.

The hand I now held was a man's hand. I had held my wife's hand often. This hand did not have that softness or delicacy, not that it was calloused like the hand of a manual worker. There was tenderness here as well but with a difference. I could feel the lines on his hand as he gently rubbed his against mine. I could sense the natural strength of its muscles. Why did holding this hand give me such a thrill in comparison to holding Ann's? Of course, it must be the fact that it was the first time I held a man's hand in this fashion, I guessed. Yet deep within me, I knew that the difference had an entirely different cause. It was a man's hand; there was no other reason.

We continued this way through the rest of the performance. The passionate violins and the mournfully happy oboes in the second movement seemed a perfect accompaniment to my mood. We even held on to each other in the face of adversity. At one point, I heard the woman to my left snort indignantly. I looked in her direction and saw that she was staring at the coat covering our hands. She then looked up at me and snorted again.

We had been caught, I knew. I looked at Audley and, through my eyes, tried to say the problem, but he just shrugged it off as if it posed no threat at all. I continued to worry, however, and the third movement almost slipped by without my notice.

The finale, on the other hand, could not be ignored. The crash of the cymbals brought me sharply to attention. It had the same impact on Audley since he squeezed my hand very tightly at that moment. We looked at each other and laughed. I felt like a giggling schoolgirl. The grandeur and triumph of the fourth movement suggested that Tchaikovsky had overcome the depression associated with his failed marriage and stark confrontation with his sexuality. Now I was openly proclaiming my perversion, albeit covered over by a shabby raincoat. But at least the woman next to us knew. There was no use hiding the secret from her. In her case, I had unequivocally revealed myself. When the end of the symphony came, I released Audley's hand from mine very reluctantly to applaud. But I could not forget the sensation of his hand in mine.

We walked quickly out of the hall—I did not want to confront the matron—and into the cool, damp night air. My date with Audley came to an abrupt end. He suggested that we head for a pub to get a drink, but I excused myself. "I don't want to be too late. I have enough explaining to do as is."

"I had a super time. Thanks for the invitation." He paused a moment and then added, "Perhaps we can do it again."

I did not take his offer seriously at first because I thought he just tried to be polite. But the fact that mere courtesy had prompted him to say that gave me much satisfaction. He could have just turned and walked off. We shook hands, holding it just a little too long for propriety, and then went our separate directions. I turned briefly to watch his retreating figure. It disappointed me that he never looked back. I caught a Circle Line train to Baker Street and rushed onto the last Metropolitan train to Amersham. When I slipped into bed, Ann stirred slightly but did not awaken. To my surprise, she did not seem angry the next morning that I had stayed out late. I long remembered that June 15 as the anniversary of my first "date" with a man. The ides of June came to have a significance to me that the ides of March did to others. In a sense, it represented a death, but a birth as well.

I was unable to spend as much time in London as I had before. With the end of June approaching, I worked less at the British Library and more at various libraries around the country, picking up a few odd pieces not available elsewhere. I only saw Audley once briefly after the concert. He seemed disappointed that I had not been around more often and that I would not be in the Golden Lion as much as I used to be. I told him that I would return after a weeklong trip to Cambridge. He promised to be there at my return.

I made an effort to persuade Ann to come along on that trip, but she had little interest. I had leased a Ford Cortina for two months so that I could gain easy access to the libraries I needed and to allow Ann and Sarah to accompany me on these various junkets. Ann's initial enthusiasm for travel, however, waned perhaps because our own relationship had progressively grown more distant. She talked longingly about our impending return to Carlisle. I also had been preoccupied both with my work and with Audley. I thought often about him and our evening together. I attempted to invent other ways of going out with Audley again. I had even considered taking him to dinner. Although I would have liked Ann and Sarah to go with me to Cambridge, I did not push it. In some ways, I needed a few days completely to myself without my family or the Golden Lion. My life seemed to be going through some sort of reorientation.

I left on Monday for Cambridge. Spending the morning getting there, finding lodgings, and obtaining entry into the university library took the better part of the day. For the next three days, I worked diligently, not only using the material I came for but also looking at works I had neglected to examine because of my frequent forays into the Golden Lion. I worked part of the morning on Friday as well, but I knew I had a mission that would consume the better part of the day.

At eleven, I gathered my belongings from the B and B where I had stayed and headed for the M11. I had carefully scrutinized the road map the night before to determine where I was headed. I exited the motorway and drove several miles along the twisting country lanes until I reached North Walden. Why I had felt the draw to the village associated with Audley's childhood, I did not completely understand.

The village itself was not particularly attractive. Most of the houses were drab brick constructed in the Victorian period. I drove around the town and then parked the car to explore on foot. The closer examination revealed just how dreary it was. I could almost understand the desperation of Aud's mother to marry anyone to get out of this trap. I could not comprehend, on the other hand, why she seemed so anxious to come back. I entered the nondescript pub and had half a lager. It had none of the excitement of the London pubs or the charm of many country pubs. It seemed as oppressive as the town itself. A few old men sat in the corner sipping beers. I made no effort to talk to them, yet it intrigued me to think that one of them might be Aud's grandfather, although I did not know his name or even if he was still alive. Slowly, Aud's world began to open up to me.

I walked outside the pub and back toward my car. I tried to imagine in which house Audley's mother had lived, where Audley had visited as a youngster. I picked a singularly ordinary house with a low white fence surrounding the small garden. Lace curtains covered the windows, concealing the life within, which made it easier to fantasize about it. I stood across the street for several moments, pondering the life that Audley must have led there. Finally, the face of an old woman peered out of the upper-story window. She obviously had noticed my loitering, and she looked annoyed. I quickly moved on, thinking happily that I had spied Audley's grandmother.

I reached the car and climbed behind the wheel. I circled the block once to get another look at "Audley's house." I then drove out to the main road again, turning northward where the signs directed me to one of the Ancient Monuments. A tape of Mozart's *Piano Concerto No. 20* playing in the deck concluded, and I fumbled through the stack of tapes and shoved one into the machine. I had trouble seeing what it was because I had to keep my eyes on the road at the same time. Just as the music began, I saw the turning for my destination.

My first glimpse of Audley End came as the strains of Elgar's *Cello Concerto* came across the radio. The mournful cry of the music matched the humors of the building I beheld. There it stood, the monument that had inspired Audley's mother. Its gray-tan stone was arranged in an irregular front typical of the Jacobean style. Two entrances stood on either side of a large window on the first floor of which probably illuminated the great hall. A series of short turrets like candles atop a birthday cake decorated the roofline. While the building had grandness, it was nevertheless melancholy.

I had stopped the car at the entrance kiosk and sat there examining the building, Elgar providing the background music. I was awakened from my reverie by a tapping on the window. The guard had been standing there, waiting to collect my entrance fee. Startled, I lowered the window to show him my pass. He directed me to the car park, which stood to the left of the house. I drove along the sweeping drive and across a small bridge spanning an artificial stream and passed the front of the house toward the designated lot. I locked the car and began the walk toward the house. The cry of the cello continued to sound in my ear. I walked through the entrance and into the gift shop, where I purchased the guidebook. There seemed to be no one else there at that time, giving me the house to myself except for the guides who watched me carelessly as they concentrated on their knitting or daydreaming.

The first room I entered was the elaborately decorated great hall. I passed through a beautifully carved wooden screen into the vast space of the hall. The walls were covered with flags, trophies, and paintings, bathed by the bright sunlight pouring through the huge window. To the left of the large fireplace on one wall were some portraits that caught my eye. Several former owners graced the wall, but one captured my attention—James I, king of England at the time when the house was first started. I laughed at the irony of seeing his face in this house associated with my Audley. I studied other items in the room and then moved toward the grand staircases. Here, I found a portrait of King William III. The coincidence of these two seventeenth-century kings, both supposedly gay, hanging together in this stately home was too much for me. I laughed out loud, exclaiming, "Now I understand everything!" I was loud enough for the guard sitting across the room to look up and frown disapprovingly.

I muttered an apology he probably could not hear and hurried to the next room. I stood in the dining parlor, not half-noticing what I was seeing. There was the answer, I surmised. Audley's mother had named him after this great house in which two notorious queers had once stayed. She, of course, had recognized the sexual propensity of her son. Although I knew this was nonsense, I couldn't wait to get back to the Golden Lion to tell Audley my theory.

I worked my way through the rest of the house. I enjoyed it thoroughly not only because of its association with Audley but also because I was able to investigate it at my own pace, not hurried along by wife or child. The contrasting architectural and decorative styles fascinated me. The elaborate plasterwork was especially intriguing; I contemplated reproducing the effect on my den ceiling. I enjoyed browsing through the library and wandering through the halls. When I got to the chapel, I knelt a moment and prayed for Audley and for me.

When I had completed the tour of the house, I walked out into the garden. In the back, an Italianate garden filled the courtyard perimetered by three sides of the building. It centered on a fountain surrounded with boxwood and similar plantings. Beyond the house, the ground rose to a hill surmounted by a small Grecian-style Temple of Concord. As I climbed the rise, I realized that on this hill Audley had played with his mother when they came for visits. I walked to the temple and sat on its platform for perhaps a half hour, surveying the scene beneath me. The strains of Elgar in my mind continued to provide the accompaniment. The back of the house was in a neoclassical style, having been altered in the late eighteenth century. Beyond the house stretched open farm country, a herd of cows on one side and bright yellow fields of rapeseed on the other. The green of England glowed brightly; I knew that I must return soon.

My thoughts turned to Audley again. I smiled to myself, thinking of the fun I would have telling Audley about the portraits in the great hall. I wondered about his mother and her use of the house's name for her son. I don't know why it was so slow dawning on me, but finally, I supposed that Audley End was the only gracious thing in her life. She lived in quite ordinary surroundings and had been coerced into marrying a disagreeable person and moving far from home in what perhaps were surroundings as drab as her original home. Although Audley had insisted that his parents lived in a posh section of Manchester, for some reason, it was not entirely convincing. That she would probably name her son Audley then seemed quite appropriate. The house had been the grand thing in her childhood; now that she had a child, she wanted him to inherit some of the grandness. Her encouragement of Audley's interest in dancing, the chances that she took so that he might be able to take lessons and perform, fit into this desire to add color to her otherwise gray life. Audley was her hope of salvation; and he had run off to London and disappeared from her life, leaving her with nothing. It was all highly speculative, but for some reason, I was sure that she could accept fully his homosexuality—if she had not figured it out already—as long as he was with her to add grace to her life. Without something, she probably had no hope of heaven.

I ended my ruminations when I glanced at my watch and noted that it was five o'clock. I had promised Ann to be back in Amersham by six. I rushed back to my car but exited from the property slowly, taking advantage of a last opportunity to study the place. The Elgar, which I had left in the tape deck, continued to play as I drove through North Walden toward the motorway and London. When I arrived home, it was nearly seven. Over dinner, I told Ann and Sarah about my trip and what I had seen. I even mentioned the fact that I had attended an Evensong at King's College, which caused Ann to frown again. I did not, however, describe the stop at Audley End. They would not have understood.

Audley did hear about that visit when I saw him two days later in the Golden Lion. He seemed to have something up his sleeve when we greeted each other, but he held back from telling me until I had completed my tale. I explained that, on an impulse, I had stopped to see Audley End, describing how I had walked around the town and had a drink in the pub before going through the great house. I started to tell him about the portraits of James and William but decided against it. I understood too much about Audley now to be flippant about that experience. Somehow that place had become sacred to me. Audley seemed puzzled why I had bothered to go there in the first place. Obviously, it did not have as much significance to him as it should.

"You know, while I was there, I got to thinking about your mother." Audley gave me a puzzled look but didn't say anything. "Do you ever think about going to visit her?"

"You know I can't go around there because of my father," he answered rather abruptly.

"Perhaps you could phone your mom and see her during the day when your father is at work. He wouldn't even have to know about it."

"That's not a bad idea. I really do miss her. She writes all the time, pleading with me to visit. I guess I really should. But I can't do it right away. I've gotten another job." He made this announcement with obvious pride.

"Are you working at the warehouse again?"

"Oh, no, this is much more respectable. I'm working at Harrods, well, at least during the sale."

"That's great news. When do you start?"

"The sale begins on July 7, but I have to begin training next week."

"Where will you be? Perhaps I'll come and buy something from you."

"I'm supposed to be in the china section, where they sell the rejects and seconds. I'd be glad to sell you something expensive. I'll be on commission, you know."

I told him that I had to go to Oxford for several days but would be sure to drop by and see him as soon as I could. I had never seen Audley look happier. Unfortunately, he admitted that it was again only a temporary position, although if he worked out well, they might hire him later on a full-time basis.

"How did you get the job?"

"Derek has a new lover who works at Harrods. His boss is a puff also and arranged for me to get the job. It sometimes pays to be into cocks. The guy thinks that, out of gratitude, I'll do a trick for him." I gave Audley a questioning look. "Don't worry, even I wouldn't stoop to please this bloke." We both laughed, and I bought Audley a celebratory gin and tonic.

I returned from Oxford the following Friday to the announcement that, the next day, we were going to the Harrods sale. "Mother sent me a letter asking me to pick up some pieces of her china pattern. Apparently, they even know about the Harrods sale in Selinsgrove," she laughed. Ann's mood had slowly improved now that the time of our departure was only a little more than a month away.

The next morning, we arose early to catch the train into the city. We arrived at Harrods at eleven, and even then, the store was jammed. I hated crowds and felt very uncomfortable fighting my way to the escalators to make our way to the second floor, where we found the sale china. All the way down to the city, I had turned over in my mind how I was going to deal with the situation of my wife and Audley in the same store and, even worse, in the same department. I prayed that Audley would be on his break or sequestered in a back room where we would not come in contact with each other. As fate would have it, I spotted him as soon as we entered the din of his area. He was busily engaged with a customer and did not see me at first. I stayed close to Ann so that he would detect her at the same time he recognized me and hopefully not make any comments. Finally, he did notice me, and a broad smile broke over his face. Ann was bent over some Royal Worcester, giving me an opportunity to scowl at him sternly. I had Sarah in hand, and he immediately comprehended the lay of the land. It did not, however, stop him from making the entire situation very uncomfortable for me.

Once he had finished with his customer, he casually strolled over in our direction. I frowned at him several times, but that did not deter him. "May I be of assistance, sir?"

"No, I think we're just looking."

"Wait a minute, young man," Ann interjected. "We are interested in getting some pieces in Royal Doulton."

I grimaced again as Audley waltzed around the counter to stand next to Ann. "Certainly, madam. Which pattern did you have in mind?" I noticed that Audley, despite his officiousness, studied her carefully.

"We wanted to get plates in the Evesham pattern."

"Certainly, madam." He walked behind Ann and looked over her shoulder to grin at me. I could feel my face go red and prayed desperately that Ann did not see. He reached under the table and pulled out a box containing plates marked heavily with wax pencil to specify their reject status. "Would you care to select the pieces you wished?"

Ann looked rather perturbed but bent over the box and began picking out the ones she wanted. Audley walked around behind me, but I did not see where he had gone since I kept my eyes firmly glued to the carpet. Suddenly, I felt a sharp pinch on my ass and gasped with astonishment. At once, I realized who had done it. Ann looked up from her searches to see what had happened. I later felt quite guilty about blaming Sarah's handling of a piece of china for my alarm. Sarah protested that she hadn't done anything, but I quickly moved her off to the other side of the room away from both Ann and Audley. When Ann finished making her choice, she motioned me over to take care of the credit card and shipping arrangements. Audley and I stood together at the counter as he filled out the information. The entire time, I could feel his body next to mine and knew that he was just a little too close to me for the sake of respectability. When he showed me where to sign, he smiled too familiarly at me. I did not know if Ann had watched this entire proceeding since I did not look in her direction. I was also terrified that Sarah would recognize him as the man we had lunch with at the zoo. Fortunately, she was distracted by the crowds that swarmed around us and didn't even look up at him.

"Thank you very much, sir. If there is anything else you want, just summon me."

"I'll tell you what I want," I mumbled under my breath and then aloud, "Thank you for your assistance."

Ann wanted to look at some other items in the department, and we tarried a few minutes more. I was aware of Audley's eyes on me the entire time. When she finally decided that she did not want to make any purchase herself, we left the room, passing Audley again on the way out. He gave us a cheery farewell as we walked toward the kitchenware. While we descended the escalator, Ann leaned over to me to comment out of Sarah's hearing, "I think the young man in the china department was a bit odd, if you know what I mean. Did you notice how he was looking at you? I wish they would stick to their own kind." I ignored her question and her intolerance, trying desperately to suppress the anger erupting within me.

Chapter XIII

Eucharist

My trips to Oxford and Aud's work kept us from seeing each other for almost three weeks. I did stop by Harrods one afternoon and talked with him briefly, but the floor manager noticed that our conversation did not concern retailing and instructed Audley to return to work. Aud promised to be in the Golden Lion the following Wednesday, and we agreed to meet.

I planned to remain for several hours at the pub that day since I had not seen him in quite some time. Moreover, our reservations back to America were now just two weeks away; I wanted to spend some time with him before I returned to my isolation. Yet Aud seemed preoccupied with and excited about something. "I'm really sorry," he said. "But I have an important engagement this afternoon at two. I had hoped we could talk longer today, but I can be here tomorrow."

I felt a rush of jealousy and anger. I knew that he had put this business engagement before our socializing. The way I reacted was irrational; after all, I had absolutely no hold on him and he no obligation toward me. Nevertheless, it hurt. "I can't be here tomorrow," I responded. "I'll be in Oxford until Saturday. I guess it will have to wait until next week."

Audley apologized again, promising that he had nothing pressing next week and that we could have longer time together. Then he asked, "What will you be doing in Oxford?" His interest in my work puzzled me. He only seemed to bring it up when we had nothing else to discuss.

"I'll be working at the Bodleian Library every day. I have enough work to keep me busy through Saturday."

He asked me questions about where I stayed and when I went to work. "Have you found a gay pub there?"

"Not yet, but then I really haven't looked." I probably was pretty cool to him, the resentment clouding my conversation. It seemed Audley noted my mood.

"I enjoyed seeing your wife. She's very pretty."

"Thank you," I replied, recognizing that he was probably lying since Ann was not above average in looks. Certainly, no gay would take a second look at her.

"I hope I did not cause you any trouble. The look on your face when I pinched you was super." He laughed, and I couldn't help smiling. "Listen, I really must go. I am so sorry about today, but this matter just came up, and it's very important. I'll tell you about it when I see you again."

I told him I understood and bid him goodbye. I remained at the Golden Lion for a few minutes after Audley left before I took my own departure. I had almost resolved never to return there again, which of course was a resolution I had broken many times before.

I failed to persuade Ann to accompany me to Oxford. I told her that she would enjoy the trip, but she protested that the exertions of packing had taxed her. She had to ship the boxes several days before our departure. Early Thursday, I drove off toward Beaconsfield and the M40 on my way to Oxford. Because I did not have the expense of Ann and Sarah on these trips, I had fallen into the habit of staying at hotels rather than bed-and-breakfasts. I needed to account for the grant money, which eased my conscience about bedding in Trusthouses rather than more rustic cottages. I therefore checked into the Randolph Hotel across the street from the monument to the Protestant martyrs of Bloody Mary. Although it certainly was not the Hilton, it was more dependable than some of the other places I had stayed at Oxford. The desk clerk apprised me of my fortune in getting a room without reservations. "This has been quite the busy year, sir, what with all you American folks traveling here this summer. What is the large group that was here not so long ago?"

"I suppose you mean the American Bar Association. They met in London in June."

"That's the very one, sir. Had quite a few stop by here on their travels. If you'll pardon me from saying so, sir, they were a rather noisy group. Kept our staff working, I'll say."

"Sounds like American lawyers to me," I laughed. "I'd recognize their accent anywhere." The clerk smiled but obviously did not understand my sarcasm.

Obtaining my key and putting my bag in the room, I went off to the Bodleian to begin work. I ordered my books and then left to browse through Blackwell's since I knew that it would take over an hour before the books were finally delivered. I purchased several paperback novels by Anthony Trollope not available in the United States and Smollett's *Peregrine Pickle*. When I returned to my desk, I found my library materials waiting.

I worked hard for the next few days, glad that I had not discovered the gay pub in Oxford. Ann knew that if I needed to work through the weekend, I would telephone her. Now it seemed I could complete the work by Saturday morning and return home in the afternoon. I rose somewhat late on Saturday morning and did not arrive at the Bodleian until nine thirty. I still felt sure I could finish my work before noon. The radical change in my plans, however, prevented me from completing my task. Not until I got home did I realize that I had failed to examine a critical piece of literature for my research. But it seemed a small price to pay.

I entered the Bodleian through the only gate opened on Saturday across from Hertford College and walked toward the main entrance. It took me a few moments to recognize the figure leaning against the fence surrounding Thomas Bodley's statue. Audley looked almost embarrassed as I approached. I was too shocked to say much of anything. All he mustered was "Hi." We stood mutely looking at each other. Finally, he muttered, "I hope you didn't mind me coming here."

"Of course not. But why?"

"I needed to talk to you. There are some things I wanted to tell you, and it couldn't wait until next week. Besides, I just wanted to see you. I know you don't have much time left in England."

"But I need to get my work finished."

"I knew you would. I just wanted to get here early enough so that I could see you before you went in. Now we can arrange to meet later."

It didn't take me long to abandon my good intentions. "Why don't we go do something, go somewhere? You know I have a car. Why don't we take a ride out in the country? Have you ever driven through the Cotswolds?"

I bubbled over with enthusiasm at the prospect of spending the day with Audley.

"I haven't been much anywhere except Manchester and North Walden outside London. I don't even know where the Cotswolds are."

"They are about three-quarters of an hour from here. Ann and I were there about two months ago for a Sunday drive. We really didn't have much time to see the area. Let's get my car and go," I said, my excitement getting the best of me.

"But what about your work?"

"It can wait."

We walked out of the Bodleian courtyard and toward the hotel. I suggested that Audley leave the bag he carried in my room. Then we went to the car park and began our drive. Only after I had found my way out of Oxford and onto the A40 did I learn how he had come to the Bodleian. "I really didn't have anything to do today, so I got the earliest train from Paddington. It got here at eight thirty. I had a hard time locating the library. I couldn't remember the name you said, but someone at the station headed me in the general direction. I had been waiting for about thirty minutes and was afraid that I had missed you. But I found out it was the only entrance to the library, and I knew I would see you eventually."

"But what if I had already gone back to London?"

"I just knew you hadn't, that's all."

"How are you going to get back?"

"I have a return ticket for the ten o'clock train to London."

"You planned to hang around all day?" I said in amazement.

"I didn't have to, now did I?"

"Guess not." It was about this time that it dawned on me that the library would not be opened tomorrow and that I should have checked out of the Randolph to return to London this evening. I dismissed practical considerations from my mind rather quickly and concentrated on the drive. We bypassed Witney and arrived shortly at Burford, where I turned north. We reached Stow-on-the-Wold and stopped to look around. Audley, who had not eaten before he left London, downed a sandwich at a small stone-encrusted pub while I drank a beer.

"There are some lovely villages near here that you might like to see. Then perhaps you will tell me your news that brought you all the way here." I had asked him while driving in the car the source of his excitement, but he wanted to wait to a more appropriate opportunity. I had a feeling that it must be another job, but certainly, that could have waited until Monday. We walked back to the car and drove the short distance to Upper Slaughter. Again, I parked; and we strolled around the village, explored the tiny church, and enjoyed the delightfully mild August afternoon. We then drove down to Lower Slaughter and left the car by the church.

"I think you will really like this one," I said. Audley seemed to be caught up in the beauty of the area, although he regarded Yorkshire equally picturesque.

We entered the church and wandered through it for a few minutes. The sun shining through the stained glass enlivened the interior of the church as it reflected off the brass, tapestry, and painted wood. After my exploration, I sat in the back pew and watched Audley scan a memorial on the north wall. I knelt on the cushion and just thought about the pleasant turn of events. Aud slid in next to me.

"You're quite religious, aren't you?"

"I'm not sure. I seem to be drawn to it despite my intellectual efforts to dismiss it. I don't know if it is just the art and music or the religious meaning of it all."

"Does your family usually go to church?"

"Not at all. My wife is rather strongly antireligious ever since our son died."

"I didn't know you had a son who died."

I explained to him the circumstances of Tom's death. "Since then, Ann has lost all religious instincts. At the most, she sees an evil and vengeful god, one who would delight in our son's sufferings."

"And you?"

"I think I may have thought something like that at one point or rejected the concept of God altogether. But I don't seem to be able to do that anymore. Somehow I get a feeling that there is someone out there who will get me through it all. There is a source of compassion in the universe."

"I haven't really given it much thought," Audley said dismissively. But I could tell he considered it carefully.

We walked from the church and down the lane toward the mill. We marveled at the roses blooming in profusion from every tiny garden and the flowers festooned in the window boxes. We watched the water mill grind noisily as the water splashed over it and down the race. In the stream not far from the mill, a few ducks swam.

"Look!" Audley exclaimed. "One's eating a worm!"

"What's so surprising about that?" I wondered.

"He might be eating Harry."

"Who?"

"Oh, it's an old Yorkshire folksong we used to sing, about a guy who goes on Ilkley Moor without his hat."

Only half seriously, I asked him to sing it to me; but it didn't take much prodding. We sat on the bank of the millstream as he began singing quite unabashedly about this poor man who died of a cold when he went on Ilkley Moor without his hat. Strangers passed us by and gave us funny looks, but it did not deter Audley for a moment.

"Where 'ast tha been sin' ah saw thee, On Ilkley Moor baht 'at, On Ilkley Moor baht 'at. Tha's been a-courting, Mary Jane, On Ilkley Moor baht 'at, On Ilkley Moor baht 'at. Tha'll go and get thi deeath o'cowd, On Ilkley Moor baht 'at, On Ilkley Moor baht 'at. Then we shall have to bury thee, On Ilkley Moor baht 'at, On Ilkley Moor baht 'at. Then t'worms'll come and ate thee oop, On Ilkley Moor baht 'at, On Ilkley Moor baht 'at. Then t'ducks'll come and ate oop t'worms, On Ilkley Moor baht 'at, On Ilkley Moor baht 'at. Then we shall come and ate oop t'ducks, On Ilkley Moor baht 'at, On Ilkley Moor baht 'at. Then we shall all 'ave eaten thee, On Ilkley Moor baht 'at, On Ilkley Moor baht 'at."

By the time he had completed singing the song, tears were rolling down my cheeks, and my side ached from laughter. Audley had difficulty singing at times because of his own efforts to stifle his laughter. And a half dozen tourists had gathered as if we were part of the provincial entertainment. When he finished, they all gave him a round of applause. He had not noticed them and was surprised when he looked up to see that he had attracted an audience. Audley did have an exceptionally fine voice; I had noted that when he stood next to me at church.

"I think we better go somewhere else," he said with a laugh.

We jumped up and started back toward the car. We entered an old schoolhouse converted into a local art gallery and examined the paintings for sale that depicted the local sights. "Where did you learn that tune?" I inquired.

"From my grandfather. He was an old Yorkshire man and loved the traditional songs."

"Your mother's father?"

"No, my guv's. He was a great old guy. I only wish my father had been more like him. Grandpa spent hours with me teaching me those songs. I know quite a few more if you have time."

"I'm not sure we should do it here and attract another crowd."

We left the gallery and headed toward the church. I thought that we would drive on, but when we came to a footpath, we decided to follow it. "When are you going to tell me your news?"

"Is the excitement getting too much for you?"

"Yes," I admitted.

"Good," Audley said with a laugh and continued walking ahead briskly.

"Now wait a minute, you got me here under false pretenses."

"All right, if you must know, I'll confess all. Actually, I have really interesting news. Do you remember last Wednesday when I had to rush off?"

I nodded without comment.

"I had gone to an audition for a dancing part in a new show that is going to open in September at the Drury Lane."

"What?" I exclaimed in disbelief. "But I thought you had given up dancing entirely."

"Well, I had. But I met this guy named Tim who has had several roles in West End shows. I told him about my training, and he suggested that I try out. I knew that I would be disappointed though."

"Well, at least you tried. You can always try out for other shows," I said encouragingly.

"No, you don't understand. I was disappointed because I'll have to give up my current situation. I got the part!" A bright grin broke out across his face, and he folded his arms over his chest in a gesture of triumph.

"What's the show? When does it open?" The questions poured from my mouth. With difficulty, I restrained my exuberance at his success. For some reason, I took it as much my triumph as his.

"It's a new show but based on old show music. There's lots of singing and dancing. The chorus is quite large, and I'll be hidden in the back row. But at least it's a start."

"Will I be able to see you in it?"

"When do you leave?"

"In about two weeks."

"I'm afraid you won't. The show doesn't open until the middle of September. But if it has a long run, who knows? You might be back again to see it."

I knew a return trip soon was unlikely, but I did not admit that to Aud. "Was it difficult to get the part?"

"There were almost a hundred guys there trying out for the chorus. I'm sure that I was one of the last picked, but the director seemed to like me."

"I wonder why," I said ironically.

"I really don't think so in this case. I'm not bragging, but I think he really liked what I could do. I wasn't a prima ballerina for nothin'."

We continued to walk along the path skirting the edge of a field, and Audley described his audition and the trauma of waiting for the callbacks. We reached a grassy spot and sat down, allowing ourselves to be warmed by the gentle sun. He continued rapidly, even nervously, about his new position and the fact that, at least for the time being, it would bring a halt to his previous occupation.

"There's something else." He paused, picking a blade of grass and slowly pulling it apart. "I've decided to move in with Tim."

At first, I didn't understand the significance of what he was saying. "Derek and you not getting along?" I asked.

"Oh yes. Derek has been very decent to me. No, I'm moving in with Tim because I've become very fond of him. He is really very kind and affectionate."

"You mean you love him?" I felt a pang of jealousy run through me.

"I'm not in love with him, but he is a terrific guy. It might move in that direction. I am fond of him," he repeated.

"And he doesn't mind about your past?"

"He doesn't know about it. I never told him how I made my living. He thought that I worked all the time at department stores. I told him that I worked at Selfridges before I went to Harrods."

"So he has no idea that you're a rent boy?"

"I just never got around to telling him the truth. He wouldn't be able to deal with it." He again picked some grass and fiddled with it nervously. "In fact, he believes that I am separating from a lover who is leaving the country." I gave him a quizzical look. "I told him I was seeing the guy—an American—this weekend for the last time before I moved in."

"You louse!"

"I hope you don't mind."

At the same time, I was furious that he would use me in this fashion and flattered that he would tell his intended of his involvement with me. Of course, Tim would never meet me and discover just how ridiculous the idea was.

"I really like the guy, and I thought if he ever found out what I had been doing, he wouldn't have anything more to do with me. I might tell him one day, but for now, I think I'll keep it to myself. You probably will never see him, but if perchance we do run into each other, would you mind being my American lover? He was quite impressed by the fact that I had an American."

The idea did not please me, although I agreed to cooperate. "But it will cost you," I quipped.

"But it won't cost you," he retorted. He smiled, but I took him seriously. "Actually, it is all in a good cause. I thought you would like me to go straight, so to speak."

"I'm overjoyed. I really am thrilled that you have left your wicked ways. I just hope you can stick to it."

"Don't get too preachy. You sound more like Father John every day. Have you been tutored by him?"

"Not exactly. But I pay attention to his sermons."

"I bet you do." We both laughed.

"I guess we had better get going again. There are any number of beautiful spots to see along the road. I need to get you back to your train on time, and I'd like to take you to dinner. After all, you are my 'lover.' That should be one of my privileges."

"I would be honored."

Audley jumped to his feet and helped me up like some gallant suitor. We retraced our path toward the car. As his lover for a day, I wanted to take other liberties such as holding his hand. I almost got the nerve to take hold of him as he had me at the concert, but discretion got the best of me. A group of schoolchildren accompanied by an adult came scampering along the path, proving the wisdom of my caution. We reached the car and drove back to Stow-on-the-Wold, thence toward Chipping Campden.

We arrived there at about three thirty, according to Audley just in time for tea. We walked through the town, examined the brownstone buildings, sat in the market for a few minutes, entered the church, and peeked discreetly into the windows of the almshouses nearby. At four o'clock, we stopped at a small tea cottage and ordered a pot of tea. Because we planned to have dinner once we returned to Oxford, we had to forgo a more elaborate tea.

"I never realized that England was quite so beautiful," Aud commented as we waited for our tea.

"But Yorkshire is lovely, isn't it?"

"Oh, I suppose so. But it's quite barren, not such pretty countryside."

"Heathcliff, Catherine, and all that."

"Pardon?"

"Oh, they're just characters from a book that takes place in Yorkshire, *Wuthering Heights*."

"I've heard of it but never read it."

"You should someday. It's quite beautiful."

"I forgot you were an English teacher. Saw you so much in the pubs that I almost forgot."

"Perhaps I don't look schoolmarmish enough?"

"How did you get into teaching?"

"I always liked to read. This gives me the excuse to do it all the time and get paid for it."

"I guess that's why I became a rent boy."

"Not anymore."

"Well, at least not as long as the job lasts."

"What about Tim?"

"There you have me. I'll just have to wait until the show closes, I suppose."

We finished our tea and began our drive back to Oxford. At Audley's prodding, I talked more about what I did at the college. Then I asked him more about the audition and the people he had met. We enjoyed each other's company immensely.

It was past seven when we finally reached Oxford. I had wanted to change before we went to dinner, but because Aud had to catch the return train to London, we didn't have the time. "Where shall we go?"

"Somewhere posh."

"I mean, do you like Indian food or French or plain English?"

"I've never been to a French restaurant. My clientele don't normally take me to places like that." Audley altered his voice into a heavy Cockney accent. "Is there one right handy?"

"We can look." I left the car in the hotel car park, and we walked into the center of town. After some inquiries of the locals, we discovered a French restaurant on a tiny side street off the High. A very formal dining room occupied the first floor for which we did not have appropriate attire, but the basement bistro suited perfectly. The latter pleased me also since the prices upstairs were equally high. The menu downstairs was rather traditional bourgeois cooking with boeuf bourguignon and coq au vin. We ordered starters and the main course, and I got a bottle of wine.

"I hope you know that I am giving up the *Saint John Passion* to have dinner with you," I said.

"I'm flattered. Did you have tickets?"

"Not actually. I planned to listen to it on the radio back in my hotel room. The BBC is broadcasting the Prom Concerts, and Bach's passion was on tonight. Have you ever heard it performed?"

"Once. My Mum took me to see it in Manchester. It was lovely, perhaps a bit heavy for my tastes though."

"I'll probably listen to the end of it after you catch your train. Or I may roam the streets seeing if I can pick up some action."

"What are you going to do when you get back to the States?"

"Well, I start teaching in September. . . ."

"I don't mean in that way. I wanted to know if you plan to hang around more gay pubs."

"Well, since Carlisle does not have one, I don't imagine I will."

"Then you plan to continue the way you are?"

"You mean randy? I suppose I'll have to. Don't seem to have much choice."

"Doesn't sound very pleasant to me. I'd go barmy."

"I think I already have several times. But there is no opportunity."

"Do you ever plan to come back here?"

"Not anytime soon. Too expensive."

"I forgot. You're one of the poor ones."

"Actually, there are places where I probably could meet someone. I go to New York or Chicago occasionally and need to find out the local hangouts. I went to a movie theater in New York once but never found a gay bar. They must exist. I just need to find the right guide."

"Won't you just find more hustlers? I thought you didn't want them."

"I'm sure that not all bars have just hustlers. I saw a film once, *Making Love*, where a guy like me used to meet men at bars and go home with them. I have been just too scared to try it myself. I've gotten over a lot of that now. I think it will be easier."

"Then why didn't you do that here—you know, this food is super, and I'm glad I thought of this place—there are plenty of pubs where the hustlers don't come."

"You know, I went to the Salisbury and the Kings Arms. I really didn't feel comfortable in either one."

"And you do at the Golden Lion?"

"For some reason. Perhaps it was because I often saw you there," I replied, only half-kidding.

Audley did not respond but just commented on the wine as he swilled down the rest of his glass.

"Shall I order another bottle?"

"Super."

"I guess I'm too old to get unduly adventurous."

"So you're going to waste the rest of your life trying to pick up something?"

"I suppose so. I don't see that I have any other option."

"Wouldn't you like to have a relationship with someone?"

"Sure. But the chances of that for me are rather slim. Where I come from, there isn't exactly a bustling gay community. What's more, I have a wife and daughter to think of."

"So . . . ."

"So when I get home, I just have to continue to suppress it until I get an opportunity to go to New York or Chicago."

"I would become a bloody nutter."

"I am already. Just talking about it can make my stomach go in knots."

"I know I couldn't do it."

"But you've had the freedom to express it. I haven't."

"Perhaps someday you will. What then?"

"I'm sure it can't be that different from having sex with my wife. All I really want to do is try it. It's just this drive to try it."

"And you think it will all go away?"

"I don't really know. But I'm sure it's the initial unfulfilled desire that is so intense. After that, it just can't have the same power over me."

"I hope you're right," he said with a smile.

When we finished our dessert and coffee, I got the check and paid in cash. Altogether, it turned out to be a rather expensive meal and left me with little cash, but I did not want to put it on my American Express for fear Ann would see it. I thought I would have some difficulty explaining. "We better get going. It's after nine already, and you have a train to catch. I hate to see you go, but we must hurry."

"We also have to stop by your hotel room so that I can collect my bag."

I had forgotten that he had left his bag before our trek to the Cotswolds. We walked out of the restaurant and into the High Street. Saint Mary's, the medieval stone shimmering in the spotlights that illuminated her, greeted us. We crossed the street and walked past the church and into the quadrangle where the Radcliffe Camera and Bodleian were located. All stood in darkness. A few people met us, walking through the cobbled streets. We entered Broad Street and passed Blackwell's and Balliol College. The whole time, I reviewed the events of the day. I knew that it was probably one of the last times I would spend with Audley. They had become precious moments to me.

We finally reached the Randolph Hotel and went up to my room to get Audley's belongings. I was choked with emotion at the thought of his departure.

Chapter XIV

Communion

When we reached the room after passing the careful scrutiny of the hall porter, I switched on the light and started to hand Audley his bag. "I see you have a radio," Audley said, pointing to the set on the bed table. "Why don't you turn on the Proms? I'd like to hear some of the Bach myself."

"But you'll miss your train."

"No. We've plenty of time. You'll drive me round, won't you?"

"Of course, I will," I agreed as I walked over to the radio. I finally located BBC 3 and recognized the music of the Passion. It was already well underway; we had missed most of the first part. The choir sang in English, and I knew that they had almost completed the section recounting Peter's denial.

The tenor lamented, "Ah, my soul, how futile is thy goal! Where may contentment find thee?"

Audley had taken a seat in the only chair in the room, and I sat on the bed. We listened to the music in silence for a few minutes until Audley rose. I thought he wanted to leave, but instead, he moved to the bed and sat next to me. He did not utter a word, however, and the music continued to fill the void. For some reason, he appeared nervous. I wanted to break the stillness, but clearly, he had something on his mind and would speak first.

When the first part of the *Saint John Passion* ended and the announcer began the intermission chatter, I finally suggested something about departing for the train station. "You'll miss your ten o'clock train if we don't hurry," I urged.

"Actually, Sim, there is no train at ten," he confessed.

"What do you mean?" I questioned. I had an inkling something significant was unfolding, and my heart began to pound.

"The last train left for London at nine fifteen."

"Why did you say it left at ten?"

"Because I had no intention of going to London tonight. Besides, I didn't even buy a return ticket."

"How will you get home?"

"I hoped you'll drive me into London tomorrow."

"Where will you stay?" I already had an idea of his answer but was afraid to articulate it.

Audley laughed softly. He apparently enjoyed the suspense he had created. "I planned to stay here with you."

"But. . . ."

"Don't you see? I want to sleep with you."

Again, I protested and almost repeated my long-standing objections to paying for sex. Audley, however, denied me the opportunity.

"You don't understand, do you? I want to make love to you." He hesitated for a moment. "Sim, I love you." His tone was almost pleading.

I was too dumbfounded to make a reply. He had only confirmed what Father John had already suspected. But hearing it from Audley's own lips still jolted me.

"You have changed my life," he continued, "in ways I didn't think possible. You showed me that there were other ways."

"I don't want you to repay me in this way."

"You didn't hear me. I'm not doing it out of gratitude. I love you."

The words only slowly penetrated. "But what about Tim?"

"I'm very fond of Tim. Perhaps it will develop into something deeper. All I really know is that I love you. I've never felt this way about another man before. I'm only sorry I didn't act on it sooner, that I didn't realize how much you meant to me. It hurts me a great deal to realize that you will be leaving in a few days. But I also wanted to change my way of life first. I wanted you to be proud of me. With the job in the show, I have some dignity now."

"So you worked all this out so that you could stay with me?"

Audley smiled broadly as if he were quite proud of himself. "I want to be the first man to make love to you. I want your first time to be special. Nothing would make me happier."

By this time, I was trembling. Audley took my hand in his. "Just try to calm down and enjoy it. Don't worry, I'll be gentle."

"But I don't even know how to begin."

"I'll show you. Once we get started, it'll come very naturally. It's best to begin with a kiss." He smiled and began to move closer.

At this point, my crisis became complete. I had dreamed of this moment; I had anticipated it for many years. Now that it had arrived, I almost drew back from it. Perhaps the first step unduly alarmed me. I had long fantasized about having sex with a man. I had imagined just about every conceivable sexual act. I had not ever considered kissing a man. In fact, the very thought was repugnant to me. Now Audley clearly expected me to respond to his embrace.

The thought brought on a feeling of terror. Audley placed his two hands on my shoulders and began leaning toward me. He slowly closed his eyes and tilted his head slightly. The whole thing took place in a moment, but it seemed to me an eternity. It was as if some movie director had photographed the scene in slow motion, like a shooting in a Charles Bronson or Clint Eastwood film where the movement of the bullet ripping through the victim's body took several minutes rather than milliseconds. Gradually, his head moved to mine; I could feel the warmth of his breath. Finally, his lips contacted mine, and I responded.

At first, our lips just touched lightly. Then he gently thrust his tongue into my mouth. The sense of revulsion quickly disappeared, and the passion within me exploded. I became acutely alive to these moments. I could feel the roughness of his beard and knew fully that I had not kissed a woman. But the dread I had initially felt had vanished. Instead, my own body responded; and within my groin, the swelling commenced.

We sat on the edge of the bed, our kisses becoming deeper and our excitement intensifying. Finally, Audley eased me down on the bed and pulled his body next to mine, practically overlapping me. His embrace consumed me, but I also watched from a vantage. I participated and observed at the same time. I transcended my body and hovered above the bed, surveying the entire transaction. The music had resumed on the radio, but I hardly heard it; the sound provided background. For a while, I was aware that Christ now stood before Pilate, the crowd demanding his crucifixion and calling for the release of Barabbas. The choir sang plaintively, "How may this mortal heart contrive to show Thee how much I owe thee? How can I hope to pay Thy benefaction by worthy action?" But the music more and more receded into the distance. Instead, I watched as our bodies become more entwined, as arms and legs became entangled, as we began to rub against each other with greater relentlessness. I heard our breathing deepen and become more demanding. Yet I was an integral part of the event, priest and victim at the same time.

I followed Audley's lead in whatever he did since I was so unsure. All I knew was that I wanted him to enjoy this experience as much as I was, that it had to be reciprocal and not just something in which I played a passive role. The more we became involved in the act, the freer I felt about it. While at first I had held back and been somewhat tentative, the more engaged we became, the more release I felt. Audley began to move his hands over my body, first across the back and then on my chest. The thrill of it was glorious. I followed suit, rubbing him in the same way. I got pleasure not only out of being touched, I found, but also out of touching Audley. I was still not sure which I enjoyed more.

Audley then let his fingers slip inside of my shirt between the buttons. He began to unfasten the shirt and push his hand farther across my chest, running his fingers through the chest hairs. He pulled back far enough to show that he wanted me to do the same. Within a few moments, both of us had our shirts entirely undone and our bare chests touching. His hands began to explore the rest of me, moving down to my leg along its length, finally caressing the inside of my thigh. The tension and excitement of what must come soon almost made me burst. Finally, he let his hand skim over my erection for the first time. The second time brought an involuntary moan from me. I opened my eyes and saw Audley grinning broadly at me. He obviously enjoyed controlling my pleasure.

I also knew instinctively he wanted me to touch him in the same way. I had held back from this final assault, this conclusive confirmation with my homosexuality, the recognition that I wanted to fondle a man's genitals. But the posture of Audley's body left me no doubt what he wanted me to do. I therefore became more aggressive in touching his body until, at last, I allowed my hand to slip over his erection. The first two times, I let my hand pass over quickly, hardly permitting myself the knowledge of what I had touched. The third time, however, I placed my hand firmly on it, squeezing it and allowing my fingers to grasp it. I could feel its hardness and size through his trousers. Most of all, I could feel the heat penetrating through the cloth. As I held it, Audley let out his own verbal acknowledgment of pleasure. Again, he smiled at me but more tenderly this time. We released our hold of each other and kissed. He then gave me a hug and murmured, "I love you, Sim." For this first time, I thought of Ann.

The choir sang, "O my soul in agony and rapture."

Audley moved his hands down to my buckle, which he expertly unfastened, and then unbuttoned my trousers. He slipped his hand inside and began to massage my erection in earnest, although he did not actually touch it but kept his hand on the outside of my underwear. But within a few minutes, his hand moved inside and grasped the shaft fully for the first time. The sensation was more fantastic than I could have ever imagined.

I too attempted to unfasten Audley's jeans but found that I did not have the talent to undo the buttons with one hand the way Audley could. He laughed and sat up. "Here, I'll get it." He jumped out of bed and turned off the ceiling light, leaving only the small lamp on the dresser to illuminate the room. He removed his shirt and pulled down his pants, revealing his fully erect penis. The sight was beautiful. I noted, at once, that Audley did not wear undershorts but did have what looked like a brass ring fitted around the base of his erection. I could not help asking about it as he stood by the edge of the bed.

"It's a cock ring. Haven't you ever seen one before?"

"This is the first time," I apologized, but Audley would not let me continue. He understood how awkward it was to me.

"It's supposed to help keep me hard."

"But how do you get it on?" I asked naively.

"Not when I'm hard, that's for certain."

I could not keep my eyes off his erection. I studied every detail of it, its length and circumference, how it attached to the rest of his body, and how his testicles hung from it. I could tell that Audley was quite proud of it and smiled at me approvingly as he observed my gaze. He leaned over the bed and gave me a firm kiss. He then reached down and pulled off my trousers and underwear. We were now both naked.

Audley got back into the bed and lay down on top of me. Our naked bodies came together, flesh on flesh. I could feel his erection push into my stomach, its warmth clearly evident in comparison to the rest of his body. "God, this is wonderful," I exclaimed. He ran his hands over my rear end and allowed his fingers to explore the crack as we continued to kiss and rub our bodies together in an undulating fashion.

Audley then reached down and began to massage my erection again. He pulled away from me slightly and watched his hand run across my groin. "You have a great cock," he said as he held it away from my body. I felt quite flattered since I had always suspected mine to be quite small in comparison to the rest of humanity. The various gay porn movies that I had viewed during my various adventures and the few gay porn books I had scanned had convinced me that all men had huge organs that swayed heavily in front of them as they walked toward the bed. Mine, in fact, compared nicely with Audley's. I wanted to ask him if he was serious but thought the question inappropriate at that particular time. Besides, Audley should have a fair knowledge of the sizes of men's sex organs.

Audley seemed to have some problem with our position. He lay on the left side of the bed and asked if we could exchange places. "Sure, but why?" I inquired.

"I'm left handed and can't get a proper grip on you this way."

He climbed over of me, and we resumed our positions facing each other. I had now learned that Audley was left handed. I marveled at the circumstances of this new discovery. We continued our touching and exploring. The guttural sounds we made became more pronounced as our passion rose. I became unaware of anything except the presence of Audley's body and the sensations of my penis.

Audley slowly pulled himself up on his knees. I wondered for a moment if he had decided to stop, and I started to sit up myself, but he just pushed me down. He leaned over and put his lips to my nipple, which he caressed gently with his tongue. No one had ever done that to me. At one time, I thought men only did that to women, but I had later seen it in the movies. My own experience with women had been severely limited as well since Ann rarely allowed me that privilege and never again after she began nursing Tommy.

I found the sensation exhilarating, but it did not compare with what Audley did next. He slowly moved his lips and tongue down my chest, skimming over the navel, and toward the groin. He brushed passed my erection and down the top of my left leg. When he had reached my knee, he ran his tongue over it as he slipped his body between my legs so that he now knelt between them. He then shifted his weight so that he could begin the return journey, this time up the inside of my right leg. The tension that had built within me almost made me burst.

The feel of Audley's lips on the inside of my thigh was overpowering. I had never known anyone who could orchestrate lovemaking the way he could. He played me like a symphony, first building me up to a crescendo and then allowing my passion to diminish to manageable levels. Just before he reached my scrotum, he sat up and looked at me while he ran both his hands along the tops of my legs. He smiled and then bent over again, this time allowing his tongue to run underneath the scrotum, perilously close to my anus. I could only groan in response while the choir managed to sing, "Away with him, crucify him!"

He then began to lick my testicles and gently rolled each in his mouth. Finally, I reached the pinnacle of pleasure as he ran his tongue up the shaft several times, the final one engulfing me. I don't want to make this sound like a cheap porno book, but the memories flood back to me as if they were yesterday. I probably could describe each move that he made, every caress, every deft movement of his tongue. I can now comprehend one of the chief reasons beyond his good looks that made Audley so successful at his first vocation. But what made it even giddier was his profession of love, which made the whole event seem not cheap but beautiful, not mere carnality but fulfillment. I'm sure one who has not experienced it could not possibly understand.

His manipulation of my erection with his mouth made me reach the point of ejaculation. Audley must have sensed this since he suddenly moved away from it and covered me with his body and kissed me. We continued to kiss for a few moments until Audley slipped over to my side. I instinctively knew that I must reciprocate. Since I did not really know exactly what to do, I did the logical thing and followed Audley's pattern exactly. He seemed to enjoy it since I heard him vocalize his feelings several times, and when I looked up at him to see how he was, he smiled approvingly. I guessed it must come naturally.

When I reached his genitals, I could distinctly smell the male musk, which I found alluring. Again, another fear had been swept away. But the wondrousness of the feel of his erection in my mouth was indescribable. The silky softness of the tip and the hot firmness of the shaft became renewed sensations to me. Although I had felt and tasted it as a teenager, it did not have the same overwhelming appeal that it had now. I was sucking a man, giving him pleasure, which was extremely gratifying to me. At the same time, I felt awe, joy, and terror.

I continued in this fashion for several minutes, enjoying the sensations within my mouth and listening to Aud's response. He then began to shift around. I ceased what I was doing, but he asked quietly, "No, please don't stop. You're super." He slowly rotated his body and lay down again, but this time, his head was at the foot of the bed. He then took my erection in his mouth. The combination of sensations was incredible: the feel of his body inside my mouth and mine in his. Our hands at the same time explored and caressed. We had become as one being in physical and spiritual union. "My spirit glad rejoices to see its steady flame."

Audley suddenly sat up and hugged me, giving me an affectionate kiss. "Bit of all right, I'd say," he proclaimed in his imitation Cockney accent. "Hold on a moment, I want to get something." He leaned over the bed, exposing his rear end to my face, and reached into his bag on the floor. After a few minutes of fumbling, he sat up with a small bottle in his hand. "Brought these along just in case." He opened the bottle and placed it under his left nostril.

"What is that?"

"Poppers. Haven't you ever used them before?"

"No, never heard of them."

"Oh, I guess you won't've. They make everything more intensified. They're great. Want to try them?"

"No, I don't think I'd better. I don't like to fool around with drugs." I remembered the time that Ann had scolded me for once trying pot.

"They're not supposed to be harmful unless you have a bad heart. Do you have heart problems?"

My heart was beating fast enough as it was; I didn't believe I needed further stimulation. "I really don't think I had better," I said tentatively.

"I guess you're right. You probably shouldn't try too many things all at once," he laughed. "Mind if I do?" he said, holding up the bottle.

"Not at all," I replied, although I would have been happier had he hadn't since I really did not understand them or their effect.

He proceeded to open the bottle again, which he had carefully closed during our discussion, and breathed heavily from it into his nose. A strong, aromatic chemical smell emanated from the bottle, filling the air with its incense. It reminded me somewhat of the airplane glue I had used as a kid, which confirmed my initial negative feelings about it. Nevertheless, Audley's reaction was almost instantaneous and intense. He resumed his sucking and pushed my head down on him. The energy that he now imparted into the exercise was even higher than he had expended before, and his vocal response to my efforts increased accordingly. Clearly, whatever the dangers, the payoff must have been sensational. But even I reached new plateaus without the assistance of the little bottle because of his ardor. With effort, I kept from ejaculating on several occasions.

Up to this point, Audley had directed our lovemaking. But I suddenly thought of something about which I had fantasized for years. *Now*, I thought, *is my opportunity.* I sat up and turned round, straddling Audley so that our genitals came in contact. I took our erections in my hand and began rubbing them together. Audley sat up and grinned at me. "And you said that you had no experience."

"None whatsoever, at least since I was a teenager. But I have a good imagination."

"You surely do!" he exclaimed and began to kiss me as I manipulated us.

The feeling of urgency began to overwhelm me; I finally cried out, "I think I'm going to cum!"

He quickly pushed my hand away. "Just relax. We have plenty of time. Are you the type that cums once and falls asleep, or can you cum again?"

"I don't really know. I was never given much of an opportunity to try it more than once."

"We'll give it a try now."

He laid me down on the bed again and moved his head toward my genitals. He placed the head of my erection in his mouth and grasped the shaft in his left hand. In this way, he began to move up and down in a rhythmic and determined fashion. The universe focused on the nexus of his head and my penis. The fluids had reached the point of demand, and again, I cried, "I'm going to cum!" But that did not deter him, and I relaxed and achieved my climax. I experienced release, followed by complete peace.

"You may end this mortal span, free from care and sorrow," the choir responded.

I opened my eyes and saw Audley looking down at me with a smile on his face. "Are you all right?" I did not have the energy to react immediately, but Audley did not give me time to respond. "My turn," he said gleefully and flopped over onto his back. I didn't need any additional promptings. I moved down on him as he had on me. I thrust all thoughts out of my head other than his body and concentrated on bringing as much pleasure to Audley as I could.

I found the effort somewhat daunting since I knew that so many other men, with far more experienced than I did, had done it before. *Would he be comparing me with them?* I wondered. That fear passed as I got into the ritual, knowing that soon Audley would react in the same fashion I had, or at least I anticipated that he would.

There is one comforting factor in having sex with another man, I thought. *Our physical responses are likely to be the same.* What gave me delight ought to give Audley pleasure as well. With Ann, I could never be sure.

I tried to concentrate on what I was doing, enjoying the feel of Audley under my touch. I ran my hand over his stomach and enviously felt the ripple of his hard muscles. Of course, I knew he was younger than I was. Thoughts darted through my mind, some related to my current pursuit, others fleeting remembrances of different times and places. Some were associated with Audley, others with my married life, and still others with my childhood. It was so confused at times that even a Joyce could not have tracked it.

I held Audley's erection in my hand and pulled the skin gently as I moved my mouth back and forth over it. My mind rejoiced. *Take, eat, this is my Body, which is given for you. Do this in remembrance of me.*

Audley began to sit up again. "Am I doing something wrong?" I asked.

"No, it's perfect. But I want my poppers." He fumbled around in the sheets for a moment until he located the bottle. After he had imbibed in the now familiar fashion, he closed the bottle and reclined. I continued what I had been doing since it seemed to satisfy. The noises he made became even louder, and I began to worry about the neighbors.

Holding hands in a concert hall is one thing, sucking cock in the Randolph Hotel quite another, I thought. Audley's body began to writhe insistently. I ran my hands over his testicles and discerned them receding inside his body. I knew the time of climax had arrived.

Suddenly, I felt a pumping begin in the shaft of the penis. I panicked, wondering how it would be like, after all these years, to taste male semen again. Before I could think about throwing up or other thoughts forcing their way in, I felt the hot, acrid liquid pulsate into my mouth. Because of the quantity, I had no choice but to swallow, but the startlingly familiar taste ran easily down my throat. *Drink ye all of this,* my mind sang, *for this is my Blood of the New Testament, which is shed for you and for many for the remission of sins. Do this, as oft as ye shall drink it, in remembrance of me.* It was finished before I could worry.

I held his throbbing erection in my mouth for a few moments and then moved to kiss him as he had done after I came. I did not think about it before I spoke. It was not just the passion of the moment but something deep within me that welled up. "Audley, I love you."

"I love you."

We lay in each other's arms for ten minutes, gently touching and kissing. At least in my case, I was overcome by the intensity and meaningfulness of the experience. I had never envisioned that it would be so different from other types of sexual experience. But I knew at the most profound level that I had experienced something of much greater depth that I had ever before. *I have truly made love to a man. I am gay.*

I heard the choir on the radio sing the concluding chorus following the Crucifixion. "My redemption Thou hast earned, my beloved Master."

Our petting slowly became more sensuous again, and our bodies began to respond to the growing passion we both felt. The soft caresses became heated once again. "I guess you were right," I said as I glanced at my erection.

"I said you would be able to get going again, now didn't I? But this time, I want you to do something for me."

"And what might that be, kind sir?" I replied lightly.

"I want you to fuck me."

I could not have been more surprised had he said that he wanted to beat me with whips and chains. My youthful experience with that sexual technique had caused me to write it out of my fantastic vocabulary. To think that I would actually participate in it again was not encouraging. "I don't know about that," I countered. "I tried it when I was a kid and didn't much like it."

"I didn't mean that I was going to do it to you. You certainly aren't ready for that yet. But I really do enjoy it. And I especially want you to do it to me. I want to get you as close to me as possible. I want to feel you inside me. Please do it for me. It may be our last opportunity."

I reluctantly agreed and did enjoy seeing Aud's face light up. "I'll be right back," he said as he jumped out of bed. He went to the bathroom, urinated, and returned with a towel, which he placed at the foot of the bed.

He then disappeared into his bag of mysteries again, this time pulling out a tube of lubricant and a condom. He applied some to me, slipped a condom on me, and then applied lube to himself. He then straddled me and slipped me inside him.

At first, the sensation was not any different from having intercourse with a woman. But the look of pleasure it brought to Audley's face made it seem quite different. He began to move up and down very slowly, but within moments, we were undulating briskly. He began masturbating, at one point stopping to repeat the ritual with the poppers bottle. That made him seem to pump all the harder. I found that moving with him was highly pleasurable, and within a short time, I had ejaculated within Audley. Although I slowed my movements considerably since by this point I was utterly exhausted, Audley continued to move back and forth on my now rapidly diminishing erection, pulling on his own erection until he finally ejaculated himself. The white fluid spurted onto my chest.

Audley slowly disengaged himself from me and cleaned us both up with the towel he had, with such forethought, provided. I told him that I felt quite lucky dealing with a man of such experience. "Did I do all right?"

"You were super. How did you like it?"

I confessed that it was good but that I was decidedly more oral.

"You have a good deal of talent in that regard," he said, and I blushed with appropriate modesty.

Audley reached over and switched off the light. We fell into each other's arms and kissed again. Within moments, Audley was sound asleep, wrapped in my arms. At first, my own head was so full of activity that sleep seemed impossible as I reviewed the events and the feeling associated with them. I recalled kissing Audley's forehead several times and running my hands across his naked back. Slowly, however, I relaxed and felt myself soothed by the closing moments of the *Saint John Passion*.

The words and music slipped in and out of my consciousness as I slowly drifted to sleep. They provided my lullaby. "Rest well, beloved, sweetly sleeping," the chorus sang. "That I may cease from further weeping. Sleep well, and let me too sleep well. The grave, which is prepared for Thee, from pain and grief will set Thee free, will open heav'n for me and close the gates of hell."

The music and the thought of what I had just done stirred my emotions. I began to cry bittersweet tears. I did not weep because of some lost innocence or because I regarded any act I committed as sinful. Nor was it out of joy for the physical pleasure I had experienced. It stemmed from an emotion I could yet not explain. I wiped away the tears so that Audley would not see them, but he was too deeply asleep to notice anyhow. I held him as tightly as I could so as not to awaken him. I felt safe.

I don't remember hearing the final chorale. It must have been completed since the radio was still on when we awoke the next morning. *"Ah, Lord, when comes that final day, may angels bear my soul away to Abram's bosom take it,* the choir must have sung. *Let then my body's anguish cease, my soul to wait the day, in peace, when Thou again awake it. Ah, what a joy it then will be the very Son of God to see, to gaze upon His holy face, my Savior on the throne of grace! Lord Jesus Christ, oh hear Thou me, Thy name I praise eternally.* I don't really remember hearing any of it. I had fallen into a profound rest, totally at peace with myself and the world.

Chapter XV

Benediction

The next morning, we awoke and made love for the last time. In many ways, it was finer than the night before. I was more relaxed about it and had gained some confidence. Nevertheless, something was quite wrong. Audley and I never openly discussed our feelings, but I suspect he also felt a new dimension not present before. I knew that I would never have another sexual experience as meaningful and fulfilling as the first one, even with Audley.

We finally got out of bed at nine and took baths to wash away the residue of passion. I wanted to get in the tub with Audley (again, satisfying a fantasy) but discovered it was too small. I waited for Aud to finish, and then I took my bath. Audley sat on the john with only a towel draped over his shoulders. He was young, animated, and sexy. I evaluated his body objectively for the first time with thoroughness and graded it extremely fine. The clearly formed *V* of his abdominal muscles I found particularly attractive. But his well-defined chest and upper torso, highlighted by small hairless nipples, were also positive attributes. Nevertheless, the discovery that Audley had never been circumcised surprised me the most.

I knew Audley was aware of my scrutiny. He did not acknowledge my gaze, however, and entertained me with the song about Ilkley Moor once again. We got dressed and walked into the restaurant for breakfast. I needlessly worried that someone would accost me about having an extra person in the room. No one paid us the least attention, and we finished an uneventful English breakfast. Between the eggs and fried tomatoes, we talked casually about his budding dancing career and my forthcoming monograph analyzing Charles Dickens's impact on penal reform in Victorian England. We returned to the room, gathered our belongings, and prepared for the journey home. Before we left the room, Audley took me in his arms one last time, and we kissed.

We chatted as we drove back toward London along the M40. After some minutes, we finally touched on the subject we had skirted all morning— what had happened the previous evening. "Well, was the first time all that you expected it to be?" Aud asked.

"What do you mean?"

"Sex with another man, was it all that good?"

"Better."

"Are you serious?"

"I'm very serious. I had not thought it would be that different from having sex with a woman. But it is. And that's sort of scary."

"Perhaps it was better because I'm so talented," Audley laughed.

"That may well be. But I've never felt such a sexual high in my entire life. And I think it can only have been the result of being with a man. There's no other explanation."

"Since my experience with women has been rather limited, I don't think I'm in a position to comment." Audley reached over and took my hand, which he held the rest of the trip. "You don't think your wife will suspect what you have been doing?"

"I certainly don't see why she would," I answered, although the question distressed me.

We rode silently for a few minutes before I finally said, "I guess this makes me an adulterer."

"How so?" Audley asked vacantly.

"Well, I'm married, and I've just had sex with you. That's normally what is considered adultery."

"I suppose so. I generally don't think about those sorts of things." He thought for a moment and then continued, "I won't let it bother you a great deal. I know what I like, and you obviously do too. I don't see how that could be wrong."

Audley's casualness about the whole affair disturbed me a little because what have occurred seemed so momentous to me. An earthquake had shaken my entire world; he seemed to regard it as the merest tremor.

Up to this point, I had been like the chameleon, changing colors to suit the environment; now I had taken a step from which I could never back away. I had leaped the abyss and landed on the other side. Certainly, Audley could not conceive of such a radical step since he had lived comfortably with his sexuality for most of his life. Now that I had crossed my Rubicon, I had to reevaluate myself all over again. I had trouble coming to terms with myself as gay; now I had to face the reality that I was no longer innocent. I had tasted of the forbidden fruit. And I liked it immensely.

I also weighed the terms of endearment Audley and I had expressed to each other. I had told Aud that I loved him. I tried to work that through rationally. I knew a good deal about Audley but certainly not as much as I knew about Ann before I made such a statement. Had I said it only responsively to his own proclamation of love? Perhaps that was possible, but deep inside me resided a gnawing doubt. I felt an emotional and spiritual tie to Audley that I had never confronted before in a relationship. It was certainly a stronger feeling of closeness and affection even than I felt toward my wife. That was a hard thing to admit to myself, but the intensity of my emotions was far more profound with him. They were at a much deeper level than I had ever experienced with Ann. I came to recognize that I could love a man in a way that I could not possibly love a woman. Again, that dawned slowly; I had almost as much trouble accepting that than I did my homosexuality. Nevertheless, it was quite true. Those few hours with Audley had confirmed a preexisting reality within me; they had not created them for me. Nor was it solely a physical phenomenon. It had spiritual and emotional dimensions, which in fact became far more significant. What startled me most was the discovery that my gayness was not just a physical desire to get into the pants of another man. I also wanted to get into his heart and soul.

We drove along the M40 past Beaconsfield, where I should have exited, and into London along the Great Western Highway. Traffic had begun to intensify as people drove into London to take advantage of the beautiful Sunday afternoon. "You'll have to tell me where to take you."

"You can just drop me anywhere. Perhaps we'll pass a tube station along the way."

"I'd like to take you where you're going, to your flat."

"I guess I'm embarrassed to show you where I live."

"If it bothers you, I'll drop you off in the center of town, near the Golden Lion. But I don't care where you live. I love you, not your living quarters." There, I said it again; it must be true.

It took quite some time to find his place on a small street in a seedy area of Whitechapel. I had never completely become accustomed to driving on the left side of the road, and driving in London was also a new and terrifying experience. I had no idea how to get around and had to depend on Audley's poor directions. He took us up two one-way streets the wrong way. We finally pulled in front of his place at one o'clock, almost three hours after we had left Oxford.

"Will you come up?"

"Just for a minute. I really should be getting home." I suddenly remembered that I had never telephoned Ann that I would be delayed. I knew that she would be concerned. We climbed the dingy stairs to the flat, and he unlatched the door. The rooms were tiny and sparsely furnished with a few chairs and a table. Audley had a room of his own, which consisted of a mattress on the floor and some boxes containing his clothing. It was the room that he first proposed we use when he thought I might be a paying customer. I had no idea that the conditions would be so rough and tried very hard not to show my surprise.

"This is home. Ain't it loverly?"

"Quite cozy," I responded.

Our entry had awakened Derek. Aud introduced him to me, but he did not seem to have much interest in talking to an American bloke. He shuffled off to the loo and shut the door. "Derek isn't very chatty in the morning. He probably stayed out late at the Vauxhall, trying to find his true love."

"I really need to leave. Will I get to see you again?"

"Of course. I don't want to send you off to America without a proper goodbye. I'll be in rehearsal every day next week. Is there an evening we could meet?"

"It would be rather hard for me to explain to Ann why I would be staying in the city late." Then I remembered that we had tickets to see *Starlight Express* on Friday evening. "I'm supposed to meet Ann and Sarah on Friday evening for a show. Perhaps I could meet you somewhere beforehand."

"Sounds super. I could meet you after half five or quarter to six."

"How about the Golden Lion?"

"No, I don't intend to go in there much anymore. Besides, Tim will probably be with me. I think I'd like you to meet him. Why don't we go to the Salisbury? That's where show people often are."

I told him that I knew the place and agreed to meet him. We then made our goodbyes. I tried to thank him for being so kind and gentle, but the words didn't come out very well. It seemed he got my drift with no help from my lack of articulateness.

"It was my pleasure. You are a very fine lover. You made me feel super." He took me in his arms, and we kissed deeply. I felt somewhat embarrassed when Derek walked out of the bath and into his room again; it didn't seem to faze Audley. "I really do love you. I want you to understand that. What happened this weekend was an expression of that. Please always remember that."

We kissed once more, deeply, passionately, and then I left. When I reached the street, I looked up at the flat, but Audley was not to be seen. I climbed into the Cortina and started the lonely long drive to Amersham. I thought a good deal about the fact that I was about to be reunited with my wife for the first time since the metamorphosis. I wasn't quite sure what it would be like, what I would say or do under these new circumstances. I knew I was the same person but, in a remarkable way, quite different.

It was after three when I finally reached home. The debris of packing cluttered the flat. Ann was quite perturbed that I had not called to let her know about my plans. She did a great deal of talking about the packing, telephone calls from home, and Sarah's runny nose. I slipped into a cocoon of my own recent memories, acutely aware of my transmutation. I worried if I looked or smelled somehow altered. Some physical manifestation of the changes wrought in me must be apparent to Ann. I felt that I had a neon sign on my forehead spelling "faggot" in gigantic red letters. It blinked every few seconds, illuminating the room. Finally, Ann asked if anything had happened to upset me. "You just don't seem yourself."

How true those words are, I thought. *Yet perhaps I am finally myself.*

I unpacked my things from the car and put them away. Then I suggested we should take advantage of one of our remaining Sundays in England to walk down to the Willow Tree Restaurant for tea. Ann complained that she had too much to do, but Sarah's excitement at the idea persuaded her. We strolled down the High Street, and I made it a point to hold Ann's hand. It felt small and insubstantial. The comparisons became insidious.

We did not have to wait long to get a seat at the Willow Tree since the warm weather and cricket matches kept most folks out of the tea cottages. The smiling manager got us situated and expressed his sorrow when we told him of our return to the States in a week. We ate our scones and drank tea as if nothing had changed. Yet the world had been recast.

Ann must have sensed something because, on the way home, she again asked, "Is something wrong?"

"Why do you ask?" I responded vaguely.

"You just seem so distant today. You're acting especially quiet."

"I really feel fine." Then I added by way of possible explanation, "I guess I'm a bit down about going home again. This trip has been quite wonderful. I'll miss England."

And Audley, I added at the back of my mind.

Ann, of course, did not understand my sentiments since she so looked forward to the return to Carlisle. "Oh, you'll cheer up once we get back. Won't it be nice to see our home again?"

"I suppose you're right." But I knew she wasn't. "Some night this week, why don't we make a point of going to the Eagle? We haven't done that in quite some time."

After we got home, I read the *Sunday Times*. At eight, we had a snack, and I put Sarah to bed. I kept trying to make certain that nothing had changed. The effort almost became desperate. I complained of fatigue and went to bed early. I felt quite guilty using such a tactic with Ann. Normally after a trip, I would pester Ann about having sex. Tonight I had no desire whatsoever to fulfill my marital responsibilities. Although I had been in bed an hour before Ann came in, I was still wide awake. I tried to make certain that my breathing was heavy so that she would not suspect.

I hardly slept that night, turning over in my mind the recent events. I had expected that making love to a man would have little impact. In fact, the more I thought, the more devastating I realized the experience had been.

The next evening, we made our way across to the Eagle. We saw a number of the friends we had made in our many visits there and bid our farewells. I made an effort to drink entirely too much beer in hopes that I would have another excuse not to perform. But I began worrying Ann would suspect something and so made my demands when we finally returned home. Ann, with her usual enthusiasm, consented. But my performance was far from adequate. I had some difficulty in maintaining my erection, which Ann with some frustration blamed on the beer. I knew otherwise.

Three nights later, I again demanded my marital due, although I had little desire. Once again, the effort had to be maintained vigorously. Only the constant vision of Audley's anatomy in my mind kept me erect. When we finished, Ann asked me if something was troubling me. "I just know something is wrong with you."

"I guess I'm depressed about going home. I don't think I'm prepared for it yet."

"You're just being silly. We've had a nice time, but it hasn't been that good."

I did not bother to respond.

The anticipation of seeing Audley again kept me going through the rest of that week. But I despaired about the fact that it would be the last time. I really never expected to see Audley again after our final farewells at the Salisbury. Perhaps that thought had interfered with my heterosexual performance; at least that was my hope.

I worked hard during the day at the British Library, trying to finish the research so that I could produce something when I returned home. I thought that immersing myself in work at Dickinson might help. I actually had accomplished a great deal despite my many forays into darkest Soho. The stack of note cards that stood in the corner of our flat were the fruits of my labors. I planned to carry them on board the plane so that baggage handlers could not lose them. The pile increased rather dramatically this last week because of my diligence. Even Ann commented on the number of cards I added to the collection each evening. I worried that she might suspect something.

Yet my work did not entirely preoccupy me. I managed to go to the Salisbury one noon to have a bar lunch and watch my fellows. For some reason, I resisted going to the Golden Lion. Somehow I didn't need to go there any longer. Nevertheless, I still felt somewhat out of place in the Salisbury; it did not have the same comfortable feeling as the Golden Lion.

On Thursday, hours before I made my second effort at heterosexuality with my wife, I reentered the Golden Lion for the last time. I hoped perhaps Audley would be there, but unfortunately, he was good to his word. Ed stood there with his pool cue and also the young man with the tattoos. I smiled at both when I saw them. *I am different now*, I thought. I was fully a member of the fraternity. I had gone through the initiation ceremony. I did not require their services any longer and stood as a peer with them. It was a very odd feeling entering that place with an entirely new perspective on life. I could even go up to the man with all the gold jewelry and kiss him as the others. I had conquered at least one fear.

Haggis walked in shortly after I arrived, and I bought him a pint. We talked for a while, and I listened to his litany of sadness. His condition had not actually worsened; but it seemed almost hopeless to think that he would enjoy any relief, at least as long as the current government remained in office. He was truly a casualty of his society. I felt much less a victim.

I finished my discussion with Haggis and walked around the pub one last time. I ascended the stairs to the lounge bar and memorized the decorations in the windows. I even arranged to urinate in the blue-lit men's room. I made a ritual of leave-taking. Finally, I walked upstairs to the bar, where I had first set eyes on Audley. I surveyed the room for the last time, trying to etch it permanently in my mind. Then I walked over to George, still lurking in the corner, and shook his hand.

"It's been nice knowing you. Hope you can make it to the States sometime. I'll show you around the sights."

George just gave me a look of bewilderment and mumbled something under his breath. I did not stick around for a translation because I feared he had had too much to drink again. I did not want another confrontation, just a fond farewell. As I left the pub, I refrained from looking back. I walked up Dean Street to Oxford Street.

I had one final valediction to make. I approached All Saints Margaret Street and stood outside the brick wall for a few minutes, rehearsing what I wanted to tell Father John. At first, I planned to tell him exactly what we had done but then decided against it. I thought about ways to suggest the reality without going into the bloody details. I entered the church and knelt. But no prayer came, just images and random thoughts. I did not know yet what to petition God for. I considered asking Him to remove my homosexuality but then was afraid he might. Finally, I asked Him to allow me to see Audley again sometime in the future.

Outside the church, I paused before the door to the church offices. I wanted to open it but couldn't bring myself. There was too much in my head to talk to Father John just yet. Perhaps I might find time on Monday to come into London and see him then. I returned to the British Library. Time for talk would come eventually but not now.

Friday was the day of our last family excursion. We had obtained tickets for *Starlight Express* and planned to meet for dinner beforehand. Ann was angry with me for getting tickets to a play just four days before our departure, but I wanted to take Sarah to see it. I dressed appropriately for the occasion in my banker clothes and told Ann to meet me at a wine bar on Ebury Street not far from the theater. Because I feared Audley might be delayed, I made the meeting time late; I wanted plenty of time to say goodbye properly.

That day, I worked hard at the library, finishing some last-minute items and tying up loose ends. I thought that I might have time to go back to the Golden Lion one last time; but my conscience got the best of me, and I stuck to my task. I checked some bibliographic references and listed some books I would have to peruse once I returned home. Perhaps it would afford me an excuse to go into Philadelphia shortly after my return to desolation. The last thing I did was clean off my shelf and turn in the books I had so jealously hoarded during my stay. I also carefully deposited the Kinsey study on homosexuality in a trash bin.

I had finished cleaning up by four thirty but sat at my desk surveying the room until the bell went off. Sadly, I gathered my things together and exited the North Library. It had become my home as much as the Golden Lion, and I would miss its mustiness and hollow echoes. It would be the last occasion I would work in this particular room since preparations to build the new library near Saint Pancras station were well underway. It just wouldn't be the same. I showed the contents of my rucksack to the guards for the last time, admiring the fact that they could maintain the same deadpan, unfriendly expression even on a Friday afternoon. I walked out of the museum and down the wide flight of stairs to Great Russell Street. I had exited the building many times before, but so much had changed. I had the feeling of making a grand final recessional.

Audley had said that he would get to the Salisbury between five thirty and quarter to six; I therefore made my way to the pub slowly. At one point, I thought of going first to the Golden Lion but decided to avoid it for symbolic reasons. Neither Audley nor I needed to go there. I walked down Saint Martin's Lane and entered the Salisbury through a side entrance.

Already, the place bustled with customers. It was much noisier and more energized than at noon. Although it always had a good lunchtime crowd, the men and women crowded around the bar and stuffed into the booths seemed more alive. At least they were animated by the fact that it was Friday. The same division of territory existed at night as during the day. The front was jammed with a mixed crowd, while the back of the main pub and the side rooms were the preserve of men.

I ordered a drink and stood by the game machines, watching the crowd. I noticed an extremely attractive man standing by the bar. I suspected that he was an American by his clothing and demeanor. Obviously, someone else had spotted him, for another man standing off to one side saddled up to the bar and, within a short time, had struck up a conversation. Not ten minutes passed before the two downed their drinks and exited the pub together. There was clearly no money involved in this transaction. I had witnessed a straightforward (well, not exactly) proposition and acceptance. It had been quick, neat, and dignified. *Why*, I wondered, *had I never succeeded to do that?* I blamed it on the fact that I had never been here at night.

No sooner had these thoughts passed through my mind than I became aware of someone staring at me. I turned and observed a younger man standing ten feet away. He looked down and contemplated his drink when I caught sight of him, but soon the eyes looked sheepishly over the top of the drink at me. With horror, I thought I recognized him as a student from Dickinson. I had been caught, I feared, just when I was about to remove myself from this evil influence. I envisioned the tale quickly spreading on campus about the professor seen in the gay pub in London.

I studied his face more closely and decided he was not the same young man. I felt quite relieved. But in the process, I had also made some serious eye contact with him, and he returned my stare with intensity. We were, I decided, cruising each other, although that had been the farthest thought from my mind. My gaze must have been too encouraging since he smiled and started to move closer, like a lion moving in for the kill.

I jumped with astonishment as Audley, standing to my side and therefore out of eyeshot, broke into my flirting. "My God, I've only been gone a short time, and you're already making time with someone else."

I turned around, completely flustered at being caught red handed. "You don't understand," I stammered, trying to explain that I was staring at someone I thought I knew.

"Likely story," Audley retorted with mock hurt. "I can't leave you alone for a minute without having to be concerned that you'll run off with the first good-looker." But he did not have to worry about any competition since the young man had beaten a hasty retreat to the other side of the bar. Later, I also observed him leave with a stranger, a turnover even quicker than the other I had observed earlier.

In my embarrassment, I had not noticed the other person standing with Audley. "Sim," Audley began the introductions, "I'd like you to meet my friend Tim."

"Pleasure to meet you," I said, somewhat ill at ease since I saw him as my replacement. I looked him over very carefully. He was about Audley's age and quite good looking if somewhat precious. There was a sweetness about him that I did not find totally attractive.

"I've heard a great deal about you. You're an American?"

We exchanged small talk as we sized each other up. I could tell that Tim felt about as comfortable meeting me as I felt about him. Audley seemed unmindful to the awkwardness of this situation. He seemed proud of his association with each of us and didn't recognize the strain.

"How have your rehearsals gone?" I said, turning my attention to Audley.

"It's quite hard work. I had forgotten just how strenuous it could be. I'm really out of practice."

"He's doing super," Tim interjected.

"That's what you think. You don't feel my muscles when you get home at night. It's bleeding hard work."

"But do you like it?" I asked.

"I love it. I've never been happier." A broad grin broke out over his face. I could tell he was being totally honest. I had a feeling that the pride came not only from his success but other changes in his life as well; at least I hoped it did.

When Tim finally excused himself to visit with some friends, I asked Audley, "May I buy you a drink?"

"No, tonight it's my turn. I've got some money now, and I owe you a few." He purchased a drink for both of us and returned to our corner. He seemed more serious than when Tim had been around. "I'm really glad that we got this chance to see each other again. You know I'm going to miss you terribly. You have meant a great deal to me. I don't think I'll ever be able to thank you enough."

"You've done wonderful things for me also." Audley smiled at that remark. "No, not just that. I mean all the times we talked together. You've helped me think a lot of things through. I really have come to grips with a great many things because of you."

"You have a great deal more to go through."

"What do you mean by that?"

"Just that it's not over for you yet. You can't go back again, you know. It's not something you can experiment with and then put back. You aren't the same man you were a week ago." He took a swallow of his drink, seeming far more mature than I had given him credit for. "And I don't mean that strictly in a physical sense. I've watched you become comfortable with gay men. When you first walked into the Golden Lion, you were an alien. Now you're one of us. If you can become comfortable with the blokes at the Golden Lion, you'll be comfortable anywhere." He laughed, but I didn't quite understand.

"I'm not sure about that."

"Just you wait and see. It won't be as terrifying for you anymore. You'll just slip into it." It was hard to believe that Audley was talking this way. He was the cocky young hustler who took none of this seriously. Now he was the sage giving me advice. "I'll bet that you can even admit to yourself that you're gay," he continued, "and, what's more, that it's not bad. In fact, it is pretty neat."

I had some difficulty admitting that he was correct. The change within me did not come because I had accepted the fact that I was homosexual. I had really known that for years and now acknowledged that there was nothing I could do to alter it. No, it really came from the fact that I could like myself the way I was and even take pride in it. That evening, I was still only dimly aware of it; but even so, I sensed that he was correct.

I looked at my watch and knew that I had to leave soon. "I've got to meet Ann and Sarah for dinner in a half hour."

"Did you tell your wife anything?"

"Obviously not!" I exclaimed, adding, "But I think she noticed something different about me." I didn't go into my marital dysfunction.

"I guess you can't live with a person that long and not notice something like that."

"I hope I can keep it from her. I don't really intend to do much about it once I get home, perhaps when I go to New York or something."

"You certainly pursued it here. I wonder just how different it will be."

"You mean, you don't think I'll be able to control myself?"

"I don't think you will be able to or want to for that matter. Someone once told me that it's like trying to put the toothpaste back into the tube.

As I recall, there was another married American interested in buying my services." He shut up quickly and looked around to locate Tim, who fortunately was still with his friends. "I need to be more careful." Aud laughed.

"I really have to leave," I interjected.

"I know you do. I'm just trying to prolong it as much as possible. Please take care of yourself. And don't try to do it on your own. You'll need help."

"You certainly have been a tremendous help and Father John also. Would you please tell him goodbye? I never had a chance to see him."

"I'll be glad to. Just remember that we'll both be thinking about you. Is there any possibility you'll get back again?"

"I've already been thinking about ways of working out another trip soon. But how would I get in touch with you?"

"Give me your address in the States, and I'll send you mine."

I got out a note card from my sack and wrote down my college address. "You will write?"

"I'll do my best. I just wrote my mum a letter, and it only took me three years to do that," he said. I smiled and put my hand on his shoulder. "I also want to stay in contact because you mean a great deal to me. I wasn't just making talk when I said that I loved you. I really mean it. What I did was because of that."

"That makes me very happy. You've made a big difference in my life as well."

"You'd better go now, or your wife will suspect something, like you're fooling around with another woman."

"I should be so lucky. That might be easier for her to take."

We both laughed and then became serious again. "Goodbye, Sim," Audley said. He leaned over and kissed me. "I'll never forget you."

"Nor I you. Goodbye."

I turned and went toward the door. Before I left the Salisbury, I looked back at Audley once more. Our eyes met and locked for the last time. It was almost like the first day at the Golden Lion, except the look we exchanged now had infinitely more depth and meaning. I could not continue to hold the gaze because my eyes began to well with tears. I waved to him and walked out of the Salisbury into the growing darkness of Saint Martin's Lane.

Today my path is clear. Then I was still confused about what the future would hold. I walked down Saint Martin's Lane toward Trafalgar Square.

In the distance, I could see the bell tower of the Houses of Parliament illuminated in the night sky. Scaffolding enshrouded the tower, except the clock face still proclaiming the time.

> Lord, now lettest thou Thy servant depart in peace, according
> to Thy word;
> For mine eyes have seen Thy salvation, which Thou hast
> prepared before the face of all people;
> To be a light to lighten the Gentiles and to be the glory of Thy
> people Israel.
> Glory be to the Father and to the Son and to the Holy Spirit
> as it was in the beginning, is now, and will be forever. Amen.

RSNOV'19

CPSIA information can be obtained
at www.ICGtesting.com
Printed in the USA
BVHW032147141119
563939BV00001B/15/P

9 781796 048223